Clouds

Clouds

Chandrahas Choudhury

ATRIA PAPERBACK

New York   London   Toronto   Sydney   New Delhi

ATRIA
PAPERBACK

An Imprint of Simon & Schuster, Inc.
1230 Avenue of the Americas
New York, NY 10020

This Atria Paperback export edition August 2019

ATRIA PAPERBACK and colophon are trademarks of Simon & Schuster, Inc.

For information about special discounts for bulk purchases, please contact Simon & Schuster Special Sales at 1-866-506-1949 or business@simonandschuster.com.

The Simon & Schuster Speakers Bureau can bring authors to your live event. For more information, or to book an event, contact the Simon & Schuster Speakers Bureau at 1-866-248-3049 or visit our website at www.simonspeakers.com.

Manufactured in the United States of America

1 3 5 7 9 10 8 6 4 2

Library of Congress Cataloging-in-Publication Data

ISBN 978-1-9821-3665-9
ISBN 978-9-3867-9707-0 (ebook)

For Amit Mahanti and Ruchika Negi and the arts of neighbourliness

for Victoria Burrows

for Ofir Touche Gafla

for Rustom, Manijeh and Sheriar Irani

for Ferzina Banaji and Shomikho Raha

for Achyut and Vidhya Das and the staff of Agragamee

for Sushma, Sheel and Sonny Khanna, for giving me a home in Delhi

*and for my late father Rahas Bihari Choudhury (1951-2002),
who taught me to love books*

Contents

Contents

Zahra

WHEN, AFTER SQUEEZING her into a small space between a bus stop and a pushcart bearing grapes, I hopped out of my Maruti 800, Zelda, on this, the very last Thursday of our good times together, I discovered that the flat tyre I'd diagnosed was all a work of my imagination. For three long minutes, I, Farhad Billimoria, had been chugging along on one side of the road in first gear, like my grandfather in the 1930s in his Morris Minor, while to my right all the aggressive new money of Bombay zipped past on hot wheels. No flat tyre here—oh no. Just the tender concern of a high-grade Parsi man for his Parsi-owned car—in automobile years as old as Queen Elizabeth and, like her, still classier than whatever came after—and now the rush-hour grime and frenzy that blew black and bilious upon my face and departing soul.

On the pushcart, the grapes of my last Indian March were big, firm and likely sweet, although nothing like the California Red Globes that I'd be scrunching next week, waltzing around my brother's spare room in my crimson bathrobe, beating time to the sounds of Coltrane and Queen or tightening my muscles in preparation for horizontal days on the beach, immersed in the sky above and the skin below—that is, if there was a clear view of these things, San Francisco being the world capital of clouds (as Bombay is the world capital of clods). But come now, Farhad, I said, it wasn't fair to apply the same standard, whether to grapes, girls or governments. This was India, and that was America, and that was now the whole argument and direction of my life. As I held a pesticide-coated bunch up to my nose—unwashed, they were the grapes of wrath—the memory came back to me (just as Proust suddenly remembered his Madeleine) of walking in my half-pant years in the heady green half-light under the trellises of the copious vines at my Uncle Mehernosh's orchards in Nasik. All the world's forms seemed to fuse: the bright chandelier on the ceiling of an apartment high above me was a bunch of electric grapes, and I remembered that the massed monsoon clouds of Bombay often looked grapey, too, and if so, the sliver of sunlight that sometimes streamed through them was the vine.

Hmm . . . the smells. After a lifetime inhaling the exhalations of our noxious city, lately named Mumbai by the nativist Marathas, and Mumabi by me as a provocation to them (they didn't seem to notice), my nose was now inured to all but the strongest, most stomach-churning vapours and stenches. Long one of Mumbai's most peaked Parsi beaks, this disenchanted nose no longer reported any news of the world and had, years before the rest of me, seceded from the Republic of India, established in 1947 with all good intentions and plenty of bad habits just *waiting* to break free. But now that it—my nose, that is, not the country—had been God-promised that the body would soon be leaving, it had come alive again and was twitching. As I took in a shot of the potent air-cocktail that would soon be removed from my life's menu, I found I could pick apart all its components: the yeasty aroma of fresh pav from an Irani bakery, diesel farts from a tempo, the diabolical and diabetical tea that Indians love to brew with milk and sugar, Amul cheese over nachos and baked beans at an Udupi restaurant, the sugarcane juice that always makes me crap in streams afterwards, dried fish, jasmine agarbattis, uncleared, well-fermented garbage and . . .

Oh Zarathustra!

. . . and mmm the riddling scent of a woman's perfume—the sort of smell for which a man's nose *always* has time. My nose knew who it was, and after a few seconds my top-five-percentile brain (two degrees, one gold medal, no children) worked it out. Unless I was very wrong, I'd just performed the olfactory equivalent of discovering the proverbial noodle in the haystack. In a city of nineteen million, I'd managed to track down a woman by her perfume, like Sherlock Holmes and the

Hound of the Baskervilles all rolled into one. And that woman was none other than—speak the words with rapturous reverence, rolling your r's all the while—Zahra, a veritable goddess from top to bottom and actually even further down, all the way to her feet.

Already, though, I could see a flaw in my scented syllogism. Was I in the vicinity not of Zahra herself but only the *perfume* she favoured? Was this another victory of the endless replicability of a capitalistic world over the particularity of human beings? (The day this tension is eliminated, humanity perishes.) If only Dior, Issey Miyake or Bulgari could assure me that they manufactured this swoon-scent in a special edition of one, I'd pay for top-ups for the user the rest of my life. My eyes searched the packed and burgeoning world, hoping, panicking, despairing, until miraculously they came to rest upon Zahra standing behind the glass door of a cosmetics shop across the road.

Hurrah for life and hey-ho to the world! It struck me that for Zahra's perfume to linger in this odour-dense place, she must have crossed the road just before I had arrived—perhaps right in front of my nose. My eyes had certainly missed her.

Zahra's back was to me, true, but there was no mistaking *that* back, possessed of more personality than so many faces that had come my way in this life. I'd studied that back, a sculptor's dream, with such wonder, such fascination, such longing—when all euphemisms are eliminated, such lust—two nights ago, when I'd seen her for the first time at the Navjote ceremony of twelve-year-old Neville, the grandson of Phiroz and Freny Irani of Rustom Baug, close friends of my late great mother and top benefactors of my psychotherapy practice.

Although Zahra's back was now covered by a white tunic that went all the way down to her knees (below which her petite frame continued towards the floor in a pair of black tights and met it in a pair of golden slippers), I knew exactly where that small beauty spot lay between those shoulder blades, for I'd had many glimpses of it courtesy of the low-backed blouse she had been wearing two nights ago with a cream-coloured, gold-bordered sari, as, escorted by a cross-eyed, buck-toothed relative, friend or lover she shimmered across the grounds of Colaba Agiary, arousing laughter and blood. But I could see into the whole of the shop: Zahra was alone this evening and there for the taking—or at least the talking. Nothing stood between us but four rows of the martial motorists of Bombay.

Oh delicious syllables! Zah-ra. Ra-zah. Zah-zah. Rah-rah. (Since I was a child, I've always had the habit of turning names around to see how they sound. Indeed, doing this to my own name—Had-fur—takes us right back to the origins of our species, to our long, epochal night as monkeys.) America! America! America! As soon as those r's began to roll, it seemed to me, life began to roll. And even before I could reach America's generous shore, swelling with the tides of human desire, rippling with the possibility of a more perfect union, it was already offering me its toothsome goods right here at my doorstep in Bombay. Because I'd known, as soon as I'd heard Zahra speak the other night, that she either had lived or did now live in the States. And then I'd literally levitated when she'd revealed—during the two distracted minutes that we'd managed to spend together, bombarded on all sides by naturally exuberant Parsis raised by good food and drink to their most boisterous—that she lived not just in any old place on that vast continent but in SAN FRANCISCO! And I'd said in return—with all the serenity of a bullet leaving a gun, or a sperm its source—that, hey, that was the very place I was headed to next week. She was about to ask why, but just then her cock-blocking companion arrived and broke us up.

And as we drifted away from one another, I knew that I had neither the confidence nor the cunning to circle back into her orbit again and that there could lie many a slip, many a slip between the Bombay cup of this evening and those Frisco lips and the fresco of Zahra and me in America. And when Zahra suddenly disappeared (why do beautiful women always leave parties before anyone else?) without me extracting from her anything like a telephone number, address or neighbourhood—and after Facebook yielded over fifty Zahras—I feared

I would never see her again. And that had added a gloomy new note to my departure, even as I put the finishing touches on my twenty-four years of adulthood in Bombay, twenty-three years of ownership of Zelda, fifteen years of marriage (and then two as a single man) and twelve years of independent practice.

The likelihood, therefore, of my running into Zahra again was even lower than that of any of my Gujarati clients paying their bills without asking for a concession. But there you have it. Every man deserves a lucky break at least once in his romantic life, and mine had come late, a few days short of my forty-second birthday.

Entering the shop, I parked myself by the small section for men, conscious of a heart flutter, of my abs retreating inwards from the waistband that enclosed them (and of some other fantastic goods, given many names by the human tongue). One of the two attendants reluctantly disengaged himself from the beauty and came over to the beast. But Zahra herself didn't turn, not even when I asked for this shaving gel and that hair cream in the suave, Anglo-accented Hindi that so impresses my clients and persuades them that I am The One. I heard her speak to the other chap about matters of great consequence—pH balance and exfoliation—in that husky voice that had given such depths of meaning to the pleasantries we'd exchanged the other night. ('Oh, Dr Billimoria, I've only been back in India a week, but I think I'm already in need of therapy. *How* do you people ever manage to live in this madhouse?')

How to move now? I was stumped. Where was the inspiration for which the Billimorias of Bombay (and before that, Surat, and before that, Persia prior to the age of Islam) had been renowned for centuries? I felt myself transported for the second time that evening into my half-pant years. In 1984, on Valentine's Day, as an ardent and acnaceous schoolboy in braces, I'd given myself ten minutes of the blackest indecision in a corner of the playground of Campion School before approaching a girl with the fourth and subtlest version of a note I'd written her. (Too subtle, as her helpless laughter showed. The art of reading was in danger even then.) I saw that the right way to have dealt with my latest challenge in romance was simply to have walked in, given myself three seconds and said, clear as a bell, like a real or Raymond's man, 'Ah! Zahra! Isn't that you? What a pleasant surprise!'

What if I went out again and got it right on take two? Even George Clooney, to whom some people have said I bear a resemblance from certain angles, presumably required one sometimes. I turned to leave.

'Dr Billimoria! Hey! Isn't that you? Remember me?'

'Oh my God, it's you!' I gasped, more surprised than even Zahra. '*Zahra*, isn't it? We met at the Navjote.'

With only a dab of make-up on, and in flats rather than heels, Zahra looked less spectacular than she had the other day, but more accessible—at a level where she could be engaged with, rather than merely worshipped. I had the curious feeling of being in a dream. I'd only met her the once, and then for two days I'd longed for nothing more than to have her face and frame in front of my own again. But now that the moment was here, I had trouble even looking her in the eye. I really was so badly out of touch with the art of romance!

'This really is so serendipitous,' I said, reaching for the word that always calms me and impresses others. 'So, how've you been? Ready to go home, or has Bombay worked its charms on you, so I'm going to discover that there's still only one member of our faith in San Francisco?'

Zahra laughed in her worldly, disconcerting way, as if able to read the panic behind my jest. 'Bombay—what a city! I'm more stressed out here than I've been at any time in the last *ten* years. I really think I need your services, Dr Billimoria.'

'Really? What happened?'

'I wish something *had* happened. I spent all of today in the court over a land dispute and *nothing* happened. Everyone just tried to get the day to end quickly and adjourn for tomorrow. I get more things done in my dreams, baba, than these people do in a working day.'

'Please call me Farhad,' I said, faintly aware of a conversation time lag—I was divided by my attention to Zahra's eyes, her nose, her mouth, her hair, her hoop earrings, her neck, her shoulders, her waist, her legs, her manner and her words all at the same time.

'Well, I'm not doing anything particular with my evening,' said Zahra. 'Shall we get a cup of coffee somewhere?'

'Um . . . coffee? Yes, coffee. Shall we?'

'Why not—if you're free? We didn't really get a chance to chat the other day at Neville's Navjote, and you said you're coming to live in my city soon?'

'Uh, coffee? I'd love you—I mean, I'd love to—but I'm headed to a family dinner in my honour in Colaba, and I'm already late.' I saw Zahra looking at me sceptically. 'Parsis aren't like other Indians, as you know. They take punctuality very seriously.'

Zahra laughed. 'Are you scared of me, Dr Billimoria . . . Farhad? Don't worry, I don't bite.'

'Well . . . why don't you come along with me?'

'I couldn't do that!'

'Well, listen . . . what do you say to . . . to meeting tomorrow evening instead?'

'Sure. I don't think I'm doing anything tomorrow after six. Are you a member of the Willingdon Club? I went there many years ago and loved it.'

'The Willingdon! Oh no, I know too many people there. It's always full of Parsis. If I get a detail of any story slightly wrong, some little old lady will come across and say, "You're wrong there, Farhad Billimoria! I know for a fact that the Bapsy Kapadia you're speaking of married Rustom Sidhwa in 1956. *I* was there." And the next day, half the town will know that we met for dinner, and the editors of the society pages will call and offer to publish a picture of us for a fee.'

'Hee hee—you're funny!'

Encouraged, realizing that it was not only himself he could keep well entertained, Dr Billimoria now chirped, 'So, no, never the Willingdon. If anything, I may be escaping Bombay primarily to escape the Willingdon. Why don't we . . . tell you what, let's go to Aer, on the rooftop of the Four Seasons Hotel in Worli. It's got a great view.'

'Air? Like what we breathe? I don't know this place,' said Zahra. 'It must have opened after I was last here in 2005.'

'Wow, you haven't been back for six years? That's right, it started after that. Are you going the same way as me? In that case, I can offer you a ride in my vintage car.'

'I'd have loved that, but I have to go the other way, to Breach Candy, to my sister's.' Zahra had a way of looking off into the far distance suddenly in the middle of a sentence. 'So I guess it'll have to be tomorrow. Where do you live?'

'Worli Sea Face.'

'Hmm . . . must be nice.'

'Yes . . . but San Francisco will be nicer.'

'How are you so sure?'

'Let's talk about it when we meet tomorrow.'

'Sounds like a—taxi!'

As the passing taxi slowed down, the cars behind it raised a storm of outraged and outrageous honking that drowned out the clarinets and trombones of my heart—while, responding to one or possibly both soundtracks, Zahra whipped open the door of the vehicle and leapt in with astonishing agility. She leaned out of the window, trying not to look extremely pleased with herself. 'All right, Dr Billimoria, so shall we say seven tomorrow at this Air place?'

'Seven, yes!' I shouted, unused to drawing attention to myself in public. The feeling was so wonderful, now that a beautiful woman was a part of the spectacle, that I added, 'That was an amazing move!'

'Thanks! I do yoga. You should try it too!'

With a wave, Zahra disappeared into the ocean of humanity—all waves tending to disappear into oceans—and Farhad, not being the same me or man who had crossed the street just a few minutes ago, was left behind to marvel at the miracle of what had just happened.

What a life! What *was* life? I couldn't work it out at all. Two romanceless, celibate, stopped-up, self-flagellating years had gone by in this city without my meeting anyone like Zahra. All that while, I'd been going to parties thrown by friends or clients, Parsi dinners and charitable functions, conferences and seminars, book readings and concerts, without ever securing the attention of someone both attractive and unclaimed from the opposite sex. (Yes, there was that swooning widow Gira at cousin Murzban's Navroze dinner last year, but if I'd gotten involved with her, my main contribution to the marriage might have been a second chapter to her widowhood.) The few single women in their late thirties or ascending forties I met were all curiously withdrawn and morose, as if being left out of the first and best rounds of the marriage carnival had subdued them for good and turned their minds to higher things such as the Art of Living or the education of slum children. Even if I found them interesting, I couldn't tell at all whether the sentiment was reciprocated—they never invited me to coffee, as Zahra had just done. We talked about all sorts of things—the weather, the Parsi Punchayet elections, the Tata succession, the Bandra-Worli Sea Link—without ever getting to other subjects of consequence. You know, the *real* subjects. And all the while, my lonely zabb—that, as you didn't know, is the lovely word in *The Arabian Nights* for the male member, which also customarily has for its delectation a whole zenana, the lucky bastard—was inflaming my brain with its white heat. I was young(ish)—and free—but what of that? It meant nothing in a world like this.

Slowly, because of these puzzling and peculiar ladies, I lost sight of what was attractive about myself—God, if I was attractive *at all*—and took to trying out all kinds of poses and roles, some of which were me and some of which were not me. I was silent one night and I was chatty the next, I dressed casual and I dressed formal, I wore my glasses and I wore contact lenses, I spoke in elevated dialects and demotic tongues. But none of these measures seemed to make any difference; it was as if a God's curse was upon me.

Oh, how I'd suffered the torments of body and soul, dick and dream! I spoke aloud to myself more than I had ever done before, trying, through stern orders and rebukes, to keep the beleaguered Farhadian soul—at some point in this dispiriting period, I'd even begun to refer to myself in the third person to create some distance between myself and my troubles—from sinking underwater. I sometimes caught myself on the border of unprofessionalism with a female client, risking, with one misstep, the cancellation of the licence and reputation I had dedicated my entire youth to acquiring. I went out by myself to late shows at the cinema and took illicit pleasure in the spectacle of teenagers making out in the dark. I gazed at bodies in newspapers and the internet, and the more real they became, the more remote did the real bodies of the world become. I even almost called up Anna to see if she wanted to get back together! Frankly, the day wasn't far when I'd be needing therapy myself.

But now, as Zahra's easy, natural conversation—indeed flirtation—with me had proved, the problem wasn't with my own nature. The problem was with a buttoned-up Bombay, enclosed in the vice-like grip of this watchdog country—it was this that was squeezing Farhad into an ever-narrower space, even as he became richer, smarter and more comfortable in his own newly single, mingle-seeking skin. I'd found out this evening that I was no monster, patriarchally projecting my desires on to the disinterested and the self-sufficient. Rather, I could see better than ever that my surmise had been correct—that once Farhad Billimoria and his environment were cleanly parted, life would begin again. And *that* emerging life, on the other side of my birthday, was already reaching out for this old one, to shake it energetically, to thrill it proleptically, in the form of this visitor from San Francisco.

It was time to make a New Deal with myself. I'd lived a life of so much learning and labour; of so much polite, domestic and therapeutic talk; of so much devotion (albeit declining by the slightest degrees till finally all dead) to a daunting and disapproving wife; up so many staircases and through so many doors; through so many doors and so many suits; past so many birthdays and so many Navrozes, without really making room for that highest of all sensual pleasures, that greatest of self-erasures. Sexually, I belonged to the middle of the twentieth century—if even that far forward. Like a Brahmin, I'd subsisted too much in mind, too little in body, too much in conformity, too little in freedom. My brain had in every sense always been Master Superior to my zabb, and as a consequence, both were, at the age of almost-forty-two, lacking in air and fulfilment. Oh Farhad! I couldn't wait to leave for the promised land. Except that I didn't want to leave Bombay either as long as Zahra was here.

But why had I been standing aimlessly on this pavement for so long?

Even as Zahra had arrived to fill the Void, another gap had appeared in the universe where Zelda had once stood.

Twenty-three years into her life as the most charming car in Bombay, my precious baby had just been towed away for the first time.

By the time my relatives let me go, it was nearly midnight—not too bad, since it was already past ten by the time I arrived at the dinner party after having rescued Zelda from the yard of the Tardeo police station. I drove back from Colaba to Worli, warm with wine and wish-fulfilment, not hurrying, true, but not feeling anywhere as nostalgic either as everybody seemed to assume I was, for these soon-to-be-forsaken lanes, these neighbourhoods and their old, resonant names, for the cuisine of my community (eggs can never fail you) and for the rest of this city. Not nostalgic for the ex-wife whom I'd romanced in cafes now closed down, and under trees now cut down, and on streets now engloomed by flyovers, and through years now marked off and museumed in neat decades—and not nostalgic for the very relatives who were assuming the presence of these emotions.

The older ones had fussed over me, and brought up the smiling shadows of my late mother and father, and chuckled over the mischief of my adolescence and the shenanigans of my youth (very minor when seen in a twenty-first-century context). And some had said: 'Don't settle down there just like your brother! We hope to see you back by the 2014 general elections latest.' And others: 'Watch out for those American broads, dikra! They're all fast, and they all wear push-up bras, and you won't know what's hit you.' (They were so proud that they knew the word 'broads'.) Cousin Gulshan, who'd had a crush on me when she was thirteen and I, twenty, had given me a card with many sweet reminiscences in it and a picture drawn with her daughter's crayons. Auntie Farzana had sold me a ticket for a charity raffle. First prize was a washing machine.

No one mentioned Anna, as if the subject was now off bounds forever, when in fact I would've been perfectly happy to discuss her, having at last attained the same detachment towards my ex-wife as I had towards my late marriage. About a month ago, a friend had told me that he'd seen Anna at dinner at the Thai Pavilion with an unknown man, and I had pretended unconcern and nonchalance. But today, I was willing not only to concede the likelihood of such an event being a date but even to hope that it was one. Why should anybody be unhappy or loveless? Tonight, I felt newly generous towards our Mumabi of many disappointments.

But hello! Returning yet again to my memory of the axial moment of the evening, I chanced upon something intriguing—and so much at odds with my impression of Zahra that it had to be true and not a figment of my imagination. I saw on her face a flicker of doubt, of anxiety, of vulnerability, as she asked, so very casually, so very naturally, if I wanted to meet her for a coffee. Could it be that . . . perhaps she, too, had thought she was never going to see me again? The entire gulf between human wants and human fears was in that instant exposed— and with that, the reassuring knowledge that we are all the same and in need of the same things. A few more days of such piercing thoughts, and I'd be ready to take over from old Osho and Deepak Chopra.

The mind—it came to me on the downward slope of Peddar Road, between Jaslok Hospital and Haji Ali Juice Centre—was like a sky. A sky, and the winds of the *cogito ergo sum* self blew thoughts across it continuously (from left to right if you were English-thinking, from right to left if you thought in Persian or Arabic). To be sure, this much had been proffered by many before me—a Billimoria never plagiarizes a thought about thought. But . . . it seemed far too simple a picture of what went on up there, in there. All thoughts were not of the same dimension or consequence, after all, and even the same thought could arrive time after time and wind itself into different clusters of thoughts or generate vastly different emotions.

No, it seemed more truthful to say that the mind was always a mind in time. The mind was less a noun than a verb—it was a series of moods and mental states. And some mental states were so dramatic they stood out just like clouds in the sky, briefly discrete and dramatic, far more immediate and important to the self than the sky-mind behind—but then also fading away. It was this quality that made the self such an interesting place—a self that appeared stable or readable to others, but that might stealthily be drifting into some new place on its own clouds.

And when the mind saw clouds drifting low in its sky, as I was now doing, it knew that something really interesting was going on in that lonesome world—that it was living a life that only it could live. And the therapeutic implication of this was that once the mind had experienced a powerful mood-cloud and perceived how many elements were in dynamic interplay in it—in my case, Bombay, San Francisco, Zahra, Zelda, memory, beauty, Zahra, laughter, farewells, rich language, dreadful puns, sexual tingles, Zahra, even the very thoughts about clouds I was thinking right now—then perhaps it could learn, self-consciously, to compound from the bewildering chaos and variety of life its own clouds of pleasure, peace or animation. Or even to dissolve thunderclouds of self-pity, rage or resentment. The sight of clouds in the sky were like a spur for the clouds of the mind—it was those hot, flat, cloudless blue skies of India that made Indians so complacent, moralistic, fatalistic, monotone. No more of that kind of humdrum mental weather! From this day onwards, in anticipation of America, I'd make every day of mine rich in mindclouds—and I'd show others how to do the same. Perhaps in ten years I'd even be credited for bringing the new art of cloud therapy to the world out of San Francisco. I saw the function in the city hall . . . I was wearing a black suit and my hair was greyer . . . Zahra was sitting in the front row . . .

Something in my field of vision loomed up close—the car in front of me had screeched to a halt. I cried out and hit the brakes, too. The world closed in upon me, and I realized, from a place of curious detachment, that I was going to crash and this was the end. Time stopped entirely. And in that moment—which afterwards seemed the most fine-grained of my entire life—the image came back of the flicker on Zahra's beautiful face as she asked me out, as if it were not just a tremor in her own being but a premonition of what was going to happen to me. And the loneliness, both of the moment and of the years just past, cut deep into me, with a relief that it would now all be over, and I felt falling over me a happiness that I was saying goodbye to life just when everything was perfectly poised, just as new love had blossomed in my heart that the passage of time might only degrade. In short, I experienced the grace that all people desire when they depart this world. Then there came a grinding noise, and my body was lifted up and sent crashing down again.

Silent was the world, but reverberating—in a way that suggested time and life. I was not in heaven but in Bombay.

The date with Zahra was on!

The door of the other car opened. A dark, good-looking man about my age stepped out. He surveyed the damage, wincing, then broke abruptly into a loud laugh. He brought his hands together in slow, apparently sarcastic, applause.

'Listen,' I said, trying to get out, but Zelda's door handle was jammed. 'I'm sorry, but . . .'

The bumpee came over, still laughing, and pulled the door open.

'. . . it really wasn't my fault,' I finished. 'You braked so suddenly and . . .'

He returned in a thick South Indian accent, 'You have done a very good job with your small car, mister, of buggering my large car. Wait, let me take a photograph.'

'Listen, sir, let's not involve the police.'

'Hmm . . . which angle would be best? I want to get Haji Ali in the background.'

'I have a flight to catch soon!'

'Calm down, calm down. By the way, I am Balu. Yourself?'

'Farhad. Dr Farhad Billimoria.'

'O-ho. A doctor. We have to send both our cars to the hospital now, no, Doctor? The problem is, this is not my, but my wife's car. And I have made so many mistakes in the past that when I make a new one, my wife gets *very* angry. If she sees the car like this, I will be . . .' He drew a hand across his throat.

I wanted to say I used to have such a wife, too, but this wasn't the time and place for male bonding, and so I said, 'You don't need to worry. There's a very good twenty-four-hour garage not far from here, and I'd be happy to pay for the repairs.'

'Really?' He paused. 'Okay, I accept your offer.'

'Great, here's my card.'

Balu's phone rang. He studied the display with a vexed expression before taking the call. An agitated voice hectored him for what seemed like an age. Balu heard him out impressively impassively, while I waited intensely impatiently.

'Just one more day, sir! The missionaries will definitely arrive by tomorrow, I promise. And they will be *fully* to your satisfaction.'

The missionaries? Oh Jesus. What was going on? For a whole year, no one I had met had so much as acknowledged that there was something like sex in this world. Then, the night that the greatest of all human forces came flooding back into my life, a chance encounter led to the revelation that even the missionaries of the world were apparently going at it like rabbits.

Balu turned to me and shrugged. 'What to do with people? Yes, sir, you were saying? Ah, your card.'

A buxom, saried, bindied lady emerged from the other door of Balu's car. She called out, 'Darling, I can't stand it in here any more. You took the key out and the air conditioning isn't working. Is it very bad?'

Balu laughed. 'Well, let's just say I can't take a car that looks like this home to Hemlata. Meet my good friend Dr Billimoria. Tonight,

God has chosen him to be a—how do you call it?—an agent of love. How about we check the car into his favourite garage and ourselves into a hotel for the night?'

'A hotel? Oh, you naughty boy! There's always only one thing on your mind.'

On any other day in the age of my recent singledom, the words of this insouciant philanderer, coolly juggling wives, mistresses and missionaries, would have provoked a stab of envy in me. But tonight, they merely reminded me I had ascended to a higher spiritual plane. And all because of Zahra.

We Are in Bombay

WHEN I OPENED my eyes after the sunsleep I had, after long hours, been able to resist no further, I saw before me Eeja, sitting erect in His chair, staring straight at me, into me. Dusk had dawned. The crow that had perched by the window all afternoon had flown off. On the bed next to my own chair, Ooi was taking sleep downstream with long, musical snores, Her unbound red, white and black hair covering the pillow, the folds of Her green sari wrinkles around Her skinwrinkles. Horizontal and vertical, the two of Them rested heavily as boulders, one to my left, one to my right.

Outside our small, bare, sad room, the spirits of night were charging at this world with their heavy, darkening mantles. The air had the sweet smell of old and high-born people, the vapours of ointments and potions, and some other thing that could only be Bombay.

As the light faded, Eeja's face grew less and less clear, but His head did not move, nor even His eyes in the middle of it, popping-peering from behind His large glasses on His nose.

Could He be dead? A tremor of panic passed through me. Eeja!

I felt a strange excitement, too—because, in passing out of this world, Eeja would at long last have done something new, and I could be home just in time for the election. I was about to rise to touch Him when a small hindwhistle escaped from Him and blew away my doubts and hopes. Nothing had changed. Everything was the same. We sat opposite one another listening to Ooi's rising and falling snores, as if passing them back and forth between ourselves like chillum-pipes, saying, 'Here, you,' 'No, brother, you,' 'All right, brother, now you.'

As with the Lord Jagannath, whose staring eyes pierce all, nothing remained of Eeja now but His gaze. He reminded me of an owl on a tree. The owl, so still—the owl, my friend. But when the wind suddenly blew, and the berries came falling like hailstones from the mahua tree, the owl remembered its wings and flew off, out of the thicket of trees and across the fields of Tininadi, over the low roofs of the village, some thatch, some brick, and past the spires of smoke rising as the first fires of the evening seized the wood. Behind the village, the Cloud Mountain rose steeply up into the sky, long and flat as an elephant's back. As far as the eye could see, the grey of dusk settled upon the greens and browns of my lovely land, but high in the heavens two fish-like clouds blushed pink, and the last rays of the sun caught the peak of the mountain and then the small blue flag of the Company planted there, as if pointing out what was wrong with the world. The sounds of night piped up and rose slowly until they reached a crescendo—all the tuit-tuits, cooees, squeaks, rustles, plops, eck-ecks, chirrups, moans and mewls calling to one another across earth, tree, mountain and sky. Far off to the west, out of the low hills where the woo-foxes had their hideouts among the copses of fig and broom-flower, two lights suddenly glimmered on the dirt track that linked the state highway to Tininadi. A jeep. Not a Company jeep, but the rattling vehicle of Bhagaban Bhai, my brother, my mentor, my friend, who could make the heaviest time light—as Eeja and Ooi, his parents, could make the lightest time heavy. He was whistling in there and singing songs to his bodyguard. Had I been around, he would be saying to me, 'So, Rabi, brother, we have succeeded in making a fine, tripping tune, and what we shall see now is a dance—nothing less than the dance of democracy. Oh, the sparks! They will light the way to the top of the mountain, where we shall plant our very own flag, that of Cloudmaker. Is there any better carnival, any bigger party, in our country than an election?'

Ah, the pleasure and freedom of travel in that wide and wonderful world—the calling out of our slogans and songs from the loudspeaker in the back of the jeep, the sudden pause of hands and legs as we passed, the dust clouds raised by the feet of the children running out of their homes, the unrolling of a white screen in clearings and compounds, the projector playing facts and footage we had gathered about the Company. The look of respect and wonder on the faces of people when I spoke my name and mentioned my village, and they realized that I was not an outsider from the city but one of them, risen to a new place of self-respect and power—both a tribal and a modern, as Bhagaban Bhai liked to put it. And the leaflets we handed out asking that, on election day, on the last weekend of March, the people ignore the bicycles and lanterns and sickles and hands they had chosen in the past, and instead put a cross next to *our* election symbol: the cloud. Such a grand occasion, one we had been working towards for more than a year, but I would not be back in time for it, caught up as I was in Bombay with two old people in whose old gaze I was nothing more than a boy, a bumpkin, a simple-minded tribal of the old times.

Something poked me in the chest—a finger! Eeja was leaning forward in the dark and His face was only a few inches from mine.

'Where—is—she?'

Yes, Eeja, life's only about what You see, what You think, what You need. I rose and switched on the light. Ooi woke with a start and looked around the room, dazed by how fast She had vaulted the fence of sleep. Her four gold bangles clinked as She raised Her hand to shade Her face.

'Where am I?' She asked.

Eeja said, 'Welcome, welcome! So, you are here, too?'

'Where else would I be?'

'Where are we?'

'Where do you think we are?'

They'd started—not a minute since She'd woken up, and They were at it again.

Ooi covered Her face with Her hands and groaned, 'Lord Jagannath, deliver me—deliver me from this world! I'm so tired of answering this question. I'm beginning to think you do it just to annoy me.'

'I'm asking for a reason. I went over to . . . to the other side.'

Ooi and I looked at each other.

'I wasn't in my body any more. I rose above myself and left.'

'Hss! You were seen by a dream.'

'What I want to ask is, am I still there, or am I back?' Eeja mused, a detective contemplating His own mysteries. 'No, but *you*'re still here . . . that means I can't be there.'

'Here, there, here, there! What other side? God knows we already are on the other side of the country. From the far east, our home, to the edge of the west.'

'I fell over, and there was a door right beneath me. Not on any wall, but on the floor. And yet, I was standing upright. I drew back the curtains and went in. Then down the long passage, the voice calling from the far end, "Ho, good soul! This way! Come this way!" Who could it have been? It could only have been Yama, the God of Death.'

'Hss! Don't talk nonsense. It was all a dream. You've been sitting right here all this time like the King of Puri in his durbar. It's your own fault for not agreeing to lie down. Look, there's so much room on the bed. It's the one thing in this wretched city that's a normal size. I lay down, and I had such a sweet, peaceful dream. The taste of it is still on my tongue. We were on a boat, drifting on a gentle current. I remember the sound of the water splashing against the wood. Across the river, under a big banyan tree leaning out over the water, was the temple of the Goddess. Waiting at its entrance was our son Bhagaban, holding two garlands of flowers—whether for the Goddess, or to receive us, or because he was about to get married, I can't tell you. We were just about to reach when, *dhssh*, Rabi turned on the light and destroyed it all. Rabi! Do me a favour and press my legs a little. All my joints have become stiff. I can't get up. No, not there. *There.*'

'Now that I'm back, I want to eat fish,' said Eeja. 'Who knows if I will get the chance again? Listen, my fellow householders! Death hangs above me, ready to swoop down any moment. Let us make the most of today.' He chortled, greatly amused.

'No, you're not allowed to eat fish.'

'Who is this fellow sitting here? You—what is your name? Where is our son?'

Ooi said, 'Our son is in Bhubaneswar on some important work. He's left us this lad to take care of us while you recover. We can't go home until you do.'

'Why not?'

'Think about it. We can't take the train because it's a ride of nearly two days across our vast country. Nor can we fly before they measure the speed of your heart once again at the hospital. Flying taxes the heart.'

'This fellow smells like a low caste. He hasn't taken a bath.'

'He doesn't smell. He takes just as many baths as you and me. More, actually, because he gets all wet when he bathes you. And he's not from any caste. He's a tribesman, beyond the pale of caste, no matter how much he may want to enter the house of Hinduism.'

'What are we doing hanging around with tribals in strange houses at our age? Let's go home.'

'Don't fuss. This *is* home—for the time being. I've tried to do my best to make it look like home.'

'This isn't home. Here, boy. You tell me, where have we landed? I'll give you a rupee if you do. Where are we?'

Ooi took a deep breath and cried, shaking with rage, '*Bom*bay, *Bom*bay! We are in BOMBAY!'

Ooi had said the very same words in the morning, and the evening before, and so many times in the last month that one could have easily thought it was Her mind that had become windy and not Eeja's. But as She said on the phone the other day to Bhagaban Bhai, 'When you live with somebody for sixty years, you repeat some questions hundreds of times. "When is the next new moon day? What will you eat? How much are they selling potatoes for? Are you asleep?" As I see it, it's just that I sprinkled my questions like salt over the months and the years, while He asks his like raindrops falling fast and thick in the first storm of the monsoon. At the end of the day, it's all the same thing.'

But no matter how often He heard the answer, not a day passed without Eeja exclaiming—as He did again now—'What! Are we in Bombay?'

What are we doing here?

Pack up your things.

Let's go home.

I knew what Ooi was going to say, too, as I knew what They were both going to say for the next hour. 'This is Bombay, the city of the rich and famous. When the hospital in Bhubaneswar said they couldn't do the operation needed for your heart, Bhagaban spent so much money to bring us to Bombay and make sure that the best doctors could take care of you. And he put us up in this house while you recover.'

Today, because She was especially annoyed with Eeja, She added, 'The same son you always thought was a good-for-nothing proved to be the very incarnation of love and parentworship. Yes, if there's one good thing that has come out of all these months of suffering, it is that our son has proved himself as worthy as any son in the great epics. And soon, he'll be a shining light not just in our eyes but before the whole world. He's going to win the election and have his photo in all the newspapers. Because he's fighting for the rights of these tribal people—the kinfolk of this boy here—who have no one but him to rely on.'

'Where is he now?'

'He had to go back. Don't make that face. It isn't his fault he's not here. Have you ever heard of an election being postponed because a candidate's father wasn't well? Don't you remember, he took your blessings before he left and wept like a child?'

'I remember going to the hospital, yes. After that, it's a blank. Is my heart fine now?'

'How does your tongue tattle if your heart isn't fine? You have a young man's heart now, ticking like a foreign clock. The doctors said so themselves. A few days of rest, and you'll be as well as you've ever been. Then we can all return to Bhubaneswar and live happily again. Oh, the days we've seen here! May no one else in our line ever have to suffer so. Even Rama had an easier time during his fourteen years of exile in the forest.'

Eeja snorted. 'Never trust a fisherwoman who says the fish is fresh, and a doctor who says you're cured. Anyway, I want to tell you both to tell the doctors that I am perfectly well. I want to go to Bhubaneswar. That's where I want to eat my next meal.'

Ooi flew into a rage and shouted, '*I want to go to Bhubaneswar, I want to go to Bhubaneswar!* There's the door! Get up! Go!'

They both fell into silence—the silence of trapped animals—with no sense that someone was watching Them or that I wanted to go back home as well. They were thinking of Bhubaneswar, and of Themselves in Bhubaneswar. If wishing for something deeply enough had ever made miracles come to pass, the will of these two old Brahmins would have turned Bombay into Bhubaneswar of the bus stand, the spired temples, the weekly markets and the share-autos, the electricity coming and going all the time, making holes in the television serials that the mind then pondered over for days. As the greater world lies behind the clouds, and what we live is only one small verse and moment in the song of creation, so Bombay meant nothing to Them, and all They saw in Their mind's eye was Bhubaneswar. How could one fault Them? They had never left Their own state until this ripe age, more fit for passing from the world than fighting to stay on in it, while, as Bhai never failed to remind me, I had already, before the end of my second decade, left my people behind once to live in Bhubaneswar with Bhai and be the face and voice of the Cloud people in our fight against the Company. And now I had assumed just as grave a responsibility here in Bombay.

Eeja said, 'Is this boy a tribal from these parts, or is he from our state?'

'I really don't know what to do with you. Here we've nearly come to the end of the Ramayana, and then you ask, who is Rama? Come, work your mind a little. Think back through the days. This boy has lifted you, bathed you, fed you, sat in a hospital chair beside you, cleaned up after you when you vomited, urinated, passed stool. We may have the intelligence, but it's his labour upon which we depend. Wouldn't it make him happy if you could just remember his name? He'd feel it was nothing short of a blessing.'

Eeja said, 'I do remember. This fellow is Ranjan.'

'Ranjan? That's not his name. That was your nephew's name. But you're close. Try again.'

'Ratan?'

'It's *Rabi*. His name is Rabi.'

'Rabi? Why, that's the name of the fisherman.'

'What fisherman? There's no fisherman by that name. In Bhubaneswar, our fisherman's name is Diba. God knows how many times in the last month he'd have come with his catch and knocked on our door. At first, the neighbours would have said to him, "They've gone away for a week or so, for sir's operation. They'll be back soon. Don't worry, don't be sad, you haven't lost a customer. Everything will be fine again." But weeks have gone by, and there's no sign of us. Maybe they think we're dead. All that wonderful river fish, sweet as nectar . . . not like the nasty fish they eat here, straight from the sea and as smelly as a dog's breath. Bhagaban told me that hundreds of years ago, this city was nothing but marshland, and the first people to settle here were low-caste fisherfolk. Between them and the British, they corrupted everyone in this city into eating saltwater fish. Some Brahmins, too. How easy it is to tempt even the best.'

Ooi stood up with a long groan and teetered on Her uneven legs. She went hobbling over to the bathroom to wash Her face, then came back and rustled in the suitcase in the corner that had all of Eeja's things. She handed Him a notebook. 'Here. Look. What's in here?'

Eeja opened the book and held it up close to His face. 'It's my handwriting,' He said, pleased. 'A Sanskrit verse on every page. This one's from the Chandogya Upanishad. Hmm. That's from the *Sarvadharmasambhava* of Madhavacharya. One of the greatest souls of the thirteenth century.'

'Whether they're from the holy books or from yesterday's newspaper,

I wouldn't know. But Bhagaban said you were to write a new verse on a new sheet every day, and then a few lines of commentary in Odia, because Hindus everywhere are falling away from Sanskrit. Then, when the election is over, he'll have it printed up into a nice book and distribute it wherever he goes, saying, "This is my father's collection. He was not just a district magistrate but also a great Sanskrit scholar." It's got to be done right away. There'll be so many things for you to attend to when we get back that you'll never have the time. Our bills, bank accounts, fixed deposits, housing society meetings . . . all the people who come to you to have their palms read.'

'Yes, why don't they come to see me here?'

'No one knows who we are here. This is a new building society. Half the flats are still empty. Else, where would we have found a place to stay this cheaply in this godforsaken city? Apparently, even beggars need to make six thousand a month to survive here. Anyway, it's time.'

'Where are you going?' said Eeja. 'Are you leaving me alone with this boy?'

'What! Are my duties to you alone and no one else? Don't you know what day it is today?'

'I couldn't tell you.'

Ooi said in a low, enraptured voice, 'Today is a very sacred day, the fourteenth day of the bright half of the month of Chaitra, the day of one of the thirteen great festivals of the year in the Jagannath temple of Puri.'

'The Festival of the Leaves!' Eeja piped up.

'You are right. From all parts of Odisha, thousands of people will flock to the Great Thoroughfare of Puri to mark the leaf-gathering of the Gods. Is there a scene like it in the whole wide world? Never. You've seen it for eighty years, you don't need to be there to picture it—the chanting and the crying, the conches wailing and the bells ringing, the smoke from incense sticks and the scent of burning camphor, the flower garlands and the holy water, the travelling preachers and Puri pandas. Since, sadly, we cannot be there, we will call Him down here, the round-eyed Lord of the Three Realms. We will call Him to our little room in Bombay through our love, through our devotion. Here. Look here. Rabi went to the market in the morning and bought me a piece of sandalwood. I'm going to sit down on the floor and grind it into a paste. I'll chop up some bananas and apples, and lay them out in my copper dishes, so that Jagannath and all the other Gods may eat to Their fill.'

'Glory be to Lord Jagannath,' Eeja conceded.

'In the meantime, you can chant some Sanskrit verses. Bhagaban said you were to do so every evening to keep your memory in good shape.'

'I don't remember anything. I want to eat fish.'

'Try and concentrate,' said Ooi, as She switched off the light. 'They'll all come back to you. Whatever you recall, say it aloud. Remember, just like us, Jagannath is feeling lost here in Bombay. He is hungry for the sights, smells, sounds, things of beauty from that distant world over which He reigns supreme. Can God exist without man's veneration? Never. When He hears you, His heart will be flooded with tenderness and feeling, even pride, and He will become Himself again. Speak for as long as you like. Rabi here is a tribal and knows nothing about the higher reaches of devotion. It will improve his mind to listen to you. Maybe you can even teach him some verses.'

'What! Teach him Sanskrit verses? Just because cows can moo, does one try to teach them to sing?'

After all these days of serving Him—or, even worse, *because* I had been serving Him for all these days—I was apparently for Eeja no better than a three-sound, four-legged animal.

'O-ho, he won't recite them. He merely wants to hear *you* say them aloud. Should we not share the riches of learning with those whose minds are blank? Come, shall I start one for you? *Eka bharja* . . . I don't know any more . . .'

'*Eka bharja* . . . *prakruti mukhara* . . .' Eeja began to chant in Sanskrit, halting and crackling like fire on wet wood, looking at me all the while.

26

Farhad in the Aer

IT WAS MY first date in eighteen years—and it was a date worth waiting eighteen years for! Even so, there was no escaping the truth and all its consequences. There's no way you can be Mr Cool on your first date in eighteen years. After a long day lost in sweet Zahric reveries, the famous Billimoric sang-freud faltered a little when I had showered that evening and shaved. My favourite clothes had been packed and sent off; I had not envisaged a situation where I'd have to look my sexiest in my last week in the city. As soon as I stepped out into the evening sunlight, I felt uncomfortable in an unfavoured pink shirt, which had become too tight for me at the shoulders, and my blue Zara jeans. Not good: unless I looked my best, how could I *be* my best self? And it was imperative that I be that, for what happened this evening could be a template for all my evenings in the next year, in search of the maps, the mysteries, of feminine flesh and feeling.

A model of how to look your best self lay in front of me in the form of Zelda who, but for a few grazes on the fender, had emerged completely unscathed from her bust-up of the previous evening. I started her up and, happy to hear her familiar hum, sailed down Worli Sea Face (beginning to swell with unruly traffic heading to the Sea Link), past City Bakery (with its cheap false-cream cakes and excellent croissants), through the crowded Naka, and finally down E. Moses Road and into the Four Seasons, which goes up and up and up till it turns on the thirty-third floor into Aer.

Emerging from the elevator, I saw that the sun was slipping past the left flank of this storied city of ours, spread out all around me in a patchwork of brightness and dark, dome and spire, splendour and squalor. There was no sign of Zahra. I ignored the waiter's predictable efforts at finding me a table facing east—the waiter's task in India, like the instinct of India itself, being to disable life and enjoyment as much as possible—and claimed one on the sea-and-sunset side. I surveyed the crowd. Some penguins in suits and ties trying to persuade themselves that they were enjoying life after a day spent discussing brand value, brokerage and boobs; tight T-shirted whippersnappers who had inherited their fathers' businesses after degrees from St Xavier's or Sydenham and MBAs from American or British universities dedicated to India; a smattering of foreign business travellers on expense accounts; and one table with what seemed to be middle-aged Russian blondes speaking in a tongue rippling with harsh sounds.

On all such evenings in the past year, the sight of so much communion around me, isolated as I was in lonely, if superior-grade, Billimorism, would have made me sad. But today, my head was in the clouds.

Unusually for March, it was overcast, and a high wind was beating at the low glass walls of the bar and tousling the tops of trees in the well of the city. Perhaps, two hundred years ago, a wind such as this had gusted down a young Bombay—an unraised Bombay of islands and marshes—and ruffled some ancestor of mine as he set out for a parlour or tenement or ship-shade for a rendezvous with an English rose or a sinning Surat wife.

I checked the time. The anticipation was delightful—Zahra was almost better absent than present.

But what if . . .?

What if for some reason she wasn't coming?

And I didn't have her number!

Just then, I heard a familiar female voice from the passage, and I sat up straight and tried to look lost in contemplation.

Zahra's voice was raised, a bit louder than if one were merely saying one was looking for somebody. She sailed into view with one hand to her ear, heart-attack lovely in navy-blue harem pants and a white, gauzy, sleeveless blouse that seemed to give her waist and bust seven planes of shimmer when she moved. Her hair was tied back simply in a ponytail. She wore hoop earrings and a silver bracelet high on her arm. Otherwise, she was free of the armada of accessories on which women seem dependent. It was as if she only needed to dress up once in her life, and the memory of that occasion, injected into the bloodstream of all humanity, would work for her everywhere, forever (it would certainly work forever for *me*). All the people on this side of Aer, and especially the women, stopped mid-sentence to examine the visitor. Zahra spotted me and waved, even as she continued speaking on the phone.

As she approached, the sunset glinting off her earrings, she said, like a stage actress acknowledging an audience by ignoring them: 'No, Mr Shroff, I want you to let him know that I will *not* be cowed down by these ridiculous pressure tactics. Hello? This is the twenty-first century—wake up and smell the coffee! Those days are gone when you men did what you wanted and then decided if you wished to involve us. Whether you like it or not, one share of the property was my father's, and so now it's mine. If *they* want to sell it, they must first ask *me*! Just because I live in a big city in America doesn't mean I'm filthy rich, like you think, or that I'm not keeping an eye on things back home. I'm keeping track of your every move. I spent my summer vacations in that place—it's mine as much as it's theirs. You have until Wednesday to behave in a more respectful way about this. Else, I warn you, I'll fight till the very end. And if need be, I'll give up my own profit share if it means that I have to stop you from getting yours. Isn't your own child a girl? What lesson are y'all teaching her with such behaviour? That she's some helpless doll who must wait for a husband to take care of her and take charge of everything that belongs to her? What? That's not my business? You know what? You're right for the first time. Sure, so that's not my business. But, Mr Shroff, this matter *is* my business. Get it? So pass on the message. And call me back if you people change your mind, else I'll sort you out in court. A very good evening to you and your crummy clients.'

She cut the call and, without breaking stride, smiled dazzlingly and said, 'Hello, Dr Billimoria—yes, I know, sorry—Farhad. I must apologize for the rudeness. I was just clearing up something important.'

'Oh no. *I'm* sorry that you're so worked up.'

'I hope you don't think I'm a demon of some kind, just waiting to drag people to court.'

'Who, me? Never.'

'It's just that, if you're a single woman in this world, you have to fight for your rights all the time. You're a therapist, you'll know. After a point, it's the world that makes us who we are.'

She was a single woman in this world! I was a single man in the very same world!

'So true, so true. Not at all. Good to see you. Is this some property dispute?'

'Yes, but let's forget it. It's not important. What a beautiful evening . . . and a beautiful view! Is that Haji Ali down there? Yes, it is. That's the pathway into the sea leading to the shrine. You know, you can never tell the real shape of Bombay from down there. Now, everything looks like it's in a different place from where I thought it was. Sorry I'm a bit late—traffic! Do you come here often?'

'Oh, almost never. A couple of my clients sometimes invite me here for a drink. To show me that they also want to be my friends, I suppose. Though it always ends up being just another consultation. People can never stop talking about themselves.'

Zahra laughed and, scanning the drinks list, told the waiter who now stood beside us, 'I'll have a—a Bombay Bellini. What about you?'

'I'll have the same then.'

'Something to eat, sir?'

'Something to eat?'

'No, I don't eat anything after six, except for a light dinner at half-seven. But it's happy hours. We can drink as much as we want,' said Zahra, in a warm-blooded way that excited me enormously. 'Sorry, Farhad. You must think I'm so cheap. But it's in our Zoroastrian blood to be spendthrifts and cheapskates at the same time, no? Or Irani blood, in my case. You're not Irani, too, are you?'

'No, proper old-school Parsi. Haughty and insular—just because my ancestors migrated here a few centuries before your lot. A slave to tradition, ritual and inbreeding.'

'Oh, come now, you couldn't possibly be like that! In fact, you must know a thousand things that most Indians don't know, leave alone the Parsis . . . because of your work in therapy. All the deepest secrets of people. Isn't that true?'

'I could tell you a few things that'd surprise you, yes.'

'There's something I wanted to ask you. I've been thinking about it all day. Tell me, is there a lot of infidelity in Bombay?'

'That depends on what you take as your base ground.'

'Don't dodge now! Tell me.'

'Yes. More than you'd think. Much more.'

'Wow, really!'

'But isn't that always the case with adultery? There's typically more of it than one thinks. It's meant to be a secret. That's what makes it exciting to everyone involved.'

'Exciting? Not for the ones who're being cheated *on*, surely? Unless they get together with each other—like the lead pair in *In the Mood for Love*. Have you seen that movie?'

'Yes. I especially love the soundtrack by Nat King Cole.'

'I love those scenes in slow motion where they go up the steps, all alone, carrying their noodle dinners. It's so romantic somehow—like they're actually together in their loneliness, only they can't see it because, of course, they don't know about each other yet. Anyway. What about incest? Is there a lot of that?'

I was delighted by the free, frank and low turn that our conversation was taking at Zahra's own bidding, and said in a whisper, 'Sssh, or in two minutes we're going to have everyone in this place sitting at our feet.'

Zahra giggled. 'What a strange lot we Indians are, don't you think?'

'I'll confess, after years of study I've come to the same conclusion—

only, now, I'm bored of such strangeness. We don't actually want more freedom, as some people imagine we do. That would be so mundane. We'd rather have a world of piety and prohibition so we can preach morality to others—all the while trying to circumvent those very same rules.'

'Hmm. So, lots of incest, too? What a world!' Zahra whistled, an act that curiously became her, the way priests can look their most charming when they run cassocked into a football game. 'Sorry if this is boring for you, Dr Billimoria. I'm just curious about these things because I've been away from India so long, and I want to know how our society is changing. And who better than you to know the secret life of the Indian mind?'

'Ah, no, I'm sure my guess is no better than any other. How long have you been away?'

'Forever! Let's see . . . I left in 1996. So, fifteen years. Yes, I know, that makes me very old. Older than you probably thought I was. But that's not such a terrible thing. A woman must just accept, at a certain point, that her best years are behind her.'

'What a shocking thing to admit. If my opinion is of any value, I don't think you'll be getting there for many years yet.'

'What a sweet thing to say. Well, I'll take you at your word and tell you how old I am. I was twenty-three when I left this city. I'll let you do the math. I left to get married, actually.'

'Really? And how was that—is that?'

Zahra laughed. 'It was like one of those diploma courses—it lasted only a year. The guy was Irani, but from Las Vegas—he worked in a casino there. Yes, I know. What *was* I doing? But I was so young. My head was full of all kinds of romantic illusions and fantasies. Eternal love and perfect union and all that.'

'Very interesting. And then?'

'Then? I already had residency when we broke up, so there was no point returning. I drifted around a bit. In the strangest places. Dayton, Ohio; Eugene, Oregon. Anywhere but Bombay. I knew that if I returned to my world of parents, aunts, uncles and cousins in Ness Baug, I'd become an object of sympathy, of pity. Everybody would go out of their way to be nice to me, and that niceness would be more terrible than anything else. In this world, it's okay to make one wrong move. But you mustn't let that lead you to another mistake.'

'How smart!' I said, with genuine respect.

'Just find some way of keeping your head above the water till you work out what you want to do next.'

'Exactly what I've said to many people who've come my way.'

'I read it in a book by Enrico Sanchez. Did you, too?'

'Enrico who?'

'Enrico Sanchez. He's a bit like—a bit like Richard Bach. Or Paulo Coelho. Only better. Those two are pop. They write for money. This man is serious. His last book was *The Secret of the Secret*. But that's not so good. His best is *What You Didn't See from the Centre of the Room*. From the mid-90s. Isn't that a great title?'

'It is.'

'It's like it arrived in my life just when I needed it. All along, I'd been in the centre of the room. And . . . you know . . . if you're in the centre of the room, why would you ever move?'

'To look out of the window?'

'Dr Billimoria, now you're laughing at me. But think about it. It's true. All my life I'd been in the thick of it. Good-looking, popular, well-connected. People around me full of love for me; doors and windows open on all sides, positive energy in every direction. Then, suddenly, something terrible happened—in this case, my divorce—and the room became empty. For no fault of mine—but that's how it was, that was the truth. To get to another room, find another centre, I had to first learn how to move around my own room. Oh, look, here are our drinks. Well . . . cheers. What shall we drink to?'

'Why not aim high? Cheers to life,' I said, with a sudden flash of happiness and optimism brought on by the face in front of me, the last rays of the sunset, and a fresh sense of the pastness of my past and the promise of my future. 'To the puzzle that is life, and to the pleasures of thinking about that puzzle. To the secret of the secret.'

Zahra laughed. 'I can't tell if you're making fun of me, but I don't care. These books changed my life. Actually, I love reading. And I love going to book launches, too. Just to see the mind of the person who made the book. I think a book becomes more interesting when you have some sense of the personality of the writer.'

'Really? I don't think I've been to more than two book launches in my whole life.'

Zahra pointed a finger at me. 'There's one in Bombay tomorrow. Want to go? A big one . . . at the Trident. My sister told me about it.'

'Sure. Whose book is it?'

'It's an Indian novelist. Very famous. He lives in America and he's visiting. Amitav . . . Amitav Ghosh! It's his new book. It's a novel . . . but a novel about things that really happened. About Indian history. History that we don't know. About the opium trade and Bombay, I think, and China. I read all about it by googling it last night. It's called *Cloud of Smoke*. And, best of all, it has a hero who is a Parsi! We must go, for the sake of solidarity if nothing else. We Parsis have no literature about us at all. Iranis even less so. Hindus and Muslims have taken over the past of this country. But actually, we've had a bigger role in its making . . . at least if you count per capita.'

Zahra's arousing laughter floated up into the sky, where the personal secretary of Zarathustra entered it in his logbook as an offering.

'Interesting. An aunt of mine, Freny Doctor, wrote a Parsi crime novel. It's called *Dikra, Your Days Are Numbered*. The title is better than the writing though. Anyway . . . I'd love to go to this Ghosh thing.'

'It's a plan,' said Zahra. 'I'd like another Bellini. What about you?'

'I'm still only halfway through this. But okay. You sure drink fast.'

'I love champagne. Don't you?' said Zahra. 'Oh, look! The sun's all gone. How beautiful it all looks. I know it sounds weird, but sometimes I think Bombay is more beautiful than San Francisco.'

'Really? Why would you think that?'

'It's more human somehow. More real. Everybody has a place here. They find a place for themselves and make what they can of their lives.'

'Even if they have no toilets, no clean water to drink, no roof above their heads, no public parks and no property rights?'

Zahra sighed. 'I guess you're right. I'm not being reasonable. When you come back to Bombay once in a while, you only see the good things. And, of course, all the memories come rushing back. When you come back to visit next year, Dr Billimoria, you'll find yourself talking like me now. Sorry for calling you Dr Billimoria. But if you don't mind, that's what I'll call you. I find it *less* formal than Farhad, somehow. I can have more fun with you that way. Maybe other people have told you that, too.'

'Maybe it's the spirits of my ancestors at work, making sure that people reach out to what is common to me and them as Billimorias and not what's particular to me as Farhad.'

'Ha! Well, what *is* particular to you as Farhad? Tell me more about yourself. I've just been talking about myself and myself. I've only asked you shallow things like what you think about incest and all.'

'*And all*? You still say "and all" after being away so many years?'

Zahra laughed. 'Well, why not? It's a very useful bit of speech, don't you think? I haven't been to your office, but I picture you now in a room with all your clients, some of them adult—what's the, you know, adjective form of adultery?—adultrious?'

'Adulterous.'

'Adulterous! Sorry, I'm not so good with words. I'm good with physical things. I picture you in a big room with all your clients, some adulterous, some incestuous, some paranoid, some deranged. Title of the scene: Farhad Billimoria and All.'

'Very charming, but too dramatic, I'm afraid. Therapy isn't like that. It's mostly long and slow and boring. Right now, the title of that scene would probably be: Farhad Billimoria *Ends* All.'

'Aren't your clients sorry to see you go? What about those who haven't got better?'

'I've agreed to continue talking to some of them on Skype. It suits me, too. That way, I can cut them off as soon as they run into overtime and tell them it was a problem with the connection.'

'Do a lot of people run into overtime?'

'Like you wouldn't believe! *Just five minutes more, Doctor. I just remembered one point that might have a bearing on the problem. For the last three weeks, my dog . . .*'

'Oh, don't be so harsh!' exclaimed Zahra, but only as a way of controlling her laughter. 'Surely there's something enjoyable in the work as well? Didn't you start doing it because you thought you'd *like* it?'

'I did, yes. Sometimes, I still do. Sometimes, it must be said, you come across honesty, candour, insight. Then you see how difficult life is, even for those people who *can see*, who aren't blinded by ego or self-deception or pain. Much of the time, though, it's all a giant mess that's never going to get much better. The best I can do is listen and make small, practical suggestions.'

Zahra sighed and looked into the distance. 'How interesting. I wish I had some kind of problem. I've never been to a therapist.'

'Well, now you know one. You can book me any time you like in San Francisco, at 20 per cent off my usual rate.'

Dr Billimoria was getting a bit daring here! But life is short, my friends. Seize the day. And should it all come crashing down, cease the day. Begin again, in a new city. Not San Francisco, though, because I've taken that already.

'You're so cheap!' said Zahra. 'But come on, Dr Billimoria, I couldn't approach you now even if I wanted to. You're my *friend*.'

'Yes, yes, but a therapist is a kind of friend anyway . . .' I teased.

'No, if I have problems, I'd like you listen to me as a friend! Not as a therapist, okay? Promise me that.'

'Okay. I'll listen to you as a friend.'

'What would the difference be, though?'

'I guess, when I listen to you as a friend, I won't be wearing a tie.'

Zahra laughed. 'You're so . . . so guarded! It's hard to know what's going on in your heart. Anyway, it's time for me to shut up for a bit. Alcohol always gets me garrulacious. That's one thing you'll have to know about me. Next time, don't let me order a second drink so fast. So. Now you tell me about *your* life, Dr Billimoria—Farhad.'

Where could I start? Zahra's interest was thrilling to the Farhadian heart but totally immobilizing for the brain. Ridiculously, I saw myself being born in a hospital.

A few seconds went by. Nothing happened, except the moon rose a mite higher in the sky.

'Well? What about it?' asked Zahra. 'It's not something you have to make up!'

'Don't you? All lives are finally the stories we tell about them.'

'Oh, come now, Farhad. Don't be boring.'

'Um . . . I'm just wondering where to begin. It's such a big question to answer.'

'Okay, I'll make it easier for you. Why are you moving to San Francisco? Next week, isn't it?'

'Next week.'

'Family? Work?'

'Family? No, I have no family.'

'You know, I sort of guessed you were a bachelor.'

'I'm not, actually. I'm divorced.'

'Oh, so we're together on that one! How long has it been? More than a decade, too?'

'Just a couple of years, actually. Why did you think I was a bachelor?'

'I don't know. There's something bachelor-like about you, I guess.'

'I see. Is that a good thing or a bad thing?'

'Oh, it's nothing. Are you upset? I'm not suggesting that I think you get no action. I'm sure you get plenty.'

'Well . . . to be honest, a bachelor is who I'd most like to be right now.'

'Really? What kind of bachelor?'

'Are there different kinds?'

'Of course. Seeking . . . or staying? A bachelor looking out of the window, checking out the chicks . . . or one curled up on the couch, reading an interesting book about Buddhism?'

'Seeking!' I declared, not wanting to seem unadventurous.

'All right then,' said Zahra, laughing. 'San Francisco is the place for you. I'll have you set up with someone sensational in six weeks, guaranteed.'

'To San Francisco!' I said, raising my second Bellini to my date, who was now offering, from the goodness of her heart—or, perhaps, because she was satisfied with the cross-eyed caresses of that popgun Parsi who had escorted her the other night—to set me up with others. 'But no, I'm not that desperate. We'll just see how it goes. Something—somebody—will come up. And if not—well, it's good to be free.'

'Hasn't something come up in Bombay? This city is full of beautiful women.'

'Yes, but single? In our—I mean, in my age group? Not many.'

'I have a cousin who's single. Jumana. She's three years older than me. Forty-one. A lovely girl. She runs her own beauty parlour in Bandra.'

'Well, thank you, but now it's too late. Perhaps if she wanted to move her business to San Francisco . . .'

'Dr Billimoria, when the mountain comes to the molehill, you're just like any other man! You men always want us women to pack up our lives and move after you.'

'Hello! I only just heard about her. I'm very happy for your cousin Jumana to stay exactly where she is.'

'You are? Cheers to that, you're a liberal man. It makes me wonder. Why would any right-thinking woman give you up in a country full of monsters and maniacs?'

How beautifully Zahra enunciated that word 'maniacs'. And what an artistic way of extracting information about my married life. The true measure of a human being lies in the ways in which she manages to be subtle—and, then, in the ways in which she is direct. In her judgement of these things. You know what I mean.

'Oh, come on,' I said, 'you know that's not how it works. People start losing sight of one another exactly from the time they start living with each other. Over the years, all sorts of troubles, and memories of troubles, and competing narratives of troubles, build up . . . and one day, you look into your heart, and you know that it's all a farce, and the show has got to end. The most wonderful people can be terrible to one another in ways you'd never suspect.'

'Dr Billimoria, you're so theoretical sometimes. Even Enrico Sanchez gives examples and illustrations for all his points.' Zahra's legs were crossed, right over left. Now she recrossed them the other way. I tried not to make it obvious that I noticed these shifts in posture. She asked, 'So, in what ways would you say you can be terrible?'

'Who? Men?'

'No, *you* as a person.'

'Oh, I'm a monster through and through . . . no, I'm joking. Maybe I'm not really terrible . . . just terrible in another person's eyes. You know, it's not only women who must fight for their spaces, their selves—although that's become the mainstream narrative of our times. Men must, too. And sometimes, when a man can no longer go forward with his partner, he must go forward by himself. And sometimes, to the partner, this can be a terrible betrayal, a rejection. An insult beyond all insults.'

'I know exactly what you mean. It was the same with me. But I don't feel bad about it any more. It's been fifteen years since it all happened. But it seems that you still feel some regret. Don't you? Just a little bit?'

'Do I? I suppose I do. It was something that lasted so long.'

'Was there another person involved in the break-up? On your side or hers? If you don't mind my asking, that is.'

'Another person? You mean was something *adultrious* going on? No, there wasn't. I'm not . . . I'm not that sort of person. It was something between us. That said, I'd be very happy to hear that my ex-wife has moved on. And I'm moving on myself by moving to San Francisco.'

'Are you going to set up a new practice there?'

'Eventually—it *is*, after all, my line. But not for a while. I just want to take a year off to begin with.'

'A whole year off? Lucky you! You must have a stack of money saved up. What are you going to do?'

'I don't know if I'm really thinking of *doing* anything. I just want to *be*. Read. Walk. Think. Travel a little. Sort of reconnect with myself. In the long years of fending for ourselves, we fall away *from* ourselves, if you know what I mean.'

'Dr Billimoria, you're a natural for yoga! You should sign up for the same yoga class as me in San Francisco. That'd be good for you, you know. Yoga is exactly for people who want to learn how to *be*, how to live in the moment. It helps reconnect the mind to the spirit. The spirit to the body. The body to the mind.' Zahra shook her hair loose and tied it up in a ponytail again, as if it had a chakra of its own that had to be opened up whenever yoga was mentioned.

'Um . . . okay. To be honest, I'm a bit suspicious of American yoga. Is the teacher American or Indian?'

'American. Does that mean you won't visit? Come, Dr Billimoria, don't be such a snob. I'm telling you, yoga in San Francisco is more genuine than most of the yoga classes you see here in Bombay—like power yoga and artistic yoga and so on.'

'If you go there yourself, I'm sure it's good. Let me think about it closer to the time—well, when is that, next week? Incredible, isn't it, that next week we'll be in the same city again on the other side of the world?'

'Yes, what a coincidence! And us meeting at that Navjote, of all places, where there were hundreds of people. We could so easily have passed one another and never met again, even if we lived in San Francisco afterwards for the rest of our lives. And perhaps, if we *were* to have met, it might have been in our fifties or sixties. When we'd be too old to care.'

'Fifties or sixties? Can we ever be that old?' I chirped, a callow under-forty-two.

'At-ti-tude! Although you might want to deny it, Dr Billimoria, I can assure you you'll get there. Those years are not far off.'

'It doesn't worry you?'

'Farhad! Age also brings progress, else we'd be on a sliding slope already. Personally, I think I'm on my way to becoming a goddess—right now, more than at any other point in my life. I know exactly who I am. I don't want to be anybody else. And that makes a human being beautiful and youthful, I think.'

I couldn't figure out what to say. It always throws me off when people praise themselves.

'But just to finish,' said Zahra, 'meeting you made me think, there must be some meaning in it somewhere.'

'Meeting me?'

'Yes.'

Zahra thought there must be *some meaning in it somewhere*. What a sea and what a sky! Even so, I couldn't resist saying, 'Do you think so? Is that what Enrico Sanchez would say?'

'Enrico Sanchez, my jootie,' said Zahra. 'That's what Zahra Irani would say, and you can take it or leave it.'

'Well, cheers to the confidence of the courage of your convictions!' I said, and it was clear I was getting a bit giddy with the mingled gusts of my good fortune, my gabbing, my glass, and—well, at least while we were in the Aer—my girl. Besides, we were still enjoying happy hours—though only for another five minutes. 'Waiter! Top up our drinks.'

'And oh, waiter!' Zahra made some strange, conspiratorial gesture to the good-looking young man who had been keeping us well-supplied with Bellinis—a chap whom, presumably, she'd never met in her life before.

'Um . . . what's going on?' I said. 'Some secret?'

'What's going on?' said Zahra. 'He's bringing us our drinks, that's what. So, Dr Billimoria, do I understand you correctly? You won't be coming to my yoga class in San Francisco just because the teacher is American?'

'Yes, that's right,' I said with a touch of pique.

'Well, it's your own loss. The place that was being held for you at Zahra's Yoga Studio will go to someone else.'

'Oh, it's *your* class? Of course. I should've realized!'

'It's too late now to change your mind. But anyway,' said Zahra, as the waiter returned with our drinks on a tray, a large parcel tucked underneath his arm.

'TAN-TA-RA!' said Zahra. 'Here, Farhad, this is for you.'

'Woah . . . what's going on? What's this?'

'I got you a little present. Welcome to San Francisco!'

'But why? What for?'

'Why so many questions? You're the one people come to with questions, isn't it? Go on, open it.'

'Okay. I'm so touched. You shouldn't have. We've only just met.'

'Oh, Dr Billimoria, must you be so formal?'

'No, of course not. Here. I'm opening it. What is it? It's in a box. It's a . . . it's a lamp! How beautiful!'

'You can switch it on right now. It's battery-operated.'

'I can? Oh cool. I love the green. I can't work the switch. Oh, I see. You turn it, you don't push it.'

The lamp came on between Zahra and me. I saw her generous green face in the light, her eyes flushed with conspiratorial pleasure and excitement, her lips slightly parted.

'Dr Billimoria, happy birthday in advance! You're leaving Bombay on your birthday, aren't you?'

Tears welled up in my eyes, and I looked away and said, 'How did you know?'

'Oh, that was easy. I saw your birthday on your profile page on Facebook. And then I put two and two together and figured that the timing of the move must be deliberate. I'm not as ditsy as I seem, you know.'

'Oh really? But when I looked for you on Facebook I couldn't find you at all,' I blabbed.

'Oh, you won't find me if you just type "Zahra Irani". You'd have to know my full name. Zahra Anahita Irani. I'm not a feminist or anything, but I do use my mother's name as my middle name. And the initials ZAI are supposed to be lucky—at least according to the Kaplan system of numerology. What is it? Dr Billimoria? Farhad! Are you all right? Why are you looking like that?'

'I'm just so tired,' I burbled—or did my heart, leaping over all Billimoric barriers and restraints. 'I'm just . . . so . . . tired. And every day that I get up to face this city, I feel even more tired. Life shouldn't have to be such a struggle all the time. And everybody who comes to me is struggling, too, even worse than I am. So how can I think of my own problems as being important? I can't take it. I haven't done anything wrong. Everything's run down in me.'

'Oh, no, Dr Billimoria, you look terrific. Honestly! If this is what you're like when you're down, I can't imagine what you're like when you're up.'

'I can't go on any more. At least not in this city. It's got its claws into everything in me that wants to live. I can't, I can't.'

'Oh, but you don't have to! You're leaving. For a place where it can't reach you. You *are* free! Oh, I'm so sorry. I shouldn't have said what I did. It wasn't to make you feel unhappy. I'm such a fool.'

'No, no. You were being nice. I'm so touched. Maybe it's the alcohol. Or it's my last week in Bombay. I'm not in control of myself somehow.'

'Oh . . . but you know what? That's so good to see! Why should we pressure ourselves to always be in control? Believe me. If you're hurting, let it out. Listen to the body! I firmly believe this—the body has a mind of its own. In fact, I'll go even further. The body *is* a mind!'

'It's a mind,' I said, perhaps not thinking of the same things as Zahra while she leaned over and placed her fingers sympathetically over the back of my hand.

'And that mind of the body has its own wisdom,' she continued. 'So, we actually have *two minds*. And often, we don't keep them in line with each other and end up building resistance. Toxins. Deposits. Negative energy. Sometimes, when we want to bring the mind to a state of equilibrium again, what we need to do first is make the body happy.'

'Make the body happy,' I quavered. 'Uh . . . another drink?'

'Another drink? Farhad! When you're in a state like this? Oh, you're mad. We should go now. Waiter! Our check please.'

'Yes, our bill,' I boomed, seeking to become a man again in my own eyes. Zahra looked at me, half-concerned, half-amused. I looked straight back at her. 'So?'

'So?'

'Nothing.'

Zahra looked away and surveyed the city lying at her feet. She gave a sigh of pleasure and said, 'Dr Billimoria, I know you're tired of Bombay and can't wait to leave, but look! It's turned into such a beautiful night. The moon's come out over the sea. A million little lights have come on in your city. People are all going home to their families, their dinner tables, their warm beds. You should count your blessings! Remember all the good things that happened to you here. Live in the moment even if you're looking forward to the future. Strange as it may sound, you won't get these days back again.'

How could I explain to Zahra that I *was* living in the moment? It was because I was living in the moment that I wanted us to keep drinking.

'It *is* a beautiful night,' I agreed. 'No, I think that if I were twenty years younger, I'd find this a wonderful place to live in. India gets harder and harder on the system as one gets older. Could *you* live here?'

'I couldn't. Especially not now. Perhaps if I'd never left in the first place. Look, let's go Dutch on this one. No? Are you sure?'

'Sir, the management has respectfully requested, if you could kindly turn off this lamp of yours,' said the waiter. 'Customers are not allowed to light their own lamps.'

'Yes, of course!' I said to him. And to Zahra, 'But only on the condition that I'm admitted to your yoga class.'

'Well, then, thank you. It's a done thing. Thursday morning next week in Haight-Ashbury. Come wearing something stretchy and comfortable.'

'A pink jumpsuit?'

'If you like. Feel free to explore your feminine side! Though pink looks good on you.' I saw Zahra appraising my chest and shoulders. 'You can carry it off.'

'Thank you,' I said, standing up on second attempt. 'Well . . . what are your plans for the rest of the evening?'

'I think I'll make it back to my sister's just in time for dinner.'

'I'll drop you back to Breach Candy.'

'Oh, you don't have to! I can easily take a taxi.'

'It's only a few minutes. Besides, here's your chance to share a part of my life that I won't be able to take to San Francisco—and this, I do regret. The queen of Bombay's streets, Zelda!'

In the lift, we stood next to each other with an Indian inter-gender distance between us. On the way down, a group of sheikhs got in, wearing enough perfume to drown out Zahra's instantly. They arranged themselves facing different directions, as if monitoring the Arab Spring from a clock tower in the centre of the Middle East. Zahra edged closer to me. Her head seemed to touch my shoulder and then right itself. I saw in the periphery of my vision the small bay of skin, exposed by the armhole of her top, rising and falling as she breathed.

'You know what?' said Zahra, turning her face to me. 'Could I drive?'

'Drive my car? Now?'

'Oh, not if you wouldn't like it. I just think it would be fun. I haven't driven in Bombay since I was twenty-one! Don't look at me like that. I do drive a car in San Francisco.'

'But it's the other side of the road here.'

'Of course, Dr Billimoria! I know I'm not an intellectual like you ('I'm not!' I protested), but don't take me to be such a fool. Come, you've almost challenged me now.'

As we approached Zelda, I handed Zahra my keys and crossed over to the passenger side. She smiled mysteriously as she opened the door and slipped in, then reached over to let me in.

It was the first time a woman had ever got behind Zelda's wheel. (Anna didn't—doesn't—drive.) And now that I thought about it, it was also the first time I'd sat in Zelda's passenger seat since the last year of my teens. The view was so different from here! Amazing how ruled, regulated, routine our lives become without us knowing it, even inside what we take to be our spaces of pleasure and freedom. ('Thought for the Day No. 42' from the bestselling Parsi-Hispanic author Farhad Sanchez. Register on 55839 for his daily text message.) For the first time in the history of the thousands of discrete moments we had spent with each other since we had met at the Navjote, I was able to observe Zahra without her looking back at me (she remained focussed, intent on showing me what a capable driver she was). In the waxing and waning half-light of the streetlights, I watched Zahra's bare arms working Zelda's steering wheel and gear shaft. Once or twice her hand brushed against my thigh, and we both murmured apologies.

It seemed such a shame that this journey would end with Zahra having driven herself home.

'So, Farhad, see? There was no reason for you to have got so worried.'

'Don't get me wrong now. No, I wasn't worried that you couldn't drive—rather, that you might find it hard to drive *in Bombay* after all these years. But you're doing perfectly fine.'

'I'm really enjoying it! I'd forgotten what it was like to drive a Maruti. My Uncle Sheriyar used to have one too. I almost wish Breach Candy weren't so close.'

'Well, why don't you take a right turn at Love Grove Junction, and we could take a spin around Worli Sea Face?' said my third drink.

'Should we? My sister's going to be upset if I get home after dinner. They eat very punctually because of the kids. But what the heck? You only have one life. Shall I take a right here?'

'Right there. Careful!'

'Sorry, it's just so exciting. Don't worry, I won't crash your Zelda. Look! Now we're driving towards the moon. Right there, behind those clouds.'

'Hmm . . . I guess the one thing I'll admit to missing about Bombay when I'm gone is the clouds.'

'Oh, don't you worry. There are fantastic clouds all year round in San Francisco.'

'Oh, of course, clouds are made up of the same kind of stuff everywhere—so, you might say one cloud is as good as another. But clouds also have a relationship to the place they are *above*, don't you think?'

'What do you mean?'

'To me, each city has its own philosophy of clouds . . . and there aren't any like the dense, dark clouds that suddenly arrive in Bombay in June, after the long, sapping summer. They have the beauty and surprise of—I don't know—comets, eclipses. It's like they're our own yearnings and doubts, the stirrings of dreams long forgotten, projected on to the skies. You can almost touch them . . . taste them.'

'Taste a cloud! Farhad, I didn't know you could be so poetic. When you say things like this to your women patients—I mean, clients—I'm sure they all fall in love with you right away. Here we are, Worli Sea Face! I haven't been here in years. Where do you live on this stretch of Bombay paradise?'

'A bit further down the road. The building's called Seven Storeys.'

'How charming! Stories as in stories? Oh no, of course, storeys! Like floors in America. How silly I can be sometimes. It's just that our entire evening has been about stories, so . . . what do you plan to do with your apartment when you leave? Is it going out on rent?'

'To begin with. Eventually, I guess, I'll sell it.'

'Have you already found someone to rent it out to?'

'Not yet. I couldn't find a party I trusted completely. A cousin of mine'll have to handle it now. Why do you ask?'

'My sister and her husband might be looking for a place just for a year because their building's going to be knocked down and redeveloped.'

'That might be a thought. Why don't you ask her to call me?'

'I could. In fact, why don't I come up with you and quickly take a look at it? Then I'll know what to tell her about it. I mean, I'm sure it's beautiful, but she has a family and two servants and all sorts of needs that require a particular kind of space.'

I don't know how long the silence lasted. Perhaps it was two minutes, or perhaps it was all in my head and I spoke up even before Zahra finished.

'Um . . . okay. It's all a mess because I'm almost packed to go, but if you don't mind that, then fine. Take a U-turn there, and then it's that building.'

A strange sense of transgression enveloped me as we entered my building compound—not least because of the look the watchman gave me as we went past. It was the first time any woman who was not family was coming to my apartment since Anna had left. I tried to think of how simple and innocent—trivial, even—such a visit by a woman would be in America, and I told myself it was my society thinking inside me, not my own self.

Zahra gave me back my car key, and we entered our second elevator. As the evening progressed, we were squeezing ourselves into ever smaller spaces. Although this was a good omen, it was—

It was getting too much for me.

I was losing all control over my face.

I could feel my eyelids twitching and my mouth freezing.

What strategy could I deploy? Ah, I had to think of my zabbalicious guest as a large, bearded man with a pot belly whom I was taking upstairs as a prospective tenant. Zahra's gauzy top, more alluring than anything any woman was wearing in Bombay tonight, was actually a threadbare old sadra. Her small clutch was a briefcase. The tiny sighs she made to herself in the silence between us were actually belches, from eating too much sali-boti.

Yes, Zahra was Cyrus. I opened the door for him.

'Welcome home! It's been a while since any human soul, other than the maid, entered this lonely den,' I half-joked and gave him a light cuff on the shoulder.

'Well,' said Cyrus, 'it's humanity's loss, not yours. What a beautiful view!' She headed for the balcony and raised her head up towards the night sky—no, he ambled out into the balcony and stood there, trying to think of what would be the right price to offer. I placed the keys up on the nail, noting with annoyance that in my haste to leave for Aer I'd not folded up the shirt I had discarded earlier that evening. Not only that, it was lying on the sofa right next to a half-open packet of chips. What a slob I'd become in my suffocating singleness!

'Look at the moon before it slips behind the clouds!' called Zahra, so I went out to join her. Zahra opened out her hair as if to tie it up again, then let the wind blow it around her face. It waved silkily, dizzyingly, against my right shoulder. *Farhad told himself to wait quietly and have patience—because while making a deal it was always best to let the other party—this fellow Cyrus—make the first move.*

But far from isolating Zahra into manageable pieces of man, I felt *myself* fragmenting before her. What did *she* think when she looked at me? We were both standing in my balcony, but she seemed far more comfortable by my side than I was by hers. That was good. Or was it? Did it mean that she had nothing to fear from me? Or did she see me just as a friend, as someone who was amusing and agreeable? She'd offered to set me up with other women in San Francisco. Did that mean she already had someone back home—a lithe Latino with a twenty-eight-inch waist, who knew how to do the salsa; or a big, beefy, business-type Midwesterner who chopped firewood, drank bourbon and was an ace at barbecues? Or, even worse, was it that Zahra was single, but I didn't even register on her metre? Wasn't I good-looking? Was my appearance too 1980s?

'It's not!'

'What's not?' said Zahra. 'Come, let's go inside. Wow, what beautiful furniture you have here! I've always loved ottomans and leather sofas. Or should one call it a leather couch instead?' She giggled.

'Thanks. One of the really nice things about being with you is that you always show your appreciation.'

'Oh really? I'm glad to hear that. One should be positive. Could I have a glass of water?'

'Of course. Excuse me a moment.' I took the chance to swoop down on the packet of chips and carry it into the kitchen. As I poured water into a tall glass and added ice, I cut up a slice of lime and threw it in, too, the way they do in American restaurants. Then I drank a glass of water myself to clear my head and dilute the fire and alcohol in my blood.

When I went back, Zahra was standing with her left profile to me, looking at the shelf of books I'd chosen to leave behind. I made a quick survey of her figure, somehow both delicate and powerful, welcoming and remote, a fragrant force field—and it seemed to me that the last three feet between my beautiful guest and me were as great a gulf as that between Bombay and San Francisco . . . or that between my great-uncle Hoshang Gustasp Billimoria (who, legend has it, had three mistresses at the same time) and Me-Billimoria (who had never in his life translated lustful thought into action with anyone other than his wife, whom he hadn't been able to keep either). I had to turn my gaze away from Zahra before my body burst into flames. Then I remembered my truant shirt lying in a heap on the sofa and turned to sweep it away. But it was now neatly folded up!

Zahra took the glass from me and asked, 'Won't you show me the rest of your apartment?'

'Um . . . sure. This way, through the corridor. Wait, let me turn on the light.'

'Oh, don't bother. I can see perfectly well.'

'Okay. Here's the main bedroom . . . a bit messy, but you'll allow that I'm packing. The kitchen and the second bathroom are here. Come this way. And here's the spare bedroom.'

'It's lovely!'

Zahra brushed past me as she went inside to take a look, neither quite touching nor really holding back. And in that instant I knew that whether or not she accepted me, she did not reject me; that perhaps her power over me was actually power that she was *giving* me in response to something *in* me; and this was, therefore, in some strange way my *own* power, asking to be given *back* in the same way. And, further, that by dwelling over my history of matrimony, monogamy and desolation, I was blowing into nothingness a cloud that I had made over the course of the evening. And, further, that my Farhadian nature was not fixed for all time to come, but was just a story that had hitherto, for reasons of both nature *and* culture, taken a certain coherent but by no means inevitable direction. And, finally, that unless I moved it forward in truthful, candid, unselfconscious practice, I would never be able to move it forward privately in thought. There was no shame or embarrassment in what I wanted from Zahra. It was just how it was in that free space between two unattached human beings. All at once, the darkness was not disconcerting; it was the canopy under which I could move on into another Farhad. I said, in an even voice, at the deep end of my range, perhaps not entirely like the man I was but like the man I wanted to become, 'You know . . . I think you're very beautiful.'

'Really? Why, thank you, Farhad,' said Zahra very quietly, as she peered out of the window at the silent frames and small, lit squares and rectangles of the buildings around Seven Storeys.

She turned around. I took a step forward.

'But Farhad,' she said, 'you should know, there are many women more beautiful than me in San Francisco.'

'Are there? But they're not Zoroastrian, surely.'

'Does that matter to you?'

'I don't know. Perhaps. I like that—I like that you're both American and . . . well . . . Indian. From there, and from here as well.'

'I like a man who is rooted, too. You have a certain . . . aura, yes.'

'Thank you,' I whispered, every bit of me beginning to tingle.

'Dr Billimoria—Farhad—I'm sorry—we have to be quick. My sister and her family go to bed by ten, and I don't have a key.'

'Yes, of course. I . . .'

I pushed the door behind me as if to shut out the ghost of Anna, and approached Zahra and gently laid my hands on her waist. Two hands came up out of the darkness and rested lightly on my shoulders. A sudden vulnerability emanated from Zahra. And a welcoming warmth—a warmth that my body had, after its long tryst with solitude, confusion and onanism, forgotten existed in human beings. A sliver of light fell across her face as we edged towards the bed. I saw a crease of worry on her forehead.

'Farhad!' she said. 'Do you . . .'

I thought of that small square of rubber that had roosted in a crevice in my wallet for more than a year, and with a sob of relief and happiness, I said, 'I do.'

We Are Not in Bhubaneswar

Hu-uc!

Hu-uc!

Hu-uc!

Hu-uc!

IN THE DARK, sounds like those that come from under the surface of a pond or waterhole. In the middle of last night, hoocups had suddenly taken hold of Eeja.

Since then, Eeja had drunk several glasses of water, eaten two spoons of sugar and one of honey, been slapped on the back, had His nose pinched shut, been made to sit up, lie on His side, speak long sentences, take a bath, recite mantras, drink milk, write in His diary. But nothing had any effect on the sounds. Like a God angry with the ways of the world and determined to disrupt it with His own sound, Eeja kept going *Hu-uc! Hu-uc!* all through the night and the morning.

Because of the hoocups, He could not sleep. And because He could not sleep, Ooi could not sleep. And although I could certainly have slept on my mattress in the kitchen, far from the hoocups, it would not have been right when it was my job to attend to Eeja and Ooi. And so I did not sleep either.

Health, peace of mind, memory, sleep . . . with each passing day, something new was taken away from one of us here in Bombay. Unclouded by these things, time became vast and unbearable. We waited, always looking at the time, living in our minds in other times, choosing different ways of making an hour or two slip by before looking at the clock or the calendar again, our only goal being to pull this rickety Eeja-Ooi-Rabi cart to a point when we could stop waiting and go home.

Today, we were all the more tense and tetchy because we had been up for so long, and because we had not heard from Bhagaban Bhai at all yesterday. The troubles that Eeja was giving us were the troubles of presence; the worries that Bhai was giving us, those of absence.

The hoocups had turned Eeja into a kind of human clock Himself. Even more so because, after a while, He spoke no words at all. We had to sit Him up in bed against a large cushion. He kept sliding down till He was not resting on His backside any more—and then I would have to haul Him up again. Light of dawn came, then light of sun. Then sounds of human activity on the other side of the door. No matter what the hour, a small look of surprise came over Eeja's face each time He hoocuped. The newspaper was delivered, and He began to read it, His fingers jerking with each hoocup. At one point, into the spaces between each *hu-uc!*, I found myself fitting in the lines of the Promises to the Dead, although I knew this was not very respectful either to the Dead or to Eeja. What could I do? Even when I tried to stop myself, I couldn't. When a sound is strong and the mind is weak, the mind catches the sound and swings upon it like a monkey across the tree branches.

> *Soon the trees of the Cloud Mountain*
> > *Hu-uc!*
> *Will drop their leaves, the slopes are bare*
> > *Hu-uc!*
> *Many more years to the top, so keep*
> > *Hu-uc!*
> *Your heads up, my drifting people*
> > *Huc!*
> *I will soon follow you into the clouds*

Eeja was thinking very hard between the hoocups, His forehead was furrowed and He was sucking in His breath noisily. Now He put down the newspaper upon His leg, stared at it with His head slightly cocked, as if it were something alive.

He said, 'There are going to be elections *hu-uc!* in our state, Odisha, this weekend. The ruling party is expected to *hu-uc!* return to power by a narrow margin, else it is *hu-uc!* to be a hung parliament. That's what it *hu-uc!* says in the *Times of India*, but *hu-uc!* they have given it only one column on the inside *hu-uc!* pages. That can mean only one thing.'

Gravely He looked at us—one face to the next. 'We are not in Bhubaneswar.'

Three hoocups tumbled out of Him at the sound of the place He wanted to be in, sometimes even thought He was in.

There was a long silence. The words reverberated between my headwalls—words given small, bright, red, angry tails by my own thoughts. Yes, we were not in Bhubaneswar—we were in Bombay. Yet inside that Bombay, we were not in Bombay. We were in another Bhubaneswar. We were neither in Bombay nor in Bhubaneswar. We were a world by ourselves, as if Jagannath and Cloudmaker had got together and decided to sport with us.

Ooi scratched Her head through Her red-white-black hair and said, 'Yes, yes, we are not in Bhubaneswar. We are in Bombay. How many times must I keep telling you the same thing.' Then, for the fifth time in the day, She said, 'I wonder why Bhagaban didn't call last night. It's the only thing he can do for us right now, so why wouldn't he do it if he could? I'm getting worried. I hope everything's all right with him. I've heard elections can be nasty business. Candidates get beaten, kidnapped, even murdered if they upset the wrong people. O-ho. O-ho. O-ho. Ever since the day he was born, this son of mine hasn't let me have more than five or six nights of peaceful sleep.' She looked at me. 'Rabi, I've no one but you to say these things to. Your Eeja doesn't seem to understand what's going on. Or if he does, he just forgets in a few hours.'

'Yes, Ma. I am listening.'

'Jagannath, Jagannath, Prabhu, every day I wonder how we got so far out here, in Bombay. And, yet, if we hadn't come to Bombay, who knows if he would still have been alive? It was the hurricane one way, the great famine the other. Anyway, if Bhagaban wins the election, it will all be worth it. Rabi, I hope your people have understood everything clearly. They *have* to vote for him and no one else. Will they know which picture to choose on the voting slip?'

'They won't have any trouble, Ma. It is the picture of a cloud.'

Eeja hoocuped and asked, 'Why does the boy speak Odia in such a strange way? Is one of his parents from another state?'

'He's a tribal. He works for our son.'

'He doesn't look it, because he wears a shirt and pants.'

'Apparently they all do these days. It's not like the old times. Things have changed.'

'Listen, boy, are you a tribal?'

'Yes, Eeja.'

While Eeja pondered on this interesting revelation, Ooi went on speaking, 'Sometimes, I think our son has gone slipping down and become a tribal as well. I still don't understand why you should fight elections if you are a Brahmin. If you're born a Brahmin, in a way that means you're already elected to a high place in the world, by virtue of your good deeds in past lives. And then, we aren't just any old Brahmins—we're Danua Brahmins. The highest of the high. Your Eeja's forebears were priests in the royal court of Banapur. After all that, can we now enter the fray against some Karana, some Kayastha, or God forbid, some Harijan or tribal, and shout from within that unholy crowd, "Choose us! Choose us!" If that's not a sign of the coming of the Age of Darkness, I don't know what is. For thousands of years, there was only one kind of order, and it was our task to obey it and keep it up. Was there really something so terrible about that world? What's so special about our age that everything has to be different? As human beings, we're supposed to bow our heads before the law of Jagannath. That's how dharma prevails in the universe. But right now, it's Jagannath who must be wondering what's going on in the world that He made. Kings have become servants, and servants are becoming kings. Brahmins are falling at the feet of tribals asking for their consent to take their seat in the natural order.'

Eeja interrupted, 'If we take the train home, we can use the special quota for senior citizens. Let's go today or tomorrow.' As though proud of getting two sentences across without self-interruption, He hoocuped triumphantly.

Ooi came back to the chief problem at hand and said, 'Ho, listen! Look here. Will you try drinking water again?'

Hu-uc!

Ooi slapped Her forehead. 'Jagannath, why do you make man suffer so? When will this strange business come to an end? It's been going on for eight hours now. I've never seen anything like it. Bhagaban hasn't called either. It's becoming unbearable.'

It was unbearable for *me* to sit there between Them, silent as a wall, not free to speak my mind. I had thought there could never have been anything in the world more spirit-breaking than the theft of the Cloud Mountain. But day after day of this pooter-patter, no tune or sense, like sun and moon each taking half the sky for day and night at the same time, was a different kind of slow death. I *had* to do something. Something that did not spring from an order. I went to the kitchen and began to heat up some mustard oil. Just looking at the flame, the oil hissing-flickering, made me feel better.

'Rabi!' Ooi called. 'What are you doing out there? Don't eat that last cucumber. Yesterday, you ate a cucumber all by yourself without asking me.'

'Ma, I'm just doing something for Eeja.'

I heard Bhai laughing as he said to me, the day before he left Bombay: 'Now, here's a little something you should know, brother, if you're going to brave it out with my mother. Maybe you already know this. It's impossible for my mother to live unless she knows what the servants are up to every minute and hour of the day, and unless she can find fault with them. She watches them like a hunter tracks deer in the jungle. Not that you're a servant, my brother. But you know what I mean. Had I brought home a bride to my mother, the poor girl would have ended up in exactly the same place—and in three or four years, I'd have had to start buying her Godrej hair dye. We all have our own vision of justice, but this truth is universally known: no one is ever more in the right than an old woman of Brahmin descent whose husband was a district magistrate for twenty years. The good thing is, her bark is much worse than her bite. So, don't get worried if you annoy her. I'm telling you—for one, you won't be able to help it . . . for another, this actually keeps my mother's spirits up like nothing else. Between that, cooking for my Pop, and locking eyes with her Gods during her daily darshan and deafening them with her conch, she's seen out seventy-five years in this world and would happily see out five hundred more.'

I came back to the room and, without taking anyone's permission, sat down on the floor by Eeja's feet to massage the oil into His legs. The skin on His ankles and feet had become almost black with age. But the soles of His feet were as fluffy and soft as a frog's underside or a broom tree flower. As the warmth of the oil began to seep into His muscles, He gave a small sigh of contentment which tripped and fell over another hoocup. *Aah-uc!*

My mind had fallen away from cloudthought for so many days, but suddenly, I began to feel the lightness coming upon me again—as if Eeja's feet were pulling me up, out of the dungeon-world into which I had descended. If you thought about it: Eeja and the Cloud Mountain were so similar to each another—one was being eaten away slowly by old age, the other by the Company. Bhai had entrusted the care of his father to me, and I had entrusted the home and upward road of our Dead, leading up the peak where the seen world touches the unseen, to Bhai. I longed to sing or to dance—at least to run down the slopes of Tininadi or to listen to Bhagaban Bhai's music system. In Tininadi, we had learnt over time not to make friends with outsiders because they could be agents of the Company. But here, in Bombay, there was no shape or shadow from that world. The men and women running the stalls down in the city market—if only we spoke the same language! Eeja and Ooi would never laugh at my jokes, but these spirited folk would have certainly liked to hear the riddles that pass in the weekly bazaar of my people.

> *What two things always hover just in front of a man's eyes?*
> *His destiny—and the tip of his nose.*
>
> *What two things always hover above a man's head?*
> *The Cloud Mountain—and the yellow bird that flies away as soon*
>   *as he looks up.*

That last one was a particular favourite of Bhagaban Bhai, and whenever he had new guests for dinner in Bhubaneswar he always made me say it after everybody had eaten, and then it was always he who laughed loudest.

Ooi said, 'Rabi! It's gone. It's gone! The mustard oil has worked. Dear God, a hundred thanks for your mercy.'

It was true. Eeja had stopped hoocuping. He smiled. He was happy. He leaned over and patted me on the head, then asked me to bring over His wallet from the table in the corner. He took out twenty rupees, then changed His mind and gave me ten rupees as a reward.

'When we are back in Bhubaneswar, come and see me,' He said. 'I will write a letter recommending you for a job in the postal or the public works department.'

Ooi said, 'Finally, I'll be able to make myself a cup of tea and drink it in peace. Jagannath, your mercy is infinite. Please, now, please send me some news of my son, else my heart will give up its beat. Listen, how can you sit there so silently? Doesn't it disturb you that something may have happened to our son, and here we are, stuck at the bottom of a well in Bombay?'

She made a strangled sound as Eeja drew in His breath and asked, 'What, are we in Bombay?'

We realized that Eeja's hoocups had kept our minds half-occupied, but now there was nothing but Bhai on our minds. I had repeatedly tried calling him during the day, but each time I heard that the number had either been switched off or was out of range.

Could the Company's goons have set up an ambush for Bhai on some remote road? Had they kidnapped him—and later, they'd spread the news that it was the Maoists who had done it? Strange, unexplained things had happened before in our part of the world, and kept happening to this day. A disappearance here, a death there. No pattern was traced from them—they were small stories on the inside pages of the Bhubaneswar newspapers only for a day before they passed on themselves. And Bhai couldn't be put in jail on a false charge, as others had been. He was too prominent in Bhubaneswar society for that, and he knew it, which was why he had been able to do many taunting and teasing things right under the Company's nose on the land it had long got used to thinking of as its own.

Ooi shook Her head vigorously and said, 'No, as long as Jagannath sits in His sanctum in the Puri temple and the flame burns at the feet of Maa Mangala in every shrine, justice will prevail in this world. Nothing can happen to either my husband or my son. Nothing. Let us take care of Eeja, which is wholly within our power, and everything else will take care of itself. Our schedule has been scrambled today. It's time to give him his red eleven o'clock tablet with a glass of Horlicks.' She got up and, wobbling like a ship on sea, disappeared into the kitchen.

Eeja explained, 'When I saw that my brother had transferred all our property into his own name in the land records, I chose not to fight a case. Can one take somebody in one's own family to court? Besides, fortune had been on my side. I had made a respectable life for myself—despite being born into the same circumstances as my brother—while he remained a petty clerk in a government office. Therefore, I bought a small plot of land on the other side of the village. This was in 1964. Many years later, when I was about to retire, I sold the land for a profit, and that's the money I used to buy an apartment for us in Bhubaneswar. In all that time, I didn't see a penny from my son. Nor did I expect any help. When a man hasn't secured his own position in life, what help can he possibly give others?'

'That was a long time ago,' Ooi called out from the kitchen. 'Remember, it was your son who brought you to Bombay, who paid all the bills at the hospital. Have you even thanked him for that?'

After just a few days alone with Eeja and Ooi, I was able to see why Bhai had never taken me to meet his parents in Bhubaneswar—until the point it became clear that if Eeja's life had to be saved, we would all have to go to Bombay—and why he only visited Them once a week for dinner on Friday evenings.

'Any more than that, brother, and they'll start getting inside my head again. They'll fill me up with guilt and doubt, the way people fill up their buckets at the water pump when the municipal supply starts in the morning. If you must pray for one thing for your next life, ask for this—never to be born a Brahmin. A single cloud, floating for ten minutes across the sky and then dying, has more happiness, more freedom than an entire Brahmin life.'

Of course, this was not completely true, considering Bhai was a Brahmin himself. But I could see what he meant. Unlike the world of my people—which knew fullness in tilling a bit of land, gazing at the clouds, eating rice twice a day with a piece of fried jackfruit and a bit of onion and salt on the side, drinking the brew of the mahua fruit, smoking a cheroot, singing songs by the evening fire, and counting down the days till the next festival—Bhai's culture was one of great expectations, great burdens, great restraints. And then there was the particular pressure of his own family. Not only had Eeja been a district magistrate, He had also participated in the freedom movement and was known as a great scholar of Sanskrit texts. That Bhai was a director of television serials about Odia society was, I knew, for his father, not anything to be proud of.

But what did Eeja think about the new turn in Bhai's life—his entry into politics? If Bhai was to be believed, Eeja didn't think much of elections, perhaps for the reasons Ooi had aired. It seemed as though there had been a certain amount of time allowed to Bhai to prove himself. And now that was past, it was impossible to please Eeja.

Ooi came hobbling back with Her cup of tea, murmuring, 'Bhagaban, Bhagaban.' Whether She meant Her son or God—for that was what Bhai's name meant—I couldn't tell. She bent down before the pictures of Her Gods and stared for a long time at the one of the blue boy Krishna. It did not seem as if Eeja or I were in the room. Then She went to Her chair and sat there silently for a long time.

She said, 'Once, when he was just a baby, we lost him in the fair at Puri. It was actually my fault. Your Eeja took him along to ride on the giant wheel while I looked at some Sambalpuri silks being sold at a discount. After a while, Eeja came back all by himself. I asked, "What, you've put Bhagaban on the ride all on his own?" He said, "No, I can't find him anywhere. I turned my head for a moment, and when I looked around, he was gone." Jagannath! My heart nearly gave up on me that day. I thought he'd been kidnapped by those nasty people always hanging around at the edge of fairs, looking for a chance to swoop down on little children. They take them away to some far-off place and send them out on the streets to beg, or they sell them to a childless couple. My son, for the rest of his life, bearing the yoke of some low-caste home and their terrible habits! I'm telling you, if we had lost Bhagaban that day, I would have left your Eeja.'

Eeja gave a snort, that of a Hindu husband saying, 'What? *She'll* leave me?'

'You don't believe me, I know. I wouldn't have divorced you, exactly, but I'd have gone back to live in my village and worn a white sari the rest of my life. And, of course, you, Rabi, would have never ended up meeting your beloved Bhagaban Bhai. Or if you had met him, it would have been in some other guise. Maybe he'd have been someone just like you. Anyway, there we were at the fair, with Bhagaban lost. We had a notice read out on the loudspeaker system, sent people out into every corner, each one shouting "Bhagaban! Bhagaban!" Some village women came up to me and said, "Ma, why are you shouting the name of God like that? He is at the temple and not at the fair." These village folk can never get their minds around anything more complicated than the four or five things they know! I told them, "You fools, it is my son I'm looking for." They thought I'd gone mad. I can still see them whispering among themselves . . . *pss pss, pss pss.* Anyway, just when we were sick with despair and fear, we came upon a fortune teller with his row of cards and his parrot. And, there, sitting sweetly by his side, like Krusna himself in the garden of Brindaban, was Bhagaban. He was saying to every customer, just like your Eeja always used to say to people on the telephone—we were one of the few families with a phone, you know—"The law will take its own course, but in the end, it's all in God's hands. The law will take its own course, but in the end, it's all in God's hands." Did you ever hear something so strange?'

Ooi shrieked with laughter. She clearly roused a bright memory inside Eeja, who began to make small, exploding sounds Himself. Like a pair of puppets connected from above by an invisible string, They rocked back and forth, neighing and snorting. The years seemed to fall away from Them, and I could see what They must have looked like fifty years ago.

Suddenly, the phone rang. I saw it on the bed, blinking among the sheets. I reached out for it before Ooi.

It was Bhai—he was alive!

'Hello . . . Bhai?'

'Cuckoodoo-coo, cloudy brother,' came the crackling, laughing voice from the distant land, so beautiful, no place like it, that was our home. 'Is everything all right out there in Bombay?'

'Yes, Bhai, if everything is all right with you, everything is all right with us. But I was—'

'It's a wonder your nature has remained as sweet as ever, trapped between those two crabby old souls. So, how goes life in the nineteenth century, brother, under the sky of Sanskrit and Bombay? Have they made you into a scholar of the palm-leaf texts yet—or a priest?'

'Rabi! I want to talk to him. Give the phone to me right now,' cried Ooi, and seized the phone with a jangle of bangles. 'Bhagaban! Son, where have you been? We were all so worried. Is it right to leave us lost like this when we are all by ourselves in this strange city, and your father so weak and poor?'

I heard Bhai's faint voice, 'Sorry, Ma, but the only cell phone tower in this neighbourhood broke down yesterday, and there was a complete blackout. I had to drive down this morning all the way to Rayagada, only to be able to speak to you. Don't worry about me. Everything is under control here. In fact, I'm having a party compared to what you poor souls are going through. And this Saturday, it's election day, and after that it's results very soon. Tell me, how is he?'

'He's not so good. What shall I tell you, he drove us all mad last night with the most terrible hiccups. Here, speak to him yourself first, or later he'll complain that he's not being respected as the head of the family. Listen! Look here. Bhagaban wants to speak to you.'

Eeja stared at the phone for a long time.

Then He held it against His mouth and said, 'Hello.'

He moved it to His ear to listen to Bhai's response.

'Leave it by your ear,' Ooi instructed Him. 'You can both speak and hear from there.'

'I know exactly what to do, so don't try to teach me,' said Eeja. 'Hello, Bhagaban, can you hear? Why are you in Odisha? Why are we here? They've got me all tied down over here. Hundreds of times every day I'm told what to do and what not to do. My leg hurts. There's no Odia newspaper here either, only an English one. It's time for us all to go back to Bhubaneswar. The matter is urgent.'

'Bapa, what can I or they do? It's the doctors who've said you're not to fly till you get better because your heart can't take it. Else you'd have been in Bhubaneswar long ago.'

'Is flying the only way we can reach Bhubaneswar? Book me a ticket on the Konark Express.'

'Bapa, on the train it takes thirty-six hours to get from Bombay to Bhubaneswar. How will you manage that? How will you use the bathroom? Anyway, listen, let's not get bogged down with things we can't help. Just four or five days more, and you're back home, I promise. Meanwhile, I've got something urgent to speak to you about. This morning, I got a call from the publisher Narottam Saha. He wanted to know what progress you'd made on the book *A Treasury of Sanskrit Verse: Our Common Cultural Heritage*. What do you think? Can you at least have twenty or thirty pages of text ready by the time I come to fetch you? Of course, it would have been best if you'd had your library around you in Bhubaneswar. But then again, you've got it all engraved in your memory, just as permanently as the edicts of Ashoka. That's why you're writing a book in the first place. For people who want a copy of *your* mind to make their own lives worth living.'

'That's how the great scholars of the West wrote their books during the Second World War—from memory,' Eeja said. 'I once read it in a report in the *Samaja*.'

'That's right. Don't let the little distractions get in your way. You've got a great task to complete. Remember, Time disappears every moment, Poetry speaks on through the ages. When the book comes out, we'll even have a note under the title that says: "Written in Bombay, all from memory".'

'I'll get down to work on it,' Eeja said, puffing out His chest. 'Ask the publisher not to make any changes to his plans, and to come and meet me in Bhubaneswar next week. Here, your mother wants to speak to you. Come soon and take us back. My blessings are with you.' He raised His hand, like the coiled head of a snake, to bless Bhai.

Ooi took the phone. 'Bhagaban, what's happening out there in those godforsaken villages? Is everything all right? Don't hang around too long in that part of the world. You've done enough now for those people. Go back to Bhubaneswar as soon as you can and wait for the election results. Where are you having your meals? Don't upset your stomach by eating at all those roadside stalls. You'll get typhoid before you know it. Those people know nothing about hygiene. I'm feeling so bad that we've taken away the boy who cooks for you. But what can we do? Jagannath is taking a stern test of all of us. Listen, there's another thing I wanted to tell you. His urine is coming out really yellow. I've forgotten if the doctors said that was a good thing. What? It is? God be praised. His memory . . . what can I say? Let's put it this way, he plays with time just like the Gods. Yes, yes, I can take care of everything over here. You concentrate on your work there. Suffering? No, no, what suffering? That's what old age is, after all. Old age looks to get three meals a day into the stomach, honour the Gods, prepare for the next world, and enjoy the success of one's children and the laughter of their little ones. Remember that last bit. Next week, Jagannath willing, we'll all be together again. You've got to go? God be with you. You'll win the elections for sure. What? You want to speak to Rabi? Here. Don't take too long. The phone's running out of battery.'

Ooi wiped a tear from Her eye and handed me the phone. These were the sweetest moments of my life in Bombay, the rebirth of lifejoy and hope. All the while, I'd been thinking: if only I could have been there for the elections! But now I knew it was good enough for me even if Bhai got through it all on his own. Even if he didn't win, it didn't matter. We would find another way to fight and triumph.

'Hello, Bhai!'

'Rabi, brother, you won't believe what I just saw this morning! On my way to Rayagada, I stopped for a tender coconut in Matihara village. And guess who I should see loping towards me?'

'I couldn't say. Someone from the ruling party?'

'What, brother, you're even more obsessed with politics than your Bhai! Remember that calf that we'd rescued a few months ago—the one that had fallen into the ditch being dug by the NREGA workers and broken its leg? It seemed certain it would die. And, now, what do I see but the very same animal, sleek and healthy, cantering up and down the lane like that Usain Bolt fellow, shaking its head and tinkling its bell? I could see that it recognized me and wanted to say thank you.'

'Bhai, I'm very happy to hear that.'

'Life, my brother, *life*. It can hold out against anything. It's the same with my father. He's lost a few battles with his body and mind, but deep down he loves life—even though he pretends, like every good Brahmin, not to care for it. It's all going well here, brother, it's all going well. I was in Tininadi yesterday, and everyone's fine there. Your people send you their love. One girl, Juari, seemed to be sending something more than just love, but I'll leave that for you to decipher when you return. As for me, I'm feeling positive. Everywhere I go in the district, people flock to see and hear me—the only person in the last twenty years to have taken on the might of the Company in Tininadi.'

'Bhai, I'm very happy to hear that. What about the people from the Company? We can't ignore them.'

'The Company's gone really quiet after I made a fuss about it supporting the ruling party with election funds. This is what I think. It's trying stealthily to sneak past the post. So, I'm trying to scale up the noise. The Bhubaneswar papers weren't saying a word about this contest for weeks, but now even they've been forced by the public to devote some columns to the goings-on. The media forgets we aren't living in the 1990s any more, when all sources of information could be blocked with piles of banknotes. This is the twenty-first century. I'm aggressively using social media to spread word in town. Some of my posts on Facebook have gone viral. We've got a chance of winning, Rabi. I'm sure of it.'

'Bhai, I'm very happy to hear that.'

'And you know what? If I win, in the next election in five years' time, you can take my place. This circus isn't for me in the long run. I'll go back to storytelling and film-making, and you can be the leader of not just your own people but of everybody in your part of the world. Take them all forward under the love and law of Cloudmaker.'

'No, Bhai, how can that be?'

'I'm serious. Can you just be a tribal all your life, brother, and fight on the tribal ticket? No, you've got to step up to bigger things, else the same old divisions will remain forever in our society and country—and no matter how much you progress, you'll stay in a ghetto yourself. Winning the Cloud Mountain back from the Company isn't the end of your journey. It's the start. So, hold the fort there in Bombay . . . because your time will come. I know it's hard for you out there. You're sounding low. But at the end of the day, no matter how much he may rebel and resist, your Bhai is a creature of the society he belongs to. I couldn't have lifted a finger here in Odisha, much less fought an election campaign against the Company, if I knew my parents were suffering elsewhere. And in my absence, you're the only one I can trust with their care. I have no one else in the world. Keep your spirits up, Rabi. For my sake.'

'I will, Bhai. Please take care of yourself. The Company can do anything to make sure that the candidate from the ruling party wins.'

'Don't worry for a moment. When you see the size of the bodyguard I've got myself, you'll know it'll be fine. His handlebar moustache is so long that, sometimes, when we're standing side by side, I can feel it tickling me. All right, brother, we'll speak again soon. I'm heartbroken that you haven't memorized any Sanskrit shlokas, but you've still got some time. Last thing: are you keeping your eyes open out there in the big city? Remember, you're in a place where nobody from the Cloud tribe has ever been before. Have you learnt something new about Bombay that you can tell me?'

'Yes, Bhai. The Marathi word for onions in Bombay—*kanda*—is the same as the Odia word for tears.'

'What a genius! Truly remarkable. I'm looking forward to hearing all your stories. It won't be long now. Speak to you soon, okay? I've got to go now. Goodbye. A cloud be upon you in Bombay.'

'A cloud be upon you in Odisha, Bhai.'

'Cuckoodoo-coo. Over and out.'

Ooi took the phone back from me, then muttered jealously, 'He speaks longer with you than he does with me.'

After lunch, Eeja was laid out flat and, having stayed up most of the night, immediately fell asleep. After watching Him for some time, Ooi lay down on the other side of the bed. Soon She, too, was asleep.

Everybody had to think so much about Them, They thought so little about others. I could not even speak freely to Bhai in front of Them, for fear that They would think I was getting ahead of my station in life.

My stomach growled. I got up and went to the bathroom. I tried to use it only when Eeja and Ooi were asleep because I knew They didn't like sharing a bathroom with a servant. As I was washing my hands with my own sliver of soap, I caught sight of my face in the mirror.

The years of being with Bhai in Bhubaneswar had changed my face almost beyond recognition. I no longer had that trusting cow-gaze of my brethren in the village. Like Bhai, I had become two-sided, one part of me happiest in a world that was not my own. Perhaps my people, too, did not quite see me any longer as one of their own, even though it was for their sake that I had moved to the city. When I'd return

this time to see them—not even from Bhubaneswar as in the past, but
from the other end of the world, from Bombay—would they think me
even more remote from them? Every day it came to me that the plane
journey to Bombay with Bhai, Eeja and Ooi had taken me above the
clouds. Was it a crime that I was the first person from the tribe to see
the clouds floating, not above, against the sky, but below, against our
wide and far-flung world? I lay down on the mattress, heartsick once
again after my little hop of happiness when Bhai had called.

As I closed my eyes, I heard a sound from the other room.

Hu-uc!

  Hu-uc!

Hu-uc!

  Hu-uc!

While My Lady Sleeps (Coltrane/Billimoria)

BEEP BEEP! WHEN Henry Ford rolled his first cars off the line, did he envisage what a wonderful post-coital pick-up driving would become, what rest and release it would offer the body? How the moving city'd shimmer with the same mystery as the lover; how the fingers would caress the wheel as previously they had caressed faces, shoulders, hips. How in his automobilic body, the car-sevak would contemplate the universe with awakened wonder after being schooled in seeing in the bedroom's darkness; how the foot would suddenly, of its own volition (the body is a mind!), depress the accelerator into the rush of an orgasm. How to be inside a car would feel so much like being linked to the force field of another human being.

And that is how, while my lady Zahra slept—having just ravished me in a haze of heat and lust and r's; then, having come, gone home to her sister's with murmured promises—I found myself unusually pleased about a new nocturnal expedition. Not with Zelda but with the Honda Civic into which I'd collided the previous night. And my nose was pointed northwards, towards a new destination far into the suburban wilderness, Borivali. Apparently, out there, an angry lady sat in a flat, waiting for her car to be returned. Balu had not turned up to claim it—perhaps the missionaries had taken their toll on him. And the garage had called, just after I'd dropped Zahra at her sister's, to present to me not just the bill, which I'd agreed to pay, but this new problem.

'Ordinarily, we would have had one of our boys drop the car home, sir. But the address we have for it is all the way out in Borivali. And when we called madam, she said she wasn't going to come all the way to South Bombay to pick it up, and I should call the man who had brought it in . . . it's all very confusing, sir. Please do something.'

Clearly, Balu had dumped all his conjugal chores on me. But this night having turned into what it had, and the lights of Bombay having become inviting and romantic again as they lit the way to San Francisco, the gallant Dr Billimoria had immediately agreed to drive the car thirty-five kilometres to its owner, tetchy from being abandoned by her philandering husband and God knew what else. Yes, I could deal with her . . . and I'd give her a peck on the cheek while I was at it and show her the way to being healed without losing a year, as I had. I could deal with *anything*. I *wanted* to deal with everything. If only they'd make me prime minister for five days, beginning tonight, I'd solve all the problems of this country in one dictatorial swoop—a bit like what Mrs Gandhi tried to do during the Emergency, except that my strategy would be emphatically the opposite of her scowling son's sterilization programme. Poverty, unemployment, pollution, caste tensions, communal violence, greed, lust, repression . . . listen, countrymen, sex is the answer.

That so many troubles could be solved by the simple fact of two people taking off their clothes and leaping at and into one another . . . it was hysterically funny, God's greatest joke on humanity, and particularly on those joyless bushbeards who claimed the right to speak in his name. Yes, sex had returned to my life with a bang. And laughter had returned to communion with sex—after a year of residing almost exclusively in sitcoms and *Prairie Home Companion*. At the confluence of these two forces, the sangam of all that is transcendent in human affairs, I became myself again. Perhaps even more than myself. I could not empathize any longer with the Buddha, to whom life seemed to be nothing but desire and suffering, necessitating self-erasure under tall trees; the spirit of the Billimorias took hold of me again, which held that life was a grand theatre and one had to act, imagine, engage, conquer . . . just spend oneself in an explosion of verbs.

Yes, Farhad Billimoria was a man again—man enough even to admit that when he'd seen a woman's cunt after such a long sexual exile, the sight had been so shocking he'd almost moved to cover it up again! The walls of the car echoed with my cackles when I remembered how Zahra had nearly kneed me in the groin when she had swung atop me, and how my fingers, caressing her hair, had got entangled in one of her hoops and nearly wrenched off her ear. Yes, as Sade had wisely observed, love was pain!

And I laughed even more when I drifted further back in time and remembered how I'd stood, just a few hours ago, quaking by Zahra's side, trying to turn her into Cyrus—and how I'd fumbled outside the cosmetics store the previous night as I had tried to approach her—and how, for months, I'd been on the verge of returning, pleading and babbling, back to Anna.

If only I'd known ... but that's the thing about life, one never knows.

Ah, the risky night-roads of Mumabi, full of madcaps. I'd bumped into this car twenty-four hours ago, now I risked bumping *it* into something else. But what could I do? Here, in the suburbs, people drove like such clods. Bandra—it had been years since I'd gone past that frontier of what used to be Bombay. Andheri, Goregaon, Malad ... what a vast new world had come up in my city in the last twenty years—and the news was that there were thousands of Mumabic apartments and offices coming up further north and east, too. I was getting out at exactly the right time. Soon, Bombay would be one vast, barbaric suburb, with a tiny fringe of civilization squeezed into the south. Only very occasionally did I have a client from these far reaches. And who could blame them for not being invested in psychotherapy, or any of the other activities that point to a human being who reflects, introspects, doubts or seeks a path unlike that chosen by his parents? As if to indicate the relative unworthiness of these northern outgrowths, the Western Express Highway steadily grew more pitted and uneven as I drove.

I looked in the glove compartment for some music to play, but there were only two CDs in there: *Evergreen Melodies of Kishore Kumar* and an odd thing titled *Susan Sontag: The Collected Lectures.* Who was this strange-looking lady with a white streak in her hair, and what was she doing in the glove compartment of a car belonging to a middle class Indian family? Between the two of them, Balu and his wife seemed to have an extremely Catholic taste in people!

When I saw a sign on the highway that pointed left for 'Borivali', I took the turn. Still on the streets—even though it was nearly midnight—were weary figures on the way home from work or eating at roadside stalls. Others were already asleep on the pavements, sometimes only just out of the range of the neon glow of the 'orchestra bars'—I had never been able to work up the courage to go into one of them, but had heard many stories about what went on in there from my clients. I.C. Colony, my destination, apparently lay deep in Borivali West. As I got closer, the roads became quieter, slopey, tree-lined, actually quite pleasant. I hoped that, now that I was here, Balu's wife hadn't fallen asleep.

The apartment building where Balu lived was called Vaastu Siddhi, after the Hindu art of construction and spatial organization, although I could see nothing very special about it. A security guard saluted when he saw the car, then saw my face and wanted to know who I was. I explained that I was a kind of delivery boy; the car belonged to Flat B19; if there was parking space reserved for it, I'd put it right there, deliver the key and be gone. I was duly let in. When my feet touched the ground again, it felt as if I'd just landed from a long flight on my new wings. On my way to the lift, I caught the wonderful waft of a champa tree, and I plucked a flower and placed it in my buttonhole.

At the entrance to the building, yet another security guard. I waltzed past him with such confidence—the body was a mind, and so it could work directly on other minds!—that he didn't make a peep of resistance, leaving me free to murder the lady for the trouble she had put me to. The lift reminded me of my previous lift ride with Zahra. It had a mirror. In it I saw my face—a most fascinating face, alive with old knowledge and new.

One of the paradoxes of the human condition: you can study your own face as much as you want, but to look that closely at another's takes so much work and requires so much permission! Like a mountain, a face becomes something else when seen up close. Much comes into view that was previously submerged by the whole. I remembered the slightly grainy surface of Zahra's perfect teeth; the glistening black curve, reminiscent of Marine Drive, of her eyelashes; the pores of her lightly rouged cheeks.

She'd promised to come see me again tomorrow—a thought that induced both pleasure and panic. What could I do, as a man, to make myself new for her? For I'd become aware from touching and tasting Zahra, as opposed to merely dreaming about her, that she remade herself every day. As I kissed her, I realized she was wearing no lipstick, while the previous time she'd definitely had some on in crimson; as I felt for her hips beneath her harem pants, I discovered I was looking for them much higher than they were because of her illusion-making top; when I pulled out the clips in her hair, I was able to reconstruct how she'd put it up with two partings. And here was a man who'd gone to the same dour barber for the last twenty years and had never deviated from combing his hair the way his mother had taught him when he was six! Zahra carried off all these changes with perfect poise, as if from a need to express the mystery and variety and depth of human nature through a constant reimagining of the surface. How could I be like that, too? Oh, Farhad, Farhad, you have a long way to go, to become the man of the year in San Francisco.

This lift was the slowest I'd ever been in. Then I realized—I'd been so busy looking at my face, I'd forgotten to press the button. Did so, reached the fourth floor in a moment. Looked at my watch. It was a few minutes to midnight. Round about midnight—my favourite hour in both life and musical history. That hour when half the great projects of humanity and almost all the great jazz records had been hatched.

The name on the door said 'KR Balu' and beneath it, 'B Hemlata'. Ah, yes . . . I remembered the line last night about not going home to Hemlata! 'Home to Hemlata' . . . now what would a song by that name be like? Even without entering, my nose—that very same nose that had, last evening, given me Zahra's whereabouts—could register the scent of tamarind and coconut emanating from this household. South India transplanted to North Bombay.

As I rang the bell, I found myself looking forward to the drive back home in a taxi, sifting through my records of the evening for all the expressions on Zahra's face. I hoped that B Hemlata would be suitably discombobulated by a visit from a strange man at such a late hour—I imagined her tremblingly collecting her key (taking care not to let our fingers touch) and letting me start my journey towards South Bombay, Seven Storeys, Farhad stories, his birthday, San Francisco, Zahra and life, tra-la-la.

I heard footsteps on the other side, and the door swung open. Hemlata—or the lady she was having an affair with after having given up on men altogether—was fair, plump and tall. She was wearing something odd like a kameez over pyjamas. Her long hair was coiled into a bun, and her owlish eyes, behind big glasses, glinted with a mix of sarcasm and contempt. Perhaps she was expecting her itinerant husband . . . because the expression on her face changed when she saw me. Then she spotted the car key in my hands and said in an upper-class South Indian accent, each word ringing loud and clear as a temple bell:

'Well, if this isn't the greatest day of my life!'

Farhad—the new Farhad—was not at all fazed and gave her a debonair smile. 'Here it is, all the way from South Bombay,' he said, handing the key over with a little bow. 'I am Farhad Billimoria, and now I shall take your leave, madam. Adieu.'

'Not so fast! Come on in. I want to ask you some questions.'

Farhad: 'Questions? What for? I know nothing.'

'Yes, yes, I've heard that one before. None of his friends knows anything. Come on in. You've come such a long way. Let me fix you a drink.'

The new Farhad, who, on principle, was duty-bound to accept any invitation from a woman for a drink, shrugged and entered. Inside, he found a tastefully furnished room, a number of lamps lighting up ornate furniture, several nice prints on the walls, one whole area lined from floor to ceiling with books, and a glass of whisky on a side-table by the sofa. Carnatic music, rather soft, trickled in from an extremely sleek sound system.

The books suggested that Hemlata was an academic of some sort. This was the household of a woman who read Susan Sontag, not *Woman's Era*.

'Whisky? Gin and tonic?' asked Hemlata.

'Oh, I'll have whatever you're having,' Farhad said, turning his back on his host to show how relaxed he was and studying a print of a watercolour of a beautiful woman painted by Abanindranath Tagore. Slowly, taking control of the room, he walked over to the sofa, which was covered with papers, some printed, some written on with a scrawling right-tilting hand. He stacked up a few and sat down.

Hemlata put my drink down on a low table within arm's reach and sat down on a chair a few feet away. 'All right,' she said. 'So where is he?'

'He, who? Your husband, madam?'

'Who else, sir?'

Farhad: 'Now, listen, I have to explain something. I've only met your husband once—when my car collided into his—and that was more than enough because, as you can see, I've been left carrying the can for him. I promised to pay for repairs, but now I've ended up delivering your car home!'

'What a convincing story!' said Hemlata. 'So, you don't know him at all?'

'Oh, come now, you have to believe me. Do I look like one of his friends?'

'All right. You can tell me one thing then. Was he with somebody when you had this . . . this accident?'

Farhad, thrown off slightly: 'Uh?'

'Was he with somebody? A woman?'

Although he had no stake in the matter, there rose up in Farhad the

solidarity that binds all men when confronted by a Female Investigation.
'Woman? I didn't see no woman.'

'You didn't see no woman?'

Farhad, melting under the heat of such a focussed cross-examination:
'I mean, I didn't see a woman.'

'You're sure?'

'I'm sure.'

'I see.' Hemlata picked up her car keys and moved casually towards
the door, like the tiger that has scented blood in the forest but wants to
make the other tigers think it's only popping down to the pond for a sip
of water. 'I'll be back in a moment. You sit here and enjoy your drink.'

'Where are you going?'

'I need to check something in the car, and then we'll know if you're
telling the truth or carrying out a con in cahoots with my husband.'

Farhad, suddenly panicking: 'Wait! I'll come with you.'

'No, you stay here,' said Hemlata sternly from the door. 'I'll be back
in a couple of minutes.'

'Listen, I have to go home!'

'Make yourself at home here.'

Hemlata closed the door behind her. I ran to open it again. As I
reached for the bolt, I heard her locking it from the outside. Hemlata's
mission was even stranger than her husband's missionaries!

The old Farhad: 'Let me out! This isn't done!'

'Ssh!' said Hemlata in a low, severe voice. 'I'll be back soon. Don't
make a ruckus, else I'll have to call the police.'

Something must have awoken in me—a self left over from the long,
raging fights with Anna—because, without willing it, I found myself
back on the other side of the room, looking for something to destroy—
anything that would serve as retribution for my sudden confinement.
I gathered up a handful of papers from the sofa and was about to tear
them up, when I stopped myself and threw them all around the room
instead. As they came floating back down, settling on furniture or falling
to the floor, laughter took hold of me again. I saw what a ridiculous

figure I was cutting and was glad for it. This really wasn't becoming of the Farhad I was becoming! What was the point of wanting freedom and adventure, and not being able to take the odd surprise? It was hard to tell what Hemlata was after—this, despite my long years in the trade and all I had learnt about marital wars and games. Whatever it was, I'd solved my own conjugal problems and had found a lovely lady to sport with and was off to San Francisco, and nothing of this other mess could in any way upset *that*.

What's more, there was free alcohol to be had in all of this. I went over to the bar cabinet and found an impressive selection of whiskies from all around the world. I chose a Yamazaki, and as I poured it out, I thrilled to the thought that this might now become a weekly ritual for me in the San Franciscan apartments of women of all shapes, sizes and dispositions. Yes, it was incumbent on *me* to cultivate a mean nature—average mean, that is, not spiteful mean—flexible enough to have some kind of fun with them all, whether carnal or non.

Sex with Zahra had clearly given me new ears, too. Even though Carnatic music has never been to my taste (to me, the American South is a place of possibilities, unorthodoxies, soulfulness; the Indian South, a place of caste marks, temple bells, tiffins and tumblers—these essences revealing themselves inevitably in their music), what my ears now heard sounded amazingly deep, rich, beautiful. I went over to the CD rack to see what I could do to show Hemlata when she returned that I'd made myself comfortable in her house, far in excess of what she had tartly suggested while shutting me in.

As I'd suspected, the music system was a Bose. On a CD rack, I found a pile of Indian classical maestros—U. Srinivas, the Dagar Brothers, Pandit Nikhil Banerjee, Ali Akbar Khan, Ustad Sultan Khan, Pandit Ajoy Chakrabarty. Interesting enough, and exponents of a venerable tradition no doubt, but all these 'ustads' and 'pandits' always annoyed me. If you're an artist who's confident of himself, stick to the name your parents gave you, and quit adding titles and honours to it. Think about it . . . did the great classical musicians of the (then fairly hierarchical) West play as Sir Bach or Pandit Beethoven?

I cracked open a Sultan Khan CD to look at the notes—and found inside Miles Davis' *Kind of Blue*. What an utterly bizarre household! Could it be that all these Indian shells were concealing fine American nuts? I opened other CD cases: not so. As I extricated our friend Miles from his sultanic embrace, I had further reason to be detained. Concealed under the CD, though not folded, was a Post-it note, with a message written in an incontrovertibly male hand: 'Hem, always I will treasure the things that we shared'. The syntax suggested that, unless he was a poet of some sort, the writer wasn't a native English speaker—but Indians didn't write English like that either. So Hemlata must, at some point, have had a non-Indian admirer or, more likely, have lived abroad for a while—perhaps even in America. My respect for my jailor went up a bit. It looked like, no matter how constricted her present, Hemlata had a past with superior men.

It seemed that, with every successive movement in this long, restorative evening in the week before my forty-second birthday, I was being initiated into some new mystery and strand of the female temperament. As the burnished sound of *Kind of Blue* rolled in, I began to feel ever more at home at Hemlata's and decided it would be even better to seek out a little snack, given that I hadn't had dinner and had burnt so many extra calories. I went into the kitchen, where the expected tiffins and tumblers were stacked up in a steel cupboard. A tulsi plant stood by the window, and a coconut and a small pile of aubergines lolled by the stove—as if, any moment, the truant husband would return with eight pals and demand that a feast be rustled up. The sound of drops, I thought, signified a leaky tap—until I realized that it was coffee, left in a South Indian filter through the night, so that a strong decoction would pool at the bottom by the morning. Half-hidden under three packets of murukku was a packet of crisps, salt and black pepper flavour. I picked this up and went back quickly to the living room, lest Hemlata return while I was away.

As I was about to sit down, a new, thrilling thought occurred to me. I went to the door and locked it from the inside, so that Hemlata would be forced to ring the bell and wait for me to open the door to her own residence, lately turned into a prison. Now the guest really was making himself at home! I stretched out on the sofa with a cushion beneath my head, food and drink at hand, and began to browse through Hemlata's papers.

And was confounded. Was this English? A photocopied essay lay in front of me, marked here and there with a red pen, titled: '(Que) eroticism: Desire and the Sublimated Object in Coc(k)teau and Amitav Ghosh' by Mihir Sharma, Duke University. Good God, was this the same Amitav Ghosh to whose book event Zahra and I were going tomorrow? I was all for eroticism flooding the night—and had added my own chapter, just hours prior, to the human collection—but not for erotic encounters that came looking and sounding like *this*. I tossed the essay aside. It was clear that Hemlata dealt in a lingo that not even the Gods could understand, leave alone poor Amitav Ghosh and Coc(k)teau.

Jazz, on the other hand . . . the magic sound of Miles and his band reverberating in the room was something any schoolboy could appreciate, if only it was put before him—which it wasn't. And that was why India was as joyless and messed-up as it was. I recalled that I used to own this CD . . . then loaned it to a cousin and lost it, and I'd never bought another copy because it just wouldn't have been the same as the first. But its reappearance at Hemlata's—this more than made up for the turn the night had taken.

And the crisps tasted wonderful . . . sex had awakened my taste buds, too. Okay, next document. I found myself facing a page from a story by a writer with a name entirely unknown to me—Saadat Hasan Manto. Hemlata had circled a paragraph in red. I read:

'Love.' What a beautiful word! She wanted to smear it all over her body and massage it into her pores. She wanted to abandon herself to love. If love were ajar, she would press herself through its opening and close the lid above her. When she really wanted to make love, it didn't matter which man it was. She would take any man, sit him on her lap, pat his head, and sing a lullaby to put him to sleep.

Well, hmm! It seemed, after all, that some writers from the subcontinent knew how to write frankly about sex, without making it a technical manual or a catalogue of acrobatics like Grandpa Vatsyayana had done, or else presenting it as something ethereal and spiritual and disembodied. *When she really wanted to make love, it didn't matter which man it was*—what a radical thought for our civilization to contemplate! Manto was my man, as was Miles. I was so very intrigued by why Hemlata had chosen to copy this out. It seemed she was as much into an investigation of the powers of the body as I was. No wonder Balu was alarmed by his wife!

I read the sentences again and saw that I'd missed a space the first time. Love in this girl's life was not *ajar*, a door that had suddenly opened, as it had for me tonight, but a *jar*, a receptacle with a lid, which made it a bit more plebeian, but that's how the writer Manto wanted it, I guess. And fair enough: when one thought about it, everything about the passage was physical, nothing was metaphysical or moony or euphemistic. (Wow, I could be a literary critic!) Even love was strangely but persuasively imagined as a kind of moisturizer or fairness cream that one rubbed into one's skin—and then, instantly, it had its effect. It was available, therefore, to all—not just to a privileged few and not just in dreams—and thrived in a free world where men and women could speak their desires to one another (even if they fell away a bit at the same time from the idea of *romantic*, stable, monogamous love), instead of growing stale in cloistered spaces marked by disabling shyness, suspicion, arranged alliances, foolish fancies and in-laws preaching and palavering all over the place.

I was for a world like that . . . I was heading next week towards one such in San Francisco! I couldn't really imagine Zahra patting my head or singing lullabies ('Dikra, dikra, drift into the night/the world is asleep, the fravashirs in flight'). But I *could* see her back home at her sister's after our private tryst with destiny, sitting now at the dressing table in the guest room (after an espresso with the family and murmured goodnights), wearing a peach-coloured silk chemise, hair down, back upright even though unsupported ('I do yoga'), shoulders bare for none to see but herself, her eyes looking into her eyes, squeezing something fragrant on to her palms from the factories of The Body Shop or Estée Lauder, and thinking, as she rubbed this in, about the previous set of fingers—the fingers of Farhad!—that had caressed her skin, roved in so many places, pulled her down later as she made to leave. That was love being massaged into her pores, too!

Now she rubbed down her legs, very slowly and mindfully, enjoying both the moment and the memories, before she raised the hem of her chemise to get to her knees and thighs.

I felt my zabb rise and swell, and I wanted to be lost again in its pleasures. Could I? There was something outrageous about contemplating onanism in Hemlata's house. But, after all, *she* was the one who'd locked me in when all I wanted was to go back to my own home, that empty room with its fragrant sheets and memories. To lie down there, and to contemplate, to caress, to study from every angle, as if for the first time, that marvellous pleasure-generating twig of flesh that was at the top of the bottom half of me and stuck out of the middle of me, as mysterious as the dark side of the moon and as persistent as gravity, as wrinkled as a tortoise born in the previous century and as smooth as the marble of the Taj Mahal, sometimes awake when I was asleep and at other times asleep when I wanted it to be awake, the fount of all creation and the root of all repression, for so many years of my twenties and thirties doing no more than chugging along on auto-pilot, and now, suddenly, one night, a few days short of my forty-second birthday, promising a revelation of nothing less than the very meaning of life itself. What went on down there, in there? What was I yet to discover about it? Where else would it take me in San Francisco? I couldn't wait to find out.

One night with Zahra had changed everything—who knew what expanses lay ahead? Expanses of not just physical pleasure but also other kinds of partnerships and discoveries. I remembered how, when we were going back to Zahra's place in the car—estranged by our new togetherness, somehow reluctant to make eye contact—I heard Zahra draw in her breath, the way she would when she wanted to say something significant.

'Farhad, tell me . . . psychoanalysis, is it a completely Western science?'

'Um, it's not exactly a *science*. But I guess you could say it's based on a Western conception of what the mind is . . . how it must work past its difficulties and traumas.'

'So, it's completely mental in its, uh, orientation? There's no place for the body in it?'

'Kind of.'

'Farhad, haven't you ever felt that's *wrong*? That one thing can't be sorted out independent of the other?'

'Yes, but . . . that's the way it's done. It's not meant to be a solution for everything. Therapy is very clear about its limitations, and that's one of its strengths, you might say, not weaknesses. It offers no big promises like these . . . these self-help books and so on.'

'But don't you think something could be added to it? To take it forward from what it is?'

'Yes, but your licence only allows you to apply certain methods . . .'

'Yes, but that doesn't have to be the *end* of the matter. That's so *Indian*! Why run away from something that might help the world? We could try to integrate psychoanalysis and the great yoga texts. Patanjali, for instance. You'll find in the *Yoga Sutra* that he thinks of yoga as primarily a science of the *mind*. Farhad, imagine if we could put our skill sets together. Like India and America coming together in an alliance! And then your clients could come to me, and mine to yours. They'd learn from both of us, and we'd both learn from all of them. Life's about learning something new every day. West and East have been separated from one another for hundreds and thousands of years. Someone's got to put it all together. It could be us.'

I saw what Zahra was saying, and it did make sense to me. It was also a sign of Zahra's trust in me—a sign that she didn't just want me for my amazing body and cock but also for my mind, my self, my work. A mature woman, girlishly excitable in such a pleasing and arousing way, but deep down wise, seeking a connection at every level.

I said, 'It's a thought.' I found her wrist with the fingers of my free hand and moved her silver bangle up and down.

Zahra squeezed my fingers with her other hand and said, 'Great! It's too late tonight, but when we meet in San Francisco, let's discuss it in detail and take it further.'

'Sure.'

'And listen. On those days, we don't make love. It's just business.'

'Of course . . . I wouldn't have it any other way.'

'Why didn't you take the right there?'

'I just thought I'd take the longer way through Cumballa Hill . . .'

'Farhad, I'm getting late!'

'Okay, okay, I'll speed up.'

'You know, out in the West, it's all become about work, about *striving*. About being tense, on edge. "Work hard, play hard" . . . what kind of philosophy of life is that, really? What we need is a new science of *stillness*,' Zahra declared, as if she hadn't been bouncing up and down on my lap half an hour ago. 'Farhad, you know, I feel strange sometimes. The yoga industry's become so big in America, you wouldn't believe it. It's worth billions of dollars. There are more yoga mats than table mats in the country! It's almost too easy for me to do what everyone else is doing, because I learnt the hard way, yet it's difficult to make the practice more challenging without looking like a fraud or crank *myself*. You know what I mean? I'm stuck between a rock and a hard place. But if I . . . we . . . don't think ambitiously now, we never will. It's come to that point.'

'Surely you could just as easily have found an American

psychotherapist for this project?' I teased. 'I believe some of them are quite good-looking.'

'Oh, but he'd be too stuck in his own world view, I think. I'm all for multiculturalism, for civilizations fertilizing one another with new ideas—which is kind of what we'd be. And don't you realize—if we work together, it'll be the first time since the Golden Age of Persia that Zoroastrianism becomes really cutting-edge! So, just for that reason, if for nothing else . . .'

Wow, could this woman riff or what! I laughed aloud, thinking of the distance I'd traversed in a single day. Miles and his merry band had moved on to the fourth track. Zahra's fingers squeezed my thigh with a mixture of friendship and desire, and then she disappeared into her sister's apartment building.

I began to sense the first promptings of sleep in my brain. Where the hell was Hemlata? I lay down on the sofa.

Above the doorway leading into the rest of the apartment, I saw a pair of photographs. They were black and white portraits of a slightly younger Hemlata and her husband. Companion pieces, with one stark difference—Balu's picture was garlanded with marigolds, as if he were dead. Smiling with that roguish impudence that was the base note of his nature, his mockery of the world was turned instantly back on himself by the ironic frame of flowers.

It seemed as if Hemlata had disappeared forever, the ogre who had locked up poor Prince Farhad in a tower and had vanished. If things didn't change soon, I'd have to cry out to Zahra, my lady in shining armour, to come and rescue me by slaying my captor. And then we'd be free and go running out into the pleasure gardens of paradise, calling out each other's names before we fell asleep at the foot of the pomegranate tree.

The Thoughts of Hemlata's Mother Narsamma When She Woke Up at 4.43 am in Her Son-in-law's Home

Oh Hemu! I knew it as soon as I woke up: this is going to be the last year of my life.

I know, I have been saying this to you for many years running. But this time, I'm sure. And I want to go. My spirit is tired, my God waits to take me across to the other world. I pray that I may pass away as peacefully as your father went, in his sleep, his arms folded over his chest, wearing his favourite veshti.

And yet, suddenly, I don't want to go. I fear for you, my daughter, my only child. Who will take care of you when I'm gone? I remember, when your father passed away and I was so worried for your future, you said, 'Don't worry, Amma. What's wrong if it's just the two of us? Can't we women be strong? Do we always need a man in the house? How will anything change in this world of ours unless we first change something in our minds? I'll tell you something. Why don't you enjoy sleeping late, making your coffee and your dosais, watching Sun TV without Appa troubling you with his silly Test matches and Twenty20? You know what? I don't want to see any boys. I don't want to marry. I don't like the boys of our community. They won't let me live my life the way I want to. I'm different, Amma. My best friends are my books, and they will be my husband and—since that is the word you crave to hear—my master as well.'

I thought you would change your mind when you went to America, but instead, you changed your mind about America itself and came back home and began your degree here. And then, two years later, you said, 'Amma, I have a boyfriend. He's doing a PhD at Kalina, just like me. I thought I'd tell you so that you don't worry. When the time is right, I'll bring him home.' I waited and waited, all the while praying that he wasn't a Muslim or a Christian. But he did not visit, and later, when I asked about him, you refused to say anything at all.

I feared again that you would decide never to marry.

But one day, when I told you about the proposal that had come for you through my childhood friend Soumya in Chennai, you sat there very quietly for a long time. I was shocked when you agreed to meet the boy! And then, when you met him, you agreed to marry him—and why not, he already had such a successful business in importing industrial machinery from Korea, and his mother gave you a bucketful of gold at the wedding where there were more than eight hundred guests, and we moved out of our tiny flat in Sion and came up north all the way to this big place in Borivali where the birds can be heard every morning—there they are, chirping right outside the window—and the security guards all salute so respectfully when I come back from the market because they know what a rich and powerful man my son-in-law is.

It could have all gone so right, Hemu, it could have been like paradise. But now it's all so wrong, and he's left the house, and you keep saying he's having an affair, and you've both said such terrible things to each other in your quarrels (I tried not to listen, but I couldn't help it).

And now, here I am, sleeping in this sad, little, silent room, and there you are across the corridor, in the room you shared with your husband for only five years, sleeping all by yourself after having sat up half the night listening to music and drinking from the bar.

I want so badly to tell you: don't take this path, my daughter, because there'll be nothing in it for you at the end.

He's not a bad man, I know that. Maybe he made some mistakes. Every man does—that's the kind of animal he is. Besides, you never gave him any children—you wanted to wait until later. A child binds a man to his home and hearth, makes him responsible, faithful. Without this, he runs wild. Man and woman were never meant to be together without children, without little feet and voices around them.

You say he wants a divorce and has agreed to leave us this house. That shows what a generous man he is!

Now, why go down a road to ruin? You have a job, you have security . . . but is that enough? Already I can see what a toll this loneliness and torment is taking on you. You forget to put oil in your hair at night, you walk around talking to yourself about the face of desire, in the morning you leave without even eating a proper breakfast. It's all wrong. We look so strange when we take a walk together in the park in the evening, like a pair of widows!

My daughter, it's not too late. Swallow your pride, let your man have his way. Speak to him, call him back. Cry if you must, show him how weak and helpless you are without his shoulders to ease your burdens—the burdens you agreed to share for life, without ever changing your mind for any reason, good or bad. And perhaps you two should also think right away of children. Once you decide to do that, I don't see anything but happiness and happiness for you.

I've decided, I'm going to tell you all this right away, before you wake up and fly to the university as if you've grown a pair of wings, your sari all over the place and your bra strap showing, only forgivable because you do it so innocently and absent-mindedly.

Oh, these tired old limbs! I'm nothing but a bag of bones now, dragging myself from room to room, meal to meal. There's no reason to knock on the door of your bedroom any more—your husband isn't here.

What . . . you're not here either! Oh my God, my Shiva. When will you send some sense into my daughter's brain? Yet again she's been drinking, and she's fallen asleep on the sofa. This is the limit. This morning I must assert my authority. I am your parent, after all. For too long I've let a circus carry on in this house, and the results are there for all to see. What would your husband—and he's still your husband, no matter how much you may deny it—what would your husband say if he were to come home right now and find you in this wretched state?

Just wait. When you wake up to someone shouting in your ear, that noise should be so loud that you are shocked back—yes, blasted back—into good sense and dignity.

Wait, it's a man on the sofa. Balu has come back! Praise be to God! Things are going to be fine again.

EEEE! IT'S A NEW MAN!

Bhagaban Bhai, Bear and Bird

JUST AS EEJA and Ooi can only escape Bombay time by dreaming all day long about Bhubaneswar and Jagannath, so, too, my life in Bombay, without freedom, friendship or clouds, is only bearable when I add Bhagaban Bhai to the frame. If, after growing up rude and wild in Tininadi, I have been able to find my feet so many times in this life, including here in Bombay, it is because of Bhai.

Like the bird that drops down for a few minutes on to earth, hopping, dust-pecking, Bhai never becomes flustered, as if he knows that he can be back in the sky any time and, for the moment, simply wants to challenge himself to learn something new about the world.

Yes, although I am not much more than a servant in the eyes of Eeja and Ooi, I feel rich and high when I remember that I am a spokesman in Bhubaneswar for all my people, and doubly so when I remind myself that I alone and none other—except perhaps the widowed social worker Sabita Swain, who stopped speaking straight to me after I saw her naked, although that was an accident—knows Bhai's true nature and deepest secrets.

The strange thing is, many people in the high society of Bhubaneswar claim to know Bhai well and often speak to others as if they understand his mind. But few of them, I notice, seem to realize that for Bhai, life is an extremely serious thing and must, therefore, be treated like a game. And that life is a game and for that reason must be taken extremely seriously.

The first thing that attracted not just me but all my people to Bhai—back when he arrived three years ago in our Cloud-Mountain-land—was that, just like us, he was always on the edge of laughter or sadness. Bhai did not—does not—feel in small measures. His body may be heavy, bearlike-lumbering, but his mind is light, even humble, and takes the cast of those he feels for. In conversation, he always tries to strike up a dance—now I take the lead, now you, faster and faster, higher and higher. It is hard to refuse his offers. He is not at all like the rest of his people, but they do not know it, and he knows that they do not know it. I know that he knows that I know that they do not know it, and so, other than the fight against the Company, this has become the secret knowledge that binds us. And if he does not always clearly reveal his heart's intent or mind's programme, it is because he has learnt—this is perhaps what makes him such a good person to have on our side—that most people are not to be trusted. Especially the Bubus (that is his mocking name for the people of Bhubaneswar high society) who had no time for him back when he was trying to be an artist and poet—'Rabi, let's give it a few more years till you experience all the moods and colours of life, then I will read you my poems'—but who now, after the success of his television serials, invite him to all their thread ceremonies, marriages, memorial dinners and ribbon-cutting inaugurations.

'Ah, the Bubus!' Bhai often cries out over his coffee, waving at some item in the newspaper. 'Oh, the Bubus are in form again!'

With such people—steeped in the pride of their ancient and grand faith, powerful Gods and world-famous temples, government jobs and capital-city wealth—I know Bhai loves to play a winking, dissembling game, repeating their most characteristic phrases for his own amusement and to indulge their puff-puff pride. There is certainly something troubling and unstraightforward about this. But only such a person, it has come to seem to me—swift as a squirrel on the branch but as rooted in his principles as a tree—can deal with the might and menace of the Company, its double war both by way of the law and around the law. Over time, everybody else had fallen by the wayside who once had thought to stand in its way.

Often, when we'd watch films together in the evenings in Bhubaneswar, Bhai would point out how shots were taken and scenes made, and how in stories it was not just the world that moved but also the eye that watched it—which is what made a good story more pleasurable than life. When I go every morning to the market here in Bombay, it makes me happy to pretend that the jute bag on my shoulder is really a film camera—that I am trying to understand Bombay as he once tried to understand Tininadi. I tell myself, I am taking what in the trade is called a 'tracking shot', just like he did for the opening moments of *Our Marvellous Cloud People*.

Did Eeja and Ooi ever see this work? I don't think so. As soon as the film begins, the camera goes drifting through our Friday market fair, dog-low among the baskets of vegetables, fish and flowers, the heaps of clothes and utensils, the fat-purse laps and legs of groups of traders from Rayagada, drinking tea as they advertise the day's prices for cheroot leaves. It could be just another village scene anywhere in India, but if you have your wits in the proper place, you are supposed to see the clue. The faces of the people sitting behind the baskets are upraised, as flowers are to the sun.

The voice in the film, which is Bhai's, speaks up: 'Ladies and gentlemen, what are they looking up at, these people who live in our own state and speak Odia just like us? Surely there is no airplane above this country market, no skyscraper with billboards full of entrancing pictures of Bollywood film stars, no political leader on a stage giving a speech? What then is the source of their ecstasy? And why do we—the people of the city, the people of Jagannath, who know that we know so much more than the primitive villagers along the furthest fringes of this holy land of Odisha—find ourselves unable to find the same pleasure and peace in that most beautiful of sights, every day the same, yet every day new, just like the river Ganga? The clouds. I bring to you, brothers and sisters, the Cloud people, their God Cloudmaker and their holy mountain or Cloudmother. And here, to tell you their story—and how, in the last decade, one mining company has with the full permission of the government begun to destroy their habitat and their culture—is one of their own, a bright youth called Rabi.'

That was the film which had first brought Bhai to us, us to the world, political parties to Bhai's door, and me to Bhubaneswar. And suddenly, after years of relentless progress, the Company was somewhat shaken. A door was opened for my people again and their ancestors, the spirits who have made our valley their home ever since they were first fashioned out of clay and straw by Cloudmaker at play—an act for which He was punished most heavily and for all time to come.

Among my people, the old have no special claim on life, and when the life-force begins to take leave of them, they retreat from the world around them and prepare for their departure. Soon after, they curl up and die, and that is when they become bright once more, in the memory of the tribe. In the Hindu faith, however, ancestor worship begins, not unjustly, with the aged who are still in this world. And so, our hands were tied when—just as the elections were around the corner, just as our years of work were to be put to the test—Eeja fell ill. Hovering between this world and the next, He sucked us all out to Bombay—nothing to be done about it. Here, He had managed to rekindle His life-spirit—though, truth be told, He had succeeded somewhat in dampening and choking ours.

What new thing have you learnt about Bombay? Bhai always asks me on the phone because, I know, he wants me to treat even these days of boredom and misunderstanding as a learning experience. I do not think I have learnt a lot about Bombay, but I have definitely learnt a lot about Bhubaneswar and the ways of the Hindu faithful. Sometimes I keep myself entertained by imagining that I am making a film—one that explains to my people, by means of close attention to the lives of Eeja and Ooi, what a tithi is and what is a gotra, what is karma and what dharma, why humanity is broken up into a ladder of castes and why the higher and even the lower castes think this is Truth and is for the good of all, why at births and deaths one earns immense credit if one feeds a group of Brahmins, why high-born people cannot touch some others in their society, and if they do, they are obliged take a bath immediately, and why, despite being divided by thousands of rule-points of purity and pollution, Hindu society, at the end of the day, is still one indivisible whole, and everyone in it knows his or her place and his or her limits.

Somewhere in the film, to be called *Our Marvellous People of Jagannath*, I will ask, 'What high wall of dread and doubt, Cloudbrothers and clansmen, stops us from opening our hearts to our brothers and sisters of a different God? Let us pause for a moment to consider this. In all our time on this earth, we have been touched by only a single great spirit, Cloudmaker, who keeps a jealous hold over our souls. But besides Jagannath, round-eyed and all-powerful, these people on the far side of the mountains have dozens of Gods, hundreds, each with His or Her dominion, either over a place or a part of human nature. Our religion has come slipping and slithering down over time from tongue to tongue, but theirs is hammered into sacred texts. They have palm-leaf manuscripts that are hundreds of years old, and each man's name reveals his entire ancestry and his tradition. Besides, they have another art by which, using the date and time of birth, their entire future can be foretold. Such is the fascinating world of the Hindus—of whom the Hindus of Odisha, vast though they may seem to us, are just one tribe, with their round-eyed God Jagannath—and you will gain much if you do not scorn it outright but try to understand it from within.'

I know that when I tell all this to Bhai back in Bhubaneswar, he will be delighted and announce that I have begun to learn a second way of seeing—which is the entire point of being a human being. Yes, it is true—after three years of living in Bhai's house and walking the paths of his thoughts, one part of me remains a tribesman of my people, under the will of Cloudmaker, but the other part has become wedded to Bhai's way of seeing, and knows that sometimes man must be a single, difficult soul, crossing swords with the laws of his group, and feeling not guilt but pride about it, sensing not lies but truth in it. Resistance is not a bad thing, though it makes for headaches and doubts—the kind never experienced by Eeja and Ooi, for whom the truth about the seen and the unseen world is transparently clear.

Sometimes, one fact disturbs me. Although he fights for my God, Bhai himself is godless—yet, again and again, for his cause, he proclaims a belief in Jagannath. (Since no one else suspects his unbelief, including his parents, this fact seems to bother only me.) Bhai, on his part, says, 'Did Cloudmaker rob me of my belief in Jagannath? No, I had given up on Hindu religion long before I came to you. Rather, all I say to the people of my state today is that if, as proud Odias, we passionately proclaim the all-encompassing reality of Jagannath, why should it be so difficult to understand the sanctity of Cloudmaker and His kingdom in a far part of our very own state? How can we watch the Company seize that realm for the sake of development, when we would never allow the Jagannath temple of Puri to be snatched for such a reason? It is an intellectual question I ask, remade for a religious herd of sheep. Unless I route this argument through the path of Jagannath, it will never be heard. Because no question is of any importance to the Odia people unless it has some relation to the worship of God.'

Round-eyed Jagannath, staring Jagannath . . . did He ever sleep? Did He even ever blink?

Ooi and I, dozing in the middle of the day, woke up when Eeja made a choking sound. Ooi cried, 'What is it?'

Eeja, wide awake, had been reading the serious limb of the newspaper. He did not seem to hear Her. Instead, He now held up one large sheet. He tore it over and over into many small pieces, shredding the thoughts properly. Even though I had never seen Him do this before, the gesture was strangely familiar to me. Bhagaban Bhai had told me that, throughout his childhood, his father had done this every time he got something wrong in his homework. I shivered, and hoped that, over our few remaining days in Bombay, Eeja would not ask me to write out the letters of the alphabet. With a snort of disgust, Eeja tossed the torn-up thoughts into the air. We watched as they came floating down, falling upon the bed, among the pictures of the Gods, on our heads, into our laps. I got up and began to collect them. While I was down on the floor, I touched Eeja and Ooi's feet.

'He's gone mad,' Ooi whispered. 'We'll have to call Bhagaban right away. Listen. Look here. What is it? Did we do something? What do you want?'

'What do I want?' said Eeja, His lips quivering like a freshpinged bowstring. 'I want the stupidity of the English-speaking people in the big cities of India to come to an end, that's what I want.'

'English-speaking people? Which ones do you meet? There's only Rabi here. And then there's me. We couldn't speak English if Jagannath Himself put the words in our mouths.'

Ooi . . . I can speak English! At least, I can read it aloud. But this was not the time to say so.

'There are dozens of English-speaking people working for that newspaper. Their brains are scrubbed clean of sense, and they've become strangers to their own culture. You, boy! Bring me a piece of paper and a pen. I have to write a letter to the editor right away.'

Ooi was tremendously happy. 'God bless the English-speaking people of this country,' She said to me. 'Give him a whole sheet of fool-cap paper from the suitcase—more if he wants. That will keep him occupied for at least an hour.'

I ran to get paper before Eeja lost any thoughts.

Ooi said, 'Tell me, what do they say in there that makes you hiss and foam at the mouth like a water buffalo?'

Eeja explained, 'One fellow writes in the editorial here, "If only the Hindus and Muslims of India would realize that religion is only a part of life, not the whole of it. That way, they can have the double dividend of being religious in their particular way but united on a secular plane, which is the point of living in a democracy, and one it is about time we learnt."'

Ooi let out a gurgle. 'What! Why do they keep mixing us up with the Musilims, as if we can do nothing without thinking about them first? Between the Musilims on the one hand and the lower castes and tribals

Clouds

on the other, we're being squeezed into the shithouse in our very own country. It's a kind of madness—a madness that will destroy everything that was once sacred. And the worst thing is, we ourselves allowed it.'

'Bravo!' said Eeja. 'One can always trust a woman to see the rump of the animal and think it the whole.'

At first I could not understand what He meant, but then I realized He was speaking Ooi down.

'There's definitely something in what you say,' Eeja continued, 'I don't deny it. If this were an examination for the civil services, you would get pass marks. But there's something even more wicked in this argument, cunningly concealed under a mask of reason. And I'll tell you what it is.'

We looked up at Him, our mouths open. It was like watching the last ball of a cricket match.

'The point is,' Eeja pronounced, 'that Hindu dharma cannot be reduced to the word *religion*, any more than life itself can be called a religion. For the simple reason that there has never been any distinction in the first place in Hindu life between what is religious and what is not. From the farmer's view of the field, to the householder's view of the family and its place in society, from what must be eaten today, to what the soul will be in each one of its incarnations, Hindu dharma is one continuous, self-sustaining system, comprehending all life, all matter, all time, all dimensions. How else is it possible that Hindu civilization has held its own over more than two thousand years, while the great civilizations of the Greeks, the Romans and the Persians collapsed? Once you start using the English word *religion*, as many educated Indians have unfortunately begun to do, you begin to smuggle Hinduism into a place where it can be compared to other systems, founded at a certain point in history by human beings like Muhammad and Jesus—systems that also call themselves religions.' Eeja made two paper balls to represent these people and threw them each into a different corner of the room. 'Religion, hss! Hindus have Hinduism. Other people have religions. The two are not the same, which is why we're not running around the world

101

like them, trying to convert everybody to the faith. If you don't know the truth about something, at least have the decency to keep quiet.'

Ooi was stung. 'I *was* keeping quiet.'

'I don't mean you. I meant the fellow writing this nonsense and the hundreds of others who think and argue like him.'

'I'm not a scholar or a pandit like you, to understand these mindmisting arguments,' said Ooi. 'For me, Jagannath, Maa Mangala, Krusna, Nrusingha, Kali, Maa Tarini, the Balmiki Ramayana and Byasa's Mahabharata, the Lingaraj temple of our Bhubaneswar and the Jagannath and Lokanatha temple of Puri, the vermilion in my hair parting, my conch shell and copper plate, my bottle of Ganga water and my precious saligrama stone, these are my religion, and I don't want to know anything more. That said, I'm sure you are right. If this fellow is babbling on and on about equality with Musilims, he's not much of a Hindu to begin with. Write it all clearly in a letter, and Rabi will find the address of the newspaper and post it. We won't leave Bombay without straightening them all out. Or else the disease will eventually spread across our land and reach the Hindus of Odisha as well. Our holy land, the kingdom of Jagannath, will be corrupted by a world that has already begun to slip into darkness.'

Eeja grunted, balanced a foolscap sheet on a notebook, placed this on His lap and began to write in His lovely hand. I watched the letters slowly form and settle down into words and thoughts on paper. Now that I considered it, it seemed that old people begin to store more and more of their essence in unseen things like the mind and silence, as if in preparation for giving up their bodies. Certainly, it never seemed as if Eeja's silences were merely empty vessels, unlike the silences of so many idle people in Bhubaneswar—I have witnessed this myself and felt clearly the absence of thought in them.

It always amazed me how focussed Eeja could become once He set His mind to think. When He wrote, all His years fell away from Him, and one forgot how He slurped and splattered food when He ate, and had to have His shirt buttons done for Him, and His leg lifted up every time He wanted to lie down, and all His waste taken care of with bottles and pots. At such times, I loved—unnoticed by Him, so engrossed was He in His own thought—to watch the flickers of His face and the switching of His gaze inward and outward, outward and inward, as dramatic as any television serial Bhai had ever made. If only Eeja could somehow be made to speak the name and cause of Cloudmaker, I knew He'd present an argument that nobody could counter, just like the one He had made now.

Eeja was the opposite of Bhai and yet, in some way, the very same. Where Bhai chose the roundabout road with jokes, with persuasion, with goading, Eeja went with arguments and high-born discipline. Both were always going someplace. Maybe this was what it was to be a Brahmin. Aged folk in Tininadi would be astonished if they saw Eeja working. What was the point of arguing with those one had never met, or putting things down on paper! The more time I spent in His presence—itself greatly diminished from what it must have been in the days of His pomp—the more I felt sure I had something of enduring value to learn from being around Eeja. Perhaps how to be sustained by a kind of wealth that no one else could touch.

Ooi sat quietly for a few minutes with Her blue gudakhu tin in Her lap, rubbing the mixture on to Her teeth with Her right forefinger. This mildly mindclouding paste of tobacco, molasses and lime was Her one indulgence, and when She took it, two or three times a day, She became as peaceful and inward as Bhai did after two glasses of whisky.

'If Jagannath wills it, we should be home in Bhubaneswar by this time next week,' She said to me through Her red mouth. 'It's not a long wait, but we've been here so many days, I can't believe any more that I'll be going home, sitting on my own sofa, making tea in my own kitchen, supervising the maid Kali . . . I hope she hasn't run off to some other house, the wretch. I've lived so many years in this world, but I've never faced anything like this—sickness and homesickness, pain and exile all combined. I don't even want to imagine what sins I have committed in my past lives for this to be brought upon me. But I tell myself, at least I am earning some merit by helping my son fulfil his dreams.'

'Yes, Ma.'

'What a strange life Bhagaban has had,' Ooi mused. 'He has no choice. More than one astrologer has told me that he was born at a most unusual conjunction of planets. I don't know if he's ever told you about his past. Till he was thirty, he did nothing at all. He turned your Eeja's hair white with worry. Perhaps a wife would have straightened Bhagaban out in his twenties. But you have to make a start in life to have a wife in the first place! After Bhagaban was caught cheating in the civil services examination, your Eeja completely gave up hope. He turned him out of the house. He shouldn't have done that. Bhagaban has always said he wasn't the one cheating. He was actually trying to help someone when he was caught. The other fellow had connections among powerful people and escaped. My poor son got beaten on the washerman's slab.'

'Yes, Ma. That was what Bhai told me, too.'

'And he never wanted to give those wretched examinations anyway. It was your Eeja who forced him to.'

Eeja grunted over His letter, as if to say there was only one course at that time and He had taken it.

Ooi continued, 'For many years, your Eeja and Bhagaban did not speak to one another. Years passed. After a while, Bhagaban stopped calling me. He said, "My pride and self-respect have been wounded. I'll only come home when I've made something of myself."

'One year, they began to show an advertisement on television, over and over again. A young man goes off to America to do one of those computer jobs they're all pursuing these days, and he comes back with a gold necklace for his mother. Did Bhagaban ever share the ad with you? No? Ask him to, when we get back to Bhubaneswar. It's as full of mother-feeling as anything in the Ramayana or the Mahabharata. We only found out from one of our neighbours that Bhagaban had made it for a jeweller in Odisha.

'And that's when he came home—like Ramachandra, victorious from Lanka, back to Ajodhya. My son had found his place in the world, even if it had taken him half his life to do so. Poor boy . . . most of his hair had fallen out by then.

'After that, he started making television serials: *The Betrayal of Jagannath, The Sounds of Family Life, My Husband Is a Stranger to Me.* He was forty before he moved out of his rented place and bought his own house in Jaydev Vihar. But, at least, after all those years of struggle, his name was on everybody's lips in Bhubaneswar. The ladies of our building would visit me every Friday, after the week's lot of episodes had been telecast, to ask what was going to happen next. We can't wait, we can't wait. I would say, "No. Wait until Monday. What's the point of telling stories if everyone knows what's going to happen next? The sense of anticipation, the feeling that everything that's important in life hinges on one decision: that's the story's claim over your hearts and minds, that's when the story takes root in the soul and makes you think about life. How do we learn how to live anyway, if not through stories? To me, there's nothing more beautiful than an unfinished tale. It's all the grace and play of Jagannath anyway . . . and the truth is, even my son is waiting for Jagannath to show him the way forward in the story."'

I was happy that, at long last, these days I was being spoken to as a human being. Edging closer to Ooi's feet, I said, 'Ma, Bhai told me he always consults you about village customs and festivals for his serials . . . because he doesn't know so much about them.'

'What? What doesn't he know? My son knows everything. If I'm of any use to him, it's only because the poor boy doesn't have a wife. So, he needs me to tell him about the feminine aspects of our culture and tradition. After all, it's man and woman who, between them, make for the stability of the world—even if a woman's share of the whole is somewhat smaller.

'But it could also be that, for a long time, my son turned his back on our world and our religion because he felt they had only given him trouble, not strength. It was your Eeja who came between Bhagaban and Jagannath by dealing with the poor child so harshly. Bhagaban had to spend many years alone in the forest, but once he found his way back on to the main path, he more than made up for lost time. As they say, the pilgrim who has lost three days to illness is the first to reach the temple of Jagannath.'

How beautifully Ooi could speak!

'But I'll tell you what upsets me today as much as your Eeja's illness and perhaps even more. It might not be exactly your fault, Rabi, but it can't be denied either that you and your people are responsible for this. Just when everything was going wonderfully for Bhagaban, and he could have settled down and started a family, he got interested in your people and landed up in the most backward part of our state, where even the days are as nights. And you know Bhagaban. Once the madness of new love seizes his brain, it takes hold of everything in his life. Since then, it's been the Company, the Cloud people, the Company, the Cloud people, day and night, sleeping and waking. God knows what these things really mean.

'And then this nasty politics, and these elections. I still don't understand it—what was the need to get mixed up in all this? You're a high-born man from a Danua Brahmin family, you've worked so hard to make a place for yourself in the capital, you're in the spring and song of your life, you're a name among the people who matter. Why go running to the edge of the world, asking low-born people to vote for you, while, at the same time, deliberately upsetting the people of your own city with all sorts of disturbing thoughts and questions? Only the moon should go backwards when it's full, not human beings.'

Why upset your own people with disturbing thoughts from the edge of the world? I saw Bhai sitting in his red velvet armchair in his room in Bhubaneswar, his drink in his hand, saying, 'Brother, let me explain something to you about the way this country works. If you set out to do something truthfully, in a trusting, straightforward way—like you Cloud people—or criticize something to its face, nobody gives you the slightest bit of attention. Or they find a way of chasing you out of the house altogether, as if you're a cat come to drink their milk. You'll be stuck in the wasteland of your ideals and principles all your life, and the only face that reflects your thoughts will be the one in the mirror. Does it make sense to go down that path? Maybe to a sage or a renunciate . . . but not to me.

'So what's to be done then? Well, the only other way is to get the attention of people from the inside, by settling in the place where they're roosting happily like chickens, and going cluck-cluck-cluck yourself. Root yourself in the world they inhabit, learn the shape of their reason, and once you have their respect, take that and run with it on to a new road. That's what Mahatma Gandhi figured out, and he was the only one in the last hundred years who managed to shake up Hindu society a bit. Only a bit. Now they've turned him into a saint as well and can afford to ignore him.

'When I realized this fairly late in life—that's how long it takes, brother, to grow a mind of your own in this world—I changed track. I stopped my empty radicalism. I began to make television serials, not about the pettiness but the majesty of our traditional culture, the pride of us Odias—which, of course, means mainly the caste Hindus, with a couple of token roles for the rest. Now, brother, although you don't come from this world—and that's as sure a sign as any that you were born under a lucky star or cloud—you've got a pair of eyes and ears as sharp as anybody, so you know that in our state there's no subject more pleasing to the populace—a sure sign of decadence—than How Great Is Our Culture and How Powerful Our Round-eyed Lord Jagannath. All our terrible habits, all our blindnesses, all our self-absorption, all our rationalization—into the story-pot I threw them, disguised as tales of our virtue, piety, pride, our love for Jagannath. The same subjects would have bored me senseless if I'd approached them directly . . . ho, what energy I felt when I threw myself into making parodies! One almost wants to say the hand of Jagannath was upon one's shoulder. And the people loved it. I gave them just what they wanted, woven into a spicy melodrama, and they never saw the joke at all. What better satire than one where the audience perceives it all as the truth? Ho ho ho.

'I laid out stories in which the rich and the middle classes were always the main characters, and the poor never appeared except as servants—and sometimes as servants who wickedly stole the household's precious possessions, a bowl here, a spoon there—much like the Muslim or, as my beloved mother says, *Musilim* invaders once raided Hindu temples and made off with our wealth. I even shook all of Odisha by making a serial about premarital sex and elopement. But in the final scene of *The Shocking Sin* it emerges that the lovers did not know that they had been betrothed to one another while they were still in their cradles, and that bond, consecrated by their wise and venerable parents, was what had led to their chance dalliance with each other's bits and bobs without parental permission. Just so no distant aunt or neighbour makes a fuss about their false fornication, they get married again, and lo, we got to shoot a great wedding scene with half the fluorescent saris and Swarovski crystals in the world, and all the characters wiggling their hips to Bollywood music under the approving watch of Lord Jagannath. I nearly killed myself laughing with that plot line.

'The more I jested and frolicked in this manner, the more I was acclaimed as a pillar of our culture. Why, when I first built an elaborate set for a temple in Lakhmi Studios, it was for a single scene in *The Golden Pitcher*—but I ended up using it so much that they didn't use that space for anything else for three years. No matter what story I chose to tell, it wasn't long before the same thing came up—cut to the temple! In fact, I've just received a letter from the Odisha Civil Services Officers' Wives Association. It says they have petitioned their husbands to build a real temple at that spot. Just imagine—my make-believe temple of ironic piety is, if they have their way, soon going to be a real temple of their faith! Truly, God is everywhere . . . one only lacks the eyes to see Him.'

I could never laugh like Bhai when he was telling these stories, because of the depth of his godlessness and his deception. It was as if he had no need for either God or man. But it did seem that Bhai's reading of the world was just, and the lonely path he had taken was the only one available—and that was brave of him, braver than I could ever have been. Bhai's God was not Jagannath, and although he spoke now in Cloudmaker's name, it was not Cloudmaker either. It was someone or something else. 'My God is my self, and to such a God, a human being can always be true if he or she so chooses,' he would sometimes say. And about that God, he could never tell Eeja and Ooi.

He looked me straight in the eye and said, 'But. There's always a *but* in every story, brother, just as there's a trace of perversion in every God. And the *but* here is this. Exactly when in the eyes of the world I had ascended the highest peak of success, and even the chief minister wanted me to be his friend and make a campaign film for him, I looked at myself in the mirror and saw only emptiness. In the long years of delighting myself by agreeing ironically with the world, I had lost sight of my own nature. I knew that if I kept going down this path, I, too, would eventually get corrupted by the perverse social order we had constructed in the name of Jagannath. Then my grand joke would be on no one but me.

'So, when I suddenly got offered the option of making a documentary film with a British NGO, I visited, as you know, Tininadi, and I learnt all about the struggle between the Company and the Cloud people over the mountain, and how the government had leased the sacred mountain to the Company so it could mine the bauxite there.

'That was the moment my soul had been waiting for. When I heard about the injustices visited upon your people, I was, of course, dismayed, but I was even more aghast when I noticed the silence around the issue. The caste Hindus of Odisha and the newspapers of Bhubaneswar couldn't have cared less for your woes, even though you people were Odia, too. For them, it was but natural that *you*, as tribals, would give up something precious so that *they* could live better and people from other states in India would respect them more.

'And I thought: I've done what I had to, to make my way up in this world. My credentials are not suspect. If I break with the status quo, they won't think of me as a leftist or a revolutionary. Rather, they'll follow me to places where the self-declared radicals can never take them. From now on, come what may, I'll speak the truth openly and work for the cause of justice.

'Of course, I don't doubt for a moment that I've taken up this cause for selfish reasons, too. I'm trying to test myself, pitting my wits against a force as many-headed as Ravana, seeking the glory that comes with victory in politics. But that's man for you, a slightly crooked and base creature, incapable of love without self-love. And at least when he knows that and accepts it, he breaks free of illusions and pompousness, false piety and parrotspeak, which are the gifts of Jagannath to our culture—which makes me think that, deep down, the round-eyed Lord might be a jester just like me.

'The fact is, man is wiser for knowing that he is a fool, and then he learns to give himself the medicine that will rein in his worst excesses. He can plan for a time when he will be rendered superfluous . . . when the friends he seeks to help in his own interest can take care of themselves.

'And that's why we need to fight these elections, brother. For, here is an opportunity for us tribals to emerge from our burrows of backwardness and introversion, to seize power through legal means and learn how to use it, to teach ourselves new principles and systems, to think of our place in the modern world and in the future. That's the real gift the Company has given us, and they don't even know it.'

'I've finished writing the letter,' said Eeja. 'Now, how is it to reach them?'

'I told you, our Rabi will post it, don't you worry. He'll write out the address on the envelope, too.'

'Really? Boy, do you know how to read and write?'

'Yes, Eeja,' I said, instead of letting Ooi reply on my behalf. 'Odia, and English as well.'

'Really? I've rarely seen a tribal like you. Till what class have you studied?'

'Eeja, till the twelfth standard.'

'Did you pass?'

'Yes, Eeja.'

'For your exams, did you learn the real meaning of the lessons, or did you just memorize what they were going to ask you? Or did you copy? Tell me the truth.'

'Eeja, I tried to study . . .'

'Really? You are to be praised for that. If you try to do your graduation, a government job will definitely come your way—they now have reservations for tribals. But few tribals have the patience or the discipline to study for years. Hmm . . . let me take a little test and assess your knowledge.'

I became tense.

'Say, now, in what year did India become a democracy?'

'Eeja . . .'

'I repeat, in what year did India become a democracy?'

'In 1947.'

'1947!' Eeja turned to Ooi, as if sharing a great joke. 'He said 1947!'

'I'm sorry, Eeja . . . I don't know . . .'

'What do you mean, you don't know? Boy, you *do* know. I was just surprised. My congratulations to your schoolteacher for doing such a good job with you.' Eeja turned to Ooi and said, 'See! This is what I always said. Once you deal with the tribals with a firm hand and show them that there's a life beyond eating and singing, hmm, beyond lolling around on the hillsides, hmm, beyond seeing signs and auguries in everything, hmm, beyond painting the outsides of their houses with rice paste, hmm, and foraging in the forest for honey and tendu leaves, hmm, and drinking themselves silly on every festival day and lying in a heap for the next three days, hmm, they, too, can come up in the world and make a place for themselves in a larger society. Maybe not a very high place . . . but a place all the same. When I was first posted in Koraput—it was the year Prime Minister Nehru passed away—the locals didn't even know the meaning of the word democracy. And it had been more than ten years since we had had the first Indian general elections! I remember one fellow thought it was a medicine for a sex disease and said, "Democracy has really healed my cock and made it big and strong again."'

Ooi's eyes opened wide inside Her round and wrinkled face. 'What's wrong with you! Why do you say such dirty words aloud?'

It surprised me, too, that Eeja could say 'cock'—a word that Bhai used so freely in his talk—but more than that, I was happy to have impressed Him with my answer to such an easy question, when so many weeks of taking care of His body had got me nowhere. School! I did not tell Him that it was not from school, but by reading the books that Bhai had given me in Bhubaneswar that I had learnt all the important dates of Indian history. As for the ideas linking the mountain to Jagannath, Tininadi to Bhubaneswar and India, and my people to Odia society, the political order, the government and the Company, Bhai poured them out of himself and into me all day long. And he was the best teacher because he was a storyteller by trade, and he knew how to make them relevant to the lives of my people.

'This *de-mo-cracy* in our land is a strange thing, Rabi. Repeat after me—for it's a word that our Cloud people must learn to befriend, as more than anything else it is what will make them agents of history. One might even say *de-mo-cracy* is Cloudmaker, come down to earth.'

I laughed and said, '*De-mo-cracy*. Why are you joking with me, Bhai? I already know this word.'

'Why, brother, that's true. You even say it like you're the one who invented it. But, as we know with bicycles and cocks, to know what something is capable of and to really make use of it are two different things. Now, what is this *de-mo-cracy*? Like that other word from which we can never escape, *fa-mi-ly*, it is something both good and bad, a basket of joys and sorrows. It's not for saints or for philosophers . . . or, for that matter, for fools. It takes place here on earth, not in the clouds. Democracy is not something to be settled between man and his God but between man and his fellow man. It's a fight, as high or as low as the participants choose to make it, to be played with all the weapons they can find, all the means they can use. If you don't fight for your share, somebody else will take what you have, and if you don't have . . .' he rubbed his fingers together, '. . . you'll be beaten, for sure.

'So, you can either sit at home with your Bhagavad Gita or your Vedas, your Ten Commandments, your Quran or your Cloudmaker, trying to get your God to make you a better world, or you can go out and learn to use the strength that the great men of the twentieth century have vested in you. Yes, you, the humble peasant, the rickshaw-puller, the prostitute, you, the scavenger, the untouchable, the tribal, in the hope that one day you will rise into the strength of it, as even the strongest warrior is better when he puts on his armour.

'Now, you may say, all that is fine. But in a democracy, if there's a dispute, what if the other side has all the power? What if the government and the Company have got together to shut out your side of the story with all the means they have, fair and foul? Then what should you do? How is democracy going to help you? Is democracy going to pipe up with the truth all of its own accord? Will it put a curse upon the rulers of the world for desecrating justice, as Brahma and Shiva used to do in the epics? No. Democracy is strangely silent. Is democracy giving you funds to fight your just battle? No. It expects you to cough up the money yourself! So, the question then is—are we really any better off in a democracy than before?

'A-ha. This is where the game really begins—so, let us first try to understand the rules. You see, brother, in a democracy, a great power, such as the Company, may be able to buy out a whole system. But—and this is such a thrilling thing—it has to tell lies to do so . . . because the truth can't be said out loud. And those lies offer immense power to those who come waving the wand of truth.

'A hundred years ago, if the Company or the British Raj had wanted your mountain, you'd have been herded out of your land and sent to live in some marsh or swamp, with sweet music being played live by mosquitoes, and boulders to squat on that turned out to be crocodiles. But with democracy, they can't do that. Now, even though they may want to kill your people, they can't use sticks or guns . . . because that's not allowed in a democracy. They can, at best, suffocate you slowly by making sweet noises—by insisting that everything they do is actually what *you* want. Land, jobs, compensation, rehabilitation, progress, development, new schools, hospitals, roads—they promise to bring you all of this if only you allow them to mine your mountain!

'Why, brother, isn't this the job of the government anyway—to provide schools, hospitals and roads? Must the government take the mountain in exchange for these basic things? Must it wipe out a God even older than Jagannath to feed and educate your children? No.

'Mother Democracy—no, let's leave mothers alone for a bit—Sister Democracy, unlike Jagannath or Maa Tarini or, for that matter, Cloudmaker, will grant you the strength to beat the sinister powers that loom above you. You and I and the people of Tininadi will do it, brother, under the law of Cloudmaker.'

'Fish,' said Eeja. 'I want to eat fish. But not sea fish. River fish.'

A Billimoria in Borivali

A DREAM, FOR sure a dream—because in it two women were talking angrily to one another, and I never let two women together into my personal space. It's dangerous. The voices were disturbed and disturbing. Even within the dream, though, I was able to back out a bit and tell my subconscious that I knew what it was getting up to. Yes, sir! Long marinated in Indian 'cultural ethos', my brain was, by inventing reproachful female voices, trying to make me feel guilty for having enjoyed myself over a night of post-marital sex and for plotting dozens of repeats of such encounters.

Oh, the sweet things my subconscious had proffered during my previous sleep, when all I'd desired was to come close to Zahra—and now, just because we'd gone from first to fourth gear, everything had changed deep down there.

Well, chatter on, ladies! I turned over to sleep on my other side. But the dream wouldn't be shaken off.

First Woman: Yes, I know, my name is not on the ownership deed of this apartment. But does that mean I stand by and watch such an outrage right in front of my eyes? I haven't grown so old that I can't stand up for my principles. And for the memory of your late father. Oh, what would he have said today if he'd been alive!

Second Woman: Ma, for God's sake, Ma, calm down! How many more times must I tell you, it's not what you think. He came to deliver my *car*. I'd never seen him before in my life.

First Woman: My own daughter, lying to me . . . if that doesn't prove that we've entered the Age of Darkness, what does?

Second Woman: Didn't I tell you, he's an acquaintance of Balu's . . . of some sort. And because I wanted to check the recording device I'd installed in the car, I left him in this apartment. I thought I'd be back in a minute or two. But, then, I got so excited by what I heard that I called Madhu right away . . . and, insomniac that she is, she asked if I could pop by and deliver the tape. Because if it had what I thought it did, it would be an open-and-shut divorce case. And then we ended up listening to the tape over and over again. I wish you could hear the stuff your son-in-law says on record . . . including one or things about *you*. Somewhere down the line, Madhu went on to tell me the story of her own marriage and divorce, and how she came to be a private investigator, and in all this drama I actually forgot about this fellow. I totally *forgot* about him. And here you are taking things to the other extreme and saying that I *brought* him over.

First: How many more times must I warn you, you are not filing for a divorce! That's like cutting off a part of your own body.

Second: How many more times must I tell you, I am! And then we'll have a flat to live in that'll be our own, and we'll have our whole lives before us, Ma, to plan, to enjoy—free of deceit, misery, anger, all the terrible things with which men control the world.

'Wake him up! Wake him up right now and send him back to wherever he came from.'

'Ssh! He's sleeping so peacefully. I can't. Not after what I did to him.'

'Tell me, in a time like ours, how could you leave me alone in the house with a strange man? For half the night, I could hear someone walking around, playing music, fiddling around in the kitchen. And I thought it was you. Imagine what he could have done to me—he'd even locked the door from the inside! Let me tell you, he made himself really happy in here. Then, clearly, he got drunk and fell asleep.'

'Ma, you've been watching too many serials. Real life isn't like that. And not everybody is like your son-in-law.'

'Already you're supporting this fellow instead of my son-in-law!'

'Ma, this is *not* one man versus another. For God's sake, why do you always have to think in binaries? This is the problem with the whole goddamn country.'

'Do this uneducated woman a favour, and don't use these strange English-literature ideas on me.'

'It's not an English-literature idea. It's a political idea, it's a progressive idea, it's a *human* idea.'

'Breakfast is a human idea I recognize. Shall I make you a dosai?'

'Yes, please. And when he wakes up, we must make him one as well to apologize.'

I slipped through the cracks that always exist in dreams into another space and remembered that I was now in possession of Zahra. And when, after the reading in the evening, she'd come home with me, it would be of the greatest importance to take things real slow slow s-l-o-w. Last night had been so frantic, you couldn't have boiled an egg in the time it took us from start to finish. I'd already forgotten what Zahra's skin smelt like, what her breasts looked like, how her lips tasted. No, tonight would be different, not just Man and Woman but Farhad and Zahra, ecstatically exploring all the possibilities of the instant, as Miles did, as did Mingus.

The tamarind whiff of sambar woke my nose up. I opened my eyes and saw a not-unknown woman sitting a few feet away from me in an armchair, eating a dosa and sambar off a plate resting on her commodious lap, and reading a book titled *The Feminine Mystique: 50th Anniversary Edition* by Betty Friedan.

Oh Zarathustra . . . it was B Hemlata!

After the first free-love night of his life and the historic decolonization of his sexual being, Farhad Billimoria was waking up into the twenty-first century on a sofa in a strange household, dressed in day clothes, without access to toothbrush or, for that matter, tongue—even someone as wordy as me could think of nothing to say in such a situation. I caught sight of my watch . . . 9.30 am on a Friday morning. And I knew at once that, no matter how ingeniously I worked it out or how much money I paid, THERE WAS NO WAY I could get back to the peace of my own apartment, through peak hour traffic and Bombarbaric frenzy, before noon.

I could've woken up this morning in my own bed. Instead—it was that kind of city—here I was being harshly penalized for doing a good turn to a stranger, and was waking up in full view of another stranger. It was like travelling second class in some long-distance train to the boondocks. Sleep is the most beautiful, the most necessary, the most sacrosanct of human privacies, to be shared only with partners and split personalities. I couldn't stop a little groan of disgust and dread.

Hemlata looked at me and said in a tone of sweet sarcasm, 'Good morning.'

'Uh . . . good morning,' I replied. 'Thank you for last night.'

As soon as I said this, an old woman—dear God, Hemlata's mother-in-law—no, her face said she was her mother—burst into the room, balancing a dosa on a spatula. She announced in an accent far stronger than Hemlata's, 'He's saying, "Thank you"! I was right. I was right!'

'Ma, no more of that . . . *please*! Ask our guest if he would like some breakfast.'

'Nonono—I have to be leaving!' I said, jumping up. 'I'll just wash my face, if I may, and be off.'

'Why? Please stay and have something to eat.' A flicker of amusement—not without a touch of malice at the sight of a member of the male tribe squirming and babbling—surfaced on Hemlata's face, as her mother deposited the dosa on her plate. 'My mother is an excellent cook. And if you don't like South Indian food, we can fix you some cereal or toast.'

'Eat my dosai,' said her mother firmly. '*Atithi devo bhava*—do you understand that, or shall I explain it in English? The guest is like God.'

I was about to stammer some excuse. But then I recalled I had woken up into a new life—the Farhad of old was a skin I was shedding with each new action of mine. Here I was, letting all the pressure flow towards *me*, when it was Hemlata and her mother who ought to have been discombobulated by this unusual episode in the history of Indian family life.

'Sure, Auntie,' I said, 'I'd love a dosa!'

'One minute then,' said Hemlata's mother happily, and disappeared with a swish of her sari.

'She loves to cook for people, no matter who they are,' explained Hemlata, before returning to her lessons in feminine mystique.

Clearly, there were going to be no apologies here! Well, I could play it cool till the other side blinked. I went to the basin in the corridor and washed my face. On my way back, I popped into the kitchen—the site of my most radical challenge ever to property rights, the theft of a packet of crisps—to take a look at what was going on and to say, 'Smells good,' to Hemlata's beaming mother. Yes, Farhad Billimoria could charm them all!

I hadn't realized the previous night that there could be another person in the house—it was just *so* silent and the atmosphere was *so* single-separated-woman! How could I have forgotten the Indian habit of having parents as witnesses for every moment of life . . . and into an advanced age!

'Nice place you have here,' I told Hemlata as I sat down on the sofa. 'Thanks.'

'I don't think I've ever been to Borivali before. It's quite far out.'

'Really? You think so? You're a townie, aren't you?'

'I live in the city of Bombay proper, yes.'

I saw Hemlata's eyebrows arch faintly. 'This is the city of Bombay proper, too.'

'Yes, of course, of course,' I said in my most patronizing manner.

'You don't think so?'

'I just told you I did.'

'Two thousand years ago, this was the centre of Bombay,' said

Hemlata, looking back into her book and continuing to read, as though I was so feeble an adversary I could be defeated while multitasking. 'Buddhist monks lived and preached only a few kilometres from here, in the Kanheri caves, in what is today the national park. In the sixteenth century, when the Portuguese wanted to construct a fort along the coast, they built it at Bassein, even further north than Borivali. South Bombay was just a swamp at that time, full of mangroves and mosquitoes . . . maybe even monkeys. South Bombay is actually a British colonial creation. Now, people are proud to live there because they think it's not like the rest of India. They don't realize how warped that stance is.'

Writing doesn't allow for split-screen narration, and ladies must always enter first, so this is the time to reveal that while Hemlata was speaking, I'd taken out my phone, as though to check for texts, to show her I wasn't really paying attention either.

Unknown number, 7.45 am: *Hi handsome stranger, how's your day going?* ☺ *A secret admirer.*

Ha, I wanted every day for the rest of my life to begin like this.

And then, from the same number, 9.22 am: *Farhad, this is your number, isn't it? I'm getting worried I texted somebody else by mistake. Of course, he got lucky! Zahra* ☺

Zahra! The poor girl was in a blue funk somewhere, thinking about me, desperate to confirm that I hadn't forgotten her and wasn't lying in the arms of another beauty, eating grapes or dosas.

I quickly texted back: *You've found your man! How did you get my number, lovely lady?* I wasn't quite sure whether to make a reference to last night, so I didn't. While the text message was still on its way, I returned to mental tennis with Hemlata and said (because agreeing with her was much more provoking to her than disagreeing): 'Yes, quite right. Very perceptive.'

'Thanks,' she returned.

'It's just that some of us were born in South Bombay and have houses there and, of course, lives, memories—so, it would be irrational to give all that up just because someone in Borivali—someone who locks people up as soon as she meets them—says so.'

'That point of view comes with so many contradictions I wouldn't even know where to start dismantling it,' said Hemlata. 'So, I'm not going to try.'

Dismantle—I saw for the first time that 'man' was at the centre of this unsettling word. Anna, too, had nearly dis*man*tled me. I said, 'You know, it doesn't really matter. I . . .'

Hemlata's mother appeared and announced, 'That dosai didn't come out right, so I am making you another one,' and disappeared again.

Hemlata called after her, exasperated, 'Ma, just give him his breakfast and then he can leave!'

'No worries, Auntie! Whenever you're ready,' I called, chirpy as a Buddhist monk on his day off in the Kanheri caves in the second century BCE. 'You know, I don't really care what's the real Bombay and what's not. It's not my home any more.'

'Really? Where do you live then?'

'America. San Francisco. I hope that, in your eyes, there's nothing warped about *that* city. If you know it, of course.'

'I lived for a year in America,' said Hemlata.

'Really? Where?'

'In New York. I was pursuing a degree at Columbia. How long have you been living in San Francisco?'

'Uh . . . well, I haven't actually lived there yet.'

'I thought you said you did. Do you have a clone?'

'I'm moving there next week, to be precise.'

'You're *moving* there!' said Hemlata and emitted a cackle of mirth. 'Future tense. And already you've started to think of yourself as American. Ma, come, you must listen to this.'

'Does it say somewhere in the law books that this isn't allowed?'

'No . . . it's just kind of funny when you think of it.'

'What's funny?'

'Well, you're Parsi, aren't you?'

'Guilty as charged.'

'Well, for a hundred and fifty years, you guys have been the most anglicized lot in this country. Since Independence, you've been the last Englishmen of India. And now you want to claim American-ness even before you get there. What's wrong with being Indian, may I ask?'

'Nothing. I've been one for nearly forty-two years. It's just that one can do better, I think.'

'Really? American is better than Indian, you're saying?'

'I am indeed.'

'On the basis of what?'

Hemlata's mother appeared, declared, 'One side is already brown, the other side is getting brown,' and left.

Emboldened by this show of maternal support—which I interpreted as partly or mainly meaning, 'My son-in-law has failed to tame my daughter, but you take over the project, and till you achieve your goal, I will keeping feeding you dosas'—I switched the play and said, 'Well, *you* say you spent a year there. Wouldn't you feel similarly? Wasn't life better there? Weren't you freer in that nation than you are as a woman in India?'

My phone beeped.

'Feeling free is not the only thing that's important in life,' said Hemlata. 'Being free is as much about personal agency as about environment. Sure, it's also linked to institutions, codes of conduct, cultural settings—but these things are being worked out here because we're a society in transition. And frankly, if educated people leave in search of "freedom", things here will never change. There'll always be a First World and a Third World.'

'Oh, agency! Institutions! Come now. I am a psychotherapist by trade, and in my line of work, I've heard the stories of hundreds of people. I know when they're trying to persuade themselves that black is white and vice versa. The truth is that this country is a dump and will always be one.'

The gold stud on Hemlata's nose rose an inch higher. 'As an upper class, privileged Indian man, it obviously won't be visible to you that America has a magnificent portfolio of injustices and repressions and hierarchies. Blacks and Latinos have to struggle there . . . and always will. And the poor. There's no real concept of social security or health insurance. It's a deeply barbaric civilization hidden behind the rhetoric of freedom . . . including the freedom to own guns.'

I opened the text message and saw that a certain radiantly beautiful woman from a deeply barbaric civilization had written: *Us San Francisco girls can find out anything we want! What're you doin'? Looking forward to tonight?*

I said to Hemlata, 'Well, so you didn't want to stay on after your one year in New York?'

Hemlata was silent.

'Was the injustice and repression there too much for you to take?'

Hemlata replied, 'Actually, I was enrolled at Columbia for a PhD. I had to leave after a year because my coursework wasn't good enough. They cancelled their offer and I had to come back.'

'Oh,' I said, suddenly feeling that I'd touched a sore spot. 'I'm sorry to hear that.'

'You don't need to be. *That* wasn't your fault.'

'But now you teach English literature here, yes? That's not bad, surely. Bombay is a centre of world literature as much as New York, it seems.'

'That's right. We even had Gayatri Chakravorty Spivak over to Bombay University last year, on my personal invitation,' said Hemlata, unable to help herself.

'Who's that? Sounds like the name of a rocket. Sputnik . . . Spivak?'

'It doesn't matter. How do you know what I do?'

Hemlata's mother appeared with a steel plate with dosa, sambar and chutney, placed this in front of me, said, 'The second one is coming,' then left.

'Some of your papers were lying on this sofa last night. I thought I might as well learn something new.'

'Don't you know that it's rude to read other people's private papers?'

'Don't you know that it's rude to lock up visitors inside your home and then disappear?'

'It was an accident. I've been under a lot of stress with this ridiculous husband of mine. I thought you were his friend. Why else would he ask you to bring my car back?'

'You no longer think I'm his friend?'

'No, I don't see how you guys could be friends. You're too different.'

'I said so last night, but you didn't believe me.'

'I had reason not to. You lied about the other woman.'

'I didn't want to get caught up in this mess. That's not unreasonable.'

'Never mind . . . I no longer need your help there.'

I quickly texted Zahra: *Boy, am I looking forward or what!* and began to eat.

'You're quite a multitasker,' said Hemlata, with the sarcasm that appeared to be the dominant note of her personality, and was probably the reason why her husband, after many such bruising encounters, had sought out more sympathetic connections—among missionaries if need be.

'Life's short. One has to keep going on many fronts at the same time,' I replied, discovering things about my new self even as I declared them to the world.

'How do you plan to go back home . . . to *South* Bombay?' asked Hemlata. 'I have to head off to work. If you want, I can drop you at the station.'

'Station? Oh, no, I think I'll just take a cab, thank you.'

'You don't take public transport?'

'Not really, no.'

'I thought so. Well, good luck then. You'll be stuck for hours in traffic. The train would be much faster.'

'I'll be able to take a little nap in the cab. For some reason that I don't quite understand, I didn't sleep well last night.'

Hemlata's mother appeared, topped up my plate with a second dosa folded into a half-moon and said, 'One more, yes?'

'No, thank you,' I replied. 'But this was delicious. I'd happily eat this every morning. Your daughter is one lucky girl!'

'Most welcome,' said Hemlata's mother. Casting a reproachful look at her daughter, she explained, 'She's a different kind of personality,' and retreated.

'You don't cook then?' I asked Hemlata.

'No. Should I?'

'Well, why not?'

'So, you think all women should know how to cook?'

'I think all *adults* should know how to cook, whether man, woman or transgender.'

'My husband doesn't know how to cook either. Why didn't you tell him that?'

'We never got that far in our conversation, unfortunately. It was just a collision on the road and the offer to pay for repairs. I never imagined it would lead me off the beaten path and towards detention and dosas.'

'Well, at least you got to see a new part of Bombay before you leave. That's something.'

'That's true. I'll never forget my night in Borivali for as long as I live.'

'Nor will Borivali, I'm sure.'

A text message from Zahra: *I want to see you every day before you leave!* The words went straight into my bloodstream where, gathering force, it began to stir a point inside me . . . the very point I had wanted to study last night. I wrote back chivalrously: *Your wish is my desire, mademoiselle.* At the same time, pointing to the photograph above, I asked, 'Why are those flowers around your husband's face?'

'Because he's dead to me. He's gone. He's the past.'

'Is he? It seems to me that you spent all of last night thinking about him.'

'One thinks about dead people sometimes . . . though it's better to bury and forget them.'

'Hm. Why did you give your husband your car anyway?'

'As you see, I wanted to dig up some stuff about his life . . . anyway, why are you interested in all this? I thought you said you didn't know him at all.'

'I'm just curious. In my line of work, I have to deal with marital strife all the time.'

'Ah, you're an expert at making marriages work?'

'If it helps, I'm divorced, too. But I have an amicable relationship with my ex-wife.'

'My mother has an amicable relationship with my soon-to-be ex-husband,' said Hemlata. 'Well . . . I can't keep making small talk. My students will be waiting for me. I have to go.'

'What a pity,' I said, standing up. 'I'd have loved to stay a bit longer.'

'I'm glad you enjoyed yourself so much. Any time you wish to repeat this experience, let me know.'

'Sure, I will. I wish you good luck with all your projects and spivaks,' I responded, the perfect gallant. Bowing before Hemlata's mother, I added, 'Thank you for the *best* breakfast I've had in years.'

At the door, I took one last look at the room where I'd spent the most surprising hours after I'd lost my virginity a second time. 'Goodbye.'

'Bye.'

Hemlata was already attending to other tasks, counting out money for what appeared to be the newspaper bill. This household read *The Hindu*.

Downstairs, one of the watchmen who had let me in last night gave me a quizzical look. What could I have been doing in there for so long? (*Listening to jazz and reading Indian literature and eating crisps and dosas, you ninnies!*) I asked him where I could get a taxi and was advised to take an auto-rickshaw to the highway and find a cab there. Oh joy!

In a rickety rickshaw, I began to think about Hemlata's sarcastic method, which—despite its apparent negativity—I'd quite enjoyed wrestling with. I wondered whether in a conflict situation it was preferable to come up against something like that compared to, say, Anna's coldness and silence, which defeated all attempts at engagement and took forever to break down. Then again, this wasn't a truth set in stone—talking wasn't always better than silence. Often, the couples who came to see me had to be disciplined into *not* saying the first thing that came to their minds, so accustomed had they become to wounding one another with words. Some of them, taking my advice seriously, voluntarily registered for yoga or meditation courses to gain self-control. I began to see where Zahra was coming from. Tacked on to one another, psychoanalysis-and-yoga could seem like just another fad; put into dialogue at their deepest points, they could be made, as Zahra had noted, to transcend the mind-body duality of Western thought. My new lover wasn't short of smarts! I wanted to text her right away and ask, '*Stay over tonight?*' so that I could hear her voice, breathe in her body, discuss yoga till even the ghost of Patanjali asked us to give it a break.

As I exchanged three wheels for four (why are Bombay taxis always so smelly?), my phone beeped. Zahra was thinking of me—could think of nothing but me. *Farhad, it turns out there's something REALLY exciting happening tomorrow! Are you up for travelling?*

She wanted to go somewhere with me! I texted back: *Sure! Where to?*

Take a wild guess! ☺

Borivali? It's got some cool Buddhist caves. ☺

No, silly. Udvada! Tomorrow. Are you up for it?

Udvada! How Zoroastrian of Zahra . . . but a little too much for me. *The religious centre of Zoroastrians in India? Can't we go somewhere a bit more exciting?*

I understand what you mean. No pressure. But it IS something exciting. Grand ceremony in Udvada tomorrow for the 800th anniversary of the arrival of Zoroastrians in India. This is our history . . . and our chance to be a part of it!!! From next week, we're in America. What say?

Ok, but how do we get there? Shall we take the car?

Oh, don't worry about all of that. Everything's been arranged.

Sounds great!

Having a facial so hv to close my eyes for next half an hour. We ageing souls need a lot of work! More when I see u at the Trident at 7! ☺ *xx*

See you xx ☺

So the Parsis had been in India for 800 years! And that likely meant 800 years of Billimorias in India, too—we would've been the sort to get on to the original ship, perhaps even the ones to make ingenious pro-immigration arguments by dissolving sugar in milk. Such a long journey that must have been . . . where was I? Still only in Malad! We were in bumper-to-bumper traffic for a mile. Gas fumes seeped in, big cars cut into our lane, every driver was honking like a goose in heat.

After an hour on the road, I was still stuck in the bloody burbs.

When I woke up in my own bed that afternoon after a long nap, I felt so much at peace with the city that I almost regretted giving it up. Who could have thought that Bombay could be so pleasurable? Suddenly, there seemed to be no difference between the dreams of sleep and the dreams of life. Dates, book launches, couch-surfing and long drives were packed so tightly into the days that I could barely keep track of what was going on. Women either came to frolic with me in my apartment or locked me up in their homes or made me dosas. Purely based on these trends, it didn't make sense to leave Bombay—which itself was a wonderful way to say goodbye to the city.

Ah, the first flush of romance! I was convinced I would feel like this about Zahra always and forever . . . but the sheer weight of human precedent indicated that this cloud of passion would gradually disappear, to be replaced by something more prosaic. And that is why I wanted to live every moment thrice over, almost dragging time back by the throat.

My phone beeped. The doorbell rang at exactly the same time. Till the very last day, the seller of pav and eggs would be sure to check on me. I got the door first.

I started, then laughed aloud.

It was Zahra, in a white top and a grey pencil skirt, her hair tied back . . . but not so neatly that little wisps didn't curl around her ears, where small blue danglers glimmered. She stood with her palm on her left hip, like a model from a fashion catalogue. Laughter sparkled in her eyes. She radiated a captivating innocence, like a teenager working on a pocket money survey in her summer vacations, fully aware of her charm and her ability to persuade the reluctant.

'Well . . . come in!'

Zahra smiled mysteriously and moved past me into the house, poking me in the ribs as she passed. I was so pleased to see her, I felt like grabbing her waist and swinging her around in the air . . . but it seemed out of line with whatever mood she was in. Maybe yesterday, when she'd dressed casual. But today, she was back to being perfect.

'You're looking great!' I burbled. 'You caught me unawares there. I haven't even begun to dress . . . I was just messing around. I mean, that's what one does at home, isn't it? And now that I'm leaving this place for good, I'm . . .'

Zahra seemed to be in some kind of pain.

'What is it?' I asked. 'Is something wrong? I'm sorry if I . . .'

Zahra's phone was in her hand, enclosed by bright red fingernails. She held it up and gestured. A text message! I threw up my hands and went over to the side table to look at my phone. I read: *Farhad! It's the day before the 800th anniversary of the arrival of the Zoroastrians . . . the beginning of Parsis in India. Whatever we do today, we must do prayerously, in a spirit of reverence. Of complete silence.*

What a charming joke. I laughed aloud again and said, 'Great . . .!'

Zahra shook her head disapprovingly and placed a finger over her lips. I mirrored the gesture to show that I had comprehended . . . the . . . rules . . . of . . .

Of the game!

I pointed to the kitchen. Coffee?

She shook her head and held up her wristwatch. How much time did we have before we left for the reading?

I mimed: About an hour? Just a bit less?

Ah, so shouldn't we be thinking more carefully about how to use our time? A delicate hand, ringed by two clinking silver bangles, pointed to the inside rooms.

Farhad: Doubles over laughing silently.

Zahra, bringing her palms together beside her face: What? I just want to sleep.

Farhad, mouthing: WHA—?

Zahra: Finger to her lips again, reproachful.

Farhad, agreeing to not repeat mistakes, with a thumbs up: Nice look!

Zahra, pointing: Nice shoulders!

Farhad: Particularly love the necklace.

Zahra: The space between my throat and the pendant?

Farhad: Yes, what about that?

Zahra, both pointing and beckoning: Exactly enough room there for your lips.

Oh, oh, what a sexy silence this was going to be! Words were falling away from me anyway; I was becoming a prelinguistic being, who knew the things of this world not as names but as shapes, colours, smells. My arm went around Zahra's waist and the other hand clasped hers as if we were about to break into a waltz. I lifted her up and carried her into the bedroom. Zahra's fingers undid the top two buttons of my shirt, even as my fingers undid two clasps on the side of her waist—enough to release her top from the confines of her skirt. As my fingertips landed on that small patch of exposed skin, I felt the most blazing attraction and the most complete immersion in the present I'd ever known. And if I'd done nothing more all evening than touch and tour those two square inches of skin, and swim in the pools of Zahra's eyes and scent, I'd have been happy—only, of course, there were dozens of similarly provoking sensual pleasures around me, for me to arrange and combine as I pleased . . . as long as I remained silent (if I said a word, Zahra would vanish into thin air like a djinn).

Even then, there were sounds, now amplified: the rustling of fabric, scratches and sighs, feet on floor, creaks of furniture, and outside the light was fading on tiptoe, the sky murmuring purple. A thrilling discovery: the language of the eyes, of gestures, of small enabling confusions—a kind of yoga of lovemaking where restraint and self-awareness opened out a new togetherness and dissolution of self. Zahra's fingers made webs across my face; mine unloosened her hair. She slipped off her top and faced me in just her brassiere, her hair falling over her shoulders. Her face and its ramparts—that exquisite nose pointing towards me; the high cheekbones and coal-black eyelashes; the bow-shaped lips and slightly pensive mouth—drifted in and out of view. Sometimes, she became nothing more than the pores of her skin, to which I added the three-second-old memory of her face.

I felt transported back to the innocence of my teenage years, when the female body was such a mystery to me that I could think about the sound of a voice or the shape of a passing figure all night long—which is a kind of gift, too. I'd forgotten that the body of a lover didn't have just one scent but two or three; we went past one to reach the next. I'd forgotten everything about sex.

I moved back and forth through these zones of thought and their cessation . . . and perhaps Zahra's passage was similar. I turned her around and my lips went all the way down her back, past the place where her flesh was slightly pinched and plumped by her bra strap. I wondered if I was the most tender lover Zahra had ever had.

As I rose up again, a mysterious hand came from around Zahra's face and touched me on the cheek. It was my own! I saw that Zahra had closed her eyes and was waiting. When nothing happened for a second or two, she opened them again and smiled and took over.

She was surprisingly strong, and when she pinned me to the bed, I found that I wasn't able to throw her over. As her hair fell all around my face, I kissed her past her nose—then she retreated. Held up straight by her, my engorged penis looked just like a rocket of love—a Sputnik. Very slowly and deliberately, she unrolled a rubber over me, smiling as I shuddered with anticipation at my coming journey into the stars.

Just like that woman in the Manto story, here was someone who knew exactly what she wanted from love. Zahra sat down upon my Sputnik, and that was it. If only time, which had taken on a new aspect in this silence, could have stopped right here, leaving the two of us frozen forever like the friezes on the temples of Khajuraho or Konark. Indeed, a sculptural stillness was the only way I could have continued to keep our asana going—for, as soon as she began to buck and heave, I no longer had control over myself, and whatever moved up through me cried out when it crested, all the more explosively because I couldn't utter a word.

Both vexed that I had come so quickly and pleased with her effect on me, Zahra threw her arms all around her like those goddesses with many hands and fell over me with balletic abandon—but so very silently that it made me laugh with pleasure and admiration.

What is human personality but the memories of the faces one has loved? I felt sorrow over Anna's bitterly locked eyebrows; I cradled Zahra close, closer in the redemptive silence.

The Company of Ooi and the
Company of Tininadi

EEJA SAID, 'I saw a dream . . . a strange, strange dream. I am going to describe it.'

Ooi ignored Him, which was something She had learnt to do, for the first time in all Their years together, during our long days in Bombay. She said, 'Rabi, now that we've been together in this city for so long, I want to ask you something.'

'Yes, Ma?' I said, while also looking at Eeja so He wouldn't think I was ignoring him.

'When Bhagaban first suggested that he'd go home to fight the election and you'd stay behind with us in Bombay, I said, never! "How will this boy take care of us in the big city? Do we even know if he can take care of himself? Wasn't it you, son, who used to say that Rabi cried every day for the first two months when he came to Bhubaneswar? Who knows what will happen once he's all alone with us in Bombay? You may think he's reliable. But it doesn't take much for someone to seem reliable to *you*, as your house is a circus anyway, and any servant you have lives like the King of Puri. Son, can't you find someone else to stay with us? Tell me, why has the saying come down the ages—*only two things are fleeting in this world: happiness, and the promise made by a tribal*—hm?"'

'Yes, Ma. I was there when you said all those things.'

'Were you? I've forgotten who was there and who wasn't, I was in such a state over your Eeja. Anyway, I want to say today that I was wrong. You aren't like the old lot of tribals. You've served us well. How many days we've spent now in this room in Bombay, keeping watch over your Eeja! And finally, She looked at Eeja and lowered Her voice to a whisper, 'we have got to the day of the election. In a day or two, we go home.'

'Yes, Ma,' I whispered back. Here we were, discussing the biggest event in our state in five years as though it were a secret Jagannath ritual that we had orchestrated! But that is how we had to speak, for fear that Eeja would become overexcited. He'd recall it was time to go home, and His mind would wax and wane like the moon, and He would again be stricken with hoocups. And truth be told, it had been so long since we had had a taste of a reality other than that of our room in Bombay that it was hard to believe there really *was* an election today in Bhubaneswar and all Odisha. It was as if we were living in not just two different worlds but two different ages.

'Anyway, Rabi, your work has not been without reward,' said Ooi. 'Your language has improved so much since we got here. You don't speak such a hillbilly Odia as you used to. I know how attached Bhagaban is to you—else, I would tell him: "Give Rabi to us. He can live with us in Bhubaneswar. Even your Bapa has got used to him now."' She looked at me hopefully. 'What do you say? Do you want to stay with us in Bhubaneswar?'

It was so hard to please Ooi—and then, when I did, there were all these new problems! She still could not see, and I myself could not say, that I was not Bhai's servant, I was his friend!

Ooi continued to think aloud: 'I wonder what sin I committed in my past life that I can't have a daughter-in-law or grandchildren. If only Bhagaban would marry, perhaps we could *all* live together in Bhubaneswar . . . and, that way, you could be with your Bhai and with us, too, taking good care of us all.'

'Ma, when we go back to Bhubaneswar,' I said, daring to be firm, 'I'm sure that Bhai will find you a first class maid. Even he has realized now how hard it is for you to take care of Eeja all by yourself.'

'You don't know anything about maids in Bhubaneswar, that's clear.

Anyway, that's not what I wanted to ask. I'm curious about one thing. When you first came to Bhubaneswar, why did you cry every day? Were you missing your family?'

Eeja's head dropped on to His chest, and a small snore came from Him.

'Ma, I wasn't crying because I was homesick. It's hard to explain . . .'

'What's so hard to explain? Speak the truth. You don't need to feel shy. When I first left my own village for Eeja's house, I was around your age. I was so homesick that I cried every day for a whole year. It's another matter than your Eeja never said a word other than, "I wonder whether I got home a wife or a puppy." But then Rama, too, was hard-hearted when Sita returned home from Lanka—he made her walk through the purifying fire. I'll tell you something—even while I cried, Bhubaneswar made me feel happy. There were so many new things to see and do—people dressed in the latest fashions, all sorts of fancy goods in the market, men and women talking to one another so freely . . .'

'Ma, in my case, it was *Bhubaneswar* that made me cry.'

'I see. Did someone make fun of you for being a tribal?'

'No . . . you see, before I came to Bhubaneswar I was . . . the village crier.'

'The village crier? You called out announcements at the behest of the village elders? Why were you sad about having to give that up? Do they give you all your food for free if you do it?'

'No, Ma . . . a *crier*. As in—crying tears. My work was to cry.'

When She understood what I was saying, Ooi swayed and shook with laughter like a tree in the wind, waking Eeja up. He looked cross, then His head dropped on to His chest again. Finally, She said, stopping to catch Her breath every few words, 'Is no one else . . . allowed to cry . . . among your people . . . and is all the work of tears given, o-ho, o-ho . . . to one person . . . like the task of cooking food . . . is given to a cook?'

'No, Ma. Among the Cloud people this is the tradition: from the first day of the monsoon to the last, when the clouds cry for the world, in every village a young person just about to come of age is made the crier. Whenever he or she sees a man or a woman or a child in pain, a bird or a beast that is suffering, he or she does not hold back the tears of pity and compassion that well up from the heart, as older people have learnt to do, but cries freely and fully.'

'But why? Why should two people cry? Does that solve the first person's problem? Isn't it enough that one person is already unhappy? Tears are so precious. Keep them for when you really need them.'

'Ma . . . can all human problems be solved anyway? One cries so that the thread of compassion that binds man to the living beings around him never breaks. Because when man loses that invisible thread, he becomes less, and not more, of a man. In my village, when older people see the crier crying, they are stirred to tears themselves, or they remember a time when they would have been moved and cry—sometimes for the loss of their compassion. And in this way, their hearts can never be hardened for good. Among our people, there is a saying, "Man's laughter can be wicked, but never his tears." Although even tears cannot completely mask the fact that man is, at root, a wicked and selfish being. And that's why, every year, the clouds come down low to cry for the world.'

'The clouds cry for the world? Silly, are the clouds really crying? They're just heavy with rain. That's why they're black. It's one thing for the old people in your village to believe all this—because they're uneducated tribals. But *you* have lived outside for so many years now. Do you really believe all this?'

I was silent. Although I had learnt much by watching Bhai prepare for debates, I still did not have his speed of thought and sense of confidence in an argument.

'Anyway,' said Ooi, 'Jagannath be praised for sending my ears something new to think about in my old age. I thought I knew about all the strange ways of the tribals of Odisha, but this is something else. So, tell me, who decides who is to become the crier?'

'The village shaman Biyagu. The face of the crier always comes to him in a dream, Ma.'

'Does it really? That's like the priest of the Jagannath temple—he sees in his dream where the neem tree—the one that'll be used to build the new idol of Jagannath every twelve years—is to be found. How long does one have to be a crier?'

'Once you are chosen, two rainy seasons. Nobody can fulfil the responsibility after that. It passes on to another person with an open and ready heart. A special exception was made for me. I left in the middle of my second crying season. That is because Bhai convinced my people that I was urgently needed in Bhubaneswar to speak on their behalf. You see, the Company had already started work on the rail line leading from the mountain to the nearest station. But, of course, when I came to Bhubaneswar, I could not suddenly stop my tears. As soon as I went out, I saw dozens of suffering people, drooping with weakness or exhaustion, or crying from hunger or pain, or begging and pleading for a bowl of rice, even trying to hide their suffering or sorrow from others. Once the tears come, there is nothing one can do, Ma. It is Cloudmaker's way of protecting man from pitch-black arrogance and wickedness.'

'What strange thoughts these are! It's a pity Eeja is asleep, else he would have loved to listen to this. But what can he do, poor man? He stays up half the night, mumbling all sorts of sense and nonsense—so, it's but natural that he feels sleepy at odd hours of the day.' Ooi went hobbling into the kitchen and came back with Her box of puffed rice. 'The village crier! It doesn't make any sense at all, but then again . . . now that I think about it, there's something like this in the Ramayana. Do you know that story?'

'No, Ma.'

'Yes, how would you know? The sage Balmiki is wandering through the forest—I can't remember which forest it is, but it's somewhere in the plains of North India.' Ooi looked up at the ceiling. 'He sees two birds above him, a male and a female, cooing and playing in a tree, making sweet sounds, cheep-cheep, cheep-cheep. Just then, the male bird lets out a terrible cry and falls to the ground, right by Balmiki's feet—it has been shot by the arrow of a hunter. Writhing and thrashing, blood gushing from its wounds, it dies, leaving its mate crying in shock and sorrow. This sight floods Balmiki with grief, and he himself cries out words of pity and compassion. He realizes that he has been speaking, without conscious effort, in a particular metre, which is the natural music of grief. And that metre becomes the metre of the Ramayana itself—a story rife with sorrow and suffering. It's the same idea as the one your tribe believes in. The only thing is that the great sage poured his grief into a story, into beautiful words and thoughts, for all time to come—while your people remain stuck in sounds, boo-hoo, boo-hoo-hoo. It's not your fault. You're tribals, after all. Balmiki was a very special person who practised austerities and possessed all kinds of secret knowledge. He could speak to Indra, Brahma and Siba whenever he wanted, and the Gods themselves always paid him their respects.'

'Yes, Ma, he was a high and noble soul.'

'That was a different age altogether,' said Ooi, staring far away, as if into the depths of time. 'I wish I'd been born then. Perhaps I was, and I've forgotten. I've lived so many lives since and committed so many sins. Why only me? Man himself has fallen a long way from the path of righteousness. And Hindu society, especially so. Between the Musilim invaders, the English babus, and the new Indian rulers with their strange new notions and their lack of respect for old traditions, Hindu society has been reduced to nonsense. It's as if, even when successive regimes were fighting with one another, they were all secretly working towards the same goal. Rabi, you know, you and your people are actually the most fortunate of all? Far more than any Hindus.'

My unfortunate people the most fortunate! I waited to hear more.

'The thing is, you tribals may be backward, but at least you are united. You stick together as one people with one mind. Hindu society lost that quality long ago. Today, all the castes are pulling in different directions, waging war on one another and disobeying the old rules and customs in the name of do-mo-cra-cy and progress. Even women end up going to school and college, and incite those who are still reluctant to rebel against the old order. What monkey-cackle! At least, because you people can only think one thing at any given moment, you're safe from this sort of turmoil. All you know is that you love and worship your mountain, and you can't let the Company have it, no matter how many rules and laws get passed in the Company's favour. Your dharma is very simple: the preservation of the mountain, come what may. While, because *we* were in charge of our society, we were the first to get attacked by the outsiders, and in trying to protect all the people of our country, our own dharma broke down. Ah Jagannath! How many misfortunes You have had to face in this world, Prabhu!'

At the sound of the word 'dharma', something flickered on Eeja's face, but He continued to sleep.

I was silent again. United? Were we united? Perhaps at one point, in the distant past, we had been. But the truth was, ever since the Company had arrived at our doorstep many years ago—when I was but a child and ran around naked with my thumb in my mouth—and had set up its operations, it had built fences not only on our land but also between us. In fact, even our own act of resistance had slowly broken the ring-circle of our hands.

In the early years, true, the shock of such a big, mysterious, threatening power in our neighbourhood had made us all form a united front, and each soul sang the same song under the love and law of Cloudmaker. But so much had happened since—so much. The great churning of our world by the Company had left everything in tatters.

Some of our people were slowly taken away by the tilted scales of time, which further strengthens the strong and weakens the weak. Holding out at first, they became convinced that we could never win against a force as strong as the Company. And if we weren't going to win, there was meanwhile no end to what we could lose—and dispossession and a new order, they decided, would be easier to adjust to than a life haunted every day by fear and trembling.

Others were consumed by greed, by the fat compensation the Company offered if they would agree to shift three kilometres west to the rehabilitation colony being set up. And if you could persuade one other family in Tininadi to do so, the compensation was double.

Other brave souls would not be persuaded by either money or fear—but after doing time in jail on charges of assault or theft or trespassing, how could they be expected to hold their resolve? The police didn't even do them the mercy of locking them up in the new local police station that had come up, right opposite the new Company gates at the foot of the mountain—a place where their families could see them. Instead, they were sent to the district prison faraway in Rayagada, and to get there, the bus fare alone came to eleven rupees. When these forlorn jailbirds returned, they were one of us only in name, their life force having been eaten by those four walls where the earth and the clouds are shut out.

As for those last few—including my late father and mother—who continued to hold up the banner of resistance and proclaim the sanctity of the mountain . . . why, these people became bitter and had harsh things to say about not just the Company but also their fellow men. They kept watch over the dealings of everybody in the village—who was, or who was said to be, seen with whom . . . when a motorcycle appeared outside someone's door . . . who was called out to a field in the next village . . . which household had suddenly bought a radio set—and became high-minded and petty all together, one the water for the other's roots.

'Ooi, You are wrong. Things are not as You believe them to be. If You like, I will tell You a story about the people of my village.'

'You want to tell me a story? All right. Go ahead. It's not as if we have our hands full with pressing tasks anyway. Just make sure you speak clearly and slowly. My old ears cannot keep up with your young tongue.'

'Yes, Ooi.'

A Great Council of our people, I said to Ooi, had been convened a few months ago. Everybody in Tininadi was given a chance to speak their mind on the great issue of the Company and the mountain. Bhai, too, came down from Bhubaneswar especially for it. But he said, 'I will not try to set the tone of the discussion. If I want to speak, I'll speak last. This is democracy set into motion. That is the most important thing. Let the deliberations begin.'

As soon as the gong was sounded, Siyap Korkori, the oldest man in the village and a singer of great renown in his youth, stood up. Holding his hand upon his heart, he said, 'As someone who has seen many generations come and go and has not yet been called away by Cloudmaker, give me, brothers and sisters, the right to your ears. My sense and my song are very simple, I know. But can anyone—even the wisest man alive—say for sure where the life-spirit of man ends and that of the world begins? No. Nature cannot resist man and man cannot resist nature. Theirs is a love that sustains this world and gives Cloudmaker the greatest peace and happiness.

'As we would not allow our own limbs to be cut off, brothers and sisters, so we cannot allow the mountain to be stripped, blasted away, cut to pieces, we cannot allow Cloudmaker's great store of clouds—which these people call *bauxite*—to be raided, we cannot allow the pathway of the dead into the next world to be torn down. Take my word for it, if we allow such things to happen, we are sure to be struck down—even before our children have had the chance to marry—by the spirits who watch us day and night, under the love and law of Cloudmaker. Then, there will be no going back.

'A tree or an animal, or even a wife, son or daughter can be replaced ... but never a mountain. I feel strange saying these words. Once we were united. Everybody used to say what I say. Slowly, everything changed. Now, when I speak, I feel so alone. Am I and a handful of believers, including one or two outsiders, really the last of the Cloud people?'

'O-ho! O-ho! O-ho!' cried Jina Bori, who with six cows, four acres of fertile land, a concrete house, a solar-powered light system and a television set was the richest among us, and had been well off even before he had become known as the 'Company man'. He stood up, sat his wife down because she stood up at the same time, and declared, 'Elder Siyap is right. May a hundred clouds bloom in the sky at the sound of his words. He has got only one thing wrong. My brothers, I fear that our refusal to properly understand the very truths that have always sustained us will, in the end, be the undoing of us people. No one in this ancient village of ours believes more deeply than me, Jina the humble, that our hallowed Cloud Mountain is, as the saying goes, "The world of our wealth and the wealth of our world". This was said by our forefathers who lived in these forests, and it was fed to us by our mothers when we nursed at their teats.

'But, my comrades, time passes in cycles, and each cycle has its own laws, just as even the oldest of rivers change course from time to time. We have entered the modern world now, and there is no going back. Today, even something that happens in distant Ame-rikia has an effect here. In turn, people from all around Odisha are going to the farthest corners of the world and bringing back prosperity to our land, building big houses in the cities, buying fine clothes for themselves and their children, and never going hungry. Why should we be left behind? If we allow ourselves to straggle, rising prices and poverty will kill us long before the spirits can decide what counts as a sin and what doesn't.

'And once we can get ourselves to see this, it will actually become clear that Cloudmaker the Playful, Cloudmaker the Wise, had in His wisdom thought of everything, at the very beginning of time. The same mountain that watched over our people for centuries has today, at the dawn of a new age, shown us that it can still be the world of our wealth and the wealth of our world. Once the Company starts running its quarry and its factory here, our lives are insured against all troubles. There will never be any shortage of work. Where, now, we are the ones who go and toil for a pittance in cities, exploited by contractors and agents, soon the whole world will arrive at our doorstep, dragged in by the Company. The bridge into the new age will be forged, our children will have access to the same schools, knowledge, opportunities as the children of Cuttack, Puri, Bhubaneswar. Tell me, could Cloudmaker have given us any greater gift than this?

'Remember, my friends, even words as simple as "do good" require man to interpret them. Try to understand Cloudmaker's grand scheme, His benediction. The dead, about whom we worry ceaselessly, will find a way to look after themselves. We, who live, must act for the sake of those who are yet to be born.'

Stick-thin and sweet-souled Garuda Magara, who had been jailed twice for leading protests against the Company and had also lost his firstborn while he had been away, stood up and said in a quavering voice, 'At the Rayagada prison, I met a man who offered me work as a gardener in an apartment complex in Bhubaneswar after he gets out in the winter. My respects to Siyap Korkori . . . but I have neither the strength to fight the great power of the Company nor the will and trust required to work for the Company. A thought came to me one night. I cannot say if it was my own or a spirit put it there. If we must leave our village, my brothers and sisters, why go to a new place so close to Tininadi that our every waking hour will be flooded by distressing thoughts and sad memories, the rage and reproach of Cloudmaker? Let us go someplace far, far away, where we can start life anew. The faster a man flees from the site of his sins, the sooner he returns to peace, even though he remains no less guilty.

'One day or another, it seems, we must give up the Cloud Mountain. Rather than see it being eaten away in front of our eyes, let us search for or ask for a new mountain in some part of the world where the Company has no intention of arriving. Once we have asked forgiveness of Cloudmaker, perhaps He will even come to join us there, and we will live in peace under His clouds. Let us have nothing to do with the Company, else our sins will become unforgivable. This is my hope for our people. If my hope is crushed, at the end of the year I will leave with my wife and daughter and go to Bhubaneswar. Do not think me selfish. As we know, to think of oneself is no crime, to think only of oneself, the greatest crime of all. If Cloudmaker wills it, in Bhubaneswar I will find work for other people from Tininadi as well. Yes, I will . . .' He began to cry and was helped back down to the floor by those around him.

Under his crown of pigeon feathers and broom flowers, Biyagu the shaman had been muttering to himself, his elbows twitching by his sides like wings—this had begun ever since Jina Bori had claimed that the words that guided us were in need of a new interpretation and had then interpreted them himself. Even before Garuda could finish speaking, Biyagu threw down his rattling staff—its dread sound was a sign that all were to be silent—and cried out in his beautiful chanting voice, 'This is for you, Brother Jina, and all those of you who would like to follow him in making new meanings—meanings that will fill your stomachs with fried food and liquor, your homes with machine music and flickering screens. As the Cloud Mountain is my witness, this staff of mine will come to you in your sleep tonight and give you such a beating, ho, such a bruising, ho, such a bollocking, ho, that you'll go running straight into the gates of the Company factory at daybreak and never dare to come out again.

'Evil spirits are swirling around us, my brothers and sisters, and a great destruction is coming, a great conflagration is coming, a great migration is coming. Now you wake up from your long slumber, now you ask Biyagu to help you. How can he? Biyagu lives half on this earth and half in the clouds. As long as you, the people of Tininadi, went down on bended knee before the unseen world, there was a chance that Biyagu could bring you its wisdom, its counsel, its protection. But the day you agreed that there was such a thing as a government in Bhubanessore, bigger than our own council—government, ha!—that there were such things as elections—elections, ha!—that there were laws other than our own laws—laws, ha!—that was the day you sowed the seeds of your own destruction and robbed Biyagu of his hemp-rope up to the spirits, to the voice of justice, to Cloudmaker Himself.

'Oh, tragedy! Oh, doomsday! Oh, gloomsong! Now that very same government, with its laws and regulu-la-lations, its district collector, its police, its courts, its jails, has given permission to the Company to come and destroy our lives. Think about it. For the Company to drop down from beyond the clouds and claim our mountain, the government had to first sell it the mountain! So we are the dupes not only of the Company but also the government. When we agreed to trust the government, and opened our doors to its ay-bi-cee classes, its malaria tablets, its census programmes and land surveys and family-planning-skims, we gave ourselves into the hands of the devil. Now all is lost, lost, lost. Ah, poor Cloudmaker! Ah, sad Tininadi! Ah, lonely Biyagu!' And with three circling leaps, each wider than the previous one, he ran out of the gathering, leaving his staff there amongst us to be his ear.

Samarupi Kul was not from Tininadi but from another part of Kashipur district—where, too, a Company had set up a factory and taken away land belonging to tribals. Samarupi, on a government scholarship, had completed a degree in management in Delhi and, for a few years now, had been the head of an organization trying to find a 'third way' of tribal development—'neither complete resistance nor complete ruination'. Every month, Samarupi would appear in Tininadi—sometimes taking a lift from Bhai when he heard from his sources that we were passing through in our jeep—to sow in our village, yet again, the seeds of his plan.

Now he spoke: 'Brothers and sisters, even clouds move when the wind comes blowing. But some of you here are hopelessly stuck in the past and are only asking to be blown away by the gusting winds of the new times. And, meanwhile, some others—I won't say who, the answer is there for all those who have eyes—think that the Company is a new deity with as much power and benevolence as Cloudmaker. Can you go north and south and still arrive at a meeting point? No, my brethren. Listen to me.

'The Company wants to take your mountain, and when we go to the government to say that this cannot be allowed, the government says that it can and will, that it is necessary for the development of our entire state. That may be true, and we may be praised for our willingness to make this sacrifice in the light of the larger good. But such development will be miniscule compared to what the Company stands to gain for itself!

'Study the facts, brothers and sisters, don't get carried away by the talk of spirits. The ancient path to wisdom may have been of help to us at one time, but now it has been thoroughly compromised by those with ulterior motives. The facts are as follows: the Company has very nearly finished acquiring all the land it wants for the bauxite factory at the foot of your Cloud Mountain, and it has said it is paying a fair market price to you, all in advance. Why is it being so generous? The answer lies in economics, in plans and calculations of the kind that you—who never think further than the next season or the next year—may have never thought of. We are dealing with people who have made plans for fifty years ahead!

'Studies have shown that, once the Company takes control of the mountain and starts a factory, for every tonne of alu-mu-nium that is produced, it will make a profit of Rs 250. And for each tonne of the same alu-mu-nium, it will give the government of Odisha a royalty of just Rs 30. How much will it be left with as profit? Even the six-year-olds in this gathering can do the maths—Rs 220 for every tonne! And there will be thousands of tonnes of alu-mu-nium, day after day, year after year! Now, how much do we—the tribals—get? One-time compensation for the prevailing market price of our land, and a house in a rehabilitation colony. Can't you see? By accepting this deal, we make ourselves the biggest losers.

'We should hold out until the Company agrees to share at least 40 per cent of its profit with us, to be handed over to the village council for roads, hospitals, schools, community centres. Only then can it be said that giving up our land has been a worthwhile sacrifice.

'This is what I wish to tell you, my brothers and sisters. If we accept the Company's present deal, our lives are worse than ever before—for, once we spend our compensation, we will have no land to fall back on. On the other hand, if we are offered a percentage of the Company's profits, as long as it keeps faring well, our people will keep getting enough to make their lives better . . . and the money is ours *as a people*, collectively. It won't merely belong to a small set of individuals with land.

'We are in the Age of the Market, brothers and sisters. It won't do to tell ourselves that we are poor tribals who know nothing about the ways of the wider world. The market, like a raging elephant, can run us all flat into the ground. But if we manage to mount the elephant, we can go wherever it goes, with whoever else it takes along. Get together and join my movement, brothers and sisters. It is the only way for us to not only survive but also prosper. Fail to follow my advice, and the day will soon come when you'll be seated in a gathering just like this one, holding your heads in your hands and saying: "Samarupi spoke the truth."'

As soon as Samarupi had finished, the village Ladder of Fertility—two grandmothers, two mothers, two young women and two girls—stood up and began a loud ululation. (I remember that in my childhood, the sounds emerged from a kind of puffcheek-blowing, after the manner of Cloudmaker . . . but somewhere down the years, perhaps influenced by Hindu women in television serials, this had changed.) They sang in one voice: 'Brothers and sisters, under the love and law of Cloudmaker, the eyes and ears around us, the snouts and beaks, the paws and wings, the airborne and those underground, all offer their prayers for the sustenance of the mountain, our Cloudmother. By the will of the sleepy bear and the pangolin, ho, the chutter monkey and the giant squirrel, ho, the tiger and the golden gecko, ho, the large mouse and the barking deer, ho, the hyena and the four-horned antelope, ho, the porcupine and the lightning otter, ho, the woo fox and the mongoose, ho, the civet and the band-snake, ho, the mountain will remain safe from all evil plots and spells, the mountain will stand for all time to come, the mountain will never stop growing clouds. The spirits have nothing to fear, the mountain will take care of us all.'

Very heart-moving it was, the Animal Benediction, and Bhai in particular loved to hear it sung. But some of the women who chanted it came from families that had chosen the Company over the mountain. They sang the song because the song was there to be sung.

Bhagaban Bhai had long been waiting impatiently to speak, and now stood up in his kurta, his gold-bordered dhoti and black mojri slippers, opened his mouth for a few moments in a dramatic pause, and said: 'Brothers and sisters, it is true I am not a tribal. Cloudmaker, in His wisdom, dropped me into the womb of a Brahmin woman many years ago. But if I speak, it is only because I have taught myself first to listen . . . to listen not only to all that has been said today in this village gathering but also to all the sounds of your world, to all the sayings, songs and truths from which your vision of the seen and the unseen world is forged.

'My friends, you are the people of the Cloud Mountain and you have always been. These forests around you, this mountain and the sky above—this is the source of your world, and from studying these things for hundreds and thousands of years, you have formed your philosophy of living.

'You should know, if you do not already, that when this country became independent so many decades ago, a pledge was made that the diversity of the many truths, the many ways of life, the many Gods of this land, would be protected and honoured. Each man could live the way he knew best, without molestation from another or the pressure to sacrifice what was sacred for somebody else's well-being. If the people who rule this state knew better, they would never have let the Company come to your door to lure you away or drive you from your Cloud Mountain, they would not remain deaf to your pleas for help.

'Why is the present state of affairs a great shame, a hideous nightmare, a gross travesty of justice? Because there are hundreds of other companies in the world like the Company . . . but only one tribe like yours. It is not enough to call you "tribals" and stop there, as the government in the capital is doing. Indeed, the very word "tribal" is a government and a state word! After a point, the word does not reveal the kind of people you are but masks it. The government and the Company have stubbornly refused, in all their papers and contracts, to call you the Cloud people . . . because they know that in doing so, they will have hacked at their own foot while striking at the stone.

'My friends, remember that the day the Cloud Mountain ceases to exist, humanity itself will become a smaller and meaner tribe, a race that has forgotten something about itself and how it should think about its place in the world. Some of you here are cowering, crying, pleading. Why? Stand tall! Among all the sects and tribes and religions of India, you are unique in being a people who live both on the earth and in the sky. You understand life as a short, transient thing. You live it as one would live a song. You see that everything has its moment of fruition, and then it passes to be reborn in another form. Your hymns and prayers celebrate a most unique view of life and death, this world and the next, man and not-man. And your source and symbol for all these truths is Cloudmaker, whose love of movement and transformation is expressed every moment through the drift and play of the clouds. Where else in our vast land can we find a people like you—men and women who love clouds, dream clouds, worship clouds? Even the mountain that nourishes and protects you, rising out of this black and beautiful earth, is viewed by you as a granary of clouds, as the fount of rain and life.

'Today, some of you here have said: "So what if we lose our mountain? Nobody can take the clouds away from us." My friends, in this very statement of apparent devotion, you reveal the extent of your breach with the Great Way of Cloudmaker! Because, for the thousands of years that you have inhabited this place, it is the mountain that has allowed *you* to see the world as if from the clouds, that has shown you man's place on this earth as it must seem to Cloudmaker in the sky. For you, the mountain is the sacred stairway to the clouds and your dead, the place from which—to borrow from one of your songs—"the near becomes far and the far near". Without the Cloud Mountain, you will never be able to sustain the philosophy of your Cloudmaker.

'My friends, we are all human beings. We have needs as urgent as those of the stomach, truths as real as those of profit and loss. Why give away your mountain—and, with it, your spirits and the wisdom of the clouds—when you can keep this *and still* make demands for jobs, schools and roads that the government and the Company are promising in exchange for your support? These things are already rightfully yours as citizens of this country. What vision of justice says that for the sake of his material needs a man must barter away his soul? Would the proud caste Hindus of Bhubaneswar consider giving away the Jagannath temple of Puri if the Company wanted that site for a factory?

'Do not let Cloudmaker be dragged down to the earth and captured, my friends. See the world from the clouds, and you will understand that your fight against the Company is, in fact, a fight for diverse ideas of humanity, for all those who have been displaced. The loss and pain you suffer today will be small compared to what you stand to lose if you abandon your world.

'I don't want to tell you what to do, my brothers and sisters, because I believe that I have learnt more from you than I could possibly give you. I only want to help you shake off your shackles, and as a city-man and a Hindu tell you how much I respect and admire your clouds, so that you can work out for your own selves, in the silence of the heart's forest, what your highest truth is and what kind of action you ought to take.

'Some people have advised you, my brothers and sisters, to give up the Cloud Mountain, so that you may enter the modern world. They are not entirely wrong. But I come with another idea, which is that you can use the rights and freedoms granted to you by the modern world—such as the right to vote—to defend your hold over the Cloud Mountain. What little power I have in the other realms of Odisha, I am happy and willing to gamble, in order to stand by you on the difficult path to freedom . . . but the will must be yours, as the wound is currently yours. Jai Tininadi! Hail the Cloud Mountain!'

Ooi said, Her eyes wet with tears. 'How beautifully my son speaks! Only the grace of Jagannath could have brought forth such moving words from his mouth. Rabi, although it's you and Bhagaban who have just finished speaking, I can hear Jagannath's coal voice and feel His grace all around me. Rabi, my heart can look into the future. With the force of Jagannath behind him, Bhagaban is sure to win the elections.'

Jagannath, the round-eyed Lord of the three realms! For thirty days and nights now He had been watching us in Bombay. When, tomorrow, the votes were counted across our state, would He give Bhai what he wanted so badly, or would He spurn him for mocking Him in secret?

The Face of Desire

A LOVELY GIRL sitting in front of Zahra and me, craning her neck like a goose, drew in her breath and crooned, 'Oh, he's *sooooo* cute!'

Flashbulbs went off. Some people stood up. Amitav Ghosh had just entered, the star of the evening, accompanied by a small gaggle of people, as politicians are, only these were not family members and acolytes but editors and publicists.

I hadn't realized until we got to the ballroom of the Trident Hotel—a little rushed after our post-yoga nap, but on time, nevertheless, courtesy a burst of speed from Zelda and some unBillimoric lane-cutting from me—what a big draw this Amitav Ghosh fellow was. I'd always viewed Bombay as basically a city of non-readers, and even my well-educated clients had confirmed this perception ('Where do I have the time, Doctor? And, also, books are *so* long. Can't you give me an article instead?'). But there were at least *two hundred* people here: little old silver-haired ladies in discreetly high-end handlooms, accompanied by grave husbands (or lovers—why be conjugo-normative?) in rimless glasses and shapeless blazers; pretty young things clutching copies of the writer's very large hardback to their bosoms, accompanied, in some instances, by handsome, middle-aged women; even a whole bunch of precocious teenagers bringing copious supplies of enthusiasm and pimples to the evening.

Mr Ghosh was indeed cute in a distinctive way—white-haired and baby-faced like an Indian Richard Gere, wearing a blue Chinese-collar shirt, a black sleeveless jacket, and pants the same colour, and carrying a small bag, as if he'd come straight to the reading from a day of poring over archives.

'That's him! Farhad! The great novelist!' cried Zahra, squeezing my arm with one hand and clutching her freshly bought copy of *River of Smoke* with the other. I felt a small stab of jealousy. I wanted to be Amitav. It was a pity that therapy was a private and not a public art; that one couldn't have a show; that one always had an audience of one; that the artist-therapist was sworn to confidentiality. My female fans were those I'd helped cure; after *that* kind of glimpse into their minds, it was hard to want to do anything with them. Thankfully, I now had Zahra and San Francisco—though, if this preview was anything to go by, Mr Ghosh had dozens of other women and—at least in a literary sense—Bombay.

Ghosh was introduced by his editor. The great novelist then briskly took control of the evening. He said a few business-like sentences about the world of the book, its double setting in India and China, and its Parsi protagonist, a man called Bahram Mody. This fellow, in the eighteenth century, moved from an anonymous life in a small town in Gujarat all the way to heading a flock of rich Bombay merchants. His vehicle: the narcotics trade run by the English East India Company, which transported opium from the fields of India to the hookahs of the gullible Chinese, often past the obstacles posed by sea patrols and sanctions. Well done, Brother Bahram! It was clearly a night of Parsi achievement all around—whether in book or audience—leading up to the crescendo of Udvada the next day.

Ghosh began to read from the early pages of the story. Zahra squeezed my hand and smiled winningly. I had a sudden and intense desire to pee. A sign of impending incontinence in old age, perhaps—or more likely that, having been put to pleasurable alternative uses, the old Billimoric pipes suddenly remembered their base selves again. I excused myself and vaulted over a few ankles, with the balletic lightness of a man who knew he wasn't going to be returning any time soon to a few wankles.

In the corridor, the publishing flunkey was packing up his operations—he'd sold every copy he'd brought. Onwards from him, the bathrooms were such a pleasure, from scent to soap, marble to music. The joys of a fine hotel. I considered booking Zahra and me in for a memorable night of seduction—and if she wanted it again, of silence—over the weekend before we left for good. I'd have to ask her first about giving her sister the slip. Or, maybe, she'd already spoken about me ('Such a handsome, distinguished man he is, and *so* funny!'), and whatever we did was kosher now.

On my way back, I abruptly came face-to-face with a wall of sheet glass previously obscured by the bookseller's table and banners—and through it, the great expanse of the grey-blue Arabian Sea at dusk, ringed on the near side by the lights of South Bombay.

I stopped in my tracks. Although I was more than thirty floors above the ocean, that trick of perspective made it seem as if the water was rising steeply and dazzlingly uphill from the curve of the coastline below. Sea and city faced up to one another, friends and enemies across the ages. I saw what had brought the Billimorias of old here—what had made them stay and thrive. I'd never thought I'd find Bombay so moving again. I laughed at the beauty and absurdity of it all, and went back in to Zahra, Amitav Ghosh and Bahram Mody.

Mody, in the meantime—time runs fast during readings of novels, and even faster within novels—had acquired a beautiful Chinese lover. A woman living in a houseboat, just off the coast of Canton. Could she have given Bahram more pleasure than the woman now affectionately patting my thigh, inches away from the spot on which she had left such a dazzling impression? I really didn't have the patience to pay attention to Mr Ghosh's rivers of smoke when my own chakras were calling out to me.

As it would have been rude to speak, I texted Zahra: *Hey, aren't we Parsi men great lovers?*

Her phone buzzed in her bag. She drew it out, laughed and texted back: *Bragger, let's see how you're doing in 2025!*

The words, a sly or sincere promise of lasting love, made me unspeakably happy. I wanted to iron out all my imperfections, be at my best every moment of my life, so as to be worthy of this angel. Ghosh finished reading and we all clapped. He said he would be happy to take questions. After that, Zahra and I had a date for a glass of wine at Pizza by the Bay before we headed home.

It seemed as if all the questions this evening were of the Parsis, by the Parsis and for the Parsis, because now a little lady in a red sari, a matching sleeveless blouse and lipstick, and a nose that could have sawn through all the timber in a rainforest, seized the mic and started, 'Mr Ghosh, hello. Rukhsana Davar here. You seem to know a lot about the Parsi community. But in your novel, your hero, who is Parsi, is married. And then he has an affair with a Chinese woman over many years and never tells his wife about it. Nor is he ever punished for his transgression. I want to ask you, when you write such stories, aren't you sending the *wrong message* to the youth of this country—and there are many young people present right here—about the duties and responsibilities of marriage? If the better-off of this world won't set the standards for behaviour and morals, what example will the poor people have to learn from? I speak as a former teacher, I'm now retired, and this is my husband here, we've been married for over fifty years, 4 March 1961 was the wedding date—though it wasn't like one of the razzmatazz weddings of today, it was something small and simple. But that's not the point, although there's a lot more I could say about it, and some of my former students have even advised me to write my memoirs. It's the young people I want to talk about.'

Zahra murmured impatiently, 'Sweetie, what's your *question*!'

'So, I taught at J.B. Petit High School, where I was known—and am actually proud of the title—as Miss MBC, Mills & Boon Confiscator. And why did I let myself become unpopular—almost a kind of scapegoat, if you know what I mean? It was for a reason. Values. Young students are at a delicate and impressionable stage of their lives. They need to have the right values and role models presented to them, not all this *bodice* ripping and heavy *petting* and phi*lan*dering. And I have another point. Why should it be a *Parsi* man who's shown as a phi*lan*derer? Why not a Hindu or a Bengali, someone from your own community?'

How juvenile, how utterly narrow-minded! We Parsis always pretended that we were so cosmopolitan and that the rest of India was a wasteland of orthodoxy . . . but someone had only to invent a Parsi character in a novel for our pathetic parochialism to pop its cover. Ghosh was just about to answer Ms Davar's question when my hand rose, and I found myself saying, 'I . . . may I . . .?'

He smiled and said, 'Sure. What's your question?'

'No, I don't have a question. I'd just like to respond, if I may, to the question asked just now.'

'Yes, of course.'

From the periphery of my vision, I could see Zahra looking up at me, her lips slightly parted. I took the mic and said, 'Ma'am, I've no doubt you were an *excellent* schoolteacher, and the values you've imparted to your students have helped them shape wonderful and lasting marriages. But let us remind ourselves that what we're talking about this evening is a *novel*, not a moral science textbook or a guidebook for a particular community. In a *novel*, as far as I can tell from my limited understanding of the form—I'm not, after all, a practitioner—in a novel, human beings are shown as they *are*, not as they *should* be. And, really, *anybody* should be able to write about anybody, men about women, women about men, Hindus about Parsis and vice versa—especially while creating stories, works of the imagination. Else we'll all be stuck in our ghettos of identity, and we'll never become an integrated society, a *real* democracy.

'I just want to remind everyone that we're all adults here, even the younger ones for whose morals you fear so much. As adults, what should be most important to us is this—having no illusions about what adult life is, what it means, all that it includes at the centre and at the extremities. The more we worry about the *message* of everything, the less space we leave for the kind of free thinking vital to adult life— even if that free thinking should lead, at some point, God forbid, to a married man or woman having an affair. Besides, in my view, false moralism is much worse, much more limiting, than real immorality, if you get my drift.

156

'I am a psychotherapist, and what my years in therapy have shown me is that by repressing something, you don't solve the problem, you actually make it even bigger. Confiscate the Mills & Boon novels all you like, I'll give you that—because they're romantic trash. But give the *really* adult books, such as the one written by Mr Ghosh here, their freedom, their right to exist. Because freely circulating stories eventually lead to a free people. That's all I want to say, and I thank you all for having given me a chance to say it.'

Everybody (including Mr Davar, excluding Rukhsana Davar) clapped, and Amitav Ghosh said, 'Actually, I don't think I can beat that answer, so I won't even try. Next question.'

A teenager stood up and asked where Ghosh got his inspiration from. Still flushed from having delivered a speech, and with lots of people looking at me, I didn't hear what the answer was.

Zahra gave my hand a tight squeeze and murmured, 'My hero.'

'Hssh, it's nothing . . .'

'Farhad, listen! We might have to take a rain check on our drink tonight.'

'My God, really? Why?'

'It's my niece. She wants me to come spend some time with her before bedtime. I missed my slot with her last night . . . and, who knows, if we get late returning from Udvada, I might miss tomorrow night, too. And, you know, I—we—only have a couple of days left here. Who knows when I'll see her again?'

'Okay. Sure. Anyway, we have the Udvada trip tomorrow, don't we? We still haven't discussed transport . . .'

'Oh, don't worry, it's all been arranged, I told you. You don't have to do anything. Honey, we're going to have a *fabulous* day.'

'Wait, I'll drop you home.'

'Oh, don't bother. You stay and take on all these stuck-up, misfiring bawas and bawis. You know, I think you've made a big impression on Amitav Ghosh! Can you get my copy of the book signed for me?'

'I will. Go home safely.'

'You're looking hot. Don't do anything naughty tonight, Dr Billimoria.'

'What, I—'

Laughing at my embarrassment, Zahra gave my hand a squeeze and got up and left in her petitely elegant, sensually silverquick way. The necks of many men in the audience craned to follow her departure. Across the rows of people, I saw Miss MBC staring beadily at me.

Amitav Ghosh declared the evening's discussion closed and said he'd be happy to sign books. Instantly, some people turned tail and sped out of the room, almost knocking one another over, as though he'd just said he was summoning a firing squad. Ah, *homo mumabicus*! Always in such a hurry to save time—to beat each other to the elevator, to the first bus or train, to getting home. I zipped off equally fast in the other direction, pushing as far up the signing line as I could, so that I wouldn't be accosted by my gimlet-eyed adversary from the Party of Morality and Marriage. When my turn came, I thought Amitav Ghosh would say something to me, but he seemed to have forgotten my defence of his art and freedom, and just murmured, 'What name?' I considered being mischievous and asking him to write, 'Zahra Farhad Irani', but settled eventually for the more thoughtful yet open-ended, 'To Zahra Irani, wishing you all the best for your ambitious new project'.

Time to go home . . . although I didn't really want to. Some day: the morning in Borivali, the long journey back through the jungle, Zahra's sudden appearance, sex without language, then lots of language and Parsis, the view of the western coastline of the city of my life. Just outside the ballroom, some people were dawdling in twos and threes. I tarried a bit, flipping through the book and watching people from the corner of my eye, especially the beautiful girls and women. I couldn't help myself—nearly three hours had elapsed since I'd last kissed a woman! Zahra had left me hungry for beauty again, hungry for life.

An elegant woman—so tall I had to lift my gaze in frank admiration—passed by, in on one side of my life and then out on the other for good. Which is one of the sad realities of this heartbreakingly beautiful world of ours, and the same thing had nearly happened to Zahra and me, too. The woman's face seemed vaguely familiar from another life and another world. As our eyes met, she stopped and said in a deep, brassy, arch voice: 'Ah. Mr San Francisco.'

It was Hemlata!

She wasn't wearing her glasses now—an absence that opened out her face and made what I'd considered her slightly owlish eyes seem big and beautiful, especially as they were immaculately kohled and framed by the long sheet of straight black hair that she'd left loose. She wore a parrot-green, gold-bordered Kanjeevaram sari and matching blouse. Ever the college lecturer, she clutched, with a gold-bangled wrist, a folder by her substantial bosom. Her small gold nose stud seemed to gleam with the same faint amusement and mockery that her eyes communicated, but the entire effect was sweetened by a jasmine scent that greatly became her. She was more beautiful and self-possessed now than she had been in the morning—and also, I thought, more striking than the woman I'd seen accompanying her husband on the night of the accident—which showed how much I had forgotten, despite being married for an eternity, about women and their outdoor selves.

Hemlata's small verbal dart was perfectly aimed and left my ego hopping. 'Ah,' I said as soon as I recovered my equilibrium. 'The jailer of Borivali.' But it wasn't as short and sharp as Hemlata's barb. It shrank rather than expanded when I said it.

'Nice speech at the reading,' said Hemlata. 'I was impressed. I didn't know you read novels.'

'Oh, one or two, here and there. And thanks. So you're an Amitav Ghosh fan?'

'I'm just a reader. Why do you use the word "fan"?'

'Just. Because it's such a long journey from Borivali to get here.'

'I came directly from the university. It's not such a long journey from Santa Cruz.'

'Ah, yes, of course.'

There was a moment's silence. 'Well,' said Hemlata, as if to say that our hostilities from the morning stood between us and always would, and that the greatest latitude they'd allow was a laboured formality. 'I must be on my way. Have a nice evening. Good night.'

'Good night.'

Hemlata and her shimmering silks glided out of sight—and the newly musical, life-loving heart of Dr Billimoria felt a twinge of regret. Women! I was so alive all of a sudden to every nuance, every gesture of the Divine Feminine—to borrow a phrase no doubt liberally scattered in the books of Enrico Sanchez, my soul brother.

As I suddenly had the rest of the evening to myself, and I wasn't all that far from Cusrow Baug, I called my cousin Gulshan to see if she was home and I could pop by for a bit. But it turned out that she was at a family dinner in Bandra. So I decided I'd go to Pizza by the Bay just as I had planned, have that drink, and watch the world—secure in the knowledge that I was no longer being left out of all the fun that men and women can think up together, and that, if anything, I was probably leading the way, my present solitude being as sleep was to activity.

I eased Zelda out of the basement parking lot and turned to Marine Drive. Outside the exit, several people were trying to flag cabs and were being turned down, probably because they only wanted the short ride to Churchgate station. Looming among them was a tall figure in a green sari. Two days ago, I'd have felt too self-conscious to consider going out of my way for any lady. Now, I pulled over chivalrously and, leaning over, said, 'Hey . . . Hemlata! Hop in. I'll give you a lift.'

Hemlata, surprised, said, 'Thanks, it's fine. I'll manage.'

'No, really. It's not a problem. You won't find a cab easily here.'

'Okay. In that case, please drop me off at Churchgate.'

'Sure. Get in.'

I pulled out quickly, pretending not to hear the 'hey, buddy, please drop me at the station, too' from a strapping man with hair growing out of his ears. Hemlata's pleasing scent wafted over Zelda country—a kingdom that was, right at the end of the *ancien régime*, suddenly welcoming women at every stop. 'Well, what a surprise seeing you here,' I chirped. 'I mean, not on the street. At the reading.'

'What's so surprising about it? I teach literature, after all.'

'What, you don't think it's surprising that we live in a city all our lives, and our paths never cross, and then we meet twice in a single day?'

'Who knows where we might have crossed paths before?' said Hemlata, enigmatically. 'For all you know, I came to see you at your practice five years ago, and you just don't remember me.'

'What? No! I remember the faces of all my clients. That way I can avoid them if I see them somewhere in public.'

Hemlata laughed, which was the first sign of a thaw I'd seen in her demeanour. She said, 'You know, I may as well say it—I'm sorry about last night. I was upset. You must understand.'

'I understand.'

'Do you, or are you just saying it?'

'I do. I've seen some rough scrapes in my time, though, mostly, they're things recounted to me at obscene length—and with no understanding of what constitutes major and minor details—by Bombayites with money to spare.'

'Well . . . I'm glad this has helped you appreciate where I come from.'

'To be honest, you've caught me at my most forgiving. It's my last ever week in this city. Next week, a whole new life begins. So why carry any bad feelings?'

'I hope you realize how lucky you are.'

'In what way?'

'To be able to pack up and leave India just like that.'

'What, you don't like India? I thought, from what you said this morning, that you loved it to bits.'

'I was just arguing with you, couldn't you tell?' asked Hemlata, as if to say that the exchange was her intellectual equivalent of push-ups or crunches. 'I don't think there are two ways about the fact that we're a terribly feudal, casteist, communal, misogynistic and, now, noxiously neo-liberal country.'

'And we can't drive either,' I said, as I missed a green light because of a car in the wrong lane.

'As for all the prejudices of our middle classes . . . don't get me started.'

'Hey, hey, don't be so harsh. You're behaving like me now!'

'Hardly. Unlike you, I'm just as harsh about America. You know, I was thinking this morning on the train, I don't believe I've ever met a psychotherapist before.'

'Ah. So you were thinking about me!'

'Must you be so childish?'

'I'd answer your question, but it seems as if we have no time. Churchgate looms . . . of course, if you're not in a hurry to get home, we could get a drink at Pizza by the Bay. That's where I'm headed anyway.'

'Alone?'

'Yes. Unlike most Indian men, I can keep myself entertained without company.'

'What about your companion?'

'She's gone home. Come on! We're two adults, after all. And last I checked, it was still a free country.'

'Yes, of course, but . . .'

'*And* we're single. Oh, you aren't, actually.'

'I am. That's really not the issue. Besides, I'm not a woman who draws such boundaries. I can have a drink with anybody whether or not I'm married.'

'Well, then?'

'Okay,' said Hemlata. 'But just one drink. I have a long journey home afterwards.'

'Sure. I have an early morning, too. So . . . U-turn then?'

'U-turn. But it's on me. To make up for last night.'

'Oh, don't worry about it. Truth be told, I already had a drink on you last night while waiting—from your bar cabinet. So this one's on Mr San Francisco.'

'I hope you know that when I called you that, I was being ironic.'

'Well, that's your problem. I was being genuine. San Francisco, watch out!'

'Well . . . if one is obliged to admire self-confidence, one is obliged, too, to puncture braggadocio. What are you bringing to San Francisco, to make a perfectly good and bright city fall at your feet?'

'Why, I'm bringing the city some new clouds.'

'*Clouds?* I hate to break it to you, but it already has enough of those.'

'Oh, not real clouds,' I said, as Bombay spun around us on the hinge of Zelda's graceful U-turn. I had lost a date and rustled another one up immediately. It dawned on me that from this juncture, for at least a few years, it might actually be harder for me to find a parking spot than a woman. Even the parking problem could be solved, if only the date took the lead—as Hemlata did by jumping out of Zelda and claiming a freshly vacant area seconds before a couple stationed ahead of us could.

Hemlata was the only woman in Pizza by the Bay wearing a sari. I followed her down the aisle with the agreeable buzz of a man who is being watched because his companion is being watched. I did not fail to notice, as she tossed her hair to one side, the green bra strap peeking out from beneath her blouse. I caught a glimpse of Hemlata's waist, too, and wondered if she was the kind of woman for whom love was a jar. She bestowed a dazzling smile, the first I'd ever seen, in the direction of the waiter who showed us to our table, and actually put her hand on his shoulder to thank him—a physicality I wasn't used to associating with Indian women interacting with those attending to them. The waiter drew back a chair for Hemlata, and as she moved back, her head bumped into my nose.

'Jeez, you're tall. What, five-nine?'

'Five-ten, actually,' said Hemlata.

'A Jim Beam on the rocks for you, sir?'

'That's right! You're a mind reader.'

'You have come so many times before with your wife.'

'Oh. I see.'

'A glass of Sula, Darpan. Red.' Hemlata broke off into a few words of resonant Tamil and received a reply in the same language (what was it with my dates and their love for bar staff?). The waiter then returned to English, said to both of us, 'Enjoy your evening,' and left—no doubt to retrieve the gift-wrapped lamp that Hemlata had bought for me earlier in the day and dropped off before the reading.

'You guys know each other?'

'I've known him for years. He used to work at the Ambassador Hotel, where my father was in the management for more than thirty years—pretty much all his working life.'

'Why did you speak to him in Tamil? Something you didn't want me to understand?'

'No, because English is more my language than his. With Tamil, there's no power imbalance.'

'That's very perceptive of you. And progressive.'

'In India, the personal is always political,' said Hemlata, a bit like an Enrico Sanchez of the Radical Movement.

'I wonder why he mentioned my wife though. My *ex*-wife.'

'Maybe he was just trying to slip in a warning to me,' said Hemlata with a mischievous smile, her mood improving by the minute in the sunlight of my companionable company.

'Oh, he needn't have worried. I'd be petrified of making any kind of pass at *you*—this time around for fear of being locked up in a cupboard in the basement of the Ambassador Hotel. But really . . . why can't people in this country accept that a man and a woman can just be friends?'

'Why can't men and women be friends? Spoken just like the protagonist of a New York sitcom.'

'What, you don't agree with me? That's a surprise,' I teased.

'Let's just say that while I don't vehemently disagree with you,' said Hemlata, 'I don't agree with you either, and think that it's too simplistic a position to take. It only seems wonderful because it sounds so open-minded and liberal. But we really don't have to limit ourselves to a pair of false binaries while thinking through such complex questions. Excuse me a moment while I send my mother a text saying I'll be home a bit late.'

It was becoming clear that Hemlata detested false binaries above everything else, perhaps even false husbands. Our drinks arrived.

'Cheers,' said Hemlata. 'To your move to America, Dr Billimoria.' Her very full lips grew redder as she drank her wine.

'A pleasure to have met you before I leave—even if it has been under unusual circumstances. And to your . . . um, what should I toast to? I don't know you well enough to be certain of what you want.'

'It doesn't matter. One happy human being per table is good enough, and a better average than that of the rest of humanity.'

'Well, how about this? Cheers to your return to singledom. I'm presuming, from my small sighting of your departing, garlanded husband—a turn of fate for which both he and you have made me pay heavily—that you're looking forward to being free of him, even if your mother isn't.'

'I like the "departing, garlanded" bit,' said Hemlata. 'As for my mother . . . she's impossible. You're right. She makes it hard for me to believe in another kind of life. But she means well. And yes, I'm looking forward to being single, so cheers to that. No self-respecting woman should have to put up with an unreasonable and unfaithful man, even if all of Indian tradition stands in support of him.'

'I hope the next man, whenever he arrives and whatever form he takes, will be both reasonable and romantic.'

'Are you being serious or ironic?'

'Serious, of course.'

'Well, that's unusually sympathetic, coming from an Indian man,' said Hemlata.

'Well, what can I say? I guess I'm a feminist.'

'Are you sure?'

'I'm sure. What about yourself?'

'What about me what?'

'Are *you* a feminist?'

Hemlata nearly spluttered out a mouthful of wine. She recovered her poise and said, 'Cute! I think I'll let you carry the flag of feminism for this evening. You're going to need all the practice you can get if you want things to work out for you in San Francisco, Mr San Francisco.'

I saw how I was once again being disarmed intellectually by my accidental, adversarial date—and, indeed, being shepherded towards one pole of a false binary. A pole where I played the flaky upper-class Indian émigré, while she spoke with the authentic wisdom of the middle class—as someone who had committed her life and soul to the pressing issues of India, no matter that all India had given her, in turn, was a job in an English department and (only God knew how such a strange couple could have come together) one husband whose dick pointed in other directions. Well, she wasn't going to win so easily!

'Hemlata, I wish you wouldn't keep referring to me as Americanized. You hardly know me, my life story or my work. In fact, if I'm moving to another country, I'd say it's because I know almost *too much* about India.'

'You know too much about India? I don't think even Gandhi or Nehru would've said that.'

'Well, you know, Gandhi and Nehru worked in spaces like law and politics . . . not therapy. After nearly two decades of dealing with Indian clients, I know how the Indian mind works, and I now wish to be rid of it.'

'The *Indian* mind? I'm not sure I believe that a billion of us have a single, monolithic "mind"', said Hemlata, filling the space between us with scare quotes.

'Well, perhaps the Indian mind is too large a term to use,' I conceded, 'though it's certainly a coherent idea structurally. Let's just say I could write long, weary portraits of the Gujarati mind, the Sindhi mind, the Marathi mind, the Bengali mind, the Punjabi mind—God, I'm almost singing the national anthem. And they're all united by one fact. These are not bright and beautiful things—the *Indian* psyche is a *terrifying* place. Even its modernity, if you could call it that, is strangely medieval. The last few years, you could give me the first three sentences of the spiel of any of my clients, and I could finish off the rest, which is a game that can only be interesting for so long. For many well-considered reasons, I need to make a clean break from Indian society—as, for instance, you need to make a clean break from your husband. Nothing else will suffice. And for all that you turn up your nose at America, my dear, at least it's a place where adulthood and freedom go together. A place that gives you a second chance when your marriage breaks up . . . unlike this one.'

'Oh, sure, a second chance!' said Hemlata through majestically disapproving lips. 'And usually a third and a fourth chance, too. The sanctity of marriage is a non-existent notion in a land that proliferates fantasies. In America, it's all about what you feel like doing when you wake up in the morning. And then there's a way of rationalizing everything—the sex wasn't perfect, like *Cosmopolitan* said it ought to be, or the dog died, or what have you. These people aren't just destroying the world with their super-sized consumerist desires and their junk pop culture and their foreign-policy shenanigans, they're infecting all of humanity with their shallow ideas of what it means to be human and to acknowledge responsibilities. And, last, please stop calling me "my dear".'

'That's just a ridiculous smear! Frankly, this seems like a serious case of sour grapes to me—given that if your American sojourn had gone as you'd wanted, you'd likely still be living there.'

'You're crossing your limits, mister!'

'Come now,' I said, both provoked and provoking. 'Let's be honest. Wouldn't you have loved to have a tenured position at Columbia University? Meet people from around the world, lunch on Broadway, and live somewhere on the Upper West Side, while checking out some good-looking men? Wouldn't that have been so cool and still so feminist?'

'I don't need your visions of what I'd have really liked.'

'Why? What's wrong with some frank conversation? Or is that condemned by our great Indian civilization? As for your straw-man argument about marriages in America breaking up because of the sex not being perfect . . . well, what's wrong with splitting with one's partner because of that? We only get this one life, after all. Why shouldn't we be as happy as we think we could be?'

'Why shouldn't we be as *happy* as we think we could be?'

'Yes, exactly.'

'Why shouldn't we be as happy as we *think* we *could* be?'

'Why do you go on repeating what I say?'

'How am I to stop, when each time around I find new bits that are intellectually fallacious, and when your entire argument is centred on an unattainable future at the cost of both past and present reality? You say you've worked with all these clients. Has it never struck you that they can *never* be as *happy* as they *think* they can be, and they should factor that into their world view?'

'Well, all I can say is that people change over time, and sometimes they have to clear the room they're in before embracing new selves—for which the spur is a vision of future happiness. As, if I may respectfully—very respectfully—say, you are doing at this very point, in deciding that you want a divorce. What? Don't look at me like that.'

'Yes, but I don't want a divorce just because I want to have sex with someone else. There are bigger issues here.'

'Such as what? That your husband's having sex with someone else? It amounts to the same thing, doesn't it? Actually, as a case study of what's wrong with Indian marriage in general, it's almost exemplary—in that it seems that he's also placed the burden of breaking up on you.'

'What a piece of work is man,' said Hemlata. 'By which I mean man as man, not as a human being. Men are never more ingenious than when making excuses for their infidelity—and then other men like you arrive to give them and the entire patriarchal order the sanction they need. So, you think the reason marriages break up has to do with the demands of marriage itself and not with men?'

'I don't think you understand, I'm actually on your side here! Hemlata, shall I tell you something? Let's take personalities out of this, and you'll be able to see the issues more clearly. Surely, as much as women accuse men of being fickle or faithless, they never fail to

give themselves the benefit of the doubt when it's they—or is it them?
—that are the guilty party. That's *human nature*, not male or female
nature specifically.'

'What's male and female nature, and what's just culture and
indoctrination, is at this moment in history a more open, contingent
question than ever before,' said Hemlata, completely rejecting my offer of
a truce. 'Till very recently, all definitions of female nature were created
by men. You'll have to give us a couple of hundred years to work out
who we are and what we want for ourselves.'

'Is that so? Well, cut us men—or at least some of us men—some
slack for those couple of hundred years then, and don't foist the
responsibility for your own confusion on us. As for me, I'd say I am
acquainted with plenty of women right now who know quite clearly
who they are and what they want for themselves.'

'Good luck with them. I think it's time for me to be going home.'

'Hey, take it easy. I hope I didn't upset you.'

'How can one be upset with a man one hasn't known for even for
a day? You came, you'll go. Excuse me a moment while I go use the
bathroom—and pay the bill.'

'Oh, you don't have to pay.'

'I insist. It was a pleasure and an education to hear your thoughts.'

'I should tell you that, at this point in my life, I have no capacity
for comprehending irony.'

'You're better off that way, I'm sure. I'll be back in a couple of
minutes.'

Hemlata flounced off, leaving me shrugging, not at anyone, but at
the clouds of banter, generosity and human communion under which
I now walked, and under which I had tried unsuccessfully to bring
Borivali's greatest feminist—only to get charged with a long list of
thought crimes.

I had already been given the maximum possible sentence, so a few
more sentences wouldn't hurt: I drew Hemlata's folder towards me. I
found three copies of a document, typed, with notes along the side
column in a hand that was not Hemlata's. It read:

Hem, this book proposal is nice, yes? It's nice. But you've got to spice it up a bit. Sure, we want to know more about Indian thought and Indian love and the body and the face. But readers also want to feel that they're connecting with a human story. Put YOURSELF in it a bit more. Wrap your adolescence, your traumas, your partners, around this. Ok? Kathleen.

So Hemlata was writing a book! I wasn't too sure if she'd be pleased to see me reading what it was about, and even women took only so long to pee, so I put the folder back on the other side of the table, just as shortly I would put Bombay on the other side of the planet. Then my curiosity got the better of me, and I slipped out one copy and stowed it into my pocket.

There my hands met my cell phone, and like a teenager who's fallen in love for the first time, I thought I'd check it for text messages from the Beloved.

Zahra, about an hour ago: *Farhad, it looks like our grand plan is off! My Uncle Sheriyar's car has broken down, and we were going to go with him. And I was so looking forward to being part of this historic day* ☹☹☹

What would be better—to commiserate with the lady and try and lure her into my bed before lunchtime; or to find a way to demonstrate that her every wish was my command. My gallant fingers typed back: *Never fear. Let's take Zelda! She's a Parsi car and wants to go to Udvada too.*

Within seconds, the reply: *Oh, can we??? Wow, that's grt!! You and me and the Parsi car and the Parsi uncle (he's sweet, and a great favourite of mine).*

And then, a few seconds later: *Petrol and lunch is on us Iranis, ok? Be ready at 7 am. See you xxx*

Hemlata appeared again. She smiled coldly and said, 'Shall we go?'

'Sure. Listen, I really want to thank you for the company and the conversation. You mustn't misunderstand me. I completely get what you say. Actually, in this city, it's not often that one finds a woman intelligent enough to have a real debate with. That's why I was just playing a bit.'

'Of course. Men must play, else they're not themselves,' said Hemlata, when just a little while ago she herself had confessed to messing with me in the morning.

'Now, now, you mustn't punish me just for being a man. Who knows when we'll see each other again? I'd like everyone in this city to be at peace with me when I leave. Come, I'll drop you to the station.'

'I think walking would be better,' said Hemlata.

'Sure, if that's what you'd like. It's a cool enough evening.'

'I don't think you understand. I mean I'd rather walk *alone*.'

Well . . . hooray for Hemlata, else I might have been beguiled into believing that I'd win the day every time I went out to play. And I had more to thank her for. It was surprisingly pleasurable to throw off the 'I-know-I-understand' attitude that I'd worn like a mask over my face for so many years in dealing with people I didn't know, and to have a good, sweaty powwow—and twice in a single day Hemlata had proved a worthy, if grumpy, opponent. All that was left of the unforgettable voice of my unusual friend—and friend she was, as all those who have passed through the best clouds of our life should be, no matter if they exit in a puff of pique—was what was in her book proposal. In the small microclimate of my last four days in Bombay, it seemed like all the sex came from Zahra, all the text from Hemlata. In my pyjamas, at the end of one of the most eventful days of my life, I retrieved the lady's book proposal from my trouser pocket—the only keepsake from our encounter, stolen from her as once a man would filch a lady's scented handkerchief or a lipstick-marked cup—lay down in bed and read:

Michel Foucault has written, 'At the bottom of sex, there is truth.'

Sex again! Hemlata couldn't stop thinking about it. It was as if she was sublimating the torment of a sexless life into a vast survey of the literature of sex—while, on the other side, I was enclosing her ruminations within my own radiantly sensual life. It couldn't be denied: how clear and lucid this French fellow was! It was what I'd been coming to all along—only something about my native Parsi garrulity and my learnt Indian bashfulness (and an attendant penchant for euphemisms and indirections) made me blubber in paragraphs what Foucault had nailed down in a single sentence of eight words.

That Hemlata seemingly endorsed the thought—so much so, she let it preface her own project—made me feel more and more curious about her sexual nature. On the face of it, it was almost as if she didn't have one, or she hid it behind a high wall as so many Indian women did. But, clearly, she thought about sex as much as or more than any other person, and when she wanted to, she could make herself very desirable. I saw that by the rules of my new, free, experimental life, I should've been inviting her back to my place tonight—if for nothing else then to enhance my knowledge of Truth in the Foucauldian sense. But the ancient default settings of my mind had, in the old manner of the twentieth century, after two balmy evenings, immediately pledged eternal allegiance to Zahra. Well, I'd never ever be getting to the bottom of Hemlata's sexual nature in person now, but I could in prose. I read on:

Michel Foucault has written, 'At the bottom of sex, there is truth.'
It might be said this one sentence, more than any other, clearly
distinguishes human thinking about sex in the second half of the
twentieth century from prior views across a whole range of periods
and cultures.

For the first time in the history of human civilization, in
the twentieth century, sex was brought out into the open in
mainstream culture and reified through all sorts of discourses—
from psychoanalysis to journalism to advertising to pornography.
As children of the twentieth century and the world that it (re-)
made, we now enthusiastically assert and reflexively assume the
primacy of the human body and of bodily sensations and pleasures,
and make it foundational to any theory of love, sex or marriage.
The old truths are already known; our chance of discovering a new
truth for our time lies here, through the ascription of transcendent

meaning to the sounds and fluids released and orifices explored by the naked body, in situations of both mutual and solitary pleasuring. Adapting Foucault, one might say now: 'At the top of truth, there is sex.'

For the most part, feminism has been sympathetic to this shift, believing that it would allow women to liberate themselves as sexual subjects, bring the bedroom as much as the workspace and the street into the ambit of productive patriarchal critique, and break down the angel-or-whore false binary about women that operates in much of everyday life.

But have we now taken the cult of the body too far? In celebrating desire's irrational and transgressive charge, one answerable to nothing but itself, have we begun to let our bodies rule our minds?

In her book The Face of Desire, *B. Hemlata collects and investigates diverse modern representations of desire in Indian literature—literature being the productive sphere where writers and readers far apart in space and time can meet to explore socially unacceptable thoughts and situations that perhaps they cannot discuss even in person. Hemlata's point is that desire—as the best representations of desire in literature, subtly but compellingly, demonstrate—is a much more ambiguous and transcendental entity than the sex it seeks.*

Miraculously, what finally disciplines the transgressive urge of desire is the face of a reciprocally desiring person. Indeed, inasmuch as human beings can never truly observe their own faces in real time, it is the face of the other that anchors the human being in full adult life, as it is the face of the parent that does so during childhood. The face is a part of the body and yet something distinct from it. If there is a place where the forces of sex and love meet peaceably and productively, it is in the face of a chosen other.

Literature shows us that it is a universal but, also, a particularly modern situation that, in answering the call of desire, human beings frequently trade the specificity of a face for a variety of bodies, to their eventual impoverishment. Hemlata argues that, in a world where desire is largely liberated from social sanctions, marriage is erroneously—because of its long history as a human institution—seen as the most conservative step taken by an adult human being, when actually it should be celebrated as the bravest and the most radical.

Not only was the idea a very surprising one, with no trace of anti-man and anti-American feeling and just one mention of a false binary, but it also seemed to me, knowing what I did about Hemlata's life, that a surpassing sadness and generosity lay beneath the argument. She seemed to be looking past the dismal facts of her own life to make a frame that could be useful and true for thousands of married people. Even I could read her thesis and flesh it out immediately with a potential face of desire—Zahra's. Not to mention a newly red face of shame and sloth—my own—for never having taken the trouble to do anything brave or radical in my chosen field, therapy. I wished I could have sent these thoughts home to Hemlata.

The Smell of Figs

'RABI! RABI! WAKE up! Rabi!'

Bangles jangling near my ear in the middle of the night, as if the Goddess Kali Herself had come to rouse me. I opened my eyes and saw Ooi's face close to mine, stretched tight so that all Her wrinkles were gone, eyes wild with fear. She was kneeling on the floor, almost falling over because Her body wouldn't keep Her upright. I sat up.

'Get up! We must call Bhagaban right away. Eeja is leaving us.'

'Is Eeja not speaking?'

'No, he's saying a lot.'

In the other room, I heard Eeja shout, 'Go away! Hss! Hss!'

'What happened?'

'He's saying terrible things. He says he saw someone standing in the corner of the room, beckoning.'

'Ma! It's nothing to worry about. He saw a bad dream.'

'Really?'

'Yes. I'm sure. Just . . . just try to put Him back to sleep.'

'Rabi! I'm frightened that something bad will happen. He's claiming that the visitor was Yama, saying, "Come away, come away, come away with me now." He says he wasn't sleeping when it happened. What should we do? I feel it myself now . . . Yama is somewhere close. It is the middle of the night. It is His time.'

Yama, the God of Death. I had often heard Him spoken of in the past, but I had never heard of Him being so close, and from someone as close to the Gods as Ooi. I jumped up and hurriedly put on my vest. Ooi was already hobbling back from the kitchen towards Eeja, Her pigtail shaking from side to side. I ran after Her.

In the main room, Eeja was sitting on the bed, holding a bowl in His raised hand as if to throw it across the room, His dhoti half-undone and streaming on to the floor, revealing a bony leg. His eyes blazed with a light I had never seen before, as though He had already passed across into another world. He saw me coming behind Ooi and shouted in a slurring voice, 'There He is! There He is! He's been hiding in the kitchen all this time!' He threw the bowl at me.

'Listen, listen, listen to me for a moment!' cried Ooi. 'Yes, this was the person you saw. But, look, it's not Yama. It's Rabi, the boy Bhagaban has sent to take care of us. An innocent boy, a tribal. He knows nothing, neither can he do anything to harm you.'

'That's a lie! Fickle and faithless woman . . . so Yama made you part of the plot as well!'

Here was a wretched new story, which Eeja could very well embellish all night long, killing all chance of sleep till morning. I came forward with my hands above my head and said, 'Yes, Eeja, it *was* me. A little while ago, I came into the room to see if everything was all right. That's when You must have seen me. I am sorry for scaring You. Come, let us all go back to sleep. In the morning, we get ready to go home to Bhubaneswar.'

'It wasn't you.'

'It *was* me.'

'Say, who are you?'

'I am Rabi.'

'Come closer. Let me look.'

'Yes, Eeja.'

I bent over Eeja, I saw His face so close. The crinkled skin, the eyes red with rage and fear, the quivering jaw.

'See, it's only me.'

Eeja lowered His voice to a whisper. 'If it *was* you standing there just now, tell me . . . why were you beckoning to me? Like this? Come, come . . .'

A chill passed through my body.

'Where did you want to take me?'

'Eeja, I wasn't . . .'

'Wait, I've thought of something else. Let me touch you.' Eeja grasped my hand, then squeezed all the way up to my shoulder, touched my face, pulled my nose. He looked at Ooi and said, 'Flesh and blood, all right. Yama, You have come prepared to confront all my tests.' He thought for a few moments. 'Nor is it Your fault. We all have our work in this world and must try to do it well. Death is Your dharma. But You know very well . . . is this life an easy thing to leave? Despite all its troubles, its pains, its agonies, the illnesses, the weakness . . . it's the sweetest thing in the world. Yama, I want to live. Just a little bit more.'

'Yes, Eeja, You must live,' I said in a grave voice, using all the power He had given me. I felt Ooi squeeze my hand to show Her assent.

'Will you make sure I go back to Bhubaneswar?'

'I will make sure You go back to Bhubaneswar.'

Eeja chuckled, clapped His hands and wheezed, 'Think of what my life has come to, when my own wife and son won't take me back to Bhubaneswar, and I have to rely on Him who takes mankind away from life to lead me back to my city. It is an act of great mercy, Yama, an act of great mercy. I just want another two days and nights in Bhubaneswar, and then you can take me away, whenever you please. Just two or three days, so that I can live my whole life once again. I'll go through everything very fast. My soul will be at peace then. You'll have no difficulty with me in the other world.'

I said in a high, Godlike voice, trying to echo the rhythms that Eeja had revealed in his shlokas, 'Why two days, I'll give You two years. Just go to sleep quietly now. Look, Your wife is tired as well. She wants to sleep, too. She's worn out from taking care of You, from waking up at odd hours of the day and night. I have other news for You. Your son Bhagaban has this very day fought the elections in Odisha. The results will be out tomorrow. Don't You want to live to find out if he has won? If You do, I have no objection at all. But first You must sleep.'

'All right, Yama. I'm trusting You,' Eeja said. 'Help me, so I can lie down on the bed. But . . . beware . . . don't take me away while I'm sleeping! Else, I'll be very angry. I want to wake up in the very same place.'

'That is just what will happen, I promise. Let me first tie up Your dhoti for You.' I secured Eeja's knot and helped Him lie down, saying, 'Tomorrow, we go back to Bhubaneswar. Tomorrow, we go back to Bhubaneswar. Yes, Bhubaneswar. Ho, Bhubaneswar. Bhubaneswar, Bhubaneswar.' It was the most words I had ever said to Eeja.

At the mention of the city He loved so much, a look of great peace came over Eeja's face. He put His hands across His chest and closed His eyes.

I heard a small, heart-rending sound behind me. Ooi had covered Her face with Her hands and was crying.

'Ma! What is it?'

'Rabi, we can't let him sleep.'

'Why, Ma? If He sleeps, He will forget what He was just saying and thinking.'

'What if he really saw Yama in this room? What if he doesn't wake up again?'

'What should we do then?'

'Rabi, we must keep him up all night, talking about Bhubaneswar, making him remember his life there. It's just a few hours before dawn. Bhagaban *will* call in the morning, and tomorrow, at all costs, we *must* go back to Bhubaneswar. I give up. I cannot keep your Eeja alive any more. If he must leave this world, let him do so in Bhubaneswar. Else, his soul will restlessly wander for all time, in and around this accursed Bombay, far from the world he loves. And I will be considered a sinner for the next ten lives. Let us wake him up again, press his legs, make him drink milk, tell us stories.'

Stories—all night long! My heart sank when I saw that there would be no more sleep. Eeja murmured something that we could not understand, then fell silent again, His face deathly in the harsh white light.

'Rabi, he's so still! Is he breathing?'

'Yes, Ma, I think so.'

'Do you think so, or do you know?'

'I know.' I raised Eeja's hand, then let it go. It fell back down upon His chest. I put my hand on His heart, but could feel no beating.

'Rabi! Is he gone?'

'Eeja . . . Ma . . .'

A storm of tears and shrieks poured forth from Ooi, and She fell down beside Eeja, a widow, shaking Her head and crying, 'It's all Bhagaban's fault, it's all Bhagaban's fault. He couldn't take us home in time.'

Eeja had left us. My heart wept for Ooi, and also for Bhai, because even if he had won the election, his victory would always be blackened by Eeja's death on the same day, and his guilt for having once again let Him down. And weak and lazy thing that man's spirit is, I was also relieved that our long ordeal was over. We were free in our own ways.

Ooi raised Her black-and-white-and-red-haired head and seemed to search the air around Her, as if something was escaping.

'Rabi, we must say the Prayer for the Dead while his soul is leaving us. Bhagaban is not here. Only a man can perform that ritual, and you're like a son to us. If you know it, say it quickly, right now.'

'Ma, I don't know it . . . it's in Sanskrit. Shall I say the Prayer for the Dead of the Cloud people?'

'No. Never.' Ooi wiped away the tears from Her eyes, and Her face become hard and stony as the mountain in summer.

'I'll call Bhagaban Bhai,' I cried. 'He will tell us what to do.'

'No. Don't call him either. Today, he has let down his father. Should your Eeja have died like a pauper here in Bombay? Listen, tell me . . . what are your mourning chants like? Are they meant to be recited when people are newly dead, or afterwards, when they are cremated?'

'They are recited as soon as the body makes no reply.'

'What a day has come upon us. Very well. We have suffered many indignities anyway. Let this be one more. Let him go away with something to light his path. Say it aloud.'

'Ma, are you sure?'

'Don't ask foolish questions. Hurry up before he leaves us!'

Crying, I picked up two hibiscus flowers from the copper vessels in front of the deities, hidden behind Their curtain, and placed them between Eeja's big and long toes. I lit a candle and turned off the light. I made a wax pool and set the candle down by our feet. Then I lay my head on Eeja's knees, close to His sweet-smelling feet, and recited in the flickering light, for the first time since my own parents had died:

Cloudmaker, You are sad,
Cloudmaker, I know You are sad,
Cloudmaker, so very sad,
  for tearing me away from my loved ones.

But Cloudmaker, I am happy,
Cloudmaker, am happy,
Cloudmaker, so very happy,
  for Your gift of days in this beautiful world.

Giving myself to earthly love,
I forgot I was not always a body, but a cloud.

'A cloud,' Ooi murmured, shaking Her head.

I threw flower petals over Eeja's body and cried:

Now, blow, blow, blow,
oh Maker,
blow, blow, blow!
Cloudlight and oozing mist come rushing in,
and into the skies I will leap,
my forgotten promise to You I will keep.
I was body, now I am cloud,
I was earth, now I am sky.
I was fire, now I am water.
I was mud-brown, now I am cloud-white.

I walked below the Mountain,
now for many years I will float above,
until I have sated my love of this world.
I was chained, now I am free.
May they not cry, but feel joy for me.

A quavering voice said, 'What . . . not a body, but a cloud?'

Ooi shouted and fell on to the floor with a loud bump, like a sack of potatoes.

'Eeja!'

Eeja's eyes were open. He said, 'What strange and gross chant is this? Who is Cloudmaker?'

'Rabi! A ghost! It's his spirit speaking!'

'What's going on around here?' said Eeja, looking around. 'Why are you two frozen like that? Don't pretend you're dead. What time is it? Bring me my spectacles, or come closer.'

'Jagannath, Jagannath, Jagannath, merciful Jagannath,' Ooi murmured, letting out a small laugh, as if everything had become perfectly comprehensible to Her. 'What a night this is . . . the strangest night of my life. Rabi, it seems your prayer has not sent Eeja into the next world, but brought him back to life. What power the soul has, both to accept and reject what is offered in its name! Son, my eyes are cloudy with weeping. Is he alive, or is he not? He seems to be, if he speaks. But I cannot bring myself to believe it.'

'He is alive, Ma.'

'God knows for how long! Oh, my boy, my good son, let us not lose him again. Let us beat him, kick him, anger him, but let us somehow keep him alive until the morning. *What is life?* I've asked myself this so many times over the last few weeks. I've even asked myself how it would matter if it came to an end. And now I know the answer. Whatever it is, it is a thousand times better than that which it is not. I will not ask the question again. Who knows what other strange things this night holds?'

'Who are you thinking of beating?' Eeja asked. 'Don't do that. As a government servant, I will be obliged to restrain you, unless you can prove that a theft occurred, or some other breach of the law.'

'Yes, a theft occurred . . . you nearly stole my life from me. Now, get up quickly!' Ooi cried.

I looked at Them, back and forth, from one face to another, not sure who knew what, which world I was in or whether I was in life or in a dream.

Eeja said, 'It'll be hard for me to do that. I'm lying here on this mattress, but I'm still drifting, somehow. I saw somebody. I met Him.'

'That was Jagannath. He gave you a glimpse of Himself.'

'If you say so. All I know is that He gathered me up in His vast embrace. Together we were floating over a vast, hilly, green land, so slow, as clouds do. I was both inside and outside myself. I've never known such peace. Shall I tell you something strange? The smell was of figs. Figs. Send me back there.'

A great ecstasy took hold of me. Cloudmaker loves the smell of figs! It was said that figs were the only things He loved even more than clouds. Every offering to the ancestors always included figs.

'O-ho, o-ho, you're going nowhere, you're staying right here with us,' said Ooi. 'Listen. Look here. Will you drink milk? Will you try to walk a little? Can you get up?'

'I don't want to get up,' Eeja croaked. 'Who was He?'

I said, 'Eeja, it was Cloudmaker.'

'*Cloud*maker? Who is that?'

'He is the God of our people. For us, the God of this world.'

'That's strange. I know a God of wind, and of the skies, and of land, and of rain, but not of the clouds,' Eeja said. 'That said, prima facie, there appears to be some merit in your claims. Say more. Who is He? How did He come into being? Is He Creation, or only a manifestation of it?'

'Eeja, I will tell you all, if you agree to sit up and listen.'

Eeja thought for a moment or two, then nodded. Ooi gave a gasp of pleasure as she saw Him so undead. Immediately we got to work, hauled Him up, and put Him back against a pillow.

'Tell him, Rabi, tell him who He is,' Ooi panted.

Behind Eeja's head, outside the window, in the sky, a sliver of the fourth-day-moon could be seen, dipping after its long night above us in Bombay—and, on the other side of the country, above Tininadi and Bhagaban Bhai. Everything was in its place. I was filled with an intense love for life and for Cloudmaker.

I began with the Story of the Creation, both of and by Cloudmaker, which I had never in my life told, only heard. 'At the beginning of time, there were on the Earth only the Sun, the Moon, the Stars and the Wind.

'For as long as He could remember, the Wind had been roving over the surface of the Earth, blowing above and through things or carrying them along under the light of the Sun and the Moon. Sometimes, He went on long, gusting runs. Sometimes, He slowed down and coasted like the birds. Sometimes, His whistling breath reached the Sun and the Moon, and moved Them to different places in the Sky.'

'Mr Wind seems to have been as giddy-headed as my son Bhagaban,' Eeja chortled, 'who has moved his parents to another city, and refuses to come and take them back.'

'O-ho, he'll come, he's coming soon,' said Ooi. 'He's on his way as we speak. Rabi, go on.'

'One day, in the middle of a great plain, the Wind came upon a vast swelling on the Earth's surface—a Mountain. The Mountain was full of tilted trees and curving streams. It was enchanted with birdsong and animal cries, brooks and groves, dark and enclosed places where even the Wind could not reach.

'The Wind went no further, but set Himself to moving the Mountain. Yet no matter how much He blew, blasted and bellowed, the Wind could not budge the Mountain. Rather, with every passing day, the Wind fell further and further under Her spell.'

'The mountain was a lady, was she? Yes, it can often be hard to get an Indian lady to move.'

'Yes, Eeja,' I said, not pleased that His jokes kept interrupting such a sacred story, but at the same time relieved since there was no better sign that He was alive. 'The Wind wound Himself around the Mountain for a thousand days and nights, caressing Her high and low, gently and then strongly, tickling Her by blowing on Her face and nuzzling Her crevices. Finally, She gave in, and let Him do with Her as He pleased.'

Eeja turned pink and said to Ooi, 'These tribals are always going at it in their stories and in their lives.'

Ooi, too, had pinkened a little, but She was happy as well, I could see, that all these changes—which are signs of a desire to live—were passing through a man who had just been dead. With a jangle of bangles, She squeezed my wrist and urged me to continue.

I went on in the same voice in which I had played Yama: 'Another thousand days and nights passed, and with the union of the Wind and the Mountain, a son was born. A child neither of the Earth nor the Sky, but somewhere in between. Nothing like Him had ever been seen in the universe. Neither this nor that, He was called Cloudmaker.

'He was never still, and no shape He took lasted more than a few minutes. His nature was movement, like the Wind or like a song. He was always at play in this world, so beautiful to begin with and now even more so when He loped and twisted in the wide open Sky, puffing Himself up into Clouds, rolling in the whistling gusts of His father the Wind or drifting before returning to His mother the Mountain.

'But Cloudmaker never knew what His limits were—in this, He was like the beings He would later create. He was both wise and foolish, generous and greedy, like man. An only child, He soon longed for a kingdom different from that of His parents, for something that was His own work.'

'Ho! This is getting interesting.'

'One day, when He was not yet fully grown, He happened to bind together, into a loose figure, some stones with a paste of mud, straw, leaves and rain, and carried it around with Him within a grey, wet, nourishing Cloud. A few months later, He was astonished to see the figure had come to life. Delighted, He set His creation down to walk on the Earth as man.'

Ooi murmured, 'When man always comes from a woman's womb, why then in all the stories of creation do men keep emerging out of all sorts of other places?'

I continued: 'But then Cloudmaker saw that man, too, would be lonely like He was if he had the Earth all to himself. And so, He made a woman, with a slightly smaller boulder He saw nearby and with what was left of the paste. He was delighted with His work—as was man. He set man and woman to work, to play, somewhat bound, somewhat free, right at the foot of the Mountain, so that He could always watch them.

'Very soon, the first man and woman were so engrossed in one another's company that they forgot totally about Cloudmaker, which caused Him both pleasure and pain.

'In the meantime, when They found out what He had done, Cloudmaker's parents flew into a terrible rage, for it seemed that He might in time flood the entire world not just with His Clouds but with His men. His parents wanted the world to remain silent and serene, just as it was at that time.

'And so, they devised a terrible punishment. They cursed Him that He would never grow up, and always remain the same—a playful child. And that He would never find a partner or a companion in the universe, but remain alone.

'And they declared, too, that Cloudmaker's men and women could live only a little while in this world before their bodies would turn back to dust and mud. That for all their happiness in this world, they would suffer terribly from disease, pain and death.'

'How harsh, how cruel,' murmured Eeja. 'All Gods must have Their consorts and companions. Siba has Parbati, Rama has Sita. If this puffing, lonely, childish fellow is your God, no wonder you people are so slow and so moody.'

Ooi sighed and said, 'Ah, poor Cloudymaker. Without a wife in this world, just like Bhagaban.'

Eeja laughed in His amused way and said to Her, 'Were we in some tribal land when Bhagaban was conceived? More and more Bhagaban seems to me like a creation of this Cloudmaker. No wonder we could never teach him the right beliefs.'

'Bhagaban has taken our sacred beliefs to more people that you ever have,' Ooi returned. 'Your son may have made some mistakes early in life, but today he is the prince of the Hindu faith in Odisha.'

I said in defence of Cloudmaker, and also to exercise Eeja's brain, 'Eeja, the great Monkey God Hanuman never had any consorts or companions either. Hanuman, too, loved to play, jump and flick his tail around things. And yet wasn't he tremendously strong and resolute, and didn't he help Rama bring Sita back from Lanka after jumping across the wide seas?'

Ooi said, 'Hanuman? No, your Cloudymaker reminds me rather of the boy Krusna who loved to steal butter from the pots of the milk-girls, and make off with their clothes while they were bathing. Listen. Look here. Do you think the Krusna story was taken to the tribals by some Brahmin Pandit in olden times, and was changed by them?'

'Very possible, very possible,' said Eeja. 'Let us hear more. It's been so long since I came across a completely new story. They are as rare as completely new worlds.'

'At heart, father and son are just the same,' Ooi murmured. 'Rabi, go on.'

'Cloudmaker may have been saddened by His parents' curse, but He remained the same—a God of movement. For Him, something that did not breathe, rise and fall, sing and play, was not Life. Even at night, when all the birds and animals would go to sleep, and the Earth would grow dark, and men and women and children would huddle around a fire at the foot of the Mountain, He would come floating above them in swirls of mist and drizzle.

'And then He would pull away His own curtain, making His creations gasp with wonder when they saw how many million stars twinkled in the vast night, how many white rods, baskets and boats there were in the heavens, how perfectly round the Moon was in a way that Cloudmaker's puffs of Cloud never could be.

'Cloudmaker's heart beat with bittersweet pleasure and sadness when He saw how, inspired by these sights they saw and their love of this world and for one another, human beings were roused to song and music and prayer. And He resolved that although their bodies would grow old and die, their souls would be drawn up into the Sky for a hundred lifetimes, and they would float there as Clouds. This way, their departure from this world would be a peaceful one, not a bitter break which would make them resent what others had and what they'd never have again. That is why the saying among our people goes: *"All souls come from Cloudmaker and go back to Him as Clouds."* The Clouds are our ancestors from hundreds of years ago.'

'It all holds together,' Eeja judged, nodding His head as if He had heard some sweet music. 'But for one thing.'

'What is that, Eeja?'

'Is the moon always perfectly round? It is only round around the time of the full moon. This is a flaw in the story.'

'Let's leave that all be for a moment,' said Ooi. 'Is Cloudymaker happy? Is He at peace? What does He want from you people? Will He be angry if you allow His mother to be desecrated, or will He break free from Her at last? That is the question.'

'There are indeed days when Cloudmaker is tremendously happy and free. Who would not be if they had the whole Sky as their playground? But at heart, Ma, He is still only a full-grown child, who when He feels one emotion or mood cannot balance it with any other. Once every year, a great gloom comes over Him when He remembers all the things that happened to Him, how He is destined always to be alone, and how much pain human beings feel when they think about death—which, too, is a kind of everlasting loneliness. Then His face turns black, He breaks down, and He cries for weeks and months at a time. The Clouds pour down with His tears, so strong that They sometimes wash away all the huts and houses, fields and fences that we human beings have made alongside the Mountain. And even the Mountain weeps when She sees how deeply He feels His plight, and She pulls Him closer to

Her, holds Him in a tight embrace, and gets hidden by low Clouds. And so, in honour of Cloudmaker's life and love and law, we Cloud people, too, proclaim a crier for these months, a full-grown child, not yet a man or woman. All of creation is then linked together by tears.'

I fell silent for a few moments.

Eeja said, 'It's so, so quiet here. Is it night outside?'

'It is.'

'Are there stars in the sky?'

'No, Eeja. There are no stars.'

'Why not?'

'The stars can never be seen in Bombay.'

'Oh, are we in Bombay?'

'Yes.'

'I forgot all about it. Anyway, what I wanted to say was—I want to see the stars and all the galaxies in the night sky, just like you described them. It's been many years since I did. Perhaps decades. I'd forgotten how beautiful that sight is. My eyes were young when they saw them last.'

Ooi said, 'Yes, yes, you must see such a sky. As soon as dawn comes, Bhagaban will call, and we can make plans to go.' She leaned close to my ear and whispered, 'Rabi, he's completely forgotten about Yama's visit. And he's not talking madness and froth either. Tell him more!'

'Eeja, in my land, one can still see all the beautiful white twinkles and streaks of night, every night, as bright as ever. Bhagaban Bhai and I will take you there very soon. You will be happy there. Man's sight travels very far in such lands, beyond himself and this world. He forgets about petty things and quarrels, and thinks about his own place in time and among other men, as Cloudmaker wants him to. It's a place meant for high people like you, Eeja.'

'If I go there when it rains, will I have to cry, too?'

Ooi hooted with laughter. Slapping Her thigh, She said to Eeja, 'You? You? When have you ever cried that you'll begin now, just because other people are doing so? I think you'll laugh instead. And not with them either, but at them.'

'I'll cry and show you any time you like,' said Eeja with great dignity. 'Ho, boy, tell me. You say Cloudmaker has never had a consort. But did he—'

'Eeja, we should say He . . .'

'All right, *He*. Did He at least fall in love?'

Ooi snorted. 'Since when did you start thinking of who fell in love and who didn't? Do people your age think of such things?'

I was impressed by Eeja's question and said, 'Yes, Eeja, in fact, He did once. And still does.'

'Really? But who was it? There's no one in His realm to fall in love with. Did He fall in love with an earth woman, as the Gods do in our Hindu epics?'

'No, Eeja, this is not the Mahabharata. Cloudmaker fell in love with someone else.'

'Who? I'm looking at the sky, and I can't see anybody around.'

'What will you give me if I tell you?'

'I will give you a rupee.'

'No . . . I can't tell you. You'll laugh at my God and my people.'

'I won't laugh. I promise! Please, please tell me.'

Ooi squeezed my hand tightly, happy to see how I was leading Eeja on. I spoke: 'Cloudmaker had been told by His parents that the Sun and the Moon had always belonged to one another, and oversaw the world by turns, passing day and night between Themselves. For the longest time, He was least interested in Them and Their life. The only thing He liked was Their light which He could play with, pass through Himself, caress and colour. He turned sunlight and moonlight into cloudlight, into beautiful shapes and shadows that fell on Earth's surface and made Him love Himself even more.'

'Cloudlight?' said Eeja. 'That's the first time I've ever heard the word. But it's true. What it describes does exist, only we never thought of a word for it. Once in a while, the tribals do hit upon something the rest of us have missed, this much is clear. But I thought we were speaking about love, not light. Though, at times, the two can be the same thing.'

'Yes, Eeja, I will speak now of love. So, one full moon night, thousands of years ago, Cloudmaker saw the Cloud people looking up at the Clouds, rapt with wonder and joy. And He was happy, and forgot about all His cares. But then He heard them praising, not Him, but the Moon. Cloudmaker flew into a rage—He saw this as an act of treachery by those He had brought to life, and He thought He would puff out a huge bank of Clouds and obstruct their sight of the Moon.

'But when He turned and looked the other way, He Himself became transfixed for the first time by the sight of the radiant Moon sailing through the heavens, regal and serene.'

'Ah, the moon, our very own moon,' Eeja said, delighted, and began to stare at the ceiling as if He could see the moon in the sky.

'And He fell in love right then and there, losing all self-love and self-possession, and His heart grieved even more for all that He could not have. And He blew thunderstorms and hailstones of rage and spite upon the Cloud people—even though He loved them, too—upset about the place into which they had led Him. And now He grew jealous of the Sun, the King of the heavens.

'What was Cloudmaker to do? He tried to get in the Sun's way and annoy Him, but the Sun sported with Him as a tiger teases a cub, and slapped Him away. In the meantime, to impress the Moon, Cloudmaker blew Himself into beautiful shapes and patterns every night, never still for a moment, just as a song is never still. And like the Moon reflected the light of the sleeping Sun, so Cloudmaker reflected the light of the Moon and suffused the entire world with an enchanting cloudlight that the Moon Herself could not ignore.'

'They're falling in love just like Radha and Krusna in the *Gita Govindam*,' Eeja crowed, His glasses slipping down His large nose. 'I feel a shloka coming to my mind, but if I focus my attention there, I'll lose the drift of the story.'

'You listen to the story first, and then I will get you your diary, and you must write in it,' said Ooi. 'Not just one shloka. Many.'

'But I don't want to steal this fellow's story. He's telling it in such good language. *He* should write or sing it.'

'Such good language! Where did he learn such good language, if not by listening to you? Don't you remember how he spoke when we first got here, in bits and scraps? Rabi, isn't that true?'

'Yes, Eeja,' I said truthfully, 'I have learnt to speak better because of you.'

A yellow-legged bird touched down on the windowsill, looked in, and flew away again. It was dawn.

'The credit for that goes to you, for which you will be rewarded in due course, as well as through the very pleasure you have gained from your progress,' said Eeja generously. 'Anyway, don't listen to her rambling. She's become old now. Continue! So the moon . . .'

'Little by little, Cloudmaker and the Moon began to come closer, playing hide-and-seek in the heavens, pretending it was other things They were after, pretending to be proud, when what They really wanted was to taste one another's embrace.

'And one night, They could hold themselves back no more, and They melted into one another, and the world was bathed with the most radiant light and fragrance. But just as They were about to consummate Their union, the Sun arrived in a terrible rage, slapped Cloudmaker many times, scorched Him so badly He turned black, not with wetness but with charring, and wrenched the Moon away.'

'Ah, Cloudmaker! Burnt for love! Take heart, take heart. You are a wet kind of fellow and that in itself will heal You.'

'Cloudmaker was distraught yet again and even lonelier than before, because now He pined for His beloved each and every moment. But where was She? For many nights, the Moon did not appear in the Sky. And when finally She did, She was a shadow of Her former beautiful self, just a tiny sliver, small and meek and downcast, giving no light at all. Cloudmaker was not even sure if He was in love with Her any more.

'On seeing Cloudmaker though, Her face brightened. And each night, She recovered something of Her past glory—until one day, She was back to Her old, round and radiant self again, and even the Cloud people on the Earth were filled with joy and relief. But as soon as He saw Her back to fullness, the jealous and vengeful Sun slapped the Moon and cowed Her down, and the next day, She appeared again, whether by will or by wit, a bit subdued and downcast, so that the Sun would not fear losing Her, and She could continue to sail across the heavens. Each day She kept growing smaller and darker till She disappeared completely, making Cloudmaker's heart sink and the Sun feel secure. But then, when She thought the Sun was not looking, She began to smile again, little by little, growing in beauty until Cloudmaker's heart nearly burst with pleasure, desire and suffering.

'And so it goes on, through the ages. Every time the Moon achieves Her full beauty and pride, She begins to rein Herself in so that She may at least continue to spend the night not far from Cloudmaker. And in Their honour, the Cloud people sing songs of how the heart cannot possess what it most deeply desires. And how in the heavens, as in this world, brute power is always stronger than love, experience always more powerful than innocence.'

'Poor Cloudmaker, poor Cloudmaker,' Eeja murmured. 'A most unhappy life. Boy, I have made a close study of the histories of different people and of their beliefs. It seems to me that ancient people took all their lessons, not from what went on around them on this earth, but from what went on above them in the heavens. And there is a deep truth here about man's past. For thousands of years, what diversion did man have in this world other than the heavens? What book did he have to read other than the book of the sun and the stars and the clouds and other heavenly bodies? What he knew from life on this earth, he saw reflected in the comings and goings of that marvellous world that hung above him. Even so, your people are exceptional in one way—for the place they have given in their system to clouds.'

In my best Eeja-like manner, I declared, 'It is said, Eeja: "Man's best self hangs just above him, like a cloud." And the light inside man's head is just like cloudlight, neither bright nor dark, but grey, always doubting, dreaming.'

'Cloudlight is really one of the best words I have come across in my entire life!' said Eeja. 'Why didn't you tell me all this earlier? We have been locked up in this house for at least three years. So many times I have been so bored.'

Ooi said, 'Were you willing to listen earlier? All you wanted to say were things about yourself. That's not wrong, as you are not just my husband and protector but the highest of the three of us. However, in any kind of coming together of strangers, it is always polite to ask about the other person, too. I knew all these things about Rabi a long time back. But that's because I asked.'

'I was ill, so how could I listen? I feel more like myself now. Boy, tell me. Is your mountain going to be taken away from you?'

'Yes, Eeja. As things stand.'

'What's going to happen to your people if that comes to be? Can they deal with it? Will they get something in return?'

'Eeja, it was the Mountain from whose womb Cloudmaker was born, and in turn man emerged. If life itself has a cloudy nature, it is because it has this root. Whenever Cloudmaker is tired, and because He is still a child, He goes back to rest inside the Mountain, and it is inside Her vast caverns that He keeps His store of Clouds. The Cloud people believe that if something were to happen to the sacred Mountain, it would also be the end of man on Earth. If the Mountain is destroyed, the Clouds, too, will disappear from the Sky forever.'

Eeja said to Ooi, 'It's a fine story, no doubt. But one thing interests me. These people are not able to make a distinction between a scientific proposition and a metaphor. It's the same thing with tribals all over the world. That's why they remain primitive.'

Ooi said, 'Only Jagannath knows what these pur-po-si-tions and moo-ta-phors really are. Anyway, Bhagaban is going to take care of these people and save them from the danger in which they find themselves. I have full faith in my son. He has the wit of Rama, the fidelity of Lakhmana and the strength of Hanuman all rolled into one.'

'I don't think he can do much,' Eeja said. He rubbed His nose for a while, then added graciously, 'But if you like, boy, when we go back to Bhubaneswar, I can try and intercede with the government on behalf of your people. I have a personal acquaintance with the collector of Bhubaneswar, Mr Nilamadhab Panda.'

The phone rang, making us all start. Ooi cried, 'Is it Bhagaban! Is it Bhagaban! Rabi, get me the phone quickly.'

After having gone so far back into the depths of time, we were being pulled back to the present again. Bhai was calling with news of the election! I swooped down on the phone and ran towards Ooi. As I passed Eeja, He held out His hand.

I handed the phone to Him.

Ooi made impatient sounds and lumbered towards Him. He looked at all the buttons and then pressed one.

I could see the call was cut.

'Eeja, the . . .'

Eeja took the phone up to His mouth and said, 'Hello.'

He put it next to His ear and was silent for a while.

He said, 'He isn't saying anything. Wasting his own time and ours. How typical!'

'The call is not on! How will the poor boy speak when you won't let him? Here, give the phone to me!' Ooi yelled.

'Why? Is it your phone?'

'Yes, it's my phone!'

'Who said it's yours? Who paid for it?'

'Rabi! Do something.'

'Eeja, if you give me back the phone, I will sing you a beautiful song about a cloud.'

'All right. Here. Take it. I just want to make sure she doesn't get too proud. Women imagine they are taking over the world these days.'

The phone began to glow and ring again. Ooi pressed the correct button and held it up to Her ear. 'Bhagaban!'

'Hello, Ma!'

Eeja ordered, 'Bhagaban! Book our tickets right now.'

'Jagannath, Jagannath the Merciful . . . my son, how are you? Have you eaten breakfast, or are you calling on an empty stomach?'

I heard Bhai howling with laughter. 'Oh Ma, will mothers never change their ways? Here I'm calling to tell you and Bapa that your son has won the election! Yes, the election! And there you are, asking if a banana or bread-piece is sitting in my belly.'

Bhai had won the election! My heart leapt with pleasure—ecstasy— pride—relief—a hundred other notes of human feeling for which words have not been found. Even so, they were nothing compared to the expression that passed across Ooi's round, wrinkled, big-eyed face. It did not belong to this world.

'What, son? No, it isn't true!'

'Yes. The collector of the district just called me with the news. The counting isn't over yet, but I have enough of a lead to be certain that I can't be beaten. It's all because of you, Ma, that I could stay here and win the election. You. And Rabi, too. Else, I'd have been a candidate just for show, to be jeered at by the Bhubaneswar papers because I thought I could dabble in politics. Now I've shown them all. Oh, I forget. How is Bapa? Did I wake you all up?'

'Wake us up? Son, what shall I tell you? We haven't slept a wink all night because of your father. And there's more, which I won't tell you about right now.'

'Really? What?'

'I can't say. You come here first.' Ooi could not stop Herself—it being human nature to reveal secrets even while concealing them. 'To sum it all up in a sentence, we were visited by Yama last night and He nearly took your Bapa away. We held on desperately in a great tug of war and dragged him back. But, son, we need to return home right away. Can you come tomorrow?'

'Tomorrow? Ma, you must be joking.'

'What! Will it be next week then? Bhagaban, I don't want to trouble you, but we are in great difficulty here. Even my gudakhu has run out.'

'Stop, stop, my heart is shaking with suffering. Ma, I'll be in Bombay by *this afternoon*. I'll get a seat on the eleven o'clock flight, so it'll be just after one when I get in and maybe two by the time I get to your door. Then we can go to the hospital tomorrow for Bapa's check-ups, and if everything seems fine, we fly home right away.'

Ooi said, 'No, no, son, don't bother coming so soon. Stay in Bhubaneswar for a day or two. All the newspapers and the TV channels will want to interview you. Finish off the Company by telling everybody what they are up to with the poor Cloud people! They need you more than us. Then come and take us back. Your old mother can manage for a few more days. Rabi is here with me. Last night, he single-handedly kept Eeja alive through the dread hours by telling him about Cloudymaker.' Ooi wiped a tear away from each of Her eyes.

'Ma, I'll handle the interviews once we're back in Bhubaneswar. Give the phone to Rabi.'

'Here.'

I took the phone.

'Brother Rabi! Cloudmaker has had His say! He's blown puffs of smoke into the eyes of the Company, puffs of smoke for a new time in history. The smoke and fizz of democracy! It's all happened for us. I have won the elections.'

'I really can't believe it, Bhai.'

'Next time, it'll be you who wins. I'm sorry if these old folk aren't letting you sleep. I know how much you love your slumber. But I'm nearly there to take over from you. Once we are back in Bhubaneswar, you can sleep for a whole month.'

'Bhai, cloudgrace and flowershowers upon you. But really, you don't need to come so soon.'

I heard Bhai's voice turn annoyed. 'What, have you all fallen in love with each other out there? Don't you want to see me?'

The voice disappeared. Was he really angry? Bhai could fly into a terrible rage sometimes.

'I think the signal is lost,' Ooi said.

'When is he coming?' Eeja asked.

'In a few hours.'

'About time, too.'

'About time to you. How could he have come before this? It's only because he stayed there, and not here with us, that he managed to win the elections. Does he have a right to make a life for himself, too, or should he only look after us?'

'He should do both in the right measure, as prescribed by Hindu dharma.'

I went off to the kitchen to heat Eeja's morning milk and make tea for Ooi and me. Back in the other room, I heard Them continue with Their argument. When I came back, Ooi was saying, 'Just once in your life, why can't you let your happiness show? That's what I want to know. If you can't be happy that Bhagaban has won the biggest victory of his life, at least be happy that you are alive, that we still have the pleasure of your grace, your words, your face. There's a bit of cream on the tip of your nose. No, no, lower down. Rabi, will you wipe it off?'

'Hmm,' said Eeja. 'Pull it, too.'

'Eeja . . . pull what?'

'Pull my nose a little. Yes. That feels good.'

'Rabi, just hold it up there until he finishes drinking his milk, else he'll dip it in there again.'

'Yes, hold on to it, but don't take it away, because what can he know who has no nose?' said Eeja, and wheezed with laughter, spraying milk all around.

Ooi made noises of disgust that showed She was more amused than vexed, and said, 'Rabi, now that he knows that Bhagaban is coming in a few hours, he's going to make things as difficult for us as he can. But you know what, son? His mind seems to have come back to him. It's this Bombay that took it away.'

'Ma, don't You want to sleep for a little while?'

'Sleep? All sleep has gone from me after I've heard this news. Why should I sleep in Bombay? Is the sleep of this place any good? It's uneasy, filled with bad dreams, fears, aches and pains. I'll sleep the fragrant sleep of Bhubaneswar, to the sounds of the cows mooing and of the water dripping from the tap in the bathroom—it's like the sacred stream of Barunei that has never run dry for thousands of years and never will, I don't know if you know about it. Bhagaban has told me many times that he'll have that tap fixed, but I always say, "No. I can't sleep without it now. Let it add a few rupees to the water bill. Eeja can afford it." Oh, I hope that the TV will be working . . . I can't bear to miss my serials for a single day more. Son, are you happy today? Your beloved Bhai, your sacred Mountain, your Cloud people . . . today all of them stand taller.'

'Yes, Ma. It is all Jagannath's doing. Are *You* happy?'

'Who, me? What shall I tell you, child? This soul has never known a day's happiness in its life.'

'Why do You say that, Ma? You have everything.'

'Yes, yes, everything . . . and nothing at the same time. Can women ever be happy? Never in our own house, always in another's . . . never living our own life, always another's. Women can only reflect the happiness of men, just as the moon reflects the sun's glow. To tell you the truth, if I have ever been happy, it is only when sadness, pain, worry, these things have been lifted from my head for a few days by Jagannath—such as today. When Jagannath does this, I know that the round-eyed Lord is filled with love and mercy for me.'

I saw how clearly Bhai had seen the truth of things when he had said, 'My mother is the simplest and happiest person I know, but it would make her very unhappy to admit it, and that is a mark both of her Hinduism and her place in history as a woman.' A feeling of love for Her surged in my heart, and I saw Ooi living quite happily with us in Bhubaneswar after Eeja passed away, as She would have had He passed away last night

The phone rang once more. Ooi picked it up. 'It's Bhagaban again. Dear Jagannath! Is he calling to say he can't make it?'

'He can't make it?' asked Eeja. 'Let me speak to him.'

'Hello? Bhagaban? What is it, son? Don't say anything terrible to your poor mother now after getting her hopes up, which she never asked you to do anyway. If we change our story again, your Bapa will throw us out of this wretched house right away. He may be old, but his thunder hasn't left him.'

'What, Ma, don't you have any faith in me?' I heard Bhai say. 'I'm calling you to say I just made my flight on time. I wanted to hear your voice again before they ask us to switch off our phones. Oh, what a feeling, what a feeling! Ma, by the way, I think I'm bringing someone with me.'

'What? Who? You have no one but us three, and we are all here. Have you found a new servant?'

'The air hostess on this flight has caught my eye. She's really beautiful. I think she'd make a great daughter-in-law.'

'Hss! Don't say all these horrible things even in jest. So what if you are in your forties now? You're now one of Odisha's most successful, most eligible men, in addition to being high-born to begin with. A matchmaker's delight. You can't bring home one of these girls—someone who picks up people's dishes. So what if she works on an aeroplane? It's just a train that can fly, no more.'

'What, Ma? I'm serious.' Wickedly, Bhai added, 'And what does a daughter-in-law in our society do but pick up dishes—especially when she goes to the house of her in-laws? So, my air hostess already has great training for her future life.'

I burst out laughing. The whole mood in our place had changed so much, now that Bhai was coming.

Ooi said, 'Listening to you is like listening to the sage Balmiki himself. You both could convince anybody about anything. If you must do such things, don't come here. Take her somewhere else. Rabi will take us home somehow.'

'Yes, let's go home right now,' said Eeja. 'Boy, bring me my shoes.'

Even to this day, I could never tell whether Eeja was actually listening to everything around Him or if He was lost in His own thoughts, and His ears only picked up certain words.

'Okay, Ma, it's time to switch off the phone. See you soon.'

'Goodbye and Godspeed. Don't eat anything too heavy because we . . . hello? Hello? It's cut. The plane must have taken off. Rabi! What are you laughing so much for? Oh, I see. It's all very funny to you, I know, but trust me, I know Bhagaban better than anybody else. If the mood takes him, he'll put a garland around the air hostess' neck even before the flight lands in Bombay, and he'll get all the passengers to be his groomgroup. Come, son, let this auspicious day not proceed any further with all of us unbathed and impure—else our Gods will be very angry with us. They probably are already, it's been so long since we got this piece of good news, and yet, while we drink tea and make merry, They are trapped in the darkness behind the curtain. I'm going to bathe quickly and prepare a feast for Them. After that, you take Eeja to the bathroom and get him ready. Today, even he must participate in the puja and offer his thanks to Them, both for his victory over . . .' she whispered the word 'Yama' to me, '. . . and for Bhagaban's victory over the Company.'

It was one of Eeja's last baths in Bombay. As if to prove that He had recovered completely and was ready to go home, He not only walked to the bathroom without any support but also bathed without any help from me. Had He really forgotten everything that had happened to Him during the night and all the places He had been to? I couldn't tell. He gently put His hand over my head while I combed His hair, and left it there. I felt blessed by a higher force, as old as the Earth.

I sat Eeja down on the bed. Ooi had got everything ready, and Herself, too. After Her bath She had put on the new sari that Bhai had given Her the day he had left for Bhubaneswar, and She had also put vermilion in the parting of Her hair, like a new bride. Perhaps that is what She felt like after Eeja had nearly died and gone away. I ran to the bathroom and bathed quickly.

'Come, Rabi.'

Ooi drew back the curtain of the Gods. They looked out at the world that had changed so much overnight—Cloudmaker and Bhai on the rise, the Company shaken, the three of us happy and eager to leave Bombay for Bhubaneswar. Eeja sat on the bed, watching approvingly.

'Ma, can I sit down behind You today?'

'Is that even a question to ask? You are the greatest devotee of them all, the one who cares for the aged and makes sure that they are able to pray. Come, sit.' Ooi began to distribute pieces of apples, bananas and oranges across the copper vessels. 'Look at what a fine feast I've prepared for Them. But you know what? If Bhagaban hadn't won, I wouldn't have given Them a single thing to eat this morning, yes. They could all have gone hungry for one, two, five days, I wouldn't have cared.'

'What, Ma, aren't You afraid of displeasing Them?'

'Displeasing Them! And shouldn't They listen once in a while to my pleas? Let me tell you, I don't fear Them at all. At my age, what do I have to fear—except for the fact that I could become a widow, the greatest of all curses? To tell you the truth, when I thought last night that he . . . that he . . . I can't say it . . . I got very angry. I may not have said anything, but They know how angry I was that They were playing with me in such a terrible way, when only a day or two remained for us to return to Bhubaneswar. Now that I think about it, maybe that is why They sent him back. If there is one thing that the Gods fear, it is the anger of the devout, who peacefully accept everything that is meted out to them in this life. Anyway, let us not dwell on all that now. We have got what we want.' Looking at the Gods, Ooi declared, 'Come, Your feast is ready. Eat! Eat to Your heart's content. I seek nothing more from You. You have given me all I need. In truth, You should not have given me so much. A little less, and I still would have been at peace.'

Ooi bent low upon Her knees and Her head touched the floor, so strangely balanced it felt like She might topple over any moment. She stayed there, rocking on Her knees, murmuring sacred and grateful words.

Eeja jumped into the silence. 'So, I said to the chief secretary, "Sir, how can I assure you that your daughter will be married off within the next year into a Kayastha family from Ganjam? It may be what is written on her palm, but a palm is only an approximate and not an exact map of life." He said . . .'

I woke up. Sunlight flooded the room. Where were we? Still in Bombay! Bhai had won the elections. Eeja had come back from the dead. Ooi had fallen asleep, right there on the floor itself, one hand below Her head and the other over Her heart. I had never seen such peace on anyone's face. Eeja was standing above Her. He must have been trying to wake Her up for a while, looking for something to eat or drink. Didn't He realize how tired She was?

I looked at Him. He pushed Her with his foot.

'Wake up, wake up.'

Ooi was not annoyed by His rude behaviour. She did not move.

'Ooi!'

Eeja looked at me. 'What shall I do now? I do not know any doctors here. I do in Bhubaneswar. But we are in Bombay.'

Honk Honk to Udvada

COME NOW, SING with me: Honk honk, bonk bonk, all the way to Udvada!

Of all the minorities in this country, where even the minorities are in multitudes, we Parsis must be the smallest. There were never any more than a few thousand of us to begin with, and, now, beyond the fringes of Bombay (which we more or less made, even if the Marathas won't allow for it now) and the towns of coastal Gujarat (where we first arrived all those centuries ago), we don't even get up to a *hundred* in any place. A family emigrating to New York or Toronto, a nasty car accident, two women marrying outside the faith—and Parsi demographics must be done all over again. Up in Delhi, a single man and his dog will constitute a Parsi mob. At our very own weddings and Navjotes, we're outnumbered by non-Parsi spouses, children, waiters— by the rest of Indian civilization, each one perfectly programmed to proliferate. Somehow, we have managed to gratify ourselves with daily infusions of fried eggs, when the rest of India likes them fertilized. Just by leaving for San Francisco on Monday night, I'd probably be tilting the scales somewhere. Possibly more Parsi men in Bombay would now be gay than not, or would live with their mothers than not.

Never a great patron of the faith, I'd always stood, from the time I stumbled awkwardly into adulthood, at a safe distance from the institutions and festive occasions of our community, and, later, psychoanalysis estranged me further from groupthink. It annoyed me that because of our declining numbers, the elders of the faith kept insisting that we had to all hold together. Past the doomsday bluster, they seemed to actually love the fact that there was a *crisis* and they were in charge of rules, prescriptions, remedies. In my head, I was a Billimoria first, a Bombayite second, and a Parsi fourth. Fifth if you ask what's third.

Except for today. For one day in my life, for the cause of romantic concord, I cheerfully submitted to being a Parsi first, keeping up his place in the trail leading to the Great Mountain of the tribe.

The Bombay-Ahmedabad Highway was a honking, trilling, swaying parade. On this one day, we pleasure-loving Parsis were laying siege to the state of Gujarat, that joyless place of prohibition, vegetarianism, thrift, riots and stepwells. The men were being encouraged to race one another; cutting in and out, they shouted friendly jibes at each other with every positional gain. Each car that overtook Zelda (I wasn't going to be driving at the same speed as some of these jokers) was manned by a beaked nose; at the windows, matriarchs and their daughters-in-law fanned themselves with copies of *Jam-e-Jamshed*, and fair, rosy-cheeked children chirped and sang; on the windscreens were Bombay Parsi Punchayet stickers and the odd one for the radical group ARZ (Association for the Revival of Zoroastrianism).

An even prouder Parsi sat by my side—Zahra Irani—in a superficially modest yet sexy black and white salwar-kameez, her hair covered with an improvised black dupatta-chador, her face flushed with contagious pleasure and excitement. And on this strangest and most thrilling of dates, we had, for better or for worse, a consignment of Parsi cargo to deliver to Udvada. In the back seat, Zahra's Uncle Sheriyar now moved his substantial frame from one window to the other and, in emphatic Gujarati, declared: 'If I'd been driving, we'd have reached Udvada by now. One hundred per cent sure, dikra, or may my balls fall off.'

Zahra gave a tinkling laugh and said in her delicious American-accented Gujarati, 'Come on, Uncle! There are only two kinds of people in the world who're always so sure of themselves: the true believer and the backseat driver.'

'What? Don't you remember when I drove you all to Udvada when you were a teenager? Out of Bombay like this and into Udvada like that, just like how babies leave the womb and pop into life. And that was on the old, bad road, before the highway was built.'

'Yes, yes, sure. But that was then. You're old now.'

'If I'm old, so is Mr Billimoria here. Take it or leave it.'

'Okay, so you're both young.'

A couple of hours into our acquaintance, I was beginning to see the competitive side of Uncle Sheriyar. When I'd met him at seven that morning, he'd seemed a mild old coot, reticent, courteous, his English a strange piece of patchwork, just like the Indian mind, his prosperous stomach a sign of both his advancing age and the success of his many businesses and projects (among them a bakery in Ghatkopar and a piggery in Karjat, I was told). Only a certain gleam in his eyes, I saw now, gave away the story of the kind of soul he really was. It was the gleam of life, of competitive life, the wish to be the wind that blows through the trees.

I had met Zahra and Uncle Sheriyar downstairs and was ready to leave, but Uncle Sheriyar had wanted to take a leak before our long journey, so I gave him the keys to my apartment, while Zahra and I waited by Zelda's side. The two of us were a bit formal with one another because it was the first time we, as lovers, were in the presence of something like family.

'So?' I finally said, pinching her arm. 'Does Uncle Sheriyar know about me?'

'What are we, teenagers?' asked Zahra. 'Of course he does. In fact, he's probably gone up as much to assess the value of your property as to pee.'

'What're you saying!'

Zahra giggled. 'Let him be. He's sweet. Actually, Uncle Sheriyar is a remarkable man. Do you know, even before he opens his eyes in the morning, he says his prayers and does his stretches in bed—all with his eyes still shut. And then he goes down to feed the stray dogs of the neighbourhood, and on the way back up he brings a pile of mail because he's also the treasurer of the housing society, and he's on the mailing list of every expo in Bombay, from furniture to heavy goods and electronics, but it's like an hour before he gets down to reading his mail because he asks all those he meets in the lift or elsewhere how they're doing, and then he gets stuck listening to their troubles. He's a bit like you in that way, only he does it all for free. He has more fingers than the world has pies . . . he's like . . . like a Ravana of the fingers. You know, Farhad, he's the most *religious* and, at the same time, the most *worldly* person I know. That's why he likes to confirm what a man is made of. I'm sure he'll be very impressed by your place.'

'Hey, is a man to be sized up by his apartment? The real goods are down here.'

'You're *so* right, honey, the real goods *are* down here, and I've been thinking about them a lot.' Zahra cuffed me on the thigh. 'But we won't be getting to inspect them any time soon . . . unless we find some place private in the crowds of Udvada. Though I don't see why the crowds would have any trouble with us doing it out in the open . . . seeing as they're always kicking up such a fuss about the need to produce more Parsis. Hey, you're so shy! You're turning red already. Come on, Dr Billimoria. Doesn't your friend Sigmund Freud say that sex is all in human affairs and everything else is a . . . what's the word? Oof, not sunscreen. A *smokescreen*?'

'Yes. But Freud never came to India. Here, I think, we choose food over sex any day.'

'You're so funny. Don't tell me your ex-wife didn't appreciate the bits of you hidden from the rest of the world. You know, you're quite a big size. Definitely in the top five percentile. Didn't she like that?'

'Uh, she . . . we didn't chat like that . . .'

'If she didn't, she was a fool. Do you still have a picture of her in your wallet?'

'No, I never did. Why do you ask?'

'Just wanted to see what she looked like.'

Uncle Sheriyar appeared again, whirling my key ring around

his forefinger like Arjuna used to spin his sudarshan-chakra in the Mahabharata television series, and said, 'Thanks, young man. Let's go.' And, winking at me, he told Zahra in Gujarati, 'It's a really nice place. At least twelve crores going by today's rates. You've found a nice, plump goose, kiddo. And in just ten days in Bombay.'

'Oh Uncle, you're so shameless! Look, you're embarrassing Dr Billimoria with your street language. He's not that sort of man, you know. He's cultured, civilized. A gentleman.'

'What do you mean, not that sort of man? There's only one kind of man, else he's not a man at all.'

'Uncle, you've got to thank your lucky stars that you were young when you were and that Auntie somehow fell in love with you . . . because, with your attitude, any girl in the twenty-first century would run *miles* from you.'

'Poof! I wish I'd been born in the twenty-first century. It's the perfect century for me. When I went to America last year for three weeks, I joined a salsa class, and all the women became friends with me on Facebook, and now they want to come and see me in Bombay. I tell them that I'd love that, but the only thing is that your Auntie won't exactly be thrilled.'

'Where *is* Auntie?' I asked as I started Zelda, sensing that only one person could rein in this most deceptively macho of Parsis.

'Auntie has a cousin visiting from Iran, and they're spending some time together, so she couldn't make it,' explained Zahra.

As we hit the main road, a long arm came out from the back seat and tooted Zelda's horn, and Uncle's voice boomed in my ear, 'Udvada, Udvada, the sacred fire of the Iranshah! Let's go with the flow, singing ho, ho, ho, honking and honking, bonking and bonking.'

After a while, I saw that my high spirits (thanks to the last couple of days) couldn't compete with Uncle's—my mood, in fact, was in danger of curdling when brought into contact with his—especially since, when I tried joining him in banter, he kept saying unprintable things that I couldn't even repeat, never having used those words my whole life.

And perhaps I became a bit tetchy, almost a Hemlata to his Farhad, especially since we had Zahra as our audience, and it was clear that she really loved her Uncle. I tried to remind myself that I had Zahra all to myself in San Francisco in a few days, while Uncle would be left behind in Bombay, expending his energies on his bakeries and piggeries and distant Facebook friends. As clouds obscure the sun to the world, so Uncle was passing momentarily between Zahra and me. Uncle could win the battle for Man of the Day, but as long as I did not let him draw me into some indiscretion, I would win the war.

And, besides, this morning, my mind had taken hold of a meditative mood—not exactly like the Buddha under the banyan tree at Bodh Gaya, but close—now that only one evening lay between me and the end of my life in Bombay. I'd woken up at five, before my alarm clock had sounded. In the pearly light of dawn, all the remaining objects in my fairly bare, goodbye-to-Bombay room—chairs, cabinets, vases, lamps—carried a mysterious charge that led me to both memories and resentments. I lay there, blown back and forth across my life, thinking of things I wished I'd said but now it was too late; watching a parade of spirits pass by, including those of my late parents; wishing I hadn't allowed Anna to exercise such power of definition of what my faults were. Doubts came seeping through my grand plans . . . because when all was said and done, my Bombay life was real and my American one still a heap of wishes and desires. And I was grateful for the security of Zahra in San Francisco.

'There's a McDonald's drive-in coming up ahead in a minute or two,' boomed Uncle. 'Let's stop there a moment for a pee and a cold coffee. It'll wake me up. I'm feeling a bit short on energy today.'

'Yes, I was kind of thinking you're not your usual self,' said Zahra. 'But it's fine. You mustn't worry about it. It happens to me too some days.'

'Does it happen to you, too?' Uncle asked me.

'Uh, I feel fine actually.'

'That's good. You'll need all your energy to keep pace with this girl here. I'm warning you from before only.'

'I'm sure I will. That's the McDonald's right here, yes?'

'Of course. How many of them can there be?' As I cut to the left, Uncle added, 'Actually, there's also another reason I want to stop. One of the girls who works here is really cute. She likes me, too. Maybe she's on duty this morning.'

'Oh Uncle, you're such a Casanova! I knew there was something fishy about all of this.'

'Wait, wait, there's also a fourth reason. Next to the drive-in, there's an emu farm. For more than a year now, on my Udvada trips, I've been keeping an eye on the baby birds, just to see how fast they grow. Pigs aren't doing so well these days. Apparently, emus are going to be the next big thing in meat. And there's nothing in the holy books about not eating emus either, the way there is with pigs.'

'Yes, emus weren't around when all these rules were being written, while pigs were probably rolling in the mud right before the eyes of those to whom the revelation appeared at the top of a mountain—or in a haze of hash,' I said wittily.

'Uncle, what a character you are! Keeping an eye on the emus, for heaven's sake!'

Uncle chortled, captivated by the force of his own reflections—and indeed, reflection, for he was combing his hair using my rear-view mirror. 'There are three of them. I've given them all names. Cyrus, Aspi and Benaifar. You'll see them in a minute.'

I wondered what the most unFarhadian experience of the week had been out of a bouquet of many: finding myself in bed with Zahra; or being locked up by Hemlata; or waking up to the shrieks of Hemlata's mother; or standing now, just off the Mumbai-Ahmedabad Highway, drinking cold coffee and watching a bunch of disgruntled emus saunter across a large, bare, grain-strewn enclosure, while Uncle Sheriyar told us all about fat and protein content in emu meat, the growth cycle of the birds, the average production cost of a kilo of emu as compared to chicken, and the PR work that would have to be done if emus were to become 'the next chicken' by the year 2020. Finally, even Zahra grew weary of the birds and said that it was hot and we should get back on the road.

'Sure, sure,' said Uncle Sheriyar. He pointed a ringed forefinger at me. 'Oye, Doctor, coming for a pee?'

'Uh . . . okay.'

We trooped over to the urinals, where we found numerous other specimens of Indian masculinity relieving themselves and cackling to one another across the stalls about cocks and cunts—a habit that has always disgusted me. The only places free were adjacent to one another. We each took one, fiddled with our trousers and, to use a Sheriyarian phrase, went with the flow. How susceptible the human mind is to the language and world view of another!

'So?' said Uncle Sheriyar in a meaningful way, looking at me over the granite partition.

'So, what?'

'Do you want to marry her or not?'

'Marry who? Zahra? But Uncle, we've just got to know each other this week.'

'When I was young, people got to know each other *after* they'd gotten married. In such matters, son, faith counts for everything, doubt counts for nothing. Don't waste any time. She's quite a catch, I'm telling you, not that I need to, as any man can see that for himself, else he's not a man but a mouse. And to tell you the truth, there's not a lot of women who are free at her age and yours. If you delay, bawa, someone else will pop the question first, and you'll have to settle for some peroxide blonde with two children, four parrots and a mortgage.'

'I'm sure you're right. But I still haven't moved to San Francisco, and it also depends on what Zahra wants and what her own plans are . . .'

'All that's beside the point. Women make new plans every day of their lives. That's how they stay young—because they surprise themselves each morning. With them, it's very simple. You've got to get them to a corner and ask, "So, yes or no? Coming with me or no?" They need to be led, else they get all confused, and then they send that confusion right back at you. Then you get confused, too, and decide to call it "respect".'

'These are very interesting ideas. But . . . I'm sure there are many different ways to reach the same goal, and what works in your view, Uncle, might not work for me.'

'You could be right. There are all sorts of newfangled theories about romance these days, which weren't there back when I did my best work. We're living in the fourteenth century and the twenty-first, all at the same time. But theories are one thing, the truth about men and women is another. All I'm saying is, you're getting a second chance in life for free, you've already done half the work in a few days, so why not finish off the job? Or are you just after a tumble in the hay, and then in America its blondes and redheads?'

'I really don't think we know each other well enough to be discussing matters in this way.'

'Okay, okay, enough of all this girl stuff. It's a holiday, let's be gay.'

'Let's be gay,' I agreed.

'Shall I drive?' asked Uncle Sheriyar on the way to the car. 'We'll get there faster.'

'If you don't mind, I'll continue.'

'Okay, hero,' said Uncle and threw himself with a resigned air into the back seat. 'Mmm! My God, how do women always manage to smell so wonderful? God was in a good mood when he created woman. Kiddo, listen, it's decided. The next time you come to India, you'll find me in the emu business. There's a charisma in these birds that pigs just don't have, no matter how much they wiggle their snouts and go oink-oink. Separately, I'm also wondering if they can be made to fight. Like cock fights. Imagine a big crowd coming together in Marine Drive or Azad Maidan for the match between Sheriyar Irani's big emu and Amitabh Bachchan's big emu!'

'Oh Uncle, it's such a historic day, the 800th anniversary of our arrival in India after we faced so much persecution in Iran, and we're going to such a big bash, and all you can think about is emus. What will Dr Billimoria think of our family?'

'What? 800th anniversary?' exclaimed Uncle. 'Silly child, what world are you living in? You've just chopped a few hundred years off our history. Darling, this is the *1,290th* salgireh of the arrival of us Zoroastrians in India, God be praised.'

'Oh, how silly of me! My hairstylist said it was 800, and I believed her. Next, I'll be saying I'm twenty years old. Isn't time strange, Uncle? Here, in our own world, we miss a human being by a moment and our lives take a different turn,' Zahra looked at me meaningfully, 'but back in those far places, you can miss the mark by 500 years, and no one says a thing. History's just a story, that's what it is, I've realized.'

'Yes, 1,290 years is how long the sacred fire of the Iranshah has been burning in the great temple of Udvada,' I chimed in, trying to keep my end up.

'What, is that what you think?' said Uncle. 'Bawa, what kind of Parsi are you? The sacred fire hasn't been at Udvada for longer than a couple of hundred years. Do you think we had it easy . . . just setting up a sacred fire at the first nice spot we found in this new country and then putting up our feet for the rest of time? That's the Parsis of today, engineering their own extinction, refusing to marry within their community, or to produce two children a pair if they do. The earlier lot, the founding fathers, the keepers of the flame, were different. Whenever they sensed danger, they ran for their lives, and everywhere they took the sacred fire with them. First Sanjan, then the Bahrot caves, then the Vansda forests, then to Navsari in the fifteenth century, then to Surat for a bit, then back to Navsari, then out to Valsad. And then, *fi-nally*, the fire was brought to Udvada in 1742, and there it's stayed for nearly two hundred and seventy years now. If I live to see the 300th salgireh of the sacred flame at Udvada in 2042, I'll believe I'm specially blessed by God. Know your history, children, know your history. Without history, man is but a condom, unrolled on to someone else's pole, but with it, he's the real thing, all swollen with pride, with energy, with willpower.'

'Oh Uncle, you say such wonderful and such filthy things at the same time.'

'What's filthy about sex? Man's generative power is to the secular world what the sacred fire is to religion. The ink of humanity comes from man, kiddo. A woman may bear a child, but she's the postman, not the letter-writer. You, Farhad! Tell me, is there anything filthy about what I said about man and history?'

'No . . . not at all.'

'Then repeat it three times, saying "wee willie winkie" in the middle each time.'

Zahra burst into laughter and said, 'I forbid you to horse around with my boyfriend like that.'

'Honk honk, then bonk bonk, all the way to Udvada, toodle-oo!' Uncle responded, leaning across and tooting my horn a couple of times.

'Why do I feel I'm lower than the two of you?' said Zahra.

'Darling, don't take my words to heart,' said Uncle. 'A woman can easily be the equal of man if she wants. Remember, I said *can be*, not *is*.'

'I don't mean it that way, Uncle. I mean for real. This side of the car is sinking. Guys, we have a flat tyre!'

'What? No!' I groaned.

'I don't feel a flat at all,' said Uncle.

'Farhad, just pull over. Uncle, will you be a sweetie-pie and hop out and check the tyre beneath me?'

'Sure thing. But if there's nothing wrong with it, you have to buy me an ice cream in Udvada for all the trouble, or send me a girl from San Francisco.'

Uncle jumped out of the car, then his head disappeared beneath Zahra's window.

'Farhad!' whispered Zahra, squeezing my hand. 'I'm sorry if he's troubling you. Is he?'

'Well . . . a bit,' I conceded, to the beat of Uncle vigorously kicking Zelda's tyre. 'But it's okay.'

'I'm sorry I brought him along. But he doesn't mean any harm at the end of the day. He's just high-spirited and maybe a bit competitive. And we won't have him around for much longer. At Udvada, he'll join his old pals, and one of them will probably take him home. Soon, it'll be just the two of us again, and I know we're going to have *so much fun*.'

The sun came out above my head, and I said, 'Okay, no worries. I'm cool with it.'

Uncle opened the back door again and announced, 'I knew it. It's a false pregnancy. The party can go on without fear . . . or speed. Driving so slowly and stopping every five minutes, it's a wonder we're not going backwards towards Bombay as the world turns on its axis. Only one force is responsible for this miracle, and that's the sacred fire of the Iranshah.'

'I'm looking forward to visiting the fire temple after so many years, sure,' said Zahra. 'But Uncle, I must tell you, what I'm looking forward to *most* is the chief speaker at today's function.'

'And who might that be?' Uncle and I spoke at the same time, only that Uncle's voice insinuated that it should've been him.

'Narendra Modi! It said so in the paper this morning.'

Uncle said, 'What! Doomsday is upon us. How could they have invited a non-Parsi to lead the function?'

'Oh Uncle, don't be so narrow-minded. He's the chief minister of this state, after all. And, let's not forget, one of the most powerful men in this country.'

'He's also a man who doesn't exactly have the best record when it comes to minorities, wouldn't you say?' I asked, with the delicacy that is my hallmark.

From the back seat, Uncle ventured, 'I wouldn't trust him with a single emu of mine. Because he's someone who wants all birds to be chickens.'

'Oh Uncle, Farhad, are you referring to those riots and stuff from ten years ago? Guys, how long can we be stuck in the past?' asked Zahra. 'If crazy people run around, intent on killing one another, how's a single man to stop them without killing a few as well? Let's look at the big picture, I say. Roads, electricity, infrastructure, jobs, business development, no corruption—these aren't things for majorities and minorities, they're the tide that lifts all the toads . . . or boats or whatever it is. *This* should be our focus. Instead, if we keep arguing and harping about the past, when will we ever get anything done? Here's what I think: what this country needs for a while is a dictator . . . then we can go back to being a democracy again. And I've been doing a lot of reading up on this man. Modi is the one for the future, there's no question about it. Gujarat is too small for him. Next stop, India.'

'I don't know what it is with you girls,' sighed Uncle. 'You're all in love with him. It's time that the vote for women was revoked.'

'What for? We women like a man who knows what he wants and sets out to get it. In fact, I might have some business with Mr Modi, just like you do with your emus.'

'What, *my* niece and *Modi* as business partners? What could you possibly have in common, baby?'

'Well . . . take a guess if you're so smart.'

'I can't think of anything in common between you and him, except for popularity with the other sex.'

'Oh Uncle, you can do better than that. Farhad?'

'Um . . . I couldn't say.'

'Yoga!'

'Oh.'

'Think about it. Here I am, Zahra Anahita Irani, a few months away from putting all my life's savings into my yoga school. And there he is—the one Indian politician really and publicly into yoga—unlike the rest who never talk about it because they think it has some link to right-wing Hindu politics, when, actually, it's a gift to all humanity. Do you know, a while ago, when Mr Modi had a brainstorming camp for all the bureaucrats in Gujarat, he made them wake up in the morning and do yoga with him? No fussing over whether it was Hindu or non-Hindu, or all that nonsense that makes us live in mental ghettos. And no one was allowed to miss it. They had to either do yoga or go back home . . . and probably miss their next promotion. Someone in my yoga group forwarded me pictures. All those around Mr Modi, poor things, looked like they had concrete in their limbs and would rather be asleep in their beds, but there was the chief minister, wearing a black tracksuit and sneakers and doing all these awesome poses.

'Uncle, if I could just find a way of getting through to him today and telling him about my yoga school in Frisco, maybe, who knows, he'd consider becoming my brand ambassador. After all, he wants to reach out to America, and he must have felt so terrible when the States wouldn't grant him a visa. Even just a personal message from his office would be cool—I'll use it on my website, send it out to the local press, and it'll make for such great PR. I'll be able to sweep up all the Indians in San Francisco . . . and then their friends . . . and then friends of their friends . . . and then the whole world will be at my door. And in turn, maybe we could raise funds for the man. After all, he'll need a pile of cash if he wants to run for prime minister in the next election. See? It's win-win for both of us, which is the first principle of business.'

Zahra's plans for world domination reverberated around Zelda's walls, wowing car and me with an entrepreneurial energy and DIY spirit the likes of which we'd never seen before. I knew that I'd certainly never plotted anything like this to widen the reach of my own practice. Perhaps it was because I came (as did Anna) from a class that was born to privilege and, therefore, to a kind of hauteur. From the time I was born, a place had been waiting for me in Bombay and in the world, and all I had to do was paddle a bit downstream, taking the opportunities laid out for me, and claim my berth. Okay, so psychotherapy had been a somewhat unusual career choice. But my first clients were friends of my family and from the families of those I'd been to school with; I had taken some years to establish myself, to be sure, but it had never occurred to me that I might go under. I was too comfortable to ever need to hustle. People came to me—those I met at dinner parties, weddings, conferences. I never chased them. And perhaps that was why I was so self-conscious about pursuing women in Bombay. I was not a bar of soap; any attempt to peddle myself would be unrefined and contrary to the discreet, sophisticated superiority I projected before my clients within the cool, book-lined, elegantly furnished room in that grand old building in Kemp's Corner—a climate that, being the opposite of Bombay's and more generally India's, allowed for a Western point of view down upon the tropical problems of those worlds.

But now that I was going out West, I could learn something from Zahra's strategic ambition, midlife energy and lack of inhibition, while showing her things she did not know—offering, in other words, a yang to her yin. Together, we could do things that neither of us could manage singly. Visions of adventures under the sun and moon of America and Zahra floated before me, and my blood tingled as I did a daring overtake, bypassing two cars and all of my former life. I longed to have Zahra's weight upon me and her face close to mine, as she narrated her plans while I stroked her back.

'. . . think it's a waste of time, but I'll see who I can get to help you,' I heard Uncle Sheriyar saying. 'Look! Finally we're in Udvada!'

And so we were. 1,290 years after they had first arrived on these shores, seeking refuge, and had settled into the Indian way and then spread their wings in the vast plain of history that lay between that moment and the present, Zoroastrians from India and all around the globe had packed themselves tightly into the streets and slopes of this tiny seaside town. There were cars bumping, jostling and tooting in the temporary parking lot behind the dilapidated villas and the sanatorium; families trooping in clusters towards the rows of tents; and banners that advertised the thousand endeavours into which our Parsi brethren had poured their entrepreneurial, eccentric and charitable hearts. I was glad I had been able to grace this occasion (as my late mother would have put it) before making good my escape from community and country, as the traveller of days past took a dip in the waters of a holy river before leaving his native place for a journey from which he had no assurance of returning. Once again, Zahra's benevolent influence was providing a bridge between my past, present and future. I would have liked to wander with her around the stalls, disappear into the milling crowds, but Uncle Sheriyar, leading the way, announced that the commemoration ceremony had already begun in the main tent . . . and if the Parsis were keeping punctual time (as, on the subcontinent, they had the unique reputation of doing), the chief guest's speech to the assembly had probably commenced.

'If I'd been driving, we'd have got here in time to find some seats. But now we'll probably have to stand.'

'Oh Uncle, don't be in such a hurry always. Let's just relax and enjoy ourselves now that we're here, okay, because isn't that the point of living?'

'When you're a man, you're always thinking of a different point of living. A two- to four-inch point that can become a six- to eight-inch point. Okay, okay, don't get all worked up now. It was just a little joke. Wow, look at how many people are spilling out of the grand shamiana. I think your Mr Modi has begun his speech. Yes, that's his voice for sure. I know it from TV.'

'Oh, let's hurry! Uncle, this is the first political speech I've ever heard live. Farhad, what about you?'

'Ditto.'

'There he is!'

'Yes, that's him.'

'It's so strange to see a famous man in the flesh, isn't it? It's almost a surprise to find out that he's real.'

'Look, kiddo, there are my pals, all gathered together. Let's go stand next to them, and they'll tell us what's happened so far. Who knows, the Vada Dasturji may have just announced the first Parsi mission to the moon, and Mr Modi may have been forced to say he'll pay for it.'

We edged up to the group of stout, elderly Parsi men standing right at the back, their trousers belted up high above their ample backsides, their necks craned to hear the speech. They were prattling into one another's ears in the usual way of the Indian crowd, never able to watch anything in silence for more than a few seconds before trying to share reactions. As a way of silently announcing his arrival, Uncle Sheriyar pinched one buddy, kneed a second right behind the knee, kissed a third one's bald spot and poked the fourth in the ribs with his elbow. They all pantomimed reactions of extreme surprise and alarm on seeing him, then cackled and made room for three of us to fit in.

'Guys, my lovely niece Zahra,' said Uncle in a stage whisper. 'And this is Farhad, the lucky man to whom she has given everything but her heart.'

'Uncle!'

'All right, what's going on? What's our noble warrior with the fifty-six-inch chest saying?'

'Oh, he's doing a fantastic job buttering them all up. They're eating out of his hand. Listen!'

Far away, on a grand stage festooned with banners and populated with blabbers, the familiar figure of the chief minister of Gujarat stood facing the audience in a grey short-sleeved kurta and pyjamas, a cream shawl draped over his shoulders. The booming voice that had captivated and, by all accounts, inflamed millions was declaiming in Gujarati: 'In the whole country, brothers and sisters, is there any community like the Parsis? A community that is always smiling and teaching others to smile, that wants no special privileges from the government, that doesn't even want an election ticket? This shows their love is without preconditions, without expectations—in other words, the purest kind of love. How did the Parsis come to be like this? There must be some great tradition alive in you that makes this possible, isn't it, brothers and sisters? There must be deep-rooted values that shape your disposition. And it is our good fortune that the fruits of these virtues have been showered here, on the blessed soil of Gujarat.'

'He can talk, I'll grant him that,' said Uncle Sheriyar to one of his pals.

'Brothers and sisters,' the chief minister continued, 'some of you have reason to believe that, by agreeing to be here today in your midst in this holy hour of your happiness, I honour you, I pay tribute to your contribution to this state. But I can't bring myself to agree with your line of thinking. After all, I'm a human being, too. Self-interest comes naturally to me. And, in coming here today, self-interest motivates me to seek out . . .'

'Dhansak?' said some wag a few feet away from us.

'. . . the blessings of the SHREEJI PAK IRANSHAH OF UDVADA,' the voice boomed. Wild cheers and whistles broke out all around me. 'I hope that your goodwill will act as the intermediary between your sacred fire and me, and the Shreeji Pak Iranshah will bestow abundant blessings upon me from this day on . . . so I become an immeasurably richer man.'

We huddled closer as more people, drawn by the crowd's applause, pressed in behind us. Uncle Sheriyar broke away and pushed his way forward, repeating the words, 'Make way, make way, every hair on this body is a sword.' As Zahra cut in ahead of me, standing on tiptoe to see better, her hands tying her hair deftly into a knot, my gaze involuntarily slipped away from the figure on whom all eyes were focussed to the one available more or less to me alone. With a sudden sensual arousal generated by the incongruous circumstances of the public occasion in which our feet were planted, conscious of my downcast gaze among so many upraised ones, almost holding my breath, I studied a small patch of skin towards the top of Zahra's back, granted a sudden autonomy and prominence by the black frames of her hair and clothing. It seemed to make a petition that was just as loud and clear as that of Gujarat's chief minister—it asked to be possessed and defended. And it engulfed me with a sense of being alive in the body and in the present moment and the conviction that things would now always be this way. I lifted a forefinger to touch Zahra's neck, when a muscle there suddenly throbbed, as if shy of my approach. The thought dropped into my head, as if from God, via Uncle Sheriyar: if we were married, I would be able to gaze at Zahra like this every day, sometimes piece by piece, sometimes as a whole. A second later, the crowd rippled with more applause, and I heard my excited lover deliver a shrill, piercing whistle.

I left the sensual world of skin and returned to the social world of speech. Mr Modi had warmed to his task. Now he repeatedly wiped his brow with a folded handkerchief, and his hands no longer buttressed his statements with polite chest-level gestures but soared above him as if he was the bright flame of the Iranshah personified. I caught the words 'Yehudi samaj' and was forced to grudgingly accept the intellectual range of this man who, at a forum as parochial as this, could get us Parsis to think about something as distant as Jewish society. Next he'd be getting the crowd to take out a collection for the embattled tribes of the Amazon rainforest or write to Barack Obama offering to broker peace between the Israelis and the Palestinians. I began to see Zahra's point about India—not that I was invested in India any more, but perhaps this gave me the distance required for a detached consideration of the subject. Maybe she was right, and the country needed an ambitious statesman such as Modi for a new time in its history. Back on the glowing train of rhetoric on which all those around me were travelling, I heard the impassioned voice say:

'On thinking about the circumstances under which you first arrived in India, my friends, trying to defend your sacred flame from persecution in your native Persia, I am compelled to compare your community to the Jews.

'How so? For hundreds and thousands of years, the Jewish people wandered around the world, guests everywhere, at home nowhere. With neither land nor friends to call their own, their sole possessions were their religion and their traditions. Round and round the world they wandered, broken up into fragments, preyed upon everywhere, always on the defensive. But throughout history, when one Jew met another somewhere in the world, he'd say to the other, "Next year in Jerusalem."

'Next year in Jerusalem, my friends, next year in Jerusalem! For 2,500 years, with the fire of the believing heart, next year in Jerusalem! Here the world was trying to extinguish the very spark of life beating in their hearts, but their minds soared far above, in a different realm, thinking of the homeland owed to their faith. And finally, in the twentieth century, we have seen the Jews have been able to realize their dream of possessing Jerusalem.'

The crowd applauded politely.

'And today, I must confess something that I have never spoken about before. I dream of the day when you Parsis will come together and, possessed by the spirit of your sacred fire, carry its light back to Iran. Aim for Iran, I say to you on this historic day, my friends, aim for Iran! The state of Gujarat and the people of Gujarat are always with you.'

Up in the front rows, there was even wilder applause, and some people jumped up and began to shout, 'Iran, Iran'.

Close to us, I heard a voice bellow like a clap of thunder, 'So he wants to pack us back to Iran and get rid of us over here? I'll take a good lunch over this speech any day!' It was Uncle Sheriyar. 'Come, my friends, let's vote with our feet,' he instructed, turning back towards us, red with anger. 'Let's not lend our ears to any more of this when there's such fantastic dhansak, patra ni machchi, jardaloo boti and caramel custard waiting for us outside.'

'Uncle, Uncle, please calm down,' cried Zahra, making her way through the crowds.

'What calm down? You calm up!' roared Uncle with perfectly lucid incoherence. 'Who here wants to migrate back to Iran and face a new holocaust? Raise your hands. I'll pay for your tickets. Let's all either head to Iran right away or head to lunch, but let's not stand here any more humouring this.'

Disconcerted, everyone began to mumble and shake their heads, before Uncle's friends took up his refrain, joking and cackling and dissolving the tension. Between them, they guided a hundred or so people out of the shamiana and towards the lunch tent. As we made our exit, Uncle Sheriyar turned back and cried out, 'Let's take Gujarat first! Then we'll head to Iran!'

After a sumptuous lunch, we split up. One of Uncle Sheriyar's grizzled friends had a sister who was married into a diamond trader's family in Surat, and her husband's brother-in-law was a part of Narendra Modi's entourage. A meeting had been hastily fixed, in the Indian way, via this insider, with pleas that he take the idea of yoga in San Francisco all the way to Modi in Udvada.

Zahra was thrilled and spent ten minutes touching up her make-up and doing her hair. As I had nothing to do with this project, I said I would, meanwhile, take a goodbye-my-country walk around the fire temple and catch up with her when she was done. I feared that Uncle Sheriyar would come with me and test me at every corner in his unique high-and-low manner—with questions about religion, history and my intentions regarding Zahra interspersed with ribaldry and scatological razzle-dazzle. But it turned out that, after all that fulmination about the speech, he wanted to accompany Zahra since he wished to ask the member of Modi's staff 'a certain important question' which he couldn't reveal until he met him.

I stood leaning against a tree trunk, as Zahra and Uncle Sheriyar headed off towards the tent specially reserved for the chief minister's retinue. Hundreds of Parsis were happily milling around me, drunk on food, religion, race-pride and family. My ears isolated this or that voice out of the general commotion and wove them into a never-ending sentence of feelings and desires that encompassed all the stages of life: 'enlightenment . . . destination . . . apricot . . . matrimonial . . . susu . . . ice cream . . .' It was a verbal carousel that threw off sparks, bright with the diversity and majesty of humanity—a truth that, for a few tired years, I had lost the knack of perceiving. If I could see it now, though, it meant that I was growing back into the world.

The largest streams of people were headed in and out of the Atash Behram temple. After its recent renovation, the great rippling white house of our faith was in a much better state than when I'd last come here in 2004 with Anna. I joined the crowd and let myself get bumped down the festive bloodstream. Inside the temple, history passed into me through the cool stones under my bare feet. I contemplated the echoes of voices, the solidity of the walls, the handkerchiefs on heads, and whether there was something intrinsically sacred about places or if collective beliefs and practices and histories made them so, and if the latter was the case, whether it was fair to call religion an illusion.

It was hard to work everything out when one was right in the middle of what was going on. Would I have a wife the next time my face was seen on these premises? Children? I didn't know. But what made me especially grateful was that life had become new not out of my own desperate making—as the Indian poor, for instance, succeed in making life palatable, no matter how terribly they suffer—but almost of its own accord. In that sense I was truly one of the faithful gathered here this afternoon, conscious of the mystery at the heart of life and the limits of human will when compared to the capricious plenitude of life itself, generating such surprising and wonderful patterns that these couldn't but be perceived as destiny.

I left my fellow Parsis behind and wandered out into the small, desolate lanes between the fire temple and the sea. Many structures here had fallen in upon themselves; all was decrepit—a sign that no young people lived any more in this tiny backwater and that Udvada would henceforth always be both spiritual centre and ghost town.

A hundred years ago, smoke would have been streaming from these hearths, clothes hanging from lines on the balconies, kites flying from the rooftops. But time had swept everything away. Who had been here before me, in the same state of expanded awareness? I felt I would give anything to swim in those temporal deeps. Perhaps an anonymous mason in the eighteenth century had decided to leave an impression of his thumb up on a high wall where no one would ever come across it. Or a woman had stowed a letter from a lover in a hole in a tree trunk the week before she was to be married and sent away, not knowing if she would ever be able to recover it again. Or a Billimoria had been here, his prayer book in one pocket, his account book in the other, trying to suss out a new bit of business that rippled across the centuries until it coalesced into my life in Bombay.

Would another man, perhaps, newly in love and newly human again, turn up here in one of the centuries that lay ahead—for, say, the fifteen hundredth anniversary of the Iranshah—and find a trace of me? Or would technology have changed human nature so much in that span of time that everything we thought of as experience, time, memory, would have altered beyond recognition? I looked up and became faintly dizzy at the sight of seagulls wheeling all the way from the town down to the coastline, no doubt agitated by the sudden invasion of their quiet world. For a second I doubted if Zahra, all my recent adventures in Bombay, even Hemlata, were for real. I fished out my mobile phone to read again the messages from Zahra over the last few days. There were two new texts, both from the same unknown number.

The first: *All ok here. Still waiting to meet the big man. Don't think it's going to work out, but that's what bizness is like. Health, happiness and propserity to you & all other Parsis on this ospicious day. Sheriyar.*

And then: *Sorry if I did anything to upset u. Don't take my words to heart. You will soon be the happiest Man in the Globe.*

I was touched that Uncle was making an effort to connect, and sent him a thank you note in return. He wasn't such a bad fellow—he seemed to be on my side, even if on his own terms.

I picked up a smooth stone and sent it hurtling all the way down into the water; I lost it momentarily in the glint of sunlight upon the waves, and then it appeared again just before it was swallowed up by the sea. Not so much thinking as being thought by the world, I registered something was saying that I didn't need a breather from life any more; that I was willing to work, build, connect, strive as soon as I got to the New World; that I was ready to write all the other chapters of the story that had commenced this week in Bombay.

I sat down on a boulder. Poetic impulses flooded me. It was almost certain there had never been anything in the life of an Indian man like the clouds of the last three days—light but majestic cargo that I would now be taking with me to San Francisco. Almost weeping with gratitude for the fact of a masculine and a feminine element pervading the world (even the land and the sea)—both principles always playing the dance of attraction and withdrawal, never fully explainable or learnable, keeping the universe going and all the beings in it, too—I began to dream about lying with Zahra somewhere in this landscape.

A text message beeped me out of my reverie: *Farhad! Where are you? Chasing lovely ladies around Udvada? If not otherwise occupied, come right away to Rm No 7 at the Globe Hotel. Someone important wants to meet you.*

I just couldn't *believe* Zahra's derring-do! Not only had she, contrary to Uncle Sheriyar's assessment, managed to get through to Narendra Modi, she had even made such a big impression on him that he was willing to meet her friends and associates. It wasn't clear what business proposal or partnership *I* had to offer Mr Modi, but it would certainly be wonderful to meet such a famous person one-on-one. And, who knew, perhaps after Zahra had told him about me, he had revealed to her he had some problem he wanted to discuss confidentially. After all, after the riots of 2002, human-rights activists had given him sleepless nights for over a decade. I looked in my wallet, but, of course, I didn't have any cards left. I had thrown away the last batch into the dustbin the day I had left my office for the last time! Well, at the very least, this meant that Zahra had got ahead with her own plans for a San Francisco life linked back to India, and if we were going to work together, those would be my plans, too.

I dusted myself off and headed back into the town at a hasty clip, stopping only for a few seconds at a water tap to wash my face. No wonder Uncle Sheriyar hadn't been able to book a room at the Globe—the best hotel in town would have been entirely booked by the VIP retinue! As I entered the premises of the hotel, still very much the same as when I'd stayed here with my parents in my summer vacations in the 1980s, I burst out laughing. The great feast organized by the flag-bearers of the faith only a couple of hours ago had clearly not been enough for the laity. More than a hundred people were packed around small tables in the hotel courtyard, noisily chomping cream buns and doughnuts, khari biscuits and nankhatai, and slurping tea and Duke's raspberry soda. One gentleman had clearly packed away some leftovers for a second go and was now delicately nibbling a leg of chicken farcha under a jasmine tree. He saw me staring and gave me a cheerful wave. Ah, the Parsis! Either they didn't know that Narendra Modi was right there on the premises or they couldn't care. Even so, I was impressed by the lack of any security cover.

I walked down the corridor and up to the first floor, where I found Room No. 7 and knocked. There was no answer, but the door was slightly ajar. I pushed it open and went in. The large room, sparsely furnished and slightly threadbare in the Globe way, was empty and dark. Only a sliver of light filtered in through the blinds.

'Hello,' I said confused. 'Are you here?'

At the sound of my voice, shrill, lawless laughter burst out from a dark corner, and I heard Zahra say in a deep faux-male voice, 'Next week . . . next week in San Francisco.' I saw her slim figure emerge from behind a four-poster bed and sashay slinkily towards me.

'What's going on?' I burbled. 'Where's everyone else?'

'Why, sweetie, who would you rather meet?'

'No, I . . . I thought . . .'

'I said someone important wants to meet you. Am I not important to you?'

Zahra's hands reached up for my face and drew me down, then her lips engaged mine in a long kiss. I caught the drift of the day and laughed in a way I did not recognize. This thrilled me almost as much as the sight, sound and scent of Zahra. I said, 'I thought you mentioned all the rooms here were booked.'

'Uncle Sheriyar had booked one of them. He said he only wanted to let us have it after he had checked you out and if you passed. Darling, you've made it.'

'Ha! I've never had any trouble impressing people.'

'Well, don't you think you should try and impress me now? This might be the only chance all our lives to make love in Udvada . . .'

'Stolen the thought off the tip of my tongue!'

I whisked Zahra off the floor and carried her towards the bed. I'd never sensed such power, such receptivity, such sexual reach course through me. I could feel myself both holding Zahra and hovering above us; making memories with a third eye even as I lived in the moment down below with my first two. I wondered why I had no previous recollection of such transcendence and saw how much there was still left to learn in this realm of mystery and self-forgetting. I had thus far barely scratched the surface of erotic life. Even the last two times I'd made love to Zahra, I'd focussed on my own body, nervous about my performance, as though appearing for an examination, rather than enjoying the totality of the experience, the vastness of the connection— something she appeared to know instinctively. Ahead of me, it seemed, lay an end not just to sexual loneliness but the much more profound isolation and discontinuity of human beings, who could not even correctly put their finger on what they were seeking, so far was the truth of their condition from the horizon of their perception.

I hoped, as I undid the cord of Zahra's salwar and watched it fall around her feet, then went down on my knees to reach behind her kameez, that I'd remember these higher intuitions later when there was no longer such a powerful physical stimulus to provoke them; I heard her groan with pleasure as I sucked on her sex and ran my fingers over her cool, taut buttocks. She pushed my face harder into her with her hands and cried out. I laughed at how fast I'd got her right to the edge of ecstasy, then rose up and took her face in my hands and kissed her gently and sensually.

As she turned her face away, I deciphered how, within the larger frame of communion, distance could be just as arousing as engagement. I resolved I'd mirror her sudden withdrawal when she moved towards me next. As she unbuckled my trousers, I lifted her up again, and her legs locked powerfully around my waist. I lowered us down on to a chair and used my teeth to ease her kameez off her shapely shoulder, even as her lips pushed away the fabric of my shirt and reached for the same place on my body—her sighs revealing that the scent of my being was as pleasing to her as hers was to me.

I pushed her back and swung her legs, which were astride me, around on her axis so that she was now sideways against my body like a mermaid, and nuzzled her neck as I slowly undid the hooks along her back, making a larger vee of exposed skin with each metallic spasm. I felt a sense of déjà vu as I saw her running her lips around my left clavicle in a way that was not only almost unbearably pleasurable but also seemed to be giving her the same amount of pleasure, which I let myself witness by drawing her hair back from her face.

Here was a microscopic universe, one where every single grain of her eyeliner was visible, and there was something especially striking about the tiny flecks that had strayed away from the rest and now glistened just above her delicate cheekbones. Zahra's kameez fell to her waist. She grasped my penis, a mysteriously large appendage that filled me, to whom it belonged, with as much wonder as the other spectator, and levered herself down upon it inch by inch, her eyelashes flapping like the wings of a bird in a cage. I wanted to enter her so deeply and fully that we were not so much one as none. I stood up again and carried her over to the sofa, impaled pleasurably on my erection, set her down and turned her around, then grasped her hips and entered her slowly from behind. My face buried in Zahra's hair, I moved in and out of her with exquisite slowness, just short of being completely still, turning away whenever she looked back at me.

And then something happened to me that I had never before experienced in the sexual act. It felt as if I was not myself but *Zahra*, pulsating to a beautiful pain and a gentle violence as I was penetrated. I was both myself and the other, both being and non-being, both awareness and oblivion, both the fruit and the vine . . .

'Farhad, stop! Stop it right now!'

'Huh?'

'Just cut it out!'

'Wha . . . am I hurting you?'

'Actually, you're not hurting me enough!' said Zahra, turning around and putting her hands on my shoulders. 'There's a reason that you're a man and I'm a woman, darling. Can't you see, behaving so sweet and tender, you're just *depolarizing* the sexual tension between us.'

'I am?'

'You are. I don't want all this, darling. At least, not all the time. Sometimes, I need you to really *do* me! Just fuck my brains out. Can you manage that?'

Could I manage that? I was determined to please. As I gravely followed Zahra's instructions, becoming smaller and smaller the more I thrashed, a strange new thought came to me.

Since Zahra was Life, and we had to keep our relationship properly polarized, what she really wanted to do was kill me.

I Am in Bombay/Pages from
Bhagaban Bhai's Diary

SOMEWHERE IN BOMBAY—beneath a manhole on a busy street or between the rocks by the sea—there is a chute down which go all the words said by someone but heard by no one. Every day, a flood of words comes pouring through—the last phrase of a suicide attempt before the chair is kicked away, the pleas of spurned lovers before they realize that the other side has already cut the call, the ramblings of old people to those who know what they are going to say, the names or greetings uttered by those who come home and find no one there, the charges of madmen as they wander ablaze and inward, the words of rage or pain uttered in crowded rooms where all have learnt how to look away so that each may have some peace, the piping of children who peddle magazines to closed windows at traffic signals, the curses of eunuchs who hustle and wiggle for a rupee, the refrains of travelling salesmen and performing showmen, the sounds of women consoling themselves, even as they realize that they are well and truly trapped and there will never be an escape, the explanations and protests of those who have just been dismissed from their jobs, the mumbles of kids huddled under flyovers and by the sides of train tracks, smoking pot or sniffing glue, the whimpers of babies left all alone when their mothers go to work or to meet a lover, the cries of cripples who fall on the streets, the whispers of the blind as they walk by themselves in the midst of hundreds, the expositions of schoolteachers as their students pass messages under their desks or play games on their mobile phones, and the pain and panic of souls that have passed away, far from home, in Bombay, and do not know their way back.

In my free hours, which should not be many—but, because I do not sleep at night, are so—I wander, wander around the crowded and cloudy city. Two things in Bombay never sleep: Bombay and me.

June 8: Hot and humid in Bombay. They say that the rains always begin in the second week of June, but this year they are not on time, as I myself could not be in returning to recover my mother from the city where she suffered so much.

Ah, Time—both the deep time of history, drifting lazily like clouds noticed by none, and the small time that is man's life and its many phases like those of the moon.

Time, history, the ego, free will, destiny, society . . . new syntheses, new combinations. When I contemplate these profound things, applying them to present-day facts and to historical situations, passing ideas through people and people through ideas, there's a crackle of lightning across my mind, like that across the wide open sky in Tininadi during the monsoons, when all of nature radiates an ineffable feeling, fragrance and fertility, like that of a beautiful woman at the peak of her pride and desirability.

To the people of the Cloud Mountain, Cloudmaker is the pleasure-loving, puff-puffing God that the Hindus and the Company want to take away from them. From my position, however, and to my mind, it seems like Cloudmaker could, from the struggle we are waging right now, emerge as the one God that the Hindu faith, with all its emphasis on cyclical time, has never had: a God of History. Not only must we protect His realm in Tininadi, we would do well to build a temple for Him in Bhubaneswar and make our faith a less self-absorbed one, in tune with history—this, not just for our own good but for future generations, the India of 500 years from today.

Bapa continues to remain very silent like a statue—but

here's the statue of a philosopher. Whether it is shock, whether it is detachment, whether it is (why should one rule it out?) peace, whether it is the forgetfulness of a mind that is no longer evenly lit by memory (like the world during the monsoons when the sun breaks through a gap in the clouds), I do not know. It's not even the sort of question one can ask the old man directly. He may reply with some story about Sage Markandeya or a verse from the Puranas or even some observation about Cloudmaker! Yesterday, as he was drinking milk, he slurped the top layer and suddenly said, 'It's like licking the cream off the tops of clouds.'

The good thing is that Sarita is proving to be a reliable maid, and he is happy to eat what she cooks (so am I). And nothing is ever missing from my desk or from Bapa's things, although it seems to me sometimes that you could steal Bapa himself and he would not be aware of any change in his environment. In fact, after hearing one of his discourses, the kidnapper would probably bring him back the very next day.

When I left Eeja and Ooi, ran away—I don't remember what happened next. I found myself at Borivali station—I jumped on the first train I saw. I did not know where I was going. Ooi, dead, dead. Eeja, alive— Ooi, dead.

Slowly, the city fell away, and some time later, still shivering from the shock of that scene, I saw to my right, steeply rising into the sky, this magnificent mountain, and atop it this temple. Ooi, dead, dead. No one had cared to stay up with Her, to tell Her stories to keep Her alive for those final hours till her son came. I sang for Her, too, the Prayer for the Dead of the Cloud people, howling, beating my chest, but She was stern and remained dead. I jumped off at the next station, Virar, and walked towards the mountain, weeping. When I came to its foot, I saw the winding stairway to the temple—more than three thousand steps, someone said—and the hundreds of people making the pilgrimage uphill. And grateful for the peaceful, hospitable company of so many strangers, I walked up, up, up with them, Ooi dead, Ooi dead, rising higher and higher above Bombay till I was three thousand steps high, almost in the clouds. From there, I could see the distant marshes and mangrove swamps, behind them the sea, down below the roads and settlements of Virar, not very Bombaylike but still a part of Bombay, and in front of me the temple of Jivdani. Ooi dead, dead.

Jiv: life. Daan: donation or benediction. Jivdani: the Goddess who grants life to the unborn, new life to the sick and the ailing. After my days with Eeja and Ooi, here was a world both new and familiar. It must have been willed by Jagannath or by Cloudmaker or by Jivdani Herself that I come here.

As ants walk up the flanks of some great beast, I take old people up and down the side of the great mountain, from dawn every day till two in the afternoon, towards Goddess Jivdani, and then back down again.

A mother, I have come to think, is like the sun. One takes it for granted that both will always rise, always rule, always animate the world with light and energy. And gradually, one stops noticing them: one sees only the rays, the things that come to life because of the sun, not the sun itself. One never believes the sun can vanish. Then, one morning, it does . . . or will.

For thousands of years, a people tucked away in a corner of the world make their own strange and beautiful religion around clouds and a mountain and never feel that the mountain can vanish. Then, one day . . .

I feel terrible now that I failed to give her the one thing she wanted above all—a daughter-in-law—so she could rest assured that there'd be someone to take care of me and, indeed, of Bapa.

Everybody is expecting me to wear a dhoti-kurta—whether in khadi or in raw silk—to the swearing-in ceremony. I think I will shock them all by wearing a suit and a tie to stand out in the assembly and, thereby, emphasize the individuality of my message and my plan for a new, rising, egalitarian Odisha.

Jivdani's shrine is as dark as night in Tininadi, but cool, fragrant, peaceful, old. People queue for hours for the chance to look into Her eyes. No one who wants to work in Her name is turned away either, which I think is one of the wonderful things about the world of the Hindus. There is always room for one more.

The first time, it exhausted me to climb all the way to the top. In fact, my legs ached for the next five or six days. But, astonishingly, many old people had managed to make it to the summit, moved by love and devotion for the Goddess. They stopped at every landing on the way to catch their breath and to sit down for a minute or two, sometimes asking their family members to go on ahead.

Even so, as much as their souls may desire it, some people just cannot climb all the way up. That is why, some years ago, the temple trust built a pulley-operated lift, seating six, which goes up the side of the mountain, from the foot to the very top. The aged and the infirm can take this if they wish.

The mountain, so similar to my mountain in Tininadi, spoke to me through the eyes of the Goddess and asked me to lay myself at Her feet. After I had served for a few days at the shoe collection counter, I was asked by the one-eyed man—perhaps it was the Goddess at work, reading my heartwish—if I would become the lift operator. I agreed.

I love my moving job and the many views of the mountain—of the top from the bottom, of the bottom from the top, of the middle from the middle, of the sky from the stairs, of the stairs from the sky. I know where the ground lifts and where it dips, whenever a new flower blooms or a birdling is born in a nest or a mongoose has burrowed a hole. Under the white clouds of late summer, butterflies and blossoms thrive.

But what I like best is hearing the old people talk, and taking their blessings when they leave the lift at the summit or the base.

June 14: Today, once again, I left Bapa in the hands of Sarita and flew to Bombay in the morning to look for Rabi—my fifth trip in two months. I thought I'd spend the day there and return by the late flight to Bhubaneswar.

Madhuri was nowhere to be seen when I boarded the flight. At once, my heart fell. Truly, when one loves with the force and simplicity of a child, one also suffers in the same fashion when one cannot have one what wants, right here, right now! Had I got her schedule wrong? I don't think so. Anyway, there was no way to deboard as my luggage had already been checked in. Thankfully I had made an appointment with the film-maker Manohar Rajguru for a meeting in his office in Chembur. I first took a taxi to his place, and we had a good chat (even he did not know anything about the Cloud tribe, he said I was a thinker of great promise).

Then I took another cab all the way to the northern suburbs and stopped at the Borivali police station.

There is still no trace of Rabi. Nor, in fact, can the police spend much time and energy looking for him. This is, after all, a city of more than 20 million people, and the police force has more work to do for mankind than even Indra or Shiva. The police inspector told me that just the list of missing people, lost and never found, in Bombay spans 77,000 names! It is not known whether these people are alive or dead. Their families have mostly given up all hope and have moved on with their lives, consoling themselves with memories and photographs.

After this, I stopped by at the apartment building where my parents and Rabi had all lived for so many weeks. The flat still lies empty. The watchman says that the landlord has found it hard to find a tenant after the news went out that someone had just died here. Some innocent lessee will eventually be found—someone new to Bombay, happy to have any kind of home in the city. The watchman says, as he has said each time I have visited, that he has seen no sign of Rabi. I told him this would be the last time I'd trouble him.

A few months ago, I didn't even know where Borivali was and had not been to Bombay for more than twenty years. Today, I have lost two people in this strange place—my mother and my brother. And only because I wanted my respected father to live, which he did and continues to do, though as another kind of half-man, deprived of the one person who shared most of his memories and could echo his talk, life and world.

In these two months, I have been everywhere in Bombay: the fort of Sewri and the fish docks of Mazagaon, the seafront in Marine Drive and another one in Bandra, the road leading into the sea at Haji Ali and another one up towards the blue-domed shrine not far away, the great temple of Prabhadevi and the quieter one outside Dadar station, the places where women's bodies are bought and sold in Kamathipura and where stocks (I still do not know what these things are, exactly) are bought and sold in Dalal Street, the seething slumtowns of Antop Hill and Dharavi, where things are almost as cheap as they are in Bhubaneswar, and the caves of the ancient Buddhists in Kanheri inside the national park.

To think that I spent such a long time without seeing anything in this city! Without knowing about its shape, its size, its nature. Perhaps we all live inside life the same way.

Everyone calls Bombay a concrete jungle, and some call it Mumbai, and the auto-drivers call it Bambai. It is ugly in the way that old people are ugly, from use and weariness. Even so, to my eye, it seems a place of mountains, rivers, creeks, groves, slopes, age, depths. The more one sees in this city and the more names one knows, the more there is to see and the more names there are to know. The city is always exhausted in one sense, and can never be exhausted in another—which, it strikes me, is an Eeja-like thought and one that He would have enjoyed.

By the time I get back home from my wanderings, it is almost three in the morning. But already the faithful are beginning to gather at the foot of the mountain for the long walk up in the dark. Next to Jivdani's temple, the trustees have built a rest house for people who come from faraway places. Here, they have given me a small room. On the other side of the wall, I can hear the old people fidgeting in their sleep, coughing, sighing, groaning, talking aloud in dreams.

And I can never sleep for fear that one of the faces that smiled at me the day before will, when the morning comes, be frozen in the mask of that sleep from which there is no rising.

June 15: As I was about to head back to Bombay airport, I got a text message. It was from Madhuri. She had had another fight with her husband—soon, ex-husband . . . they're in the middle of a divorce—and he left a bruise on her face, and she had to miss her flight. She said she'd be on the same route the next day. Human and sexual nature being what they are, a woman who is oppressed by one man seeks not just respite from him but a friend in another man. And a man who sees a beautiful woman unhappy with another man yearns to become her saviour. Also, I think she sees that I can never be violent. She senses, perhaps unconsciously, a future with me and my destiny, with not just Bhagaban the film-maker but also with Bhagaban the member of the assembly and the talk of Bhubaneswar's hi-fi society.

I cancelled my flight and decided to go back to Bhubaneswar one night later, when she'd be back at work. I booked myself into the Ibis Hotel next to the airport, had a couple of drinks at the bar (they had a single malt that the barman said was 'peaty', which is how most Odias pronounce 'pity'), then jumped into a taxi and told the driver to take me wherever he pleased. In other words, to imagine that he was the director of a film in Bombay (the people of Bombay only think about films, and through films) and his brief was to show his audience all the facets of the city—but in a silent film. I wanted to be alone with my thoughts, my anxieties, my fears, my joys, in this, the strangest month of the strangest year of my very strange life in the new India.

Eeja must be back in Bhubaneswar now. But is He alive or dead? There is no way of knowing. Has He moved in with Bhai? What does He do during the day? Who takes care of Him? Has His mind come back to Him in Bhubaneswar, or has Ooi's death deranged Him even further?

How I would love to take Him to the top of the mountain to meet the Goddess and watch His face as we rise up!

With Eeja and Ooi—two people always dreaming of returning to Bhubaneswar—I became a new person in Bombay against my will, and learnt so much about faith and love and human nature. Now I must make myself again in this very same place, nowhere else, for it is curiously liberating not to be a tribal carrying the yoke of his cause, only a human being carrying the flag of his self. There is so much to learn from Bombay, as there was once so much to learn in Bhubaneswar from Bhai.

It is as if Cloudmaker Himself whispers all these things in my ear, happy—after thousands of years in quiet places—to float above a great and noisy city.

O my beloved cloudy brother, where are you? Somewhere close—on a street, on a train, in a restaurant, on a field—but concealed by these cacophonous hordes? My helpless and arrogant body may long for the touch of a woman, but my soul longs for nothing more than news from you, to hear once again all your strange and vivid thoughts, to be a young man through you. Are you alive or dead, in Bombay or in Bhubaneswar? What are you thinking, what are your plans? Do you want me to find you? Did I pass you on the street, only I was looking the other way? Or have you left some clue that leads to you but that I cannot read?

Are you angry with me for placing the weight of my mother's death on your innocent shoulders?

Have my parents come between us forever, leaving us doomed to wander restlessly along our separate paths? Will you punish me for a few days, weeks, months, or is to be forever, just like the wall my mother has put between herself and me? Is this your punishment, that I must celebrate my victory—our victory—all alone and hear the curses of your people for taking away their young cloud prince and losing him somewhere in a far corner of the world?

I feel like abandoning all my unbelief and going to a temple somewhere in Bhubaneswar or Bombay to pray for your return.

It is so very different to look at the world from the top of a mountain than to see it from the bottom. I did not know what it was to fall in love with a mountain, until I fell in love with *this* mountain.

In Tininadi, the Cloud Mountain was our joy, our pride, our everything. But although it loved us, it was distant from us, a bit like Eeja. We gazed at it and sang songs in praise of it and Cloudmaker every day of our lives, but we never walked on it or up it except on one or two festival days—for the power of the Cloud Mountain lay in the fact that it was mysterious.

Here in Bombay, however, I go up and down this mountain all day long—on the winding trail of one side by foot, on the straight line of the other by the lift—and there is something now so familiar and affectionate and old-young between us, as there was with Ooi.

The mountain is free for anybody to use, on sacred days and plain ones, for sacred causes and stomach ones. Beggars live and prosper in its nooks, children have climbing competitions from one point to another, small men and women sell godstories and prayer books, incense sticks, medicated oil, snacks, and religious pictures, the jobless come to pass their time, and lovers know that they will not be disturbed or harassed (as they are on the sea-facing streets of Bombay) if they include Goddess Jivdani in their quest. When, by dusk, the crowds begin to thin and retreat, the mountain becomes peaceful, and the most reflective walks can be taken at this time.

A mountain, like life, has only a few flat places. The rest is all uphill or downhill, and man must keep his balance as best as he can.

June 25: I got a large envelope in the post this morning—a Company envelope—signed personally by the CEO. The letter congratulated me on my victory in the tribal regions and said it was a very big achievement both for me and the Cloud people, a sign of the deepening of Indian democracy and a fructification of the vision of the founding fathers at the time of Independence. It urged me, further, not to let the marvellous beliefs and folklore of the Cloud people remain isolated in a distant corner of Odisha, and suggested that if we joined hands, we could bring them all the way to Bhubaneswar, where the people of the capital could take pride in the diversity and exotic colours of Odia civilization.

To this end, the Company proposed to set up a fund to build a Cloud Museum at some well-located central spot in Bhubaneswar. It said that the chief minister had already agreed provisionally to give his permission for such a venture. Some people from the Cloud tribe would be educated and assigned the task of giving talks and demonstrations at the museum, so that they could be suitably empowered and uplifted. The exhibition room of this centre would be a version of a planetarium in which a cloud machine imported from Denmark would blow clouds across the 'sky', and viewers would first be taken through the myths of the Cloud people and then the actual science of clouds as climatic creatures rather than as puffs of the breath of Cloudmaker.

What a laugh Rabi and I would have had to read this fantastic missive, a sign of the Company's great power to mine for not just metals but also myths! Instead, there was no one to share this piece of literature with except the four walls of my room, as talking to either Bapa or Sarita about it would be akin to speaking to a tree and expecting it to answer, 'Ho ho ho, what a piece of work is man.' I put the letter away and thought I would give myself a week to compose a reply.

For the first time, Madhuri and I are meeting by ourselves tomorrow, without anyone to disturb us or any troublesome passengers to be fed while they go gudu-gudu-gudu in their chairs like cranky chickens. As there is no way she can come home, with Bapa here, we have decided to meet at Cafe Coffee Day. I wonder if I should buy her some roses . . . but how would she take them home?

I had to lie to the sarpanch of Tininadi on my trip there on Tuesday and Wednesday, and say that Rabi had stayed on in Bombay to do a short two-month course in English and human resource management so that he could prepare for a future in politics as an empowered, and not just as a symbolic or ceremonial, mascot of his people.

Rabi! I feel sure you are alive, and on a train back to Bhubaneswar right now.

This morning the air was cool, the sky grey, the birds strangely silent. Even the chambers of the temple, the water-spilled paths and the petal-strewn resting places, were dark. Inside the sanctum, I spent a long time looking into the eyes of the Goddess, who sees everything and knows everything, listens patiently to all and says nothing in return, letting each one release his burdens as clouds release rain. It is we, as human beings, who have made Her what She is, have granted Her Her awesome power and pledged to Her our devotion, so that both man and God may not be lonely in this world. The black, sticky slabs of the sanctum and the crumbling steps of the mountain stairway are marked unmistakably by Her touch and radiate Her presence and power. All those who begin the climb far down below find the strength, somehow, to make it to the top, hauled up by Her.

As I left the temple, a rumble sounded close to my ear. I turned my eyes and saw right above me: Cloudmaker!

The dark clouds had come bounding in from the sea, as the goats gallop in one direction at the lash and call of the herdsman, and were swimming in the air all around me, waxing and waning as if to mimic the moon. Somewhere behind them, He laughed and played puff-puff—for the first time, it seemed hard to think of His dark form as sad—moved to tears by His own happiness at having found a new mountain to play around. Soon, He'd be dropping pearls of rain upon the world.

A language came back to me, and feelings, that—soaked morning and night in the Odia of Eeja and Ooi, and the small and then vast world of Bombay—I had long forgotten. My mind moved and drifted of its own free will, sparking like lightning, and my face longed to be uptilted for the rest of its time on this earth, watching the clouds, only the clouds.

July 1: My first day in the assembly. It's quite something to enter 'the grand chamber of the people' and realize that one is part of such a select group of people and in such poor company at the same time. Sitting in the place marked out for me and listening to the sermons and oaths of the chief minister and his cabinet made me sleepy, and thinking of Rabi and my Cloud people in order to wake myself up made me shed a tear or two. The members of the opposition who saw me wiping my eyes thought that I had become emotional because I had become an MLA for the first time, and they burst out laughing. The speaker reprimanded them, and they pointed at me, saying it was all my fault. It felt like being in school all over again.

This sorry bunch claims to know what the right religion is and the right morality, what man's dharma is, and what policies should be proposed so that all classes of society can prosper and progress. They last thought a thought devoid of self-interest or scheming twenty or thirty years ago, if ever. Yet they view themselves as being exceptionally sophisticated, worldly and wise, always with some pious thought upon their forked tongues. Ah democracy! You imagine the just order of wise citizens, then you validate the buffoonery of a cartload of clowns.

Even so, I saw a few village-type legislators in their midst, still untouched by big money or megalomania, wearing clothes long past their best days, their old shoes concealing grass-roots dreams and cracked heels. So there is hope. It is my dream that the next time a new assembly is convened, Rabi will sit on this chair on which I sit.

My eyes (and, no doubt, the bulging eyes of many lecherous legislators) picked out the one beautiful creature in this landscape: Madhuri, in the visitor's gallery, sitting next to Bapa. They were both waving at me. I felt inexpressibly happy. As I waved back, I remembered Ma—who always insisted she'd not had a day's happiness in her life—and felt that on a day like this she could not have held on to such a preposterous claim any more.

Under clouds, we realize that what we thought of as the look and colour of the world is only a trick of the light. That when the light changes, all things change. That the idea of one truth is a lie, and seems true only because the light from above does not change or is not allowed to change.

The Vaitarna river can no longer be seen from the top of the mountain. The rain is closing in. As the first heavy, spitting drops beat the earth, some run for cover, some raise their faces to the sky.

The arrival of rain clouds marks the only time when the Bombay person spares a moment or two to look up at the sky. Every pulse quickens with the cooling and darkening of the air and the thought of rain. People who never say a word to one another suddenly begin to marvel in the up-looking company of strangers.

July 10: These Cloud people are really beginning to annoy me now. They just can't make up their minds about anything at all. It's like their brains are clouds, too, so the ones that promised something on Friday have long disappeared by Tuesday, and you have to begin all over again, explaining how the world works for the millionth time.

They're suspicious. Every time I insist that we should go forward with something right away, they say, 'Let Rabi come back, we will ask him first. What are we? Poor, uneducated village folk. He has seen the world and come on TV in Bhubaneswar and is learning new things in Bombay. Can't we wait a little, brother?'

Do they really want to save their Cloud Mountain, now that we have a chance to oppose the Company not just on the streets of this district but in the heart of power in the state, in the legislative assembly?

Suddenly, they are not so sure! They want the Mountain to be as is, but they don't really want the Company to go either! They've got far too used to watching TV off the satellite dishes of those neighbours who've sold land to the Company. They've begun to see that they can eat goat curry not just once a month but every Sunday, maybe even twice a week. They like the fact that educated, well-dressed engineers and workers from the city come and hang out at the one tea shop around the corner of the Tininadi road, even if these outsiders won't say a word to them!

Just so they could also begin to educate themselves about the world of the city and feel at home there, I organized a skills camp in Bhubaneswar for all the women of Tininadi, where for the first time they would live by themselves for a few days, away from their men. And in the evening, after they were done with classes on home-oil extraction from rapeseed, broom-making from the broom flower and small business management and rudimentary accounting, they could go out into the city and see how it worked, so they would not be intimidated by it any more. All the women agreed, from the teenagers to the grannies, and were so excited about visiting Bhubaneswar for the first time, the grand, distant capital. Of course, I was excited, too—we were all thrilled, and it felt just like the times when Rabi was here.

Come the morning of the trip, the big bus that started from Bhubaneswar the previous day pulled up outside the village—and then the stories began! Oh my, oh my. Someone had a terrible stomach ache, another one hadn't cooked rice for the day because her husband woke up late, a third suddenly had her sister visiting from the next village, a fourth's son had fallen ill.

By the time we could round up the few who did agree to go, it was late afternoon, and then we had to stop three times on the way for snacks and meals and because they wanted to buy

*things like soap, shampoo and bindis in the markets of the small
towns. If I'd agreed to halt each time one of them wanted to eat,
pee, shop or vomit, we'd have reached Bhubaneswar in the same
amount of time that it took Alexander to reach India. I cursed
myself a million times for joining this sorry parade, but who
else could I have entrusted with this work? Rabi is the only one
who could have done it, and done it well, but the moron ran off
somewhere in Bombay—doubtless seduced, the same as this lot, by
the bright lights of the big city. I should at least thank Jagannath
or Cloudmaker that he lasted with my parents for so long and left
me one alive to bring back home and saved me the guilt of being
thought an ungrateful child.*

Everywhere I have been in my life so far, it has been clear who is an
outsider and who is not. But in Bombay, it is somewhat different. Here,
as soon as one stops thinking of oneself as an outsider, one stops being
an outsider.

This does not mean that the city is welcoming—no. Only that it
does not really care, and that its rules and its language can be quickly
learnt. All may speak good mother tongues at home, but in public they
speak the same broken up, pav bhaji language of the city, rich in cut
up words, curses and codes.

I specially love to eat vada pav with mint chutney and chilli powder
for seven rupees outside Dadar station. And to walk on the railway
overbridge of Wadala, down into the night market along the tracks,
where the earth shakes every time a train thunders by, as do the dead
fish on the boxes, the cabbages in the baskets and the clouds in the sky.

*July 31: Whoever knew that as a legislator one had to read so
many papers and documents, all bursting with gibberish or at
best with vague, obscure and opaque phrases designed to conceal
the truth of how power works in this world? My brain is well
and truly fried, just like that of a goat in a Muslim restaurant
in Bombay (what a meal that was in Noor Mohammadi last*

week!), by reading this day and night . . . even in my dreams I find myself repeating the most common phrases I've read over and over again, until they become a kind of nonsense verse. Truly, if meaningfulness is the standard, the best writers in a society are the poets and the aphorists. If obfuscation is what is desired, no one can do it better than lawyers and accountants.

It was one thing to be able to attack the Company from the outside with questions, pointed arguments, exposés of discrepancies between what they were doing and what they were saying they were doing, satires, or paeans in praise of the lore and culture and magic of the Cloud people. It's quite another thing to work against them now from inside the system—to read all the MoUs between them and the government and various government departments, to search for inconsistencies between the principles articulated ('articulated', see how my language has changed!) in PESA or the Land Acquisition Act and the agreements signed between the Company and individual members of the Cloud tribe in Tininadi, and then to find simple and compelling ways in which to articulate (there I go again!) the meaning of these slippages in op-ed pieces in Odia newspapers, even while using the Right to Information Act to procure police FIRs used to imprison people in Tininadi and bringing together the testimonies of different witnesses to show that these were trumped-up charges.

I sometimes have the paranoid feeling that this fight against the Company is a conspiracy set up by my biggest rivals in the Odia film and television industry—Gangadhar Jena, Ramakant Behera—so my faculties get eaten up from within by the linguistic termites of business, politics and the law.

Yesterday, I finally managed to have Bapa's collection of Sanskrit shlokas, culled from the great texts of our literature, released in Bhubaneswar. The chief minister agreed to be the chief guest at the launch and even postponed a trip to see his daughter in California in order to do so, and we got so much coverage in the papers that Bapa hasn't moved from his chair from seven in the morning today. He reads one report of the function after another, by which time he's forgotten that he's read the first, and so he reads that again. And in this way, by being, at once, Mr Memory and Mr Forgetfulness, he's gone through the entire day, nodding and murmuring to himself, without even feeling hungry or thirsty.

Last night, I was completely exhausted by my many worries (Bapa's health, the Cloud people, the Company, Rabi, Madhuri), and I saw Bapa's book lying on the table and, just like that, I opened it and began to read.

Truly, what a language Sanskrit was! Reading its literature is like falling in love with a statue—one knows that it's not for real, but it's all the more real precisely by virtue of its perfection. In the silence of the night, I could hear so clearly the metre of the lines and the elegant drape of the language upon the form, like a sari upon Madhuri's figure. Perhaps it's not because our civilization was so Sanskritic that it became hierarchical and decadent, but rather because we fell away from the power and rigour of Sanskrit to lower places. Could someone who knew all these verses and think all these marvellous thoughts about love, piety, duty, divine law, caprice, wealth, families, time and fate really be such a bad person? Or, rather, would his weaknesses stem from the fact that he was lost in his own world of beauty and truth (in a way, like Cloudmaker) and blind to some of the problems just outside his immediate province . . . much like Bapa all his life?

One of the greatest triumphs of any person in Bombay—and one of the surest ways of earning the city's respect—is being the first to leap on to a train as it comes rumbling into the station.

At first, one is amazed by it all, laughs at how stupid and desperate people can be, risking their lives or legs just for two buttocks worth of territory with a moving view for an hour. But, after a few times, it all begins to make sense, and one begins to see no harm in it. In time, I have become quite good at this sport myself.

Although, to those watching, it all seems to happen so fast, the experience is very different from the inside. Ages pass by between leap and land—as though this isn't just an attempt to spring a few feet in the air but Hanuman's vault across the length of India to get back the sacred herbs from the Sanjeevani mountain. There is the thrill of flight, and then there is the thunder of landing. And if it is the last—and therefore the first—stop, a man has two or three seconds to choose which window seat he wants before the rest come pouring in: sunny side or shady side, platform side or track side, river side or mountain side. Those few seconds offer the most blissful solitude in the midst of a crowd—one can survey vast expanses, as Cloudmaker does from the sky.

This (and other such things) is the trademark of a city that fights for everything in life and tries to shave a few seconds off every one of the day's tasks.

If the clouds were any closer to the earth, the people of Bombay would find some way of fighting for and in them, too.

August 13: It was a hot afternoon when I went into the district jail to inquire into the case of Sabu Dadara, upon whom the Company has slapped fresh charges of intimidation and destruction of property after having let him and others go a week after the election, probably as a peacemaking overture.

I had hoped to be out in ten or fifteen minutes, but the constable on duty offered to take me on a tour of the jail, and I agreed. As we walked, many prisoners cried out piteously to me from their cells, shouting, 'Babu! Babu! Have mercy on us. If you should will it, we can definitely be free.' Much like the rich, the poor believe there is nothing like the law in this country . . . only power matters!

My heart grieved when it heard these sounds—but then I reminded myself: man being what he is, these people could be the most cold-blooded murderers, rapists or thieves. I conducted an impromptu inquiry session, so that any soul who managed to persuade me that he was innocent could be listed on a piece of paper—and this sheet could be taken across to the Bhubaneswar NGO that offered to give free legal representation to those charged by the Company.

When I came out after a couple of hours, my mind was still stuck in that dark, accursed place, smelling of violence, desperation, urine and fear. Raising my head as any man would do, I came face-to-face with that one thing that had been taken away from the prisoners. The sky. Space. Room to think, imagine, dream. Dark clouds were rolling in from the west at a very fast clip, like travellers in olden times who had to get to a certain place by nightfall, and as I watched spellbound, a streak of lightning cut the sky into two, lighting up the entire fallen world.

I felt like the man who looked up and saw this scene for the very first time in human history.

Here, in Bombay, the clouds, rain and wind come and go in gusts all day long, attacking sharply without warning, then fading away just as fast. June went this way, now July, and likely all of August. Sometimes one can hear the rain recede just as clearly as a song coming to an end. It is as if Cloudmaker is so excited and disoriented by life above the big city and by the thousands of pockets of people He can see that He tries to sing and dance for them all. Sometimes He tries to throw them off course by sending marvellous shoals of dark clouds—bigger than the greatest buildings in Bombay—that loom just above the eyebrows of all in the city, but do not release a drop of water, and only rumble a bit, then dissolve. At other times, the rain arrives from nowhere, and the clouds seem to form in the sky only in its wake, as if it were the rain that made clouds and not the other way round.

These are the moods of the city where one cannot always say what one means or be what one is, and one must sometimes do the opposite of what one wants to do to reach the place one wants—pretending not to notice a girl in the bus, for example, so that when two seats fall vacant in different places she takes the one next to you. When the bus suddenly lurches through a pothole, the fleeting touch of that foreign arm upon your own is just as thrilling as Cloudmaker's sudden feathery caress must have been to the Moon (before the Sun took Her away).

September 11: Today, in the morning, I got some news from Madhuri. She is pregnant!

When I heard these words I was consumed by a strange mix of surprise, pleasure and embarrassment. She had only got divorced from that fellow Kaushik three weeks ago, and they hadn't been able to have a child through their nine years together! And we had been using protection all the time . . . except on that one night when things got a bit out of hand.

Truly, strange are the ways of God or whichever other CEO or Great Leader there is who runs the affairs of this world. There is still plenty of time for us to marry before the bump begins to show, but when the child arrives—I know it will be a son, my instinct in these matters has never failed me—our mischief will become clear to everybody. Never mind, they will all say, Bhagaban has always done everything his own way.

I would have shared this happy piece of news with Bapa, but who knows what he will say? For fear that his reaction could somehow spoil my private joy, I've revealed nothing to him.

Instead, when I got the news, I went into the puja room and knelt down in front of the picture of Ma (who always assumed such a serious face for photographs) to ask for her blessings. I prayed to her to look after this one aspect of my life, which I had longed for for so long but had somehow never been able to work out. The older I grow, the more I begin to feel that Ma was right, and there is such a thing as fate or destiny.

And while I was down there in that unfamiliar position on my knees, something else happened. I found myself saying goodbye once again not only to my sainted mother but also to something more abstract. My youth has lasted very long, longer perhaps than in the life of any other man in the history of Odisha. For nearly twenty-five years I have carried on with my acts of subversion in one way or another, laughing at the very people who swallow my jest whole without digesting the real meaning behind it.

As it turns out, in the end, it was no act of will but the transference of a few drops of viscous (some words pop up in the brain so suddenly after they are learnt and forgotten in school!) fluid from a hard, impatient to a soft, welcoming place that brought about this change in my life. Or Life, with a capital L. Even the man most firmly attached to positivism (to borrow a word from Western philosophy) cannot fail to sense something sacred and mysterious in this existence, and give up his sarcasm and his scepticism before the wonder and transcendence of moments such as these.

I must try ever harder, now, to remake this iniquitous world, so that it may be a better place for my child and for the children of the Cloud people to grow up in. And to thank the Cloud people for all that they have taught me about Life and living, I have decided that the little one will be named Meghdoot or the Cloud Messenger.

If nothing else, this Sanskritic name, alluding to Kalidasa's great play from God knows how many thousand years ago, will definitely please his grandfather.

Today I am a father!

I thought that I had come to Bombay with three others: Eeja, Ooi and Bhai. But I actually came with four.

Cloudmaker came with me, too. And as my people say, 'He who rises above the clouds, never returns.'

Farhad on the Ground

AH, SAN FRANCISCO! City of vertiginously slopey roads and dazzlingly warm colours, bards and banterers, Spanish names and Indian ones, the Twin Peaks and the Sutro Baths, environmentalism and experimentalism, bay love and gay love, Google and so many other human search engines.

I tell myself I am happy, that having waited so long for this moment to arrive, I must honour it by trusting it. Already, just by the fact of having made it out here, I have understood newly what man really seeks out of life, and therefore, also of a city—a sense of freedom and possibility; a sense that he knows who he is and yet has much to discover about himself; a sense that other people are also engaged in this search (in the real business of living, not just existing) and that he is sure to find them on every corner.

This sense is no longer present in Bombay, which long ago dipped below the poverty line existentially . . . and, therefore, the very root of life is missing in that city. Those who continue to abide there have forgotten what life is all about and perceive it merely as instinctive, ravening competition and endless, pointless conflict—the emblems of which are the car horns that sound all day long and the people who lose their lives every day crossing the railway tracks. A city that, like a difficult wife, demands to be left.

Goodbye to all those things of which Bombay has been, perversely, so very proud. Goodbye, fatalistic-heroic philosophy of stoicism and suffering; the veneration of the tawdry and sweaty; that mockery of all that is beautiful and sophisticated as elite and effete; the raucous and raggedy patois that, at its very root, means nothing else but 'look at me, I'm a Mumbaikar'! For a few hundred years, the Billimorias had given the city their best, but in the end that was not enough—and in the face of such a battle could never be enough.

So enough of that.

Or, at least, that's what I'd be feeling when I'd be sitting two days from now on the shores of San Francisco—as opposed to shitting this very moment on the shores of Bombay—which wasn't me, but the many people down below the promenade at Worli Sea Face, between the rat-infested rocks, in the early minutes of my forty-second birthday—yes, even at this odd hour, a few minutes after midnight, when it comes, it comes.

I really shouldn't have been up at this hour, even if I'd gone early to bed with a headache after my return from Udvada. But I'd woken up again at eleven, and that was all that sleep would give me of herself, perhaps having decided that my slumber was depolarizing the late weekend snoozes of the worthy citizens of San Francisco.

No matter how much I tried, I couldn't stop replaying that dispiriting incident at the Globe, even though Zahra had seemed to think nothing of it afterwards . . . and so, I couldn't bring it up either. In fact, on the drive back, Uncle Sheriyar had been so poignantly funny while retelling the story of his marriage to a beautiful Iranian girl that I'd almost forgotten about the episode. I'd even promised to meet Zahra in the morning for coffee before I left for the airport. But as soon as I was alone, it came back to me. For a long time, I fretted in that dark and empty room, thinking dreadful thoughts about life.

What did I want? What did I have? What could I trust?

Finally, I dressed and came down to the sea.

And here it gradually dawned upon me, as the dawn gradually dawns upon the world, that over the last few days I had let myself be drawn out into a very strange place and that I wasn't in the mood for any kind of exchange with any woman, Parsi or gentile, yoga or mocha, until I had rowed myself safely across to the other bank. So I sent Zahra a text message stating: *Sorry, not feeling so well, might have to take a rain check on tomorrow. See you in San Francisco. Safe journey.*

A masterpiece of male understatement, especially since in its wake—Zahra didn't reply and was probably sleeping—my resentment grew ever more tempestuous, like those clouds that would soon be whipping themselves into rumbling black squalls in the sky of Bombay. And in a rage, I had just sent her another text message, right now. I couldn't believe I'd actually sent it, but then I checked my 'sent' folder, and there it was: *In fact, let's not meet for a while in San Francisco either. Don't want to run the risk of accidentally depolarizing your ladyship's cunt in that city, too.*

Shame, Farhad, shame! Now his only hope was that the Indian telecommunications network was as unreliable as everyone said it was and that, somehow, the message hadn't gone through. But could he be faulted? There were so many other ways in which Zahra, too, could've got her message across to him. But such were the shackles on human understanding that it didn't even seem to have occurred to Zahra that something had gone wrong—perhaps fatally wrong—between us.

But really—what did Zahra matter? A week ago, I didn't even know who she was! All the prospects and pleasures I'd contemplated for my future life when Zahra-less, all of them still existed. Nice sky. Dark. So happy to be going to San Francisco. Oh, what a wonderful city it was, a place for the cutting edge of humanity. Craft beers and cool cafes at every corner. Women! Always complaining about the violence done to them by men, but under cover of their rights and their freedoms and their resistance to patriarchy and God knew what else, sneakily managing so much violence of their own. Preying, just like men, on the meek of the other sex, those souls who were most willing to listen sympathetically. And, so, where they should have helped lay the foundation of a new consensus, they merely repolarized the world of the sexes. The division would never dissolve, the war would never end, men and women would wear each other out no matter what. San Francisco. A port city, full of maritime lore just like Bombay, and probably written of by historians with better prose styles and narrative capabilities . . . books waiting to be read on evolution, astronomy, quantum physics, all those things I knew so little about. And new kinds of psychic turmoil to be contemplated and healed in an experimental society—who knew if I had the mind to detachedly digest some of the stories waiting for me in my chambers there? But, first, the task of setting up a new apartment, all by myself, taking advice from nobody. The curtains could be pink, the divan gold. And if anyone didn't like it . . . they were welcome to leave. So much furniture in America had to be home-assembled. Like it or not, I'd have to brush-up on my DIY skills. Wasn't I a real man? She seemed to be saying as much. But if men were, in every situation, supposed to be as men were supposed to be, how could they ever be anything else? When not pinned back to their own corner by polarity, they were returned to it by those other beings who, for their own part, made such a fuss about being imprisoned by gender stereotypes. This wasn't a good place to be in. Make a joke . . . but what joke? Check-in at two pm. Should've really flown first class on such a long journey, just me being cheap because I wouldn't be making any money for a while in America. Now, suddenly, the prospect of recycling all these wretched thoughts twelve hours from now, boxed into a corner for nearly a full day by some obese person; or being bored to death by an inquisitive auntie; or getting up from an aisle seat like a battery-operated toy all day and night as the other two in the row took turns to visit the bathroom . . . what a wretched, soul-destroying combination of birthday clouds that was going to be!

Two raindrops, or some other form of precipitation, fell on to the back of my hand, which rose up to stop them at source. And suddenly I knew I really couldn't fly to San Francisco tomorrow in economy class . . . or in any class to any city where Zahra was scheduled to turn up soon. And I saw how I had almost destroyed everything that I had so carefully set up for a second go at life, and that I would have to now find a *third* way and be a *third* man in a *third* city. How? Where? There was no escape. I was grateful that it was dark and quiet while

I wept . . . suddenly it seemed best not to hold back the tears, and time with tears appeared to be moving forward in the way that time without them had not.

A shadow fell upon my arm. A croaking person said, 'Spare a rupee or two, sir? Any small change for a cup of tea?'

'A rupee or two?' I replied in a voice just as cracked. 'Think money grows on trees? Learn to work for a living.'

'I'd have happily done so, sir. Unlike some others on this beat, I'm no shirker. But what can this wretched soul do? Blindness has cast a shadow upon his every thought.'

'Hah! Dude, you're looking straight at me as you say this. Think I was born in Alibaug?'

'Sir, it only looks like I'm looking at you because my face is pointing towards where your voice is coming from.'

'Listen, friend, I can see your eyes looking at me quite clearly.'

'All right, sir. Just as you wish.'

'What do you mean, just as you wish?'

'What can I say? Not only am I blind but I also have the further misery of hearing the sighted of this world force a false sight upon me. I'll take myself away from here. Although every place is the same to me, so I could be back here again soon.'

'Hello . . . hold on! You talk a good talk. Just for that, and because it's my last day in this ridiculous city, I'll give you something. Here, take this five-rupee coin.'

'Please drop it into my tin, sir.'

'Playing it up till the very end! Here, then. Into the tin of deception it goes.'

'Thank you, sir. To tell you the truth, deception can be of many kinds. Even sight can be a kind of deception, which means that sometimes the blind are fortunate to be able to see past sight. There are so many mysteries in this life that sight fogs up.'

'What rubbish! Get going right now before I take my money back.'

'Goodbye, sir, and God be with you. Come back soon. This city always takes care of its own.'

Off he went jangling his coin collection, the Baude-liar of Worli Sea Faece. Just the sort of ragged philosopher, it seemed to me, that Zahra would have been terribly impressed by. 'Oh Farhad! He's so real! He's dealt so bravely with all that life has had to throw at him, and his blindness has become a boon, a road to wisdom and fortitude. Let's give him a thousand. It's only fifteen dollars anyway.'

But I couldn't take pleasure in my own jokes, which was something I'd been able to do for so many days and weeks now, building up from the time I'd set out to leave Bombay. And this and so many other things were disturbing signs that my new self and wisecracking ways were going off the rails, or had just been an interlude between two laboured lives. The very Farhad who had thought and done so many wonderful things and formed a liberating philosophy of clouds was himself no more than a cloud! He was dead and gone. I was performing the last rites for him right here before I departed for San Francisco.

Voices came to me from the distance. A crowd, marching down Worli Sea Face, chanting something—God knows what and why, seeing as it was the middle of the night. And the shrill, high-pitched voices of the women were completely drowning out those of the men—no better symbol of the times. I snickered and turned around so I could watch them.

As they drew closer, I realized that my condition was even more serious than I'd first suspected, for I was hallucinating. Every single person in this mob was a woman! And they were all heading straight for me, as if seeking to capture me and haul me off to some kangaroo court. They were wearing saris, salwar-kameezes, jeans and tops, even nighties with dupattas in the Bombay way. A fly perched on my tongue before I could spit it out, and I realized that my mouth was wide open. I registered what the mob was shouting, alternately in Hindi and Marathi:

The night! The night! We are the women of the night!
The night is ours too! Give us back the night!

A new crusade! Yes, the night is yours, the day is yours, the world is yours, ladies, everything is you and yours. As they passed me, I contemplated taking a picture of this silliness, but I feared the mob would turn upon me—a man making merry in his patriarchal night. I needn't have worried—they were so possessed they didn't even notice me. They marched past, set to tear the whole world down.

As I turned away again, a figure detached itself from the group and I heard a familiar voice saying: 'Why must men always sit with their legs spread wide open?'

It was Hemlata! It was strangely reassuring to see again one of the cast members, even if an inadvertent one, of my greatest ever cloud. Just like me, Hemlata was much changed. She wore a black T-shirt and blue jeans, and had her hair tied back into a ponytail. Her face was flushed with pleasure and excitement, as after a good workout. For once there was no sign of paper on her, unless they were all in the jute bag on her left shoulder. She looked more attractive with her glasses on than she had two days ago without them . . . or maybe it was just because my vision was fuzzy from crying.

Wiping my eyes quickly, I returned, not with my usual élan but passably, 'Professor, aren't you lot always saying our brains are down here? How will they work if they don't get some fresh air?'

Hemlata laughed and said, 'Touché, Dr Billimoria! Is this what the civilized people of SoBo do at night? Hang out on the waterfront and ruminate on the lost days of the Raj?'

'Before I answer, my dear, does your mother know you're out so late in the night?'

'Very funny.'

'Anyway, what's all this? What's going on?'

'Is it so hard to understand? We don't want to be second-class citizens in our very own republic—or have only half the day available to us when men can have a full one. Have you ever thought about why we can't wander at night or sit on our own by a promenade, just like you're doing right now?'

'Yes, but it's not my fault. You're more than welcome to sit here as long as you like.'

'This isn't about personalities, it's about structures. If men won't give us our night, we're going to get together and take it. Not just women of a certain class. All of us.'

'All right. That makes sense.'

'Great to see that an idea has passed your exacting standards. All right, Mr San Francisco. I've got to join the group. But before I go, I want to say sorry for getting into such a huff yesterday.'

'No need to. I apologize for getting you into such a huff.'

'It seems like whenever we meet I say I am sorry for being rude, and then I'm rude again, and then we meet again. Before I'm rude once more, it's time to break this cycle. Goodbye.'

'But we . . . but we won't be seeing each other ever again,' I blabbed. 'Don't you know, I'm going away today!'

'Well, if you're so keen to chat, why don't you come join the march?'

'Me? But I'm a man.'

'So what? We're not against men, only against patriarchy and double standards. And a token man in our midst can only be of help to us. Too many—yes, that would disrupt the message.'

'But I've never been part of a rally . . . people will stare at me . . .'

'Oh, grow up. Look at it another way. It'll feel like you're the only man left in the world. Isn't that every man's dream?'

A familiar hot spring of pleasure bubbled up from the dark well that was my soul, and I chirped, 'Wow, sounds like a thought. All right. Girls, girls! Wait, I'll protect you.'

'Just make sure you don't get too excited. I won't be able come to your aid if it turns out that you "accidentally" gave someone a poke.'

'Oh, there's no fear of that. My Sputnik is very well behaved with Indian women.'

'Your night in Borivali seems to have had quite an effect on you. So, it's given itself a new name in preparation for good times in America, has it? Or should one say hard times?'

'Your mother will be shocked to hear such thoughts, and for her sake, so am I. But why just it? All of me looks like I'm set for hard times.'

Hemlata rolled her eyes and announced, 'Hello, everybody, this is a friend of mine who wants to be part of the agitation. He says he believes completely in our cause. Let's test him out. Repeat after me, *Give me my rights, give me my nights! I deserve a night too!*'

'Give me my rights, give me my nights!' I said experimentally, setting off a flurry of thrilling, even arousing—despite my black, now grey, mood—female laughter around me.

Hemlata laughed, too, and said, as we walked on, 'You're a natural activist! If only you'd stay and commit yourself to the cause, Dr Billimoria.'

'Seeing how much pleasure you get from exposing my class biases, I'm almost inclined to charge you to talk to me. Or perhaps we could monetize our disagreements with a television series: *Farhad and Hemlata.*'

'Ha! Who'd do the writing?'

'How about I get to write your lines, you get to write mine. That way, when it looks like someone has won the war, it's an act of generosity, not aggression.'

The expression on Hemlata's face changed. 'Listen, I just want to say something. I'm not the sort of person you think I am. Even though it doesn't make any difference what you think.'

'Really? What sort of person do you think I think you are?'

'I'm serious. I'm not a man-hater or an angry person or a sour bitch with a midlife crisis. That's just a side of me you got to see.'

'Is that so . . .'

'Though maybe you bring this out as well with your terribly annoying "I'm so smart, I'm so witty, and only a country like America deserves me" air.'

'Is that how I come across?'

'That's how you come across.'

'Well, I don't know how to change that—since it's probably true.'

'See!' said Hemlata. 'I can't believe you're a psychotherapist. Do you come across like this to your clients, or is it a role you play just with me?'

'You'll have to work that out for yourself. The way things are going with the gender wars, soon it's us men who'll have to cultivate an air of masculine mystique. Anyway, I want to say sorry to you, too.'

'Sorry for what?'

'For making fun of you. To be honest, I'm also sorry *for* you. I already realized you weren't the sort of person you thought I thought you were.'

'What do you mean, sorry for me? Do you pity me? I don't need that.'

'I know that you're unhappy, and your marriage is about to break up, and it's not your fault, but our society being what it is, you'll be the one who suffers most from it. I was too caught up in my own happiness earlier to understand your distress.'

'Okay, apology accepted. I'm sorry, too, for saying sarcastic things about you and your life choices. Each one should be able to decide what's best for him or her. I thought about it later. It was just me being jealous of other people's happiness, of the fact that someone else has the freedom to make a new start, and I don't. That's the truth.'

'That's very gracious of you. But, my dear, you *do* have the power to make a new start. Everyone does. Even in India.'

'Why aren't *you* making one here then?'

'I thought we agreed not to criticize one another's choices.'

'We did. I'm . . . no, I'm not sorry.'

'Anyway, tell me, what's the point of us marching like Subhas Chandra Bose's army this late at night? We may have the night, but not the ears of those we want to reach.'

'Oh, this is just the last leg,' said Hemlata. 'We've been walking for hours.'

'Where, up and down this stretch?'

'No, silly! We started in the slums of Ganesh Nagar in Wadala, broke up into three groups, went through all of that neighbourhood. I stepped into a pile of shit at one place, which probably taught me more than any other step in the last five years about the reality and materiality of our city. What're you edging away for? Anyway . . . so we caught up again at the junction that goes up to Antop Hill. Walked across the railway overbridge and past Five Gardens into Matunga. It took us a while because they were selling fish cheap in the market beneath the bridge, and some of the women didn't want to miss out. In Matunga, we took a break and had Punjabi Chinese for dinner. Then we headed off towards Dadar station and set up stall for a bit outside Pritam Hotel. There I got into an argument with a man who was standing around making sarcastic remarks about us. It had been such a long time since I had tried to both control my tongue and use it in Marathi. One of the ladies said we should call the police, but that would have just got us all kinds of negative publicity. I asked him only to think about what we were saying and why he was against us, and to try not to make up his mind before next Sunday, that's all.'

'Really? I'm shocked.'

'Shocked by what?'

'You're so gentle while correcting everyone else, so harsh only with me.'

Hemlata ignored me, as one ignores the buzzing of a mosquito, and continued, 'Then on to . . . ah yes, into Prabhadevi, and now here. That's a good distance for a thought to have walked. At least 5,000 people heard us in one night. As for neighbourhoods, let me see, we did Tamil, Dalit Buddhist, Konkani, Maharashtrian and a small patch of Gujarati, Koli bastis . . . what was your day like?'

'Oh, nothing too dramatic. Drove to Udvada for a ceremony commemorating the 1,290th year of the arrival of the Parsis in India. Listened to a speech by Narendra Modi. Walked all around the town and by the sea. Checked out an emu farm on the way. These birds are going to be the next chicken, I'm telling you. Oh, and in the midst of all of this, got my Sputnik into a bit of a pickle while making love to a lady. I think I won't be seeing her again.'

Hemlata looked at me suspiciously and said, 'I can never quite tell when you're being serious and when you're not.'

'It's all true!'

We had reached the Ruia College junction. The leader of the party, a stout lady in a maroon sari, shook her fist—perhaps I should say Her fist—and glanced at us with what one could call a 'movement smile'. She shouted, and we both shouted after Her, 'Tonight's a new night, tomorrow a new dawn!' This must have been the point at which the procession had agreed to disband, because the women began to say their goodbyes and disperse in groups of twos and threes. It seemed as if they didn't yet trust the city enough to go home alone. Even so, I felt happy to have played a part in this little piece of Bombay's social history.

As she bid adieu to a few ladies, Hemlata said in charming Marathi, 'Yes, a friend of mine. No, not of my husband's . . . *mine*.' They all looked at me a bit suspiciously as they departed, leaving us together—showing that they still had a long way to go in the night of their own minds.

'Well?' I said.

'Well, if it's really your last night in Bombay, shall we get a drink? This time it's my invitation, so I won't have to say sorry via email sometime next week.'

'Sure. Where would you like to go?'

'Wasn't that Udupi restaurant we just passed still open? I'm craving a chikoo milkshake.'

'A *milkshake*? Um . . . okay. I'm more hungry than thirsty, so maybe I'll have a dosa. I fell asleep before I could eat dinner.'

'As you please. By the way, if it really is your last night in Bombay, what were you doing sitting there all by yourself?'

'Why, waiting for you to turn up.'

'No, seriously . . .'

'Well, saying goodbye to the city and my life in it.'

'Were you feeling sad?'

'Uh . . . you could say so. For over forty years, this was home.'

'Did you say goodbye to your ex-wife?'

'No. I didn't want to spoil the good feeling. I'll write to her once I've made good my escape—oops!' We bumped into one another entering the restaurant through the narrow space between the juice counter and the pav bhaji one.

'Who knows, maybe she's emigrated to America, too,' said Hemlata mischievously. 'Well, what about your companion from the other night? Where's she?'

'Who, Zahra?'

'If she was the one sitting next to you at the reading, yes.'

'Ah, yes . . . I went with her to Udvada. I only just met her though.'

'You went out with the same woman two days in a row? She must be really special. So how're you going to keep it up if she lives here and you're leaving?'

'Oh, that's one thing I don't have to worry about. She lives in San Francisco, too. She's just visiting.'

'Oh . . . so you're moving to be with her?'

'No. Strangely enough, I was already about to move, and then I met her.'

'You men tell so many lies! What's the harm in admitting that you're moving because you're in love with her?'

'There'd be no harm in it . . . except that it's not true. It's not like that between us. At least, not yet.'

'Have you guys already slept together?'

'*You* seem very interested in this relationship.'

'I'm just very interested in modern Indian sexual mores—in part because of a book I'm writing,' said Hemlata. 'But not so much the younger generation. Our generation, the ones who missed the sexual revolution. And now we have a second chance, but this involves unlearning all the old truths.'

'Am I a sort of case study?'

'You should be flattered that I'm curious.'

'Well . . . to respond to your question, of course we have.'

'Okay, so why be so shy while saying so? When was the last time you did it with someone other than your wife?'

'Um, there . . . there hasn't been anybody else. Anna was my first love, and I believed in being faithful.'

Hemlata burst out laughing. 'Really, only one woman in forty years? What was it like with your new squeeze then? Was it a shock?'

'A shock in every way you can think of. I'm still reeling from it and don't know if I'll ever recover.' I took the menu and began to fan myself for dramatic effect. 'You speak, dear Hemlata, as if you've made love to dozens of men.'

'I certainly hadn't had sex with just one until the week before, I can tell you that,' said Hemlata, greatly pleased with her victory in the war, if not in the battle. 'Ah, my milkshake. Want a sip?'

'No, I don't. I'll eat my dosa. Well, I hope you won't judge me because I'm using a spoon and fork.'

'What other way can there be to eat a dosa or a pizza?'

'So you have no new, um, *squeezes*? A nice professor at the university? Someone wanting to end his life as a bachelor or widower?'

'No. You know it as well as me, I'm sure. It's hard for people our age to make a fresh start in life or meet someone new in this city.' Hemlata saw the glint of victory in my eyes and said hurriedly, 'That doesn't take away from what I said when we last met, that it's *too easy* in America. I'm sure you'll get married at least three times in the next decade. Look . . . look how excited it's making you.'

'What can I do? These visions are making me so randy.'

'Yes, when men sleep around, they're just being randy. But when we do it, we're just being randis.'

'Never in my universe, I can promise you that. I want everybody to enjoy free love. I know it's hard to find someone new. But if it's any consolation, at least in your line of work you have access to people who're not going through a personal crisis. How about a nice *student* at the university?'

'Don't be ridiculous. This is all a big joke for you, isn't it?'

In between my cackles, I said, 'Why should you be the only one exercising your imagination? And what's wrong with it? *I* could see myself having a crush on you at twenty-one. Don't be so closed-minded.'

'I hate to break this to you, but twenty-one is the age you've stayed.'

'No wonder I'm such a fantastic lover. Anyway, as this is question hour in our parliament, allow me one or two more queries, although I know you don't like talking about your husband now that you've garlanded him in a photograph as well as in real life. What kind of business does he have?'

'Oh, he's an engineer by training. Actually, he's very bright with everything except gender relations. Now he imports heavy equipment into the country from South Korea. Stuff they use in steel plants, construction. Very boring to those of us in the humanities, but I'm sure it's a fascinating field. Very lucrative, too. Why do you ask?'

'I was just curious because I heard him on the phone the other night saying something about missionaries.'

'Missionaries? That's ridiculous. There's no slander I won't believe about him now, but I'll guarantee that he has absolutely nothing to do with convents. There's no heavily made-up woman to be got there, after all . . . nor orders for heavy goods. Those are the main things that interest him.'

'How strange!' I repeated from memory in an accent approximating Balu's: 'I'll supply the missionaries, I'll supply the missionaries.'

Hemlata let out a shriek of laughter, unsettling four men hunched conspiratorially at the next table. 'No, silly! It's *machineries*. He always uses the plural when he's speaking about machines. His English isn't his strong point.'

'Oh really . . . how disappointing! I'd have loved an evening of communion with a nice missionary. I'd never say no to a nun.'

'The question is whether she'd say yes to you. I can just see her finding out about your sexual history and saying, "Dr Billimoria, get a life!" In fact, the same criticism applies to your ears as well. Don't tell me you've never heard people speaking in a South Indian accent before . . .'

'No, I have. Just not about . . . about missionaries.' Hemlata exploded with hysterical, unwomanly laughter every time I said the word—so, happy to play the fool, I kept saying, 'Missionaries . . . machineries . . . missionaries . . .' till the effect wore off. 'I'm just curious about how the two of you got together. I never saw a couple more different from one another.'

'More different? What're you saying?' asked Hemlata with deep irony. 'Same mother tongue, same caste, same class, same Gods, similarly enthusiastic parents—everything important was the same. A perfect match.'

'Yes, but how could someone like *you* have had an arranged marriage?'

Hemlata shrugged. 'What can I say? It's no excuse, but I guess I was depressed. I'd just come back from America after failing at Columbia. My dreams were shattered. There wasn't going to be a second chance. I wasn't getting younger. There was pressure on me from my parents. Then, this proposal came along. He had a business of his own, was "settled", was the right caste—the things that parents go for. We met a couple of times, and he was fine with me working after marriage, which some guys still aren't. As long as literature was something I played with and didn't bring into the rest of his life, it was all fine with him. Same old Indian story—I couldn't see any great harm in marrying him. I guess, you have to live it to find out if you can live with it.'

'True, true.'

'And, to be perfectly honest, part of the blame is mine for succumbing to the temptation of the security of a rich husband.'

'Wow, that's big.'

'Bit by bit, we've got ourselves into that terrible place where we take pleasure in slighting or hurting one another, and every action is just one more chapter in a long saga of prosecution. You're the first person I'm telling this to,' said Hemlata, pausing to make some slurring sips with her straw, 'but, suddenly, after my long walk today, I don't feel so punitive towards him. I'm done with that. In fact, if I just have an honest chat with him, and we agree to separate in a civilized way, I know there's someone wonderful waiting for me on the other side. Someone I used to know.'

'Ah, so there *is* someone!' I cried, remembering the writer of love notes in Hemlata's CD collection. 'Who is he?'

'It's not a *he*.'

'You're going to get yourself a dog! Hemlata, this is so disappointing.'

'I'm going to go back to myself,' said Hemlata, absorbing the jest with dignity. 'I'm going to leave my house and make a world that supports the person I used to be, before I got married and embedded into the bourgeois mores of the middle class. Think of what we're doing right now. I can do this every day. I'm going to be free to walk, wander, think, stay out late at night, meet new people, read and write, work on a book. If this isn't a legitimate recipe for human happiness, why should anything else be?'

'Won't you want someone to share it all with?' I asked, jealous on the one hand, for I had never thought about Bombay in this way, and disbelieving on the other, for I did not believe Bombay could support such dreams of pleasure and independence even for a man, much less for a woman.

'Perhaps someone will come along. But it'll have to be someone with no illusions about what he's getting into. Or, at least, someone with a good pair of walking shoes.' A sudden glimmer appeared in Hemlata's eyes. 'Or maybe I could just lock him in for the night, so he doesn't get up to any hanky-panky, and head out for a wander!'

'Oh my. What will he get in return for such a great sacrifice?'

'He won't have to worry about that, there'll be plenty,' said Hemlata. 'Anyway, Mr San Francisco, what about *your* love life?'

'What about it? I'm alone, too.'

'I thought your lady love is waiting for you in San Francisco.'

'Yes . . . that's the problem.'

'How is that a problem?'

'Well . . . suddenly, I'm not so sure about her any more. Things may have become a bit strained between us. At first I thought she was going to be the muse for my new life in San Francisco, the heroine of the *Farhadnama* . . . just as Dante wrote *The Divine Comedy* out of love for Beatrice, and Proust wrote his masterpiece guided by a vision of Madeleine. It was she who gave me new insight into not just life on earth but clouds. But, suddenly, I'm wondering if she's going to be good for me. Perhaps, if I could just be alone for a month or two . . . what're you laughing like that for? It's not funny, it's tragic. Did I laugh even once while you were talking about your troubles?'

'Proust's Madeleine?'

'Oh, don't go all French on me now . . . Proust's Made-*leyne*.'

'Proust's Made-*leyne*?'

'For God's sake! Isn't that the name of the girl in his famous book . . .'

Hemlata gave a shriek of laughter again. 'So you think Madeleine's a person?'

'Why, is she a cocker spaniel?'

'Madeleine is a kind of French biscuit!'

'What! A bloody biscuit? Who'd have thought . . . no, you're joking with me.'

'You've been caught out, hotshot. I bet you've never read a page of Proust, you charlatan Charlie.'

'Um, I . . . I don't really have the time to read novels . . . who was it who said that Madeleine was a girl? Was it my ex-wife Anna?'

'Don't try to pin the blame on a woman! You men are all such poseurs.'

'Well, what can I say?' I said, raising my hands in surrender. 'I always thought the French were crazy, and now I know it's true. You'll never catch a real man getting into such a state over a biscuit. Although I suppose we Parsis have our passion for eggs and mawa cakes . . .'

'Well, one thing's for sure, Farhad. You're going to keep your little friend in San Francisco well-entertained,' said Hemlata, as she drained her glass. It was the first time she'd called me by my first name, which suggested that I had been appointed a Friend.

'Don't call her little. She's petite.'

'I'm sure you're a great hit with your female clients, with all your fancy talk about missionaries and Madeleines. I can see lots of rich

Bombay ladies speaking to their friends about wanting to be as beautiful as Proust's Madeleine, courtesy your little scam.'

'It was the first time I ever brought it up, I swear. Just for you because you love literature. The next time, I'll stay within my areas of real knowledge, which are vast. Anyway, biscuit or no biscuit, it doesn't change the fact that I have to figure out what kind of man I am, or want to become, in peace. We men have our own nights to reclaim, even if they are metaphorical ones.'

'I'd agree with that, at one level . . . it's actually a more stressful age for men today than for women,' Hemlata said. 'Those of the old school, like my husband, are flummoxed by the changes on the other side and think the world's gone haywire. While those men who view themselves as feminists find that the feminism of the other side continues to remain oppositional, or that women have left them behind once again, by dint of the natural velocity of their journeys, and have become post-feminists.'

'When will it all end? Isn't it the responsibility of thinking women with feminist partners to become . . . *masculinists*?' I asked, inventing the term that would become the legacy of this particular Billimoria to the world, as confirmed 200 years later by Yazad Jal's *I Egg to Differ: A History of the Parsis* (Simon & Schuster, 2211 CE).

'You don't ask bad questions,' said Hemlata. 'I'm beginning to think you play the fool partly because you underrate yourself intellectually. Well, do you want the easy answer or the radical answer?'

'It's my last night in Bombay. The radical one.'

'Well, in that case—it might be an idea to completely abandon words like *man* and *woman* and start off again with new words that don't carry the social and historical baggage of these ones. If we, as women, don't want to be held prisoners by the matrix of assumptions associated with the word *woman*, maybe we should free men from the yoke of the word *man*, too. Else, like the monkeys of Gandhiji's story, we'll always be biting off more on one side or the other in an attempt to even things out. We all acknowledge that our history comes in the way of a new compact between the sexes, but what we fail to see is that our language itself, and not just what it describes, carries the burden of this history.'

'But how can we wipe out words?' I argued. 'Will men and women stop thinking of themselves as such from 1 January next year?'

'It might be too late for that. But they could rear their children with new words . . . as one brings up children today to think in ways that are different from those of the past.'

'It's a thought. My dear, you need to start a commune or a kibbutz or a panchayat or something, where all of this can be tried out on a test basis. How about setting up a little radical colony in Borivali National Park . . . like Gandhi's Tolstoy Farm?'

'Oh, we academics are much too lazy,' said Hemlata, stretching her arms. 'I think I'll just drop the idea into a book and let someone else take it up. You, maybe. San Francisco is supposed to be the place for grand experimental ventures.'

I asked, as did the disciples of the Buddha, 'What other things do we need new words for?'

'Masturbation,' declared Hemlata. 'It has too much baggage attached to it as well, which makes so many people feel guilty about something that can be educative, not to mention socially useful. Yes . . . let's, by all means, forbid masturbation, as the church fathers and the Hindu sages recommend. But not the practice. The word.'

The men sitting at the next table jumped up and marched out, muttering darkly and looking back at Hemlata. I laughed so much I nearly coughed up my dosa as upma.

'Listen,' I said, 'this is good stuff. You've got to get to America. No one's going to take you seriously here, but you could make a big stir in the Bay Area. You can even stay at my place, if you want.'

'I'll have to stay at your place tonight if we keep nattering away like this . . .'

'Roll along!' I chirped.

'. . . and I miss the last train to Borivali. I'm just going to go use the bathroom. I'd pay, but since it's your last night as a gentleman of the old world . . .'

'Or perhaps even as a man . . .'

'Or perhaps even as a man, yes. Why don't you settle the bill as a man for the last time?'

'Sure thing, madam . . . er, nameless being.'

'Man or no man, it's clear that nothing can separate you from your dreadful jests.'

'Mummy!'

'Stop horsing around now. Here's something I'd like you to read while I'm gone. It's only one page.'

Hemlata dipped into her jute bag, handed me a folded page and disappeared, clipping my ear with her left hip as she passed. I was just about to look at the sheet when my phone beeped. Text and more texts, all chasing me. I looked at my phone and read: *Farhad, hello, dikra! Hope this is not waking you up. Just wanted to say, if it's not too late, it'd be so wonderful if you thought a bit more about this leaving Bombay business. For my sake, and for the 32 people involved in our chess games, including two beautiful queens. Love, Uncle Percy.*

What a sweet gesture. I was gratified that I remained in the thoughts of so many people. And perhaps my own texts hadn't reached Zahra, after all, and I could offer a more dignified explanation in the morning, neither closing the door on her nor leaving it as wide open as it had been. I looked at the next message: *Oh my God! Dr Billimoria, I thought you were a gentleman. But it looks like you're just like any other common man!!! Please don't waste my time in San Francisco, unless you're willing to provide a sincere apology. I'm giving your place in my yoga class to someone else. Z*

Zahra had once again made a man of me and wanted an apology and had even expelled me from her yoga class! I laughed and, restraining my fingers from sending back a reply, turned to read what Hemlata had given me.

But, for once, something Hemlata had written held no surprises. That wasn't because it was dull, or because I'd become a sophisticated thinker in her company, but was because it was the synopsis of her book *The Face of Desire*, which I had already read earlier. But, of course, a couple of nights ago, I had been a *spy* on that world, while I was now being invited to *share* it and even *comment* on it, which meant that Hemlata was paying me an oblique compliment. As I had fallen in Zahra's world, so I had risen in Hemlata's. Oh Farhad! For the first time, I saw that the cloud of the last few days in Bombay had not been about Zahra, with Hemlata thrown in on the side, but about *both* Zahra and Hemlata. Each had been as important as the other, teaching me something about ladies, love and life, and so what if only one of them had seen me naked . . . the other one had seen me asleep, and eating a dosa twice.

All the more tragic, then, that while I was leaving to become the Indian sage of San Francisco, poor Hemlata had no one to share her ideas with other than her own books and papers, and everywhere else in this society, she was merely what the topmost layer of her seemed to suggest she was: a upper middle class South Indian woman, nearly divorced, with a university job. She deserved to be heard, engaged with, respected, far more than she was being, and were it not for the fact that Borivali was so far-off and unfashionable, many intellectuals with more prestige and influence than me would be eating her mother's dosas. I wondered how many people existed around us for whom real solace lay only in the life of the imagination or the intellect, in visions of another world different from the brisk, banal and heartless Bombay that had emerged from history and now rippled with a persistent reality! I was relieved, too, that after the nullity and numbness of recent hours, language was again throwing sparks inside my mind, and in joining the women's march to take back the night, I had taken my own night back from those forces that had menaced it.

And returning to the moment, I saw that I'd goofed-up once again and that Hemlata was paying the bill. I picked up her things and went to join her.

'Farhad, I can't believe it takes you so long to read a few paragraphs.'

'But there was so much in them to think about!'

'Let's rush now! Else I'll miss the train.'

'I'll drop you to the station.'

'You don't need to. This is Bombay.'

'It's not about your safety. After all, it'd be a rash man who'd try to mess with you. Just courtesy, if such a thing exists in the future world that we're trying to bring into being.'

'All right then. Come along.'

We went out on to the street—to the very same spot near the Flora Chinese junction where, as a sixteen-year-old, I'd first hung out this late in the night with friends, and gone home to find my father waiting for me outside the building with a stick. It was wonderful to contemplate how life had progressed, and I was now free to go wherever I pleased, and my late Pop couldn't say a thing.

We flagged down a screechy cab and settled into the tattered and smelly back seat, below which lay buried gold or the potholes of the street.

Hemlata said, 'Did you like the synopsis? Is it interesting?'

'Interesting? You bet! I've never seen anything like it before.'

'Do you think it engages too much with sex?'

'Of course not. In fact, I want more.'

'Come on, if you're following the argument, how can there be more? I'm saying the key word is *better*, not *more*.'

'Yes, I can see the seed of something very big in it. And it's very moving, too, at a human level. Especially in the light of your own marriage.'

Hemlata reddened and said, 'In literary criticism, which I consider the most ethical way of reading the world, that argument would be called a biographical fallacy. But as we're friends, I'll grant that this is my way of ending my marriage while constructively examining its wider possibilities.'

'It's a most intriguing thesis and one that I'd love to apply to my practice as and when I take it up again in America. Or disseminate it widely in the TV series carrying our name.'

'Very funny, Monsieur Madeleine. That's what your name for the show will be.'

'I promise you I'll read *all* of Proust in the next six months, Miss Parle-G. How much of your book have you written?'

'Quite a bit. I should be done in a few months.'

'Maybe, after it's published, you'll become a huge star like Susan Sontag.'

'Ha! I'm surprised you know the name.'

'I'm very interested in her ideas.'

'We should definitely discuss some of that over email. Farhad, I know we've had our disagreements, but in the end, it was a pleasure meeting you. I'm serious.'

'I know you are.'

'Cocky till the very last, I see. Here, keep my card.'

'Thanks. I'll be sure to write as soon as I reach.'

'There's the train pulling in on Platform 1!' shrieked Hemlata. 'Let's run for it.'

'Don't! It's not safe!'

'It's better than waiting four hours for the next train!'

'You go on, I'll pay the cab off and join you.'

Who'd have thought that Hemlata could run so fast? In the few seconds it took for the cab driver to give me the sixty back from a hundred, she'd already made it to the platform. She was going to catch the train after all, although I had secretly hoped she wouldn't. I sprinted after her, past the terrible tableau of crushed vegetables and prostrate bodies left behind by the day, running—my body told my mind—for the first time in more than a decade.

'Did you buy a ticket?' I panted, as I caught up with her by the open door of the compartment.

'I have a pass! Well, Mr Madeleine, what can I say? Sometimes cities and husbands yield surprising things. Good luck with your life. Call me if you're ever back in Bombay.'

'Good luck with yours. Wow, so many women in the ladies'

compartment at this hour. I wonder if they'll let me join the crowd like the last set did.'

'You're free to get on, actually. It becomes "general" after midnight.'

'I think I'm about to have a heart attack from running so fast.'

'Well, hop on, and we'll take care of you.'

'No, I can't . . . I've got to pack!'

'Well, bye then!'

As the train began to move, Hemlata held out a hand of friendship and parting. I reached out to clasp it but missed the red fingernails by a couple of inches. My fingers began to chase hers, but they picked up speed—life always being a tease—at the same rate as me. I looked up and saw Hemlata staring at me goggle-eyed, the reason for which I discovered the very next moment when I found myself flying, tripped up by a vagrant shoeshine box. I fell, skidding with my palms on the platform, saying fuck for the first time in my life. What a terribly embarrassing vision of oneself to leave a lady with!

Looking up, I saw Hemlata still at the door of the train, but she had turned her head away in the other direction. The direction of her future—I was already in the past.

Then she leapt deftly off the train, facing forward in the manner prescribed by the laws of physics and Bombay, and went running a few more steps with a clacking of her slippers before coming to a practised halt—only then to slip through some sludge and land heavily on her backside and, I suppose, her Bombaywoman's pride.

Bleeding and guffawing, I got up and ran over to help her up.

'Why did you jump?'

'Don't ask stupid questions!'

'Okay, okay, I won't. Come, let's go to my place and patch ourselves up. What? What're you looking at me like that for?'

'I just want you to know,' said Hemlata sternly, 'that we're nothing more than friends.'

'Of course, of course,' I said, as I held her hand. 'What sort of man do you take me to be?'

Acknowledgments

MY FIRST BOOK, *Arzee the Dwarf,* was written entirely in Bombay. But then a great wanderlust took hold of me, and *Clouds* was written in eight years mostly on the road, often in the homes of friends. My thanks to Amit Mahanti and Ruchika Negi; Subhashim Goswami; Rustom, Manijeh and Sheriar Irani; Shomikho Raha and Ferzina Banaji; Sonia Faleiro and Ulrik McKnight; Amit Varma and Jasmine Shah Varma; Aditi and Brian Saxton; Christopher Kloeble and Saskya Jain; Delna and Kersy Dastur; Vikas Bajaj; Akshay Shah, Geetika Rai, Sanah Shah (a promising young writer) and Kyra Shah; Ros Schwartz and Andrew Cohen; Jui Chakravarty and Aveek Das; Rohit Chopra and Gitanjali Shahani; and Molly Sugarman and Cooper the cat for their love and hospitality over the years.

Drafts of different sections of the book were also written at the International Writing Program at the University of Iowa; Sangam House Writers' Residency; Art Omi Writers' Residency in Ghent, NY; and Toji Cultural Foundation, South Korea. I am grateful to these institutions for their support and the chance to exchange ideas and stories with wonderful writers from around the world.

Thank you also to Aditi and Brian Saxton, Sabina Dewan and Gavin Steingo for making the time to read draft versions of the manuscript and for useful comments.

Working with Dharini Bhaskar on the manuscript was one of the most stimulating editorial experiences of my life. My deepest gratitude to my wonderful editor and publisher for all her enthusiasm, energy, hard work, and commitment to this book from the moment it dropped on to her desk to the day that it went to press. Thank you also to the entire team at Simon & Schuster: Rahul Srivastava, Sayantan Ghosh, Bharti Taneja, Richie Maheshwary, Yatindra Chaturvedi, S. Senthil, Swati Lingwal, Sonam Agarwal, Sagar Tanwar, Daman Choudhary, Kamal and Mahinder (aka Dhoniji). Before they all came on board, my agent Jessica Woollard was a great help with work on this story.

A book is much more than the words that comprise the text. Thank you to Golak Khandual for painting the beautiful image that adorns the cover, and to Rajinder Ganju for his excellent typesetting.

There are few novels that don't touch on the notion of family, and I would like to thank all those who make up the meaning of this word for me in my own life: the late Bhaskar Sarangi, Krusnapriya Sarangi, the late Rahas Bihari Choudhury, Sindhubala Choudhury, Chitrangada Choudhury, Aniket Aga, the late Lalitbala Mishra, Ajaya Kumar Mishra, Shubhra Mishra, Pradyumna K. Mohapatra, Aarshiya Mohapatra, Siddhant Mohapatra, Shweta Mishra, Soumitra Budhkar, Parth Budhkar (a promising young reader), Purnendu Kumar Sarangi, Archana Sarangi, Pallavi Sarangi, Sonal Sarangi, Aswini Kumar Sarangi, Sudha Sarangi, Amlan Aswini, Sarat Kumar Sarangi, Satati Sarangi and Sambhav Sarangi.

Last, a writer is, in one view, a privileged and powerful creator of worlds; in another view, he is no more than a humble boatman on life's river, developing a narrative vision and worldly philosophy from the people who give him something of themselves and become clouds that are always drifting in his sky. I owe more than I can express to Victoria Burrows, Arshia Sattar, Mette Moestrup, Aamer Hussein, Dr Pushpesh Pant, Golak Khandual, Sudeep Sen, Charlotte Chalker, William Dalrymple, Olivia Dalrymple, Namita Gokhale, VK Karthika, Manasi Subramaniam, Saugata Mukherjee, Dr Philip Lutgendorf, Dr Tapan Basu, Dr Rekha Basu, Srimanjari Basu, Dr Tarun Saint, Sunil Dua, Ros Schwartz, Andrew Cohen, Leo Schwartz, Chloe Schwartz, Sabina Dewan, Shakti Maira, Swati Chopra, Samrat Choudhury, Indira, Erika Kinetz, Dino Prevete, Aarti Shah, Jui Chakravarty, Aveek Das,

Acknowledgments

Vikas Bajaj, Cheryl Tan, Christopher Merrill, Natasha Durovicova, Amit Patani, Pinaki De, Alaap Mishra, Gautam Siddharth, Asiya Zahoor, Madhavi Bhargava, Mohita Modgill, Tulsi Badrinath, Himalee Vyas, Karuna Nundy, Catriona Mitchell, Arati Sawant, Amlan Goswami, Aparna Sanyal, Meghna Dutta, Piyus Agarwal, Phyllis Granoff, Adrian Poole, Jatindra K. Nayak, Himansu S. Mohapatra, Anant Mahapatra, Atul Nayak, Srinivash Das, Kulaswami Jagannath Jena, Mrs Kanak Mani Das, Chandan Singh, Pintu Nitturkar, Pompa Ghosh, Dibyendu Ghosh, Sarit Sangam Sarangi, Gaurav Mishra, Jaya Mishra and Sridala Swami. Separately, the people who over three decades have constituted my school in Bombay and taught me much of what I know about that city: Rustom Irani, Amit Varma, Jasmine Shah Varma, Sonia Faleiro, Ulrik McKnight, Rahul Bhatia, Richa Nigam Bhatia, Rupesh Pai and the staff of Quick Bite restaurant, Aparna Pai, Rucha Pai, Parimal Singh, Vikram Chandra, Mayur Ankolekar, Uma Ankolekar, Shaila Ankolekar, Shachi Ankolekar, Jai Vasantlal, Subhash Nagwekar, Naina Nagwekar, Vedika Nagwekar, Sayali Nagwekar, Srishti Nagwekar, Quais Fatehi, Charulata Moorjani, Sanjukta Sharma, Sammit Das, Noyonika Sharma Das, Asad Lalljee, Vinee Ajmera, Salil Kawli, Delna Dastur, Kersy Dastur, Ranjit Hoskote, and Nancy Adajania.

A final note: The passage from Manto is taken from *Bombay Stories* by Saadat Hasan Manto, translated by Matt Reeck and Aftab Ahmad, Penguin, 2013.

Some real-life people make guest appearances in this book, including Amitav Ghosh and Narendra Modi. The excerpts from the speech by Mr Modi in the Udvada scene are based on a speech given by him in Gujarati at a public function in April 2011 when he was chief minister of Gujarat, to mark the 1290th anniversary of the Shreeji Pak Iranshah at Udvada.